VICTORY OF THE LAMB

VICTORY OF THE LAMB

Lamb of God Series
Novel Two

K. S. MCFARLAND

Softcover

ISBN: 979-8-9881298-4-4 Softcover

CONTENTS

PREFACE

VICTORY OF THE LAMB is the second book in the LAMB OF GOD Series. I strongly suggest reading WAY OF THE LAMB before you read this novel. The sequenced set is historical fiction that focuses on the mission of God's Anointed. Both novels are written with a constant eye toward the four Gospel testimonies but integrated into one seamless story—a task that required meticulous attention. The plot is based on biblical facts and the historical context of his time.

The Scriptures have been interpreted for meaning, insights, and ongoing themes in order to create this fictionally rendered novel. In Scripture, you will find that the cast of characters named in Jesus's story are given no details concerning their history or personality. Rather, the Scripture is presented much like an eyewitness testimony as it would be given in a court of law with just the facts. It lacks the personal details that make you feel a part of the story. Therefore, I have tried to develop interesting characters to enliven the novel yet remain true to the facts provided in the testimonies.

There a several important biblical characters that bear the same name. This can make the storytelling confusing. I have used slightly altered names to differentiate those characters (i.e., Mary, John, Simon). I hope this will be helpful to lessen the confusion of 'who is who' while reading the novel. Please see the character cross reference.

The first novel, WAY OF THE LAMB, ends with an emotional turn of events that plunges Yeshua into the heart of a heated conflict with the powers and principalities of his time. Buckle up. While the first half of the journey was hardly easy, it is safe to say the journey is about to become even more treacherous.

CHARACTER REFERENCE

Yeshua	Jesus
Miriam	Mary, the Mother of Jesus
Yosef	The Human Father of Jesus
James	Brother of Jesus
Si	Simeon, Brother of Jesus (Simon)
Jose	Brother of Jesus
Jude	Brother of Jesus
Hannah	Sister of Jesus
Yohannan	John the Baptizer, Jesus' cousin/relative
Yohan	John, a Disciple of Jesus, the son of Zebedee
James	Brother of Yohan
James	Disciple of Jesus
Simon (Rock)	Disciple of Jesus called 'Peter' or Cephas
Andrew	Disciple
Philip	Disciple
Nathaniel	Disciple, also called Bartholomew
Thomas	Disciple
Thaddeus	Disciple
Simon (Zel)	Disciple called 'The Zealot'
Matthew	Disciple also called Levi
James(Alfie)	Disciple Son of Alphaeus
Judas	Disciple Son of Iscariot
Mariamne (Mari)	Disciple called 'Magdalene'
Cleopas	Uncle of Yeshua
Mary	Aunt, Wife Of Cleopas

Lo-Rahamah	The woman at the well
Deborah	Wife of Simon Peter
Abigail	Mother of Deborah
Decimus	Centurion in Galilee
Jairus	Capernaum Synagogue Leader
Lazarus	Disciple from Bethany
Martha	Sister of Lazarus in Bethany
Simon 'The Leper'	High profile religious leader in Bethany
Caiaphas	Serving as High Priest
Annas	High Priest (Emeritus)
Herod Antipas	Tetrarch /A Son of deceased Herod the Great

DEDICATION

To the glory of God our Savior

in the person of Jesus the Christ.

Who is like you—LORD majestic in holiness,

awesome in glory and in the working of wonders?

There is no one like you. You alone are God.

When I consider your heavens,

the work of your fingers,

the moon and the stars, which you have set in place,

I wonder what is mankind that you are mindful of us,

human beings that you care for us?

You created us in your image,

though lower than the angels.

You crowned us with your glory.

You honored us with your grace,

salvation, and presence.

Lord at your feet I bow and pay homage to you.

PROLOGUE

Father, you are my shepherd;
you guide me, and I lack nothing.
You lay me down in green pastures,
you lead me by quiet waters,
you refresh my soul.
You guide me along righteous paths, for your name's sake.
Even though I am walking through the darkest valley,
and death stalks me wherever I go, I will fear no evil.
You are with me;
your rod and your staff, they comfort me.
You have prepared a table before me
in the presence of my enemies.
You have anointed my head with the oil of your Spirit,
my cup overflows with your power and grace.
May every step along my way,
leave a trail of your goodness and love behind me,
for all of the days of my life,
for when all is done,
I will dwell with You in Your house forever.
Amen
Psalm 23 (rewritten with I and you pronouns)

Yeshua stared out into the night sky. He was always on the move, always sleeping on a bedroll stretched out under the night sky, with no comforting place to lay his head. Sometimes, his exhaustion overwhelmed him.

Tonight, though he was drained, he could not sleep. Yohannan, his relative, closest friend, and ally in his mission, had been beheaded by Herod Antipas and his wife, Herodias. Although he had suspected Yohannan's life would end in martyrdom, his cousin's death had greatly affected him with strong emotions. Just like him, Yohannan had entered his predestined mission with the foreknowledge of its cost, danger, and the probability of how it would end. They had both understood that in the world of good vs. evil, one had to incessantly battle for that which is good. There could be no compromise, no moments of weak resolve, no going with the flow, not if one wanted eternal life.

Despite that knowledge, Yeshua felt his resolve slipping. The battle was too hard, and the cost was too high. And, although he had sought to escape the crowds so he could regroup, he had been caught by the masses and a full day of ministry. Finally, here on this rise overlooking the Sea of Galilee, he found the solitude to allow his tears to flow freely. Now that Yohannan was dead, he would be next in the long line of his Father's slaughtered servants. It was all part of the plan. He was overwhelmed by how much more he had to accomplish before the day of his death. By his estimation, he had a year and a half. Passover. He counted off the remaining months.

Until then—he would execute his plan, finish his work, and fulfill all that had been prophesied about him. He made a mental list of the things he had to complete: He had to finish training his men for the mission they had yet to understand. He would confront the powers at work in the world while remaining blameless in the face of constant temptation. He would circumvent Herod Antipas, Rome, and the horde of religious leaders until that date. Finally, he would overcome his ancient enemy. Satan had been trying to murder him since his conception, but he would escape him until the day of his darkness came. The work would only get harder; the pressures increase.

He had to pull himself together to finish the work of making the only way for God's salvation. He needed his Father's supernatural help. He turned over to bury his face, and he began to pray.

EPIGRAPH

"The kingdom of heaven
is like treasure hidden in a field.
When a man found it,
he hid it again,
and then in his joy
went and sold all he had
and bought that field."
Matthew 13:44

~ 1 ~

GOD OF THE ENOUGH

How will he not also, along with the Son,
graciously give us all things?
Romans 8:32

When you pass through the waters, I will be with you;
and when you pass through the rivers,
they will not sweep over you.
When you walk through the fire,
you will not be burned;
the flames will not set you ablaze.
Isaiah 43:2

Yeshua had preached for eight hours straight. His stomach rumbled, reminding him that he had not eaten all day. His energy flagged. His disciples wore signs of exhaustion, as well as the crowd. He stopped preaching, gave a benediction, and dismissed the crowd. Taking his leave, he began to climb up the slope behind him. His disciples followed his steps. But as he looked back, he found the thong of people were still pursuing him like sheep following their shepherd. Their faces were expectant, as if they were waiting for his next words.

Looking to the west from which the crowd had appeared, Yeshua rubbed his chin. The sun would set soon. Even if the people left immediately, there were no stops for refreshment along the way.

He remembered his time in the wilderness and how difficult it was to think when one was starving and hungry. Satan had used his misery and need to taunt his Father's words. He thought, 'I can't let that happen to these people today. What shepherd would have his sheep travel hungry? I have fed their souls, but now I must feed their bodies.'

Philip was considered the most resourceful and willing of his men. Not even Philip was creative enough to do his work without dependency on the Father's help. He saw the opportunity to give them another important ministry lesson concerning their dependency on the Father for all needed provision.'

"Philip, where can we buy bread for the people?" He sounded like he was confident Philip could handle the need.

Hearing his question, Judas straightened to signal Philip with an alarmed shake of his head and a beseeching look.

"Lord, two hundred days' wages wouldn't buy enough bread for all these people to have even a bite." Philip shielded his eyes since he was silhouetted against the approaching sunset.

Philip wondered, 'Does he now expect us to become a catering service to the masses?'

Judas unconsciously hugged the money bag a little closer to his side, "I don't think our bank can support that."

"Huh. Really?" Yeshua asked, as if surprised. "You and the others should go see what foods you can rustle up amongst the people."

His disciples were speechless. Lunch was long passed. People normally carried one meal on a day trip.

Philip sensed this was some sort of test. Obediently, he had the other disciples filter through the crowd to ask, "Does anyone have any food?"

One young boy whose mother had generously packed more than enough for him was the only one willing to offer up his food. Philip brought the boy back with him, unwilling to take the big-hearted child's only food.

"Look!" Philip said, "We only found five barley loaves and two small smoked fish. But it is all this boy has. Should we take that from him?"

The boy smiled and opened the basket to show him.

Yeshua smiled a grateful smile at the boy and placed his hand on his shoulder. After asking the boy's name, he asked, "So he was the only one with something to give?"

They blinked at him mutely.

"Well, I suppose that will have to do."

The disciples looked at him as though he was addled. "Just send the people away. It is already getting late!"

With complete seriousness, Yeshua said, "We can't send them away empty. You give them something to eat."

Twelve incredulous eyes stared back at him; their mouths hung open with confusion and skepticism. Usually, his men jumped to do his bidding. But now, they ran their fingers through their already unkempt hair.

Finally, Judas spoke up to challenge his words. "So, you are saying you want us to go and buy two hundred days of wages to buy enough bread to give them little more than a bite to eat?" His eyes were wide and hardened; his composure was slipping.

Yeshua slapped Judas on the shoulder. "Okay, since you are so worried about it, bring me whatever you can find; gather it in this basket."

But, the people held their bags close to their sides, unwilling to share them. So the disciples returned once again in frustration, "Master! We got nothing. Only these five loaves and two fish! That is all! The people have eaten everything they had."

Yeshua lacked any concern. "Okay, bring it to me."

Holding the meager bundle in his hand, he said to the disciples. "Now go and have everyone sit to eat in groups of fifty. While they did this, Yeshua continued to hold up the one small basket.

The people took their seats, eager and hopeful, seeing Yeshua with the lifted basket.

Finally, he prayed, "Blessed are you, Adonai our God, Sovereign of all, who brings forth bread from the earth and at whose voice all that exists came into being."

He sat down upon the rock to break the bread and the fish into bite-sized pieces, tossing them into the baskets of the disciples. From the one basket, he filled their twelve lunch baskets with fish and loaves. His men stared with wonder at one another before they began to distribute the food.

People reached in and took as much as they wanted.

When the next person stuck their hand in the basket, they also took all they wanted. Soon, the whole hillside was munching like grazing sheep, contented and filled with wonder.

The disciples returned to Yeshua with astonishment. "How...How did you...?"

Yeshua held up his hand to quiet them, "Look, the people are full. Go now and gather up all of the leftovers. Make sure you pick up all the pieces; leave nothing behind."

They found the uneaten pieces and refilled their lunch baskets.

Yeshua watched as groups of people began to form, then break apart, only to regather again with someone else talking with such animation. He felt the energy changing, and he knew what they were purposing to do. They were preparing to declare him the Messiah—their king—publicly. There appeared to be a whole regiment of Roman soldiers surrounding the perimeter. Such words would force them to draw their swords, viewing their actions as an uprising.

He heard the excited shouts, "This is the Prophet that Moses said was to come into the world!"

"No, no, no!" he shook his head, fearing the blood bath that might ensue. He could not allow them to take this action now, for fear for their lives. This was not their place or time. Only my Father has the right to choose the time or to declare me the King of the people!

He looked around and motioned his men to him, also knowing this kind of public proclamation would fill their heads with ready expectations.

Abruptly, he told them, "Go quickly! Hurry now! Go to the boat and set off. Take your baskets with you and go to the other side of Bethsaida towards Capernaum. I will stay and dismiss the crowds."

His disciples looked confused and dismayed.

"Do as I say! Hurry!"

Philip asked, "Wasn't he just wanting to stay and feed the people? Now, he wants us to hurry to go!"

They were concerned, but his urgency finally made them do just as he asked.

During the sudden diversion of their run for the boat, the people turned to watch them, thinking Yeshua was among them. Meanwhile, Yeshua disappeared into the twilight of the night. When they didn't see him with the disciples or on the boat, they turned to search for him, but he was gone.

A little later, after the people had dispersed and it was dark, Yeshua climbed to the peak of an overlook. There, he fell face down before his Father, overwhelmed by his exhaustion and sorrow. He was reminded that he had not eaten. This reminded him of his time of hunger in the wilderness. Satan had tempted him to turn stones into bread. He had also offered to give him the kingdom of this world and all that was in it—today had been no different.

The dam that had restrained his devastated emotions broke open, and the torrent was released in tears until he was spent. He thought of Yohannan ..., he thought of this latest temptation. He leaned into his prayer, grasping at the tender blades of spring grass. He begged his Father for his help and guidance through all that lay ahead and expressed his every jumbled thought and concern until, finally, peace overtook him to push away his fears. His words began to transition into words of thanksgiving.

He was grateful that throughout the day, his Father had been with him, strengthening him and helping him to teach, train, and protect his disciples. His Father had been present in the miracle of feeding the masses and in all of his thoughts and discernment. He had held him up and kept him from falling. He was so grateful. Once again, his Father had helped him to walk the tightrope of his humanity and his divine calling. He had kept him from slipping and falling.

"Thank you, Abba, that you never leave or desert me! Continue to empower me for this work you have prepared for me. I can do nothing without your help. Just as without my Spirit, my disciples can do nothing. Ours is mysterious union indeed."

Eventually, he raised his head with renewed awareness. He did not know how long he had been praying. A strong gust of wind caught and pulled hard against his dew-dampened ringlets, causing strands to whip about like a flag.

The Wind.

When had the wind arrived? He had been so entrenched in his prayers that he had not even noticed the wind until now. He peered out into the darkness below. He felt the strength of the straight-line winds, the high clouds parted momentarily, allowing the moon to cut a path across the churning waters of the sea. It was as if it were a beacon of light meant to draw his eye.

He saw the small boat of his disciples being pushed back, unable to advance at all. The men appeared to be working hard at their oars, but the strong western wind resisted them. They had made no headway. They were being tossed up and down like a toy boat, pounded by the wind-roughened surf. Yeshua saw their struggle, and he hurried, making a quick descent toward the lake. Purposefully, he strode out across the raucous waves. With every stride, the waves lifted anxiously to meet his feet. He cut a direct path toward his men.

He arrived to find them fearfully huddled and hanging on.

For hours, they had struggled and wondered, 'Where is Yeshua when we need him?'

But, when they saw the form of a man advancing across the waves towards them, they couldn't imagine it was him. Instead, old superstitions arose to frighten them.

"What is that?"

"A specter or a demon that has risen from the watery pit below?" Lake lore had it that on such a night, the ghosts of those who died within these waves would awaken at the wind's fury.

Thomas was confident, "It is a ghost!"

They felt the terror of the apparition. Would it come to drag them down into the depths of the abyss of the dead?

When Yeshua saw their fear, he shouted, "Take courage! It is I! Don't be afraid!"

Simon grew excited, recognizing his voice. Yeshua! He was the only man he wanted in his boat in this storm, and here he was, walking on the water. Seeing what he could do, Simon immediately wanted to do it too. Hadn't he said they could do the same things he did?

"Lord, if it is you, let me know that is indeed you, and let me come to you," Simon called to him.

Amused at Simon's lack of understanding and bravado, he laughed to himself, 'Rock! How I love that impetuous guy! He will even climb out of his boat in this storm to be by my side! He wears his heart on his sleeve! But he doesn't realize it takes faith to walk on water.'

"It is I. Come," he shouted to him and held out his hand.

Without hesitation, Rock stepped out of the boat, and with excitement and wonder, he began to walk toward Yeshua like a child taking his first tentative steps, and excited by his new freedom. The men on the boat had tried to stop him, but Simon had pushed them off. Now, seeing Simon's feat, their mouths hung open in absolute wonder.

"You're doing it!" Andrew shouted.

At his words, Simon glanced back with excitement toward Andrew. Simon saw the boat being tossed on the waves, and he felt the gusting wind. He floundered, wondering, 'What was I thinking?'

A terror shot through him, causing him to lose his footing. Unbalanced, he was undone. Panicked, he sunk feet first into the cold depths of the water. The next large wave swallowed him.

He came up spitting, searching desperately for Yeshua.

"Lord, save me!" He cried and reached desperately toward Yeshua. Just then, another wave crashed over him, taking him back into the depths yet again. Buried in the churning darkness, Simon became twisted around. He didn't know which way was up; he was lost in a dark sea of confusion. He—a fisherman—was going to drown on his stomping grounds. Something grabbed hold of him, pulling him. Would he be dragged into the abyss after all?

But when his head broke through the water, it was Yeshua's face that he saw. Unbelievably, he was able to pull him back up on his feet. While Simon coughed, gasping for air, he clung desperately to Yeshua. There, in the midst of the waves, face to face with his savior, Yeshua spoke to him as a father would an untrained child. "Hey! Hey! Hey! You are okay; I am with you. Simon, you have so little faith! What made you doubt? Didn't I say I would be with you through the waters? They will not pass over you?"

Trembling and cold, Simon 'the Rock' clung to Yeshua's strong hand, and all the way back to the boat, he kept his eyes on him, afraid to look at anything else. His friends hauled him back into the safety of the boat, and Yeshua climbed in behind him.

Yeshua raised his hand, and the winds ceased, and the sea calmed. The astonished faces of his men welcomed him.

He pushed his wind-tossed hair back from his face, "Why are you looking at me like that? After the miracle you witnessed today, are you so thick that you still do not understand?" He stared at the bottom of the boat and shook his head. How long would it take for them to understand who he was, or how they were to walk by faith? They were constantly with him. They had seen *all* of his signs and miracles.

But they had also seen all his discomforts, his weakness, his exhaustion, and his humanity. It was too confusing for them. No matter his marvels, something new would come along to distract them, causing them to fall back into their former state of amnesia, and they forgot the marvelous deeds he had performed.

But then, when he looked up from just thinking this, he was encouraged. Because all of their eyes were on him, and starting with Rock, then Andrew, James, Yohan, Philip, until all twelve knelt before him at the bottom of the drifting boat with lowered heads. They were all quiet for a moment, not daring to look any higher than his sandaled feet standing in the drifting boat as if he were a king. Although his feet looked ordinary, familiar, and human, they knew that the waves had raced forward for the chance to uphold those same two feet. With their heads pressed together in a tight circle of worship, they said, "Lord, you… really are…the Son of God."

$\sim 2 \sim$

GRUMBLERS

Don't grumble ... brothers and sisters, or you will be judged.
The Judge is standing at the door!
James 5:9

The following day, a number of people still lingered on the mountainside, watching for the teacher but finding only wildflowers and birds.

"Where is he? He did not get on the boat last night. He stayed right here!"

"Well, I am telling you he is not here. I can feel it."

A boatload of people from Tiberias disembarked and looked around expectantly, including a group of Pharisees and Scholars, "Where is that teacher, Yeshua of Nazareth? We received word that he was here."

"We don't know. We are looking for him too. Yesterday evening, he fed over 5000 of us right here. We were hoping to find him this morning."

As the morning wore on, a messenger came to the gathering crowd. "If you are looking for the Nazarene, he was spotted in Capernaum."

The men in the crowd said, "See, I knew we should have made him king yesterday! Now he is on his way to only Elohim knows where, and here I stand hungry once again."

"If we leave now, we can make it by the next meal."

The mournful man just threw up his hands as if he were put out.

The Pharisees and scholars returned to the boat, speaking rudely to the oarsmen, "We have been misinformed. The man is not here. Deliver us to Capernaum straightway."

As they traveled, they discussed Yeshua.

One of the Pharisees said, "We can't find anything for which we can condemn him if we can't hear him. We have our orders."

"Yes, but every man has said or done something that can be used against them by wiser people," the scholar rebutted.

"It is all a matter of who has the better connections," the man with the taller hat chuckled. "And it appears he has no champion in high places, no relatives or friends among the High Priest and his closest allies."

"True, I know of no one among our people who is willing to support him. And, none among our scholars have taught him. No wonder he behaves as he does; he doesn't *know* the law!"

The Pharisee sniffed, "It is my understanding that he is of peasant pedigree from Nazareth, and he has had no formal education."

The scholar was sure, "We can catch him in some real error of some blasphemous teaching. Unwashed hands and eating heads of grains in a field on the Sabbath won't be enough to turn the masses from him or to condemn him to death."

**

Yeshua sat on a stone on the beach, eating a piece of fish his men had caught right before the boat landed.

"Umm, this one was really tasty!" He said after swallowing, only to take another torn and steaming piece between his fingers, waiting like a delicacy to be enjoyed. He looked up to see a boat land down the beach a ways. He watched with a wary foreboding as the boat unloaded its patrons. He recognized some of the people from the day before, as well as some Scribes and Pharisees from Tiberias, a delegation of trouble. They looked around with a determined glint in their eyes.

Someone pointed his way. Yeshua hurried to gobbled down the last remaining bites of what was to be his breakfast. His eyes were still puffy and reddened from his prayer time with his Father the night before. An ache lingered in his head. He was not in the mood for the confrontation he felt coming. The men advanced towards him in a double-lined processional with careful steps over the pebbled beach. They stopped, then peer suspiciously at him, while the ring leader adjusted his phylactery. He rested his hands on his protruding stomach.

"What is it that you seek?" Yeshua asked.

"Would you like some of our breakfast?" He pointed to the spit, where several fish were still roasting.

One Pharisee looked at the fish with disgust. "We do not eat with defiled hands as you do."

Yeshua tossed the remaining tail and bones of the fish into the fire. Wiping his hands on a handkerchief, he flashed them a curious smile and waited without speaking.

The men who had arrived from the day before pressed around the Pharisees.

"Here you are. When did you come here, Teacher? We have been looking for you."

"Ah, yes! Of course. But were you looking for me, or simply more fish and loaves? Are you here searching for bread for your stomachs or your souls?"

The men looked at one another, surprised at his direct assessment. They answered defensively, "Well, you gave food freely yesterday. It cost you nothing; why wouldn't you give it to us again today?"

"At no cost, you say? You have failed to understand the meaning of the miraculous sign," Yeshua said, staring at the hole he was poking into the sand below the pebbles.

Then, with resolution, he stood to his feet to deliver his words of challenge, "Listen to me! You should work to eat, but not to feed your ravenous appetites with food that spoils overnight! If only you were searching for food that can sustain your life eternally. There is a food that never spoils or grows old."

"Some of that fish would do," the other man offered boldly, licking his lips.

Yeshua moved a step closer to the man. His voice rang with authority and clarity, "The Son of Man can give you food that doesn't spoil because the Father has placed his seal of approval upon him." He searched the man's face for a sign of recognition to find only a dull irritation.

Seizing the opportunity to engage Yeshua in a discussion concerning the law, one of the Pharisees asked, "What sort of thing should *we* do to satisfy Yahweh's requirements?" The man was confident he could argue any side, any time, and very well. Rarely did anyone outwit his intellect. He stood a little taller for having pressed his challenge.

Yeshua stepped toward the man so quickly that the man flinched and stepped back.

"Believe in the One he has sent."

"Believe? If you have revealed yourself with miracles, then what is this miracle they speak of that we should believe you? What demonstration of power will you show us?" the Pharisee asked as if he had heard nothing.

The man hoping for food said, "Obviously, if Moses gave bread in the desert to our ancestors, then, if you were the Son of Man, you could give us heavenly bread to eat daily."

Both delegations waited with cat-like smiles, demanding this proof, demanding bread.

Yeshua heard the subtle temptations in their words. He even glanced behind them as if expecting to see his desert nemesis. He paced out a circle around them as if to cordon off an evil influence. He spoke as he went, "This is the truth! Moses did not provide the people with *heavenly* bread, but only a foreshadowing of that Bread of Life that would one day come. Now, today, that bread is being offered to you, the true bread which comes down out of heaven to offer life to the world."

The men who had come to fill their stomachs said, "Sir, give us this bread from now on!"

A crowd was growing, and the people were quick to join the men in their request.

Yeshua stepped back as if to leave in frustration, 'Will they never hear me, see me, or receive me?'

He raked his hand through his unruly black curls before he turned to walk a good five paces away. He stopped, and then he spun around as if desperate to make them see.

He declared with his hand on his chest, "I am the Bread of Life." He reached toward them in an invitation, "Whoever comes to me will never grow hungry. Believe in me, and you will never thirst."

The hungry men and the men from Tiberias did not move, nor did they look convinced. They maintained their attitudes of dis-belief—moments passed by in silence.

Finally, Yeshua spoke to the men he had fed the day before, "But no. Even though you have seen and heard me for yourself, even though you have seen the sign, you do not believe!"

The hungry men became angry that he was not providing the bread they hoped for.

"No, you do not believe. Why am I surprised?" he asked the pebbles on the beach, raising his eyebrows with a deep breath.

He looked up and told them, "If my Father had chosen you, you would have come to me, but you do not. Anyone who comes to me, I will never send away! Do you think I have come from heaven to do your will? Or even my own will? No, I tell you! But the will of my Father in heaven who has sent me. His will is this, 'Everyone who sees the Son and believes in him will receive eternal life.' And I will raise them at the last day."

The Jews from Tiberius began to grumble, "Who does he think he is?"

"Isn't he the son of Yosef of Nazareth?"

"Yes, his mother and father are known to us."

"What is to be believed?"

"Maybe he is possessed?"

"How can he say he came down from heaven?"

Yeshua held up his hand to an unseen force of demonic influences, commanding them, "Stop your grumbling."

The grumbling ceased.

"Do you not wish to live?" He asked them. "I am offering you the Bread of Life. I am the Bread of Life that has come down from heaven. I offer up my body, which I will give for the world."

A commotion broke out among the people.

"What?" they shouted, faces twisted in disgust. "Who would offer their own body as food?"

Even the two men, who had searched for him, cringed and held up their hands, backing away, "No, we are not that desperate. Why would we eat your flesh!"

"We are not cannibals."

"I tell you the truth," Yeshua said, "Unless you eat of this body and drink of my blood, you cannot find eternal life. But if you do believe and eat of my flesh, I will raise you to life on the last day!"

Beating his chest, he shouted above the rebellious din. "Whoever eats this bread will live forever!"

At those words, those gathered around him took a barley loaf from their day bags and threw it at him as a sign of their unbelief.

A man shouted, "He has acted strangely before, but what kind of talk is this? He had crossed the line. Who would associate themselves with this lunatic?"

**

Yeshua left the beach and proceeded onward toward the nearby synagogue. Only his closest disciples trailed behind him. They were also clearly disturbed by his words. Judas, most of all, since Yeshua's words made for bad publicity. They were anxious for Yeshua to explain his meaning, but he offered them no instruction as they moved on.

Walking behind him, Judas began a whispered revolt. Going from disciple to disciple, he built a case that Yeshua was destroying his mission. "We need to reason with him. What kind of deliverer would speak of such things!" He whispers, adding to their agitated state.

"What does he mean by such words?" he asked them. "The leaders are right. He *is* talking nonsense. We need the Pharisees and the scholars on our side, but Yeshua constantly confronts them as if they were his enemy. How will this behavior ever advance his cause?"

Moving to the next, he said, "What do you think? Is the pressure and Yohannan's death too much for the Rabbi right now?"

To another, he asked. "You agree, right? I mean, this is a very difficult message. Was he being literal or talking in a parable? If so, why doesn't he just say what he means? Why such a strange story? Why doesn't he just speak plainly?"

"Can you blame the leaders for doubting him? Shouldn't we leave, too?"

Judas barraged the Twelve with every doubt, a grumble here and a grumble there. In very short order, he had spread his doubts and dissatisfaction to every man, goading them to add their doubts to his.

Yeshua heard bits and pieces of what was happening behind him as he walked, allowing Judas to challenge them all. It was not the first time, nor would it be the last time they were tempted to doubt him. But, when they finally arrived at the synagogue, Yeshua stopped to stand just outside the threshold. He turned to face them all.

They halted abruptly, bumping into one another. They were brought up short by the pain they saw burning in his eyes.

"What?" His voice boomed, "Have I offended you too?"

Those who had trailed behind him hid their guilty faces from him, staring guiltily at their feet.

"Tell me, what will it take for you to believe me? What if I just ascended to heaven in front of your eyes? Would you believe me then?"

No one spoke. Nervously, they exchanged sheepish looks with one another.

"No. It takes the Spirit to give life to a body; a body without the breath of God is not alive. It cannot accomplish anything of its own," he muttered as if reminding himself of the things his disciples could not understand.

Agitated, he started again, "Listen to me! My words...."

Realizing that he was speaking too loudly, he dropped his voice, "My words are both Spirit and life. But some of you are refusing to take my words into your being. Instead, you argue against me and resist what I say. You refuse to believe!"

He speared Judas with his eyes. Then, looking around the circle, he asked them directly, "Do you also wish to leave? You can only come to believe in me if my Father has provided you with a certain level of faith. This is a moment of decision for you. Do you have faith in me? Do you trust my words, even if you don't yet understand them?"

Confused and guilty faces stared back at him.

"We are crossing a threshold," Yeshua spoke metaphorically while motioning to the doorway that stood before them. "It is not going to be easy! It will only get harder as we press forward. For your survival, it is critical that you believe what I say. So, if you have doubts about me and want to leave, do it now. Don't waste your time or mine." He motioned towards the open spaces. "I will not force you to go on a journey you don't believe will be worth it."

His disciples stood meekly while they pondered his challenge. They admitted, if only to themselves, 'Yeshua is a hard teacher to follow, but I would not consider any other teacher after following him, even when I don't understand.'

They felt small and unworthy under his rebuke. Never had he made such an ultimatum. It was hard to stand by him while he challenged other people because his words always spoke the same hard truths to *them* as well. Now, his words were personal, directed at them, and they were well deserved. They were caught red-handed in their gossip, folly, and disloyalty.

Those closest to him placed their hands on their hearts, feeling the cauterizing tip of the sword of his words pointed at them. His pain joined to their own. Had they learned nothing from their lesson on the sea from the day before?

Yeshua drew in a deep and cleansing breath, seeing the signs of their remorse. As he blew his breath out slowly, he worked to calm himself and forced his hands to stop shaking. His heart began to regulate from its painful pounding; his psychic pain began to ease. He drew another deep breath and, looking desperately towards the heavens, then let it go with a loud sigh. With it, he released a private and plaintive prayer, 'Father, I feel so alone in this. Will they ever believe in me? At least I have you with me; for now, that is enough.'

When he had collected himself, he looked purposefully into the eyes of each disciple—both the men and the women. One by one, they tentatively met his eyes as if they were looking into the sun, feeling guilty and repentant. His eyes asked the sad and silent question, 'Will you leave too?'

Each one remembered their initial encounter with Yeshua, their subsequent calling, all they had seen him do, his lessons, and their many amazing experiences with him.

Even they wondered to themselves, 'Why *is* it sometimes so hard to believe? Why *do* I forget? Why do I *listen* to the voice of doubt?'

A few stragglers toward the back fell away as if it were too much for them. But none of the twelve, nor the women who followed, budged. They waited, wondering if he had changed his mind about them.

"Here is your chance to turn back. You are either with me or against me." He spoke again into the silence to make clear their choice.

Finally, Rock could stand the intensity of his scrutiny no more. Once again, he felt unworthy to follow Yeshua, but he simply could no longer imagine any other life. He knelt before his master, his eyes on his travel-worn feet, wondering where they might lead him. Even so, he knew he had to follow them. His hand was still pressed to his smarting heart when he meekly said, "Lord, where else would we go? To whom could we go to be shown the way? You ... you alone have the words of eternal life! We have come to believe.... and are convinced that you are the Holy One of God."

Yeshua held out his hand of reconciliation to Rock with a sigh of great relief and renewed gladness. All his emotions glistened in his eyes, "Rock, I am so glad because I chose you." He took Rock by surprise when he grabbed his face and planted a big kiss on his broad forehead as if to say, "I love you, brother!" His face was filled with genuine gladness.

He drew back to shout to the rest, "Didn't I choose you all?"

All the faces brightened and moved closer to receive his touch as they entered the synagogue. One lagged but finally entered the synagogue, feigning innocence, his countenance unmarked by concern. Yeshua watched Judas step across the threshold, once more assured he had chosen the right one to betray him.

Yeshua straightened then, watching him go. Under his breath, he uttered, "Yet one of you is a devil!"

~ 3 ~

THE SENDING FORTH

See, I am sending an angel ahead of you
to guard you along the way
and to bring you to the place I have prepared.
Pay attention to him and listen to what he says.
Exodus 23:20-21

The fields were growing white with the crops planted in the fall, and most of the tablelands were finishing their harvest, but there was now no time to waste. Over the winter months in Judea, Yeshua had taught his men the preaching basics. They had taken turns preaching various messages to people in the Judea wilderness. Yeshua had wondered, at times, if they would ever be ready. They had heard his words, but too often, it seemed they did not understand his message. He had to trust that, in time, the words would spring to life and grow to fruition.

Now, he could wait no longer. It was time to send his men out into villages throughout Israel to preach the same message he had been preaching. He had one more full season of harvesting souls before his time would come. He brought the Twelve together to give them their final instructions.

He began with a special prayer over each one of them, laying hands on them and anointing them with oil of the Spirit. He conveyed upon them words of power and authority.

His charge was this: "Proclaim the kingdom of God is drawing near and ready to come to them. Tell them to be cleansed in baptism, make their lives right, and turn back to God's commands. God is holy, and no unclean person may enter into his kingdom. Drive out their demons and cure their diseases."

They looked at one another with shock and surprise.

Thomas blurted out, "But we can't do the things you do."

Yeshua answered, "All things are possible with God. Together, you will do even greater things than I."

"But what if the religious leaders come after us? Or the Romans?"

"Do you think I would send you to your death after all this time I have invested in you? My Spirit will be with you. Be strong and courageous! Still, I understand why you ask me this. The kingdom of heaven has been subjected to violence, and violent people have been raiding it. If they hate me, they will hate you too. Do not be afraid of them, for nothing is concealed that will not be disclosed or hidden that will not be made known. Don't worry about what to say; my Father and I will give you the right words at the time. If any place rejects your message, shake the dust off your feet and move on. They have received their opportunity. Pray for your mission every day."

"Where should we go?"

"Go to the lost sheep of Israel. You have received from me freely; now freely give. Take no money with you in your belts."

"What?" They exclaimed in unison.

"But how will we eat or get what we need?" Judas asked, visibly upset.

"Money will only cause problems and make you more vulnerable on the road. It is better to fall upon the goodwill of grateful people."

"Who then can be trusted with the money bag?" Judas wanted to know.

Yeshua gave him a look that closed Judas' mouth; he huffed silently.

"When you enter a village, choose a righteous person in that town to offer you shelter. Eat whatever they sit before you. No grumbling, no picky eaters. Extend to them your peace and stay in that same home until you move on. Don't insult your host. If someone turns down your request, don't let that upset you; just let your peace return to you. The synagogue leaders may question some of you; don't sugarcoat things in fear. I will speak on your behalf. Speak the truth I have taught you. Don't be afraid of those with the power to kill you; fear instead the one who has power over your body and soul. Whoever acknowledges me before others, I will also acknowledge before my Father in heaven. But if you disown me before others, I will disown you."

They had endured the difficult work but never ventured far without Yeshua as their leader. They depended on him for where to go, what to say, and how to get out of difficult scrapes. Their faces reflected a gambit of emotions, true to their personalities. Rock looked eager, and Andrew looked at his brother. James and Yohan looked ready to face any adversary. Philip looked thoughtful. Thomas looked resolved. Bartholomew looked nervous. Simon looked passionate. James and Thaddaeus looked unsure. Matthew and Judas looked warily at one another, thinking they had each drawn a short straw for a mission partner.

To assure them, Yeshua said, "Look, the Spirit of your heavenly Father will give you the words you are to speak. You are going to upset the apple cart! Some people will love you, and some will hate you! No student is above their teacher. Remember, I didn't come to bring peace but a sword. My words are divisive! My words will turn every relationship one way or the other according to what people believe or don't want to believe about me. I can't pretend this will be easy for you. But no matter what, you are meant to be a peaceful revolution—the exact opposite of the rebellion of this world. Stand firm to the end, and when you are persecuted in one place, flee to another. Just keep doing the work for which you have been sent. If they welcome you, they are welcoming me. I will be close behind."

Thaddeus spoke up. "My father has been sick, and he is near his end. I feel I should stay near to bury him."

"Thaddeus, you must make up your mind. Who do you love more? If you put anyone else before me, you are not worthy of me."

Yeshua looked around at the stunned faces and added the clincher, "Anyone who does not take up their cross and follow me is not worthy of me. If you have found your own life, you must let it go, and whoever loses that life for my sake will find their ultimate life."

They blinked, trying to take in this manifesto. Was he calling them to give their very life for him? Yeshua sounded like a king for the first time, with every right to call his men into his mission and go to battle. Men die every day for King and country. He was asking nothing less.

That night, they slept little, knowing that tomorrow Yeshua was sending them out, as he had put it, 'like sheep among wolves,' two by two, across the battle lines of society. After his "pep" talk, they did not feel particularly hopeful. Instead, they all began to feel woefully ill-equipped and filled with trepidation.

The next morning, after a time of prayer, Yeshua watched as they all departed in their separate directions, off to the four winds. It was a dreary and windy day, and their cloaks beat their legs with each step as if their abuse could dissuade them from their quests.

Magdalene came and stood next to Yeshua with her arms wrapped around her, watching them go.

"Why did you only send the men? We, women, have listened to your words and are just as ready as they are. Maybe the men would not listen to us, but the women would." she said plaintively.

Yeshua turned his gaze from his men to her with some amusement, "Will they?"

She was certainly a woman to be reckoned with, both strong and soft at the same time. She thought she was equal to any man.

"You will get your opportunities in your turn. My words are no less true for you, but it is not yet your time. Besides, who will join me in prayer for those greenhorns if you women are out there in the heat of all the action yourselves? You know how dangerous it is out there. For now, our prayers will call my Father's power forth to protect and help them."

She thoughtfully mulled that over, yet to be convinced.

He chucked her chin.

"Hey, isn't that what a 'watch tower' does? Watches and waits? Prayer is often the greatest work one can do. It is the source of all success and blessing! Without prayer, any work or sacrifice remains flat, useless, and endangered! Everyone has their role to play in what is happening now, and it is all-important."

"What are you going to do now that they are leaving?"

"I am going to pray, and when I am done, I will take a nap."

She narrowed her eyes on his back as he turned and entered the house to find a dark and private corner.

"Hm-m-m!" She thought, then rejoined the women.

"Ladies, let's all take some time to pray for the men. Yeshua is not going to send us today."

Susanna and the others looked relieved. They did not want to take to the road. Only Magdalene felt so motivated.

Magdalene wondered at Yeshua's desire to sleep while his men went out into the wild. She did not know that when Yeshua went into a deep sleep, his unconscious mind was temporarily reconciled with his cosmically divine mind. In his sleep, he was unified with his Father. Things were being ordered within his mind and mission. This was part of the mysterious work of the embodying Holy Spirit, which was at one with his own Spirit and the Father. His rest was not wasted but critical time. This was how he often foreknew what was coming, how he knew what he needed to do next, and how he overcame the evil purposes that were always in play around him and his men.

When Yeshua awoke, he was rarely conscious of what had happened in his sleep or dreams, but he was aware that his Father and the Holy Spirit were with him. He didn't always know what would happen but could discern the events around him. His work and dreams mainly remained in his subconscious mind—showing and instructing him as he went on his way, much like the imprinted words of scripture were accessed from within. The two never seemed to be far apart. And… whatever he heard or knew to be confirmed between the two, he obeyed.

After some lengthy prayer for his men, he relaxed into a deep sleep of physical exhaustion. With the men gone, Capernaum was oblivious to his presence in his darkened corner. In this way, he was fighting for his men and upholding them all.

The women gave him space and sat out in the courtyard, grinding grain and weaving cloth, talking and laughing softly and lifting their prayers for the disciples on their journeys.

The women prayed for the disciples' needs, shelter, friendship, wisdom, right words, safety, health and strength, traveling mercies, sustainable food, opportunities to speak in the synagogues, healings, deliverances, repentance, and acceptance.

Most of all, they prayed for people to come to believe in the exhausted man snuggled inside, sleeping so hard that his mouth hung slightly open and he emitted soft snores. His all-seeing eyes moved rapidly back and forth under his closed eyelids, and a bit of drool pooled at the corner of his mouth.

~ 4 ~

MY HEART IS AWAKE

I slept, but my heart was awake. - Song 5:1

"The women are my daughters, the children are my children...
Come now, let's make a covenant, you and I,
and let it serve as a witness between us." - Exodus 31:43-44

"Praise be to the Lord,
who this day has not left you without a guardian-redeemer.
May he become famous throughout Israel!" - Ruth 4:14

They remembered ...
that God Most High was their Redeemer. - Psalm 78:38

When Yeshua awoke later that evening, it took a moment for him to discern the time of day. He had slept particularly hard, and the lack of light filtering into the room disoriented him. His head cleared to the sweet aroma of roasting meat wafting in the air. When he walked out into the courtyard, he was met with an assembly of abnormally quiet women at work to put together the meal. They were talking in whispers. But that changed when they looked up excitedly to see he was awake.

"Finally! It has been impossible to keep the laughter and conversation down so you could sleep." Magdalene said happily.

He was surprised to find his sister sitting with his mother and the women who followed him regularly. There was also Deborah, Abigail, his Aunt Mary, Sarah, Salome, and her daughter Lydia. There were twelve in all.

"How was your rest?" Asked his Ima, who had just returned to Capernaum.

"I brought you a surprise!" Miriam beamed, motioning to the infant asleep in his sister's arms.

"Hannah has just been purified and was allowed to travel."

Magdalene came to him. "We have prepared a special dinner for you this evening, considering our company from Cana. We are so excited because we women never get to have you to ourselves with all your men about to occupy the conversation. So, we decided to claim this time for us! You are our secret for the next few days."

She beamed and turned to the other women, who agreed, giggling like school girls.

"Well then, how in the world could I say no? I say, let the feast and celebration begin!"

He wiped his still sleepy eyes and beamed back.

He came to his sister, who stood quickly to hug him. Without hesitation, he took the little one into his arms.

Studying him closely, he said. "So, Yosef bar Zerah, we must stick together as the only two men amongst so many women!"

He offered his finger to the tiny hand that closed around his finger. With great tenderness, Yeshua bent his head to kiss the soft, downy forehead and whispered his blessings upon the child.

"Oh," Hannah said to her son, moving forward. "I can see that you have already taken my place in Yeshua's affections." She reached to take her son.

But Yeshua lifted the babe away from her, placing him high in the cradle of his arm. "There is enough of me to go around; don't be jealous now," he said, flashing her a grin.

The other women were busy finishing their collective feast.

"Seriously, it is so good to get some private time with you now that you are so popular with the people and traveling all over Israel," Hannah said, taking a seat next to Yeshua.

"You look well," Yeshua observed. "Better than well."

"I am recovering pretty well from the birth of Yosef. Ima never told me how hard childbirth would be."

"And why should she? There was no need for you to worry about it in advance. Every day has worries of its own." Yeshua said, touching his sister's hand and inspecting her closely.

"Zerah. He is good to you and happy to be a dad?" He asked.

"He is wonderful. He dotes on us both. You will see him soon. He is here in Capernaum with James and his family. He insisted on coming with us. But... Ima and I wouldn't let him come to our girl gathering tonight. Do you think us selfish?"

"No, it will make him miss you like crazy. It will be good for you both."

The table was quickly laid out and laden with nuts, olives, roasted vegetables, loaves of bread, dips, roasted meat, an apple mixture, curds, and honey. They gathered around the table. Miriam blessed the food and the drink, adding, "Blessed are you, O LORD our God, who gives us sisters to share life with, and allows us to eat freely from your table, and share life with you."

Yeshua looked around the table of women and felt the power of their love and affection. But soon, he found all of the women asking him so many questions that he could hardly take a bite or chew his food. They were all vying for his attention and wanted answers.

Finally, he laughed, holding his hands drawn back as if in surrender.

"I will answer all your questions after I have finished my meal."

The women laughed good-naturedly to one another, then began talking with one another without missing a beat.

For a time, he ate, and the women chattered on and on. The energy grew louder and louder as each fought to get their turn to speak. Yeshua listened with genuine interest to what was going on in their lives and the myriad of concerns they freely shared. They often glanced his way for his reaction, for his nods of approval, seeking his expression of concern and compassion. He was unsurprised that each woman had strong opinions, deep insights, and wisdom to share. Amongst the men, women were rarely allowed to speak their piece.

He greatly appreciated their conversation, which was quite lively and different from that of the men. He found himself interjecting comments despite himself. The women talked of the cost of goods at the markets, political uprisings, events in town, breastfeeding, child discipline, and marital dilemmas.

Suzanne said, "News arrived from Jerusalem from the women Mari taught in the women's court. They have sent their regards. They truly miss her insights and leadership. They are longing for her to return to them."

Mari looked torn. "Now I have more to teach and to share than ever. But, for now, I would not take anything for having this time of discipleship." She glanced toward Yeshua, "Because of the Lord's teaching, I finally have something worth giving them."

He said, "Don't worry, you will surely teach again."

Then Salome asked him the question every woman wondered about, "Why are women treated as second-rate citizens in the faith? Men can enter the women's courts, but women cannot enter the men's courts. The men run everything, whether they deserve to or not."

All the women turned to Yeshua expectantly, and the table grew quiet.

"You mean beyond the curse that has rested on women since the fall?" He rubbed his brow in thought. "It is complicated, partly because of the constant slaughter of animals. Men have always served their families by making the required sacrifices. Sabbath gatherings at synagogue and temple weren't always meant to be separated." He told them. "Though our faith has always been patriarchal, sabbath gatherings and instruction were meant for the whole family. There are always those who love to oppress others, even the women in their households. Control is the human equivalent of power, and people love power. Surely, you have noticed that some men can hardly share power with other men, and women refuse to share power with other women. Some women, in an effort to overcome their powerlessness, lust for power even more than some men. Their need to feel in control can become a stumbling block. Sexual attraction is one of the ways women have been able to feel powerful. Lust and power make for a dangerous combination. After Jezebel rose to power over Israel as priestess of Ashtoreth, some women joined with her to become a stumbling block to the community of faith. For most men, it takes little to nothing to cause his lust for women to become a stumbling block to them.

"During King Jehoshaphat's reformation movement in Judea, he separated men and women as a hedge of protection for both of them. Judah had begun to emulate the ways of the Northern Kingdom's Baal and Ashtoreth worship. Inappropriate sexual rituals were taking place between men and women influenced by pagan worship. By separating women and men, Jehoshaphat had hoped to end the sexual rituals and abuses, including flirtatious behavior within the synagogues and temple. It was not to make women second-rate citizens, but rather, it was enacted to help preserve holiness during worship.

"But as you know, each law meant to stymie sin often comes with a circumstance. Jehoshaphat's reform made women feel separated from God's worship as if they were second-rate citizens to my Father, but that is not true. But take heart: the curse will not last forever. I have come to remove that curse. In the meantime, guard your hearts. Do not be deceived as Eve was. Trust in my Father's word and his purposes for you.

"Faith is to be central within the family and communal worship. Women need to know as much as possible so you can create a godly atmosphere in your home and train godly children and participate with modesty within the holy bounds of community life."

He looked at them all and said, "Never underestimate your purpose. Value your childbearing and your godly influence with the men in your life and with one another. Women's roles are crucial to the family life, salvation, and in the work of building of the kingdom."

Deborah said, "Please come and remind me of that when I am in over my head with a sick child, and Simon is off somewhere with you."

Yeshua nodded, noting her hardship. "Yes, there are many days like that for you as mothers. And I won't forget your sacrifice."

"Are children our only purpose?" Hannah asked him. She was a young woman looking down the road of many years of childbearing and rearing.

"Right now, this young man is one of your most important purposes. Who can care for him better than you?" he asked, glancing up at his sister. "But to answer your question, no, women have many godly purposes within their families, amongst their friends, and within their communities. Never mind that your husband depends on you to use your discernment and intelligence to help govern the family. He looks to you for things that even he does not know he needs."

He gently rocked the child in his arms for a moment and then looked up again at Hannah and the others, "Still, even that is not all that you are. You are the royal daughters of God. You share in the building of the kingdom. You have an important role in your Father's house and the community. And the community of God, each of you comprises a special part of the bride of God. As such, you have everything you need to help you become equal partners in your marriage. When you submit to your husband, he will grow to love and trust you all the more. Then he will be willing to submit to you as well. That is how you become a strong family. Love and respect heal the pain of sin between the two sexes. Your husband will depend on you in more ways than you know. Am I right, Ima?" He directed his question to his mother, who was lost in reflection.

She was startled by his question. His words had caused a flood of memories from the past and her marriage to Yosef. How much she missed him. She remembered the delicate balance of give and take within their relationship. Neither one of them was perfect, but together, they were perfectly at peace and comforted. Not that there had not been standoffs, demands, raised voices, and harsh words from time to time, but they had worked through all conflicts until a rich, abiding love remained. Called back from her memories, Miriam's eyes shimmered, grateful yet grieving.

She could see that her son had read her thoughts, and she nodded. Mari Magdalene squeezed Miriam's hand to comfort her sadness.

To change the subject, Mari asked, "But what about me? I have no husband. I have no children. Now, I have no business to run, no students to teach, so what purpose do I have?"

His eyes met hers with a particular tenderness, understanding her singular and lonely life. Their eyes held, and something deeply personal passed between them.

He answered, "Then the Lord will be your husband."

Mari gasped, surprised by the effect of his words. Confused, she wondered if she had received them more intimately than he had intended them. But, his gaze was still on her. Everyone felt the spiritual fervor and the transcendence of his words. They looked down discreetly, allowing them the intimate moment.

Finally, Joanna said, "Tell us a story, Lord. I can never get enough of them."

Yeshua settled back to make himself comfortable, still snuggling baby Yosef to his chest. He tucked little Yosef under his chin. "Let's see..."

They all waited.

"Finding your purpose is crucial in a happy and well-lived life. My Father has prepared a purpose for each of you. Purpose gives you a sense of fulfillment, belonging, and a feeling of personal value. If you know your purpose, you have found your intended path."

He motioned to the luxuriant headpiece that framed Lydia's face. It was covered with small coins attached to the headscarf. The coins had been given to her by her husband for their betrothal.

"Suppose a woman has ten silver coins, but she loses one. Doesn't she light a lamp to sweep the house, searching carefully until she finds it? Because that coin is of utmost value to her."

Lydia reached up to touch her coins.

"Her coins are a symbolic gift meant to show how much her husband values her. Lydia must be valued very much indeed. His love for her makes each coin so valuable to her.

"It is that way in the kingdom of God. You are very valuable to my Father. If you get lost, he will search high and low for you until he finds you. And he will give whatever it takes to have you back, even if it takes everything that he is.

"Likewise, if you value your closeness with the Father, you will give up whatever it takes to be with him."

He gazed up into the soft evening sky and smiled. Then, he contemplated the sleeping infant in his arms, his expression tender, "Each child is of infinite value to him."

He looked up at the women and began again, "The kingdom of heaven will be like ten virgins who took their lamps and went out to meet the bridegroom."

All of the women sat up to listen. What woman doesn't like a good wedding story?

"Now, five of the bridesmaids were foolish, and five were wise. The foolish ones remembered their lamps, but they forgot to take any extra oil for them. But the wise ones took along extra jars of oil for their lamps just in case..."

The older women cut their eyes at the younger women, who giggled together, knowing they could easily forget the needed things like lamp oil.

Abigail and Miriam laughed, acknowledging that as responsible as they both were, when they got in a tizzy of distraction, they could forget the extra oil.

Yeshua grinned at their inferences, then continued, "The bridegroom was a long time in coming. The bridesmaids grew tired of waiting; since they were exhausted, they fell asleep.

"At midnight, the cry rang out, 'Wake up, here is the bridegroom! Come out to meet him!'

"All of the virgins woke up to light and trim their lamps. But when the foolish ones saw they didn't have much oil left. They said to the wise ones, 'Give us some of your oil so our lamps won't go out!'

"'No,' the wise virgins replied, 'we don't have enough oil for us to share with you. You will need to get your own oil. Go to those who sell oil and buy some for yourselves.'

"While the foolish virgins went out to buy the oil, the bridegroom returned for the wedding banquet. The virgins who were ready went in with him, and the door was shut behind them.

"Later, the foolish virgins arrived to beat on the door. 'Lord, Lord,' they said, 'open the door for us!'

"But the doorkeeper replied, 'Truly I tell you, I don't know you. The wedding party arrived some time ago, and everyone has been admitted. Am I to believe you were left behind?'"

The women whispered their comments.

"Keep watch, therefore, because you do not know the day or the hour that the bridegroom might come for his betrothed."

Lydia laughed nervously.

Hannah said, "That was my favorite part of my wedding, all the lanterns lighting the way. It was so beautiful!"

"Yeshua, who is the bridegroom in this story?" Joanna asked.

"Who do you think the bridegroom might be?" he asked her with a tilted brow.

Joanna's eyes were wide with wonder, but instead of speaking, she looked toward Mari for confirmation.

"According to the Law of the Covenant written on Mount Sinai," Magdalene stated, "the Bridegroom is no less than God, himself."

Her eyes met Yeshua's across the flames of the fire warming the courtyard, and she remembered that Yohannan had referred to Yeshua as The Bridegroom.

Yeshua offered her a nod of approval.

Was it her imagination? His eyes seemed to dance with flames. Or, was it just the reflection of all the lamps scattered around the space?

Salome commented, "The covenant was with the people of Israel."

"The prophet, Jeremiah, tells us that a new covenant will be written for all who receive the Messiah," Magdalene added.

"So, what is the lesson of the story?" Yeshua asked the women.

"Keep plenty of oil in your keep." Abigail laughed, thinking of the first time she had to borrow oil to fix dinner for Yeshua.

"And, take extra oil with you," Salome laughed, "so you can sell some to the other bridesmaids for a hefty profit."

They all laughed at Salome's humor, but they knew there was a serious message in Yeshua's story.

Hannah could wait no longer. Her full breasts needed relief; she came to take her son from her brother. Little Yosef startled awake and began to cry, unhappy at his disturbance.

"I can't believe he has slept so contentedly in your arms. It is way past time for him to eat." She felt her milk let down, and quickly, she turned away to feed the child.

"I seem to have that effect on babies. I think he was eating his fill of spiritual food. Little Yosef will make a good disciple one day," Yeshua laughed. "But a growing boy must eat."

That night, Mari lay awake thinking about the women's happiness to have the Rabbi all to themselves. Their evening with the Lord turned out to be a special gift to the women. She missed her work among the women in Jerusalem. She was learning new things every day; she felt like a pitcher being filled to overflowing. Her soul was stirred with gratitude for her discipleship. She lay awake meditating on all his words. And yet, beyond all the laughter of the wonderful evening, there still lay the stark reminder of the night the somber news had arrived about Yohannan.

'How long will we have with him?' she wondered.

Her old nemesis 'anxiety' stirred, leaving her feeling restless and tense.

Finally, fearing all her tossing and turning might awaken the other women, she went outside for some air. As she passed by the stairs leading to the rooftop, she paused. She wanted to talk with Yeshua. She placed her foot on the first stair. Thinking better of her impulse, she reluctantly removed it. It would be improper to go to him. What? Would she wake him from his sleep?

Instead, she moved out into the now-darkened courtyard. She looked up into the night sky and wrapped her arms around her shoulders. She thought, 'I should have grabbed a wrap.'

A voice spoke from the shadows, "You can't sleep either?"

"No," Mari said with a sigh. "Are you praying for the men?"

"Yes. It was like sending out sheep amongst the wolves. It won't be easy for them out there, you know."

"No, I suppose not." She followed the sound of his voice to find him sitting on the long bench against the wall, also looking up at the night sky.

His arms were raised triangles; his hands cupped the back of his head as he rested against a pillow. Mariamne came to sit at his feet. He motioned to the unoccupied length of the bench. She sat, also tucking her knees up and turning towards him so that she could see his darkened profile. She rested her head on a pillow also against the wall. They remained that way for some time. Neither spoke. She was waiting for him to admonish her, to tell her that her presence here with him at this hour was inappropriate, improper. But he did not.

Yeshua spoke first in a low voice, "I believe our time together is limited. Soon, you will need to return to Bethany to be with your family."

"I am not ready to return, not yet, Lord." She said.

"Things are going to change with the men going out. After them, I will send out more men, and I will go out on the road, visiting from town to town. We will be confronted with all kinds of conflict, and Herod Antipas will become more and more agitated by my presence."

She leaned her head on her raised knees, listening.

"I will need you and the other women to be safe so my mind is free to do what must be done. You have heard my teachings. You know what I am about. But now the disciples and I won't return to Capernaum nearly so much. We may even need to make a quick escape into other territories. I can't leave my daughters vulnerable."

Mari noticed that tonight, he spoke to her as a concerned father.

"You know, I don't want to go, not yet. I feel like I just got here. How long do…you…have?"

He knew what she was asking.

"I still have one more Passover left before…" his voice dropped with resolve.

Mari counted off the number of months and grimaced. Dread and the cool night air made her shiver. Yeshua reached over to cast his cloak over her. She snuggled into it, inhaling his scent. She leaned back against the wall, watching him. His cloak evoked the memory of that day at the temple when he had saved her from death and how he had covered her shame with his cloak. Even on that horrible day, the scent of his cloak strengthened and reassured her.

After a time, she said. "How do you know?"

He sighed, "I know through scriptures, premonitions, dreams, and visions. I was born to be the Passover Lamb/the Atonement Lamb all rolled into one."

Closing his eyes, he said, "After Yohannan's death, I have known my time of ministry was half over."

She leaned up again from her pillow to better see his face, trembling at the horrible thought of that day. "What will I do then? Not to be selfish, but..."

"You will wait and watch what happens to me; you will be one of my witnesses."

She looked up, "What do you mean?"

"Magdalene—that will forever be your name because you will be a watchtower that watches over my death on that day. You will root yourself like a tower, then standby to watch and take note of everything, first my death, then my resurrection, then when I return to my Father, when he sends you his Spirit, and finally, you will watch for my return."

"Resurrection?" her eyes looked hopeful.

"Yes, resurrection. You will trumpet these things that will begin the spread of the good news of God's salvation to people everywhere, beginning from the tomb, then to the other followers. Afterward, your words of resurrection will expand from Jerusalem to Galilee, into the wilderness, to Samaria. Your message will become an ever-expanding advance."

"What are you saying? How can I do all of that? What about the others? How can you ask me to watch you die?"

"All things are possible with God, Mari. As 'Magdalene,' you will stand as my faithful witness."

"Surely, not just me..."

He inclined his head, "No, not just you, but all who earnestly believe will do these things with you."

It sounded too mysterious for her to understand, "Lord, though I don't understand what you are asking, I will try to do my best if you show me. I could never say no to you."

She felt she might never get another moment like this, one where she could speak her most inward heart to him. She struggled to know if she should tell him, but the moment felt safe. She pushed away her indecision, "Lord, I don't know what will come or if I may ever have another chance to tell you..." Her words were softly whispered like a prayer.

Yeshua waited for her words, and he felt his heart beat a little faster.

"What I mean is, I can't let you do what you are going to do without telling you that I have placed you like a seal on my heart." Tears began to trace a path down her cheeks. "I want to always stay at your feet because I know my life is in your hands. I need you."

Her voice became thin and reedy, fraught with emotion, "I have placed myself under your authority and offered my life to you. And, tonight, right now, I feel like Ruth with Boaz, as if I am throwing myself at your feet on the winnowing floor. I am at your mercy to survive what is coming. If I could be with anyone forever, I choose you." She covered her mouth, trying to contain the sob of her emotions.

Yeshua moved to face her and to wipe the tears from her face. He caressed her cheek. His own deeply felt emotions filled his eyes. He pressed his forehead to hers and spoke her name, "Mari."

They sat like that for a moment. Mari felt safe enough to finish what she wanted to say.

"If only you could be my kinsman redeemer like Boaz was for Ruth," she whispered sadly.

Yeshua lifted her chin and looked into her eyes. "I Am."

She went still, barely breathing.

"I will be with you forever. Never fear." He looked into her eyes and promised her.

Then he dropped his hand and leaned slowly back against the stone wall.

He explained, "I am your Kinsman Redeemer; you are under my care, now and forever, and I will redeem you."

They sat quietly while Mari wondered at his words, knowing he meant what he said, though intuitively, she understood that she was just one of the many he would redeem. Still, she had spoken her heart, gave voice to her desire, and he had received her devotion gratefully.

Finally, she asked, "So why were you out here?"

"Because we needed to talk."

"You were waiting for me?"

"Something like that."

"You knew...?"

He said earnestly, "Sometimes, it feels like you are the only one who understands me or my purposes in this world, but I don't want to confuse you. My mission on earth will be completed. Then I will return to my Father. Even then, I will be with you; I will return *to* you. Then, when the time is right, I will return *for* you. You will come to understand there will dimensions in our spiritual union, but you will never be alone. Even when your physical death comes, I will never leave or forsake you. Until then, you will be an important part of the movement and a spiritual mother to many.

"Your devotion is a great comfort to me. You don't look at me like I am crazy. You don't doubt my methods or question my mission. It pleases me that you are always attuned to me and my thoughts. You constantly and willingly support my cause with all you have. Knowing that you believe in me and my words makes the trials I face easier. I am grateful."

To her ears, it seemed strange for Yeshua to make such a personal and human confession. She understood he was God. She collected all his promises to her as precious, personal, and to be believed. She was still basking in the warm promise of his words when his tone changed.

"But I must warn you now, Mari, in the future, your knowledge and thoughts will be tested. You will be tempted to forget what I have shown you, what you now know, and the things I have told you. You will have tribulations of your own that will make you doubt my promises and will require you to keep the faith at all costs, just as I do. It has been easy for you to believe in me up to now. It won't always be that easy."

She felt a weight of sick dread, and she stared up into the sky to ponder his words. What did the future hold? But Yeshua would never tell her. Up to now, his teachings have been like a salve for all her hurts and sorrows. She wanted to focus on those words and ignore his warnings, at least for tonight. She resolved herself to trust him. Hadn't he promised to be with her?

Peace permeated her soul. Old feelings of abandonment and deprivation evaporated in his presence. Satisfied that her devotion had pleased him, her eyes drifted closed, and her breathing evened out. She relaxed her arms between them. Her hand fell limply toward his foot that still rested on the bench. She sunk deeper into her pillow. Her hand slipped forward and found its anchor on the top of his foot. He sat still watching her sleep. It was as if reflexively, she was holding on to him as if to keep him from going. Her small unconscious act felt like a prayer to him.

$$\sim 5 \sim$$

THE RETURN

I will give them a heart to know me, that I am the Lord.
They will be my people, and I will be their God,
for they will return to me with all their heart.
Jeremiah 24:7

Those who go out weeping,
Carrying seed to sow will return with songs of joy,
carrying sheaves with them.
Psalm 126:6

Simon and Andrew were sent off into the region of Philip in Gaulanitus to hunt down pockets of Jews that were dispersed in those areas. These were hard-core places, surrounded by Gentiles and pagan beliefs. But when the Jews *were* found, they were surprised that anyone had even remembered them or thought to seek them out.

They even asked, "Why would *you* come out here to *us*?"

The response was positive, and they rejoiced at the good news of the coming of God's kingdom. They were eager to be baptized.

The two brothers found a family willing to give them a sheltered space to sleep and share their meals. It was in that family that the first healing took place, a child with a misshapen foot. With the healing, the boy was free to play with the other boys.

Word spread quickly after that, and more people came to hear them. They worked long hours, remembering and imitating what Yeshua had done before them. They remained for the designated time frame; by that time, many of the pagan neighbors began to question what was going on among the Jews. Several Roman soldiers showed up to see what was happening and to break up the crowd, sending people scattering in every direction.

Simon and Andrew decided it was time to return to Yeshua. Yeshua never remained so long as to bring the people trouble. With rejoicing, they returned to Galilee.

Just so, each pair of men returned to tell of their exploits, successes, failures, moments of triumph, celebration, and moments of fear. Each had experienced various obstacles along the way. They could hardly believe the awesome things Yeshua had sanctioned them to do in his name. They couldn't stop sharing their incredible experiences with Yeshua, one another, or their friends. Their excitement was contagious, causing other followers to long for the same experiences.

It was not long until the others came to Yeshua, saying, "Lord, send us out too! Let us go out in your name!"

Yeshua was encouraged by their enthusiasm. "Yes, I will send you, too!"

Matthew and Judas returned last, having had a challenging time. Most of the conflict had been between Matthew and Judas because of their very different viewpoints concerning ministry. Judas had left Matthew to do all the talking and healing while he constantly worked on ways to collect benefits or payments.

Matthew had admonished him for trying to get financial gain for God's grace, "Yeshua never charges the people for their healing or his help!" Matthew found himself shouting at Judas in frustration, "He will not be happy to hear what you are doing."

"Please! What are you so upset about? You were a tax collector! Would you dare to judge me? Besides, we need money for ministry. Yeshua thinks money will appear out of thin air. You don't have to live in fear there won't be enough, but as the money keeper, I do." Judas said.

"No! My life was driven by money in my former life before the Rabbi! I have seen how it affects one's reputation. Money makes people do things they should not do. Have you forgotten what Yeshua said? 'As you have freely received, freely give.' We are not to be like the temple priests."

"Look, someone has to fund our missions. It is up to me. Yeshua appointed me. He just doesn't know how much it takes to keep it all going! Didn't he throw us out here amongst these people to do the work he didn't want to do? Why shouldn't I draw a wage for that? Don't you think his way is harsh and restricting?"

"I will have no part of this," Matthew said. "I am leaving to-morrow. You can either go with me or stay."

Judas had looked at him with disgust. But when the morning came, he went with Matthew. Figuring it was better to cut his losses. When Matthew and Judas returned to Yeshua, Matthew was happy that he had been able to do miraculous deeds and help many people. However, Yeshua sensed Matthew was carrying some burden of guilt and shame from his time apart. Yeshua caught him sitting slumped and alone as though he was mulling over a worry. Matthew looked at Yeshua sheepishly as he approached and sat up a bit straighter. They sat side by side for a while without words. Then, Yeshua turned and looked closely at Matthew, "Did you have problems out there?"

Matthew nodded.

"Do you want to talk about it?"

"I would, but I don't want to be a snitch. I feel dirty for having been with Judas. There is only one thing that he thinks about."

"You will not be held guilty of his sins. Sometimes, the former sin wants to spring back up to accuse you or to tempt you. That is when you have to raise your shield of faith to repel the low blows and potshots."

"Yes, you are right, of course."

"Do not fear; the Father knows your heart, and Judas' too. Rejoice in the good you were able to do. You have proven yourself faithful. I am proud of you."

**

That night, Yeshua told his disciples a story, "The coming of the kingdom will be like a man leaving to go on a journey. He called his servants to him and then entrusted his wealth to their care."

He poked at the ground with his walking stick, building a little suspense to get their full attention, "To one servant, he gave five bags of gold, to another two bags, and another one bag, each according to his ability. Then he went on his journey."

He paused again, ensuring everyone, including Judas, had tuned in.

"The man who received five bags of gold went at once to put his money to work, and through his efforts, he gained five bags more."

He looked up at those who had fully committed themselves to their mission and work, making eye contact with them. He saw they seemed confused that he was talking about gold.

"So also, the one with two bags of gold gained two more."

He looked at those who had been more tentative and unsure in their approach and skill but had been productive nonetheless.

"But the man who had received just one bag of gold went off, dug a hole in the ground, and hid his master's money." He looked at Judas; he stared back at him with real interest since the topic was gold.

"After a long time, the master of those servants returned and settled accounts with them. The man who had received five bags of gold brought the other five they had gained from their efforts.

'Master,' he said, 'you entrusted me with five bags of gold. See, I have gained five more.'"

All eyes were riveted quizzically on Yeshua as he continued. He lay his staff aside.

"His master replied, 'Well done, good and faithful servant! You have been faithful with a few things; I will put you in charge of many things. Come and share your master's happiness!' And Yeshua clapped his hands joyfully. He looked at those who had deployed their skill with abandon, having taken the risks and put themselves out there for his cause.

"The man with two bags of gold also came. 'Master,' he said, 'you entrusted me with two bags of gold; see, I have gained two more.'"

He looked at some of the men who had not been quite as successful. They bowed their heads, humbled that they had not produced more but still very grateful for the returns they had gained in their ministry efforts. They were glad for their experiences.

"His master replied, 'Well done, good and faithful servant! You have been faithful with a few things; I will put you in charge of many things. Come and share your master's happiness!'"

Again, Yeshua clapped his hands appreciatively at those who had felt insecure in their ministry but conservatively put their skills to the task; they had been obedient and stepped far outside their comfort zone.

He stopped clapping and took up his staff again, bracing it in his right hand like a king.

"Then the man who had received one bag of gold came, saying, 'Master, I knew you are a hard man, harvesting where you have not sown and gathering where you have not scattered seed.I was afraid to put your gold to use, so I went out and hid it in the ground. Here is exactly what belongs to you.'"

Yeshua directed his eyes on Judas, "His master replied, 'You wicked, lazy servant! So, you knew that I harvest where I have not sown and gather where I have not scattered seed? Well then, you should have deposited my gold with the bankers so that I would have received it back with interest when I returned."

Judas looked surprised.

Yeshua continued, "He spoke to his other servants, saying, 'Take his bag of gold from him and give it to the one who now has ten bags.'"

Pausing, he maintained his uncomfortable eye contact. Judas squirmed under its fierce intensity, 'Wait, is he speaking about me?'

An unreasonable fear filled him. Everyone in the group looked from Yeshua to Judas and back again, as his prolonged and stern stare made his displeasure known.

Judas looked nervously toward Matthew, wondering what he had said. But Matthew looked neither jubilant nor remorseful but sat listening alertly.

"Master, is this story about making more money?" Judas tried to prepare a defense.

"What do you think? Is it about money?"

Judas looked confused.

Yeshua looked back to the others, "For whoever has received wealth from the master and put it to practice will gain more, the more they believe, the more they will gain, and they will have an abundance to show for their efforts."

Looking back to Judas, he said, "Whoever has not received, or obeyed, even what they have will be taken from them." Yeshua raised his staff, then drove it decisively into the soil like a king rendering a decision with his scepter. "And the king will say, 'Throw that worthless servant outside, into the darkness, where there will be weeping and gnashing of teeth.'"

The disciples shivered at 'the Masters' verdict, not wanting to be that man. They understood this story had been told to inform them of an important kingdom truth, not mere entertainment. He used them to teach touchy and complex subjects and to illuminate spiritual truths.

When his story was finished, Yeshua began to sing a psalm, and a few joined in the celebratory tune, and the disciples eased back, meditating on the story for more of its significance. A muscle worked in Judas' cheek as he silently gnashed his teeth together in anger. He didn't appreciate being called out, even if it was indirectly. He simply refused to acknowledge he had done anything wrong.

~ 6 ~

SCATTERING SEEDS

(The righteous) have freely scattered their gifts to the poor,
their righteousness endures forever;
their horn will be lifted high in honor. - Psalm 112:9

The voice of the Lord strikes
with flashes of lightning. - Psalm 29:7

That spring, Yeshua visited the towns where he had previously sent his men to announce his coming kingdom. To the people, it was a new world order, and they were anxious to hear him. He never tarried long. He had too many towns to visit. His window of opportunity was already closing, so he worked all the harder to reach the dispersed Jews who lived within Israel's borders. They would be critical to the future of the movement. A network of people was already working strategically together to expand and multiply the kingdom.

The seeds of the gospel were being scattered everywhere, springing up in the soil of unexpected places like the wild mustard seeds, traveling great distances as if carried on the wind. Not everyone who heard the good news of God's kingdom was happy about it or ready to receive it. Still, the seeds of his kingdom fell upon the hardened hearts just the same as the prepared hearts. They fell on the ears of those who lived and moved in thorny places, places where many factors simply overgrew the words of hope with the weeds of concern and doubt. The seeds were often attacked by the Pharisees, who picked away at the words like greedy birds, snatching them up before they could take root. But some people were like fertile soil, plowed and ready to receive the seeds of his words and believe in him with real joy.

Yeshua prepared and sent out seventy-two other disciples with his most basic and introductory message, targeting every prominent village to receive an announcement of the good news.

"Repent," his messengers shouted, "for the Kingdom of God is coming to you. Get ready for the Messiah is on the move."

With so many preachers afoot, it became really hard to track Yeshua as he went from place to place. No one knew where he was, and it was clear that the seventy-two didn't know what his schedule might be. This kept the authorities confused because he had effectively multiplied his presence and message. He had given his disciples his authority. So their words resounded with the weight of his glory, striking their intended targets like flashes of lightning. Meanwhile, Yeshua prayed for the presence of all evil to be subdued, to clear the path before them.

He stayed on the move with hardly any identifiable rhyme or reason. The twelve and Magdalene and Susanna traveled with him from place to place. Joanna had returned to her husband. Magdalene and Susanna made themselves useful by ministering among the women of the towns and offering them his special encouragement concerning their lives.

Finally, Yeshua and the seventy-two met up at the designated time with great excitement and joy, ready to share their stories, "Lord, even the demons submit to us in your name," they exclaimed.

The Lord rejoiced with them, "Yes, I saw Satan fall like lightning from heaven. I have given you authority to trample on snakes and scorpions and to overcome all the enemy's power so that nothing will harm you."

But quickly, the disciples began to exhibit an unhealthy sense of competition rather than humble encouragement and support of one another. Their stories began to take on a sense of propriety rather than praise, as if they had done their miracles on their own. Their excitement began to veer precariously towards pridefulness.

He warned them, "Do not rejoice that the spirits submit to your commands. Instead, rejoice that your names are written in heaven."

**

When all the missionaries were safely regathered, their excitement became explosive. Everyone talked over one another to share their stories. Each disciple could feel the kingdom of God was really alive and powerful, and it was advancing exponentially.

When Yeshua stood up before them, an expectant hush fell across the crowd. Full of joy through the Holy Spirit, he lifted his eyes and hands towards heaven in a prayer of praise.

"I praise you, Father, Lord of heaven and earth because you have hidden the kingdom from the wise and learned; instead, you have revealed it to little children. Yes, Father, for this is what you were pleased to do."

He gazed around at all seventy-two, his twelve disciples, and the women. His heart was full of love and joy. As he spoke, his voice sounded as if he were standing next to them, speaking directly to each one of them or even from within them, making his words feel very personal, "All things have been committed to me by my Father. No one knows the Son except the Father, and no one knows the Father except the Son and those to whom the Son chooses to reveal his Father."

The disciples wore expressions of seriousness and pleasure, knowing they had been chosen for both revelation and mission.

"Blessed are the eyes that see what you are seeing. You can't imagine how many prophets and kings wanted to see what you are seeing now, but it was not time. They longed to hear what you hear but did not hear it."

Being called 'little children' was insulting to Judas, he interrupted peevishly, "Lord, why do you call us little children?"

Yeshua called to Rock's daughter Ana. She ran to him joyfully, leaping up into his arms. He lifted her and held her high. Her face hovered just above his. She took his beard in her chubby little hands and tugged playfully until she lay her face to his, eye to eye.

Yeshua laughed. "Ana, who do you spy with your little eye?"

"My Yeshi!" she crowed happily, soundly patting his cheeks.

He hugged her to him, then twirled her around, causing her to giggle and squeal with happiness.

Then he answered Judas and addressed the gathering as he took his seat with the child on his knee.

"I am telling you a kingdom truth: Only those who come when they are called like little children will ever enter the kingdom of heaven.

"Therefore, whoever welcomes the kingdom of God with the abandonment and joy of a child, without distaining his lowly position, is the greatest in the kingdom of heaven."

Judas chewed his jaw and fought the need to roll his eyes. He did not care for children; they were loud, noisy, dirty, and troublesome. And, they were of no benefit to him.

He looked away to brood, 'Yeshua lives with an irritating view of the world! Still, his movement is expanding. People are all too happy to offer up their money in appreciation. I can't quit now. If I can keep skimming some off the top, I'd be a fool to leave. And who is the wiser? Look at him! He is too lost in his childish illusions to care.'

When he looked up, he found Yeshua's eyes were upon him. He offered him a nonchalant smile and a nod, thinking, 'Yeshua is simply too lucrative. I can't walk away, not yet.'

**

In Magdala, the temple tax collectors boarded a ship traveling to Capernaum. They were to go and gather back taxes, specifically from Yeshua and Simon and a few other disciples who had been remiss in making the required tithe.

One of them was so intent on his goal that he forgot to have his fare ready as he went to board the boat. People waited irritably behind him. He asked his co-worker to pay his fare, and he would pay him back once they boarded the boat.

But once he was on the way, he forgot to pay the man. Before they drew near their landing, his co-worker reminded him of re-imbursement.

"Don't you think I am good for it?" the man huffed testily.

His partner stared at him pointedly, holding out his hand.

He threw down his day bag to rummage through it, pulling out a handful of coins to prove his ability. His hand laid open before his partner as proof. The boat lurched unexpectedly, knocking him off balance and causing a large four-drachma coin to fall from his hand. It rolled across the floor. He clamped his hand on his other coins and shuffled to reach it. Unfortunately, it landed with barely a splash into the Galilean Sea. He looked on with regret as his glittering coin sank into the water.

Still sputtering, he turned back to his insistent partner with accusation, "That was a four-drachma coin! Now, I will never see that coin again!"

A sizable fish saw the large glittering object and swam directly for it. Thinking it was a smaller fish, it opened wide to take the coin into its mouth. He tried to swallow it with a gulp, but it was not a fish. It did not go down, and now, it seemed he could not release the coin either. The poor fish swam away with the coin trapped in its mouth.

**

A bit later, Rock opened the door to find two official-looking characters looking down their nose at him. This could not be good.

"Simon bar Jonah?"

"Yes?"

"We have come to collect your two-drachma tax. You are past due."

Rock knew they meant business, "Sorry, I have been out of town quite a bit lately."

"So it would seem. We understand you are a disciple of the Rabbi called Yeshua. Be that as it may, that hardly removes you from your duty to pay the temple tax, now does it? A devote man gladly pays his dues."

The other man sneered, "And, what about your Rabbi? Does he pay his temple tax? Or, does he teach you that you do not have to pay the temple taxes? It seems he has been conveniently "away" as well!"

"Yes, of course he pays his taxes!" Rock defended his Master. "We will come to the synagogue and pay you..."

"Don't you have it now?"

"Well, I don't have that much, but I will get it," Rock assured them.

"See that you do. Otherwise, we will send someone to persuade you."

Rock closed the door and sighed heavily before returning to Yeshua inside.

"There is always one more looking for their pound of flesh!" he said with disgust. "I am just a fisherman!"

Yeshua noted Simon's anxiety, "What do you think, Simon? Do kings tax their children or people they do not consider family?"

Rock answered, "Other people."

"You are right, but so we do not offend the temple tax collectors, go to the lake and throw out your line. Take the first fish you catch and open its mouth. You will find a four-drachma coin. Give it to them to pay for my tax and yours."

"Why not ask Judas for it? Doesn't he disperse the money we need? Or is he crying bankrupt yet again?"

Yeshua gave Rock a prolonged glance but did not remark.

Rock did what Yeshua commanded. He went down to the shore and cast his line into the water. It was really not too long before he got a hit. He could tell that it was a sizable fish. But surprisingly, it did not take long to pull it in, "Ahh," Rock talked to the fish, "so you have no fight in you."

Landing the fish, he remembered to open its mouth. Awestruck, he pulled the large four-drachma coin from the fish's mouth. As soon as he did, the fish squirmed and slipped from his hand to splash into the water to swim away.

Rock laughed, "For your service, you get to live another day! Thank you!"

He held the coin up to the light.

He surprised the tax collector when he found him and placed the coin in his hand.

"How did you get this?" The man frowned as if to say, "I know you are wretchedly poor."

Rock said, "It was a gift from God."

The man clucked his tongue. He had no idea he was holding what had been his own coin to carry back to Herod's temple.

**

It was around noon when Yohan came racing to find Yeshua, "Herod has sent some of his militia to Capernaum. I just saw them asking for your whereabouts. From what I could gather, Herod has summoned you. We all know what that means. Look at what happened with Yohannan. Reports of the missionaries throughout his region have him trembling in fear. He fears our movement is subversive and will lead to an insurrection. He wants to see for himself that you are not Yohannan risen from the grave."

Yeshua narrowed his eyes, "Of course, some things never change."

Yohan awaited his instructions. His youthful face was full of fear.

"The time has come to leave this region for a while. I will take the road towards Syria." Yeshua said, gathering his satchel, filling it with food, and grabbing his skin and filling it with water.

"Go get the others and scatter, get out of town. Each of you should travel separately. They will be looking for a group or a pair of you on the highways. Do not return to this house. Take only the essentials for the journey. I will meet you along the road to Syria. When we have regathered, we will travel northeast from Herod's jurisdiction. He has no attention span for such pursuits; if the threat disappears, eventually he will give up."

Yeshua was once again grateful for the guidance of the scriptures that gave him direction. When Elijah had fled from Ahab, he went to stay among the Gentiles. It kept him safely out of Ahab's reach, "Once news of our mission dries up, he will get bored and move on."

Still, Yeshua did not waste time preparing to leave.

He instructed Yohan, "Also, go tell Magdalene Herod is in pursuit. Tell her to take the other women and return to Bethany. And, tell them not to worry."

Yohan responded, "You can count on me."

Yeshua donned his cloak, then quickly disappeared into the streets, heading for an indirect path out of town.

Yohan ran to locate the others. As he entered the main street, he saw Herod's men striding towards the now-emptied house of the disciples. How fortuitous that the women were gone to the market. Herod's soldiers barely glanced at him. He had to admit that his youthful appearance was a benefit sometimes.

After Herod's men had passed, Yohan picked up his pace to locate the women and the rest of the men.

~ 7 ~

THE CHANGING SEASONS

Surely you will summon nations you know not,
and nations you do not know will come running to you,
because of the Lord your God, the Holy One of Israel,
he has endowed you with splendor."
Isaiah 55:5

Yohan appeared on the road below. Yeshua let out a sigh of satisfaction. He was the last one. All twelve had all made it safely out of Capernaum. Now, the whole group could head out upon the high road towards Tyre and Sidon.

After several days of hard travel, they made their way through the hilly terrain to the intended destination between the two coastal cities, the ancient town of Zarephath. The same place where miraculously his Father had provided a hideout for Elijah amongst the Sidonian people.

In this region, the culture was utterly Hellenized. Every nation in the Middle East had adopted the Greek language and culture under the rule of Alexander the Great. The maritime city was wedged between two bustling seaports. Zarephath had always been a major point of convergence, and it was well known for its industry of purifying crucibles for ores harvested from the hills. The city's name meant 'crucible.' It was a town of iron works, purified minerals, pottery, and purple dye. It had one of the worst red-light districts on the coast. It was a port where seafaring men enjoyed feminine comfort and pleasure.

The women in this area were understandably rough around the edges. They painted their eyes and wore colorful and sleeveless tunics that revealed their tattooed skin. The women went about with unveiled hair.

The village borders stretched out toward Tyre to the south and toward Sidon to the north. Both of these two cities had personalities and energies of their own, filled with all kinds of Greek entertainment, such as theatres, sports arenas, feasting establishments, a variety of shrines to the gods and goddesses of the nations, libraries, and educational institutions. Both cities had adopted impressive Greek-style buildings, complete with amphitheaters, baths, and trickling fountains. Mansions of wealthy tradesmen were large, well-manicured, and walled away in the cities. On the north side of Sidon and the south side of Tyre were the large country estates of the ruling classes who wished to be as far from Zarephath as possible. Wealth was on display everywhere within these two cities.

The families of seafaring men and the serving class lived in rough little hovels in Zarephath, near the highways, for ease of commute. Small pockets of Jews lived there, but they were so Hellenized that it was hard to identify them. The disciples caused a stir. Their Jewish attire looked oddly out of place. Not only did they feel conspicuous, but they were also more than a little bit disoriented by the sights and smells of the village market. The cloying scent of the exotic spices mixed with the aroma of roasting pigs and shellfish. It was a stark reminder that they were not in Galilee anymore. But it was for this very reason that Herod would not think to find them there. They passed through the market quickly to escape notice. But as always, there was a man who had recently traveled through Galilee who recognized them and began to spread the news. Notoriety was not all it was cracked up to be.

Almost immediately, the news of Yeshua's arrival began to spread among the other Jews.

Upon reaching their destination, their Jewish hosts ushered them quickly into their sufficiently sized home with an unexpected delight. After the welcoming cleansing ritual had been administered, Yeshua and his men were seated for an impromptu meal of bread and watered wine meant to hold them over until the evening meal was prepared.

His hosts, Rivka and Iason, wanted to be happy at Yeshua's visit. But he explained to them that his presence in Sidon was out of necessity rather than a social visit. They couldn't ignore the ominous undertones when he told them what had happened.

"Herod sent his men for me," Yeshua said. "We just need to lay low for a bit until things cool off."

"Herod thinks he is the Baptizer come back to life," Andrew added.

They were surprised and anxious. Still, they agreed, "You can stay as long as you wish. We are honored."

"Thank you. We will do our best to keep our presence hidden," Yeshua assured them.

"Of course, of course." His hosts nodded sagely, not wanting Herod's long arm of wrath to touch their home.

"Thanks." Yeshua offered a wan smile.

Iason led them through the inner courtyard to a large private room. "I think this will work well for you and your men; if you need more room, let us know. But you may sleep here and take your comfort in this room; it is our largest guest space. It will give you privacy. Our son and his wife began here, but then he built his own home just down the street."

Yeshua looked around the large room, thinking it was the same size as the home he had grown up in.

"This is more than sufficient. Thank you!"

Iason led them back into the courtyard, "And you are welcome to use the courtyard and inner porches, which are hidden from view of the street. You should not be detected here."

"We are very grateful for this space. It will work out splendidly."

But word *had* spread that the Jewish Messiah was hidden somewhere within the village. People were watching for him. That night, the disciples spoke honestly with Yeshua about their concerns of speaking openly in this place.

"There are too many Gentiles here," Nathaniel said without diplomacy; his nose curled as if at a bad smell.

"Please keep your voice down. Do you wish to insult our kind hosts?"

"Well, I, for one, am confused; Yeshua had us go out to share his message with our Jewish brothers and sisters, not to the Greeks or the Syrians," James said. "Remember that we were only to take our message to Jews?"

"Not completely true!" Rock said adamantly. "Remember when he healed the Gerasene demoniac, and Samaritans, and ..."

"And the tax collectors and women." Matthew cut in to finish for him, knowing he and his ilk were still not fully accepted by the other disciples. His point rested uneasily among them.

Chagrinned Rock said, "It is just that I feel the same way here as I felt near Gera. These people creep me out. Did you see that snake handler today? I swear the serpent hissed and lunged right at me. I hate snakes. What kind of people make them their pets?"

Yeshua overheard their whispers. "I have a story to tell you," he said, stepping into the room.

The men turned his way, anticipating another kingdom lesson.

"Great, I could use a good story about right now," James quipped.

Yeshua sat, then leaned back to relax upon the Greek settee. The lantern light flickered and danced across his weathered features, shimmering in his eyes and the gloss of his beard. In his repose, he had the appearance of a sage king.

He began, "There was a certain man—a King—who put in motion the preparations for a great wedding feast for his son." Yeshua began.

"He prepared a long list of persons who he hoped would come and share in his joy," he paused, stroking his chin thoughtfully, "When the banquet preparations were complete, he sent his servants out to those he had invited to say, 'Come to the feast, for everything has been prepared.'

Some of his men remembered being invited to Hannah's wedding. They nodded, remembering they had been favored as Yeshua's guests.

Yeshua continued, "But one by one, they all began to make excuses. The first said, 'I have just bought a field, and I must go and see it. Please excuse me. Another person said, 'I have just bought a yoke of five oxen. I'm on my way to try them out. Please accept my apologies.' Still, another said, 'I just got married, so I cannot attend.'"

The disciples thought, 'Those seem like legitimate reasons. But who would say such a thing to a king?' Each man recalled how he had almost declined the invitation to Hannah's wedding because of their other responsibilities. It was his first miracle, and they would have missed it. They leaned forward wondering, 'Where is he going with this?' They recalled all the other men who had followed Yeshua for a short period, only to leave with excuses.

Yeshua looked around the circle, studying the effect of his story. "Now, his servants returned to the king filled with trepidation at delivering such a report to the king. Only a few had responded with enthusiasm.

"The king became livid at this lack of reverence for him. He ordered his servant, 'Go out quickly into the streets and alleys of the town; bring in the poor, the crippled, the blind and the lame.'

"Sir,' the servant said, twisting his hands before him, 'what you have ordered has already been done, but there is still room.'"

The disciples thought of their trips to the villages and remote areas of Galilee and the lack of response. "Then the master told his servant, 'Go out on the highways and to the country lanes. Compel the people to come so my palace will be filled.I tell you, not one of those who were invited but had more important things to do will get even a taste of my banquet.'"

Their faces reflected alarm, 'Is he saying what I think he is saying?' But then they realized, no one could dishonor a king in this way and expect less?'

Yeshua sat quietly, chewing on the edge of his beard, letting his silence settle.

Then, he spoke so softly that his men strained to hear his words, "When the barley harvest has ended, the wheat harvest begins."

They looked about confused. Both the barley and wheat harvests had passed for that year. What was the Teacher talking about?

Rock held up his hands in exasperation, "What are you saying? What do barley and wheat have to do with your story?"

Yeshua took a deep breath and let it go with a slow patience, "Our people, the Jewish people, have received their invitation, but few attend the banquet. Now, the harvest has begun its transition; the opportunity is shifting away from the Jews toward the Gentiles." He stared into the future. "But there is still a bit of scattered barley yet to be brought in."

No one questioned him further, knowing it was another riddle to chew on when they weren't so tired. Yeshua was tired, also.

He thought, 'The Jews have historically held on to Yahweh as if he were their God alone, who they are unwilling to share. Yet they don't want him either. They have failed to understand that he is the LORD of all the nations, of all people everywhere, whether they know him or not. They have failed to foresee that Yahweh would open a doorway for all people. Didn't he charge Israel to be a light to all the nations?'

**

Bernice looked down upon her sleeping daughter; the fierceness of her love for her child sometimes made her heart hurt. Fatoula had just turned five. She was beautiful and sweet-natured, but Bernice was forever watchful. A horrible destructive force seemed determined to steal her child away. One moment, Fatoula would be playing happily, and the very next, she would be struck down and fighting for her life. Bernice dreaded the sudden look of terror right before her little cherub would fall to the floor to twist in agony. Her eyes would roll back in her head, and her mouth would foam, and most times, she would wet herself or worse. She had even momentarily quit breathing, and her lips had turned blue. Bernice was hyper-vigilant to intervene and refused to leave her alone for a minute as if her constant presence could ward off death.

When this occurred in public, people fled, screaming and pointing at her suffering child. Bernice's world shrunk to this constant state of anxiety. She was exhausted and fearful the next time her child would be stolen away from her.

She had gone to every healer and diviner of the gods in the hope of saving her, but no help was found. Deep down, Bernice felt her daughter's illness was somehow her fault. She had displeased the gods, and Fatoula was paying the price for her offense.

She racked her memory, wondering, 'Haven't I done everything the gods had demanded of me?'

She remembered the time her husband had placed their perfect first-born son into the arms of Baal, and he had melted into the flames. She had been inconsolable. The ritual had felt so wrong to her. He had sacrificed her perfect son. She had begged her husband not to do it. But he had insisted this would give them favor with the god of prosperity. Once they became wealthy, they could have a houseful of children. But she often woke in a sweat, in tears, hearing again and again the drums of the temple musicians and the screams of her son. Wasn't this more than any god should demand of a mother? Yet, where was the reward he had promised her?

Her second pregnancy had been hard. Both Bernice and her daughter had almost died from the labors of childbirth. The midwife had pushed and prodded her abdomen until she thought she would be torn asunder. Still, the child could not come.

As a last resort, the woman had placed a crude instrument up into her body to grasp the child's head, trying to turn her. The pain had been excruciating. Finally, the child's release had come, and she had slid from her womb—a girl. But the child did not cry or make any sound. She was sure the child was stillborn. After examining the child, the midwife found the child was alive, but she believed the child had been too traumatized by the birth and she would not survive. She insisted the child should be taken and left on the rocks as an offering to the sea. But Bernice had adamantly refused. She could not allow the loss of another child.

"What have I done to anger the gods?" She had cried out.

As Fatoula grew, she never made a sound. She was still an infant when the seizures began. Bernice tried everything, but nothing worked. Exhausted by the constant needs of their strangely muted child, her husband had divorced her, saying she loved the child more than him. He turned her and the child out onto the streets.

She had come home to her mother and father. It was a lot to ask of them. Initially, they feared their granddaughter, but in time, they had softened their hearts. They saw the child's pain and sought to relieve it as much as they could.

Two days before, one of Bernice's Jewish neighbors had told her they had heard of a Jewish Rabbi who had come to town and was known for producing miracles of healing and driving out demons.

"They say no one has ever spoken with such words of authority as his. He was spotted in the village market recently with his men."

Bernice's heart skipped a beat. "Then...you must tell me when you find him. I will go to him straight away. He may be my last chance before one of these fits takes Fatoula from me forever."

Now, looking upon her sweet child, she bowed her head and prayed to the unknown Hebrew God, "Please. I beg of you, although

I am unworthy to ask it, please have mercy on me and help me to find your Healer! You are my last hope."

Fatoula stirred a little and smiled up at her mother, the smile of an angel. And Bernice's heart quickened with a beat of hope.

**

Bernice carried the basket of food filled with kosher fruits and vegetables on her shoulder. In another basket, she had a container of fresh curds, a package of goat cheese, and a dozen eggs. Her mother had insisted that *she* take this to the house of the Jewish woman who paid well for her produce.

"Please!" her mother urged her, "My arthritis is bothering me badly today." Bernice grimaced to see her mother hobbling about, holding onto her hip and back.

"Look at Fatoula!" Her mother pointed. "She is doing fine, and I promise I will watch her as if I were you! It will only take you a few minutes. It will do you good to get out of the house for a while."

Bernice agreed. Still, she hurried along the narrow street, anxious to make the delivery and return home. It took several knocks before the door opened. The maidservant ushered her into the storage keep to complete the transaction.

While the servant counted out the objects and prepared to make payment, Bernice glanced up to look through the interior door into the inner portico. She saw a group of men sitting around a low table in the courtyard, enjoying their midday meal. She could see that they were distinctively Jewish.

"You have company." She observed, staring.

"Yes, visitors who wish to preserve their privacy. So please, keep their presence to yourself?" she asked, pressing an extra coin into Bernice's hand rather pointedly.

Bernice looked at her host. "Would that be the Healer from Galilee?"

"You have heard of him? He has come to seek asylum, though he has done nothing wrong. Please do not tell anyone he is here. Or, my mistress will have my head," She begged the girl.

Before her words were out of her mouth, Bernice bolted into the courtyard, coming to stand directly beside the man with gentle eyes, who was obviously in charge. She fell face down before him, taking hold of his feet.

"Lord, Son of David, have mercy on me! My little daughter suffers terribly from a demon."

As soon as the woman touched him, Yeshua felt the power of her faith lifting him as if a portion of his spirit had separated from his body. Although he was seated at the table, he was simultaneously transported to a room several blocks away.

Seeing the strange expression on his face, Thomas called out to him. "Lord!"

He turned to the other disciples, "What is that woman doing to him? Look!"

Even though Yeshua was in the distant room, Yeshua was also aware of what was happening with the woman and with the disciples. It was as if he was in two places at the same time. Everything seemed to slow down as if moving in slow motion.

In the distant room, a young girl sat playing quietly with her doll. Her grandmother got up to go into the kitchen. But as soon as she went, the child's eyes filled with terror as two dark spirits pressed in around her. One grabbed her head and squeezed it as if it were gripped in a vice. The child fell to the ground, thrashing and fighting. The other spirit grabbed at her throat and began to strangle her. Her eyes bulged with terror before they rolled back into her head, and her mouth foamed, and she shook all over.

Anger and compassion consumed Yeshua. "Be gone from the child!" He commanded the spirits with a low growl. Surprised, the demons looked up, shielding their eyes from the brightness of his light. They began to spit and curse, but their grip upon the girl was broken. In a flash of power, they were thrown across the room away from the child.

"Do not touch this child again!" Two flashes of lightning escorted the two demons from the room.

Just then, her grandmother stepped into the room, shocked and frantic to find her granddaughter lying limp on the floor. "Oh no-no-no-no-no!" The elderly woman screamed, "Fatoula! Fatoula!" How had this happened? She had only been gone a moment. Filled with self-blame, she lifted her limp granddaughter into her lap, listening for her breath, fearing she was dead.

"Awaken, Fatoula," Yeshua commanded her.

The child's eyes opened, and she sucked in a purifying breath. She saw the Man of Light who had driven the dark spirits away, "Look, Grandmother, the Man of Light!"

The girl reached toward Yeshua. He took her hand and stood her on her feet. Holding his hand, she basked in his light.

Her grandmother looked around the room and did not see anyone, though she could feel the benevolence of his presence. It was only then that she realized that her little granddaughter had spoken for the first time.

"He is here!" The child exclaimed, motioning to the air in front of her.

Fatoula spoke to the air, "You drove them away!"

"Yes," he answered her, "The darkness has no place in your life anymore. You, Fatoula, were made for light. Isn't your name Fatoula? God is light."

"I like your light. Can I be light like you?" She asked shyly.

"Why yes. I like your light, too. Do not be afraid. Those creatures of darkness will never appear to you again." He could tell by her relieved expression that she believed him.

Meanwhile, blocks away, the woman was still kneeling at his feet, sobbing with grief and hope. She did not even lift her head for fear of his rejection. She held on to his feet, refusing for him to flee before she got her blessing. She pled her case, desperate for her pain to be heard.

Rivka ran into the courtyard, her hands to her face in embarrassment at this intrusion.

The disciples came to their feet, preparing to drag the small woman out of the house.

"Should we send her away, Lord? If she keeps crying out like this, the authorities will come, and the whole city will discover we are here."

Now collected to himself once more, Yeshua looked around the circle of anxious men, wondering, 'How can they not feel her pain?'

This was a teachable moment, one that he hoped they would not soon forget. He let out a heavy sigh and shook his head, "No."

Bernice sought his face, her tear-filled eyes pleading silently.

Scripture had been clear that he *would* become a light unto the Gentiles, but he had not expected this to begin so soon. His focus had been on the lost sheep of Israel. But even now, the pagan world was seeking his light. He whispered more to himself than to anyone present, "Was I not sent to gather the lost sheep of Israel?"

"Lord, please help me!" She begged.

He looked towards his men and considered the moment. He said, "Should not the children eat their fill before I take the children's bread and toss what is left to the dogs?"

The disciples' mouths fell askance as if hearing their own cruel and prejudicial remarks for the first time.

Beatrice didn't care. She would reason with this holy man. With determination, she sat back onto her haunches, waiting like a persistent dog at his feet. Faith and hope radiated from her face. She refused to take "No" for an answer. She opened her hands as if ready to receive, "Yes, but Lord, even the dogs eat the crumbs that fall from their masters' table."

Yeshua's eyes left the confused faces of his men to look upon the woman. Her lip trembled with fear and determination. His face turned soft, and he reached out and touched Bernice's face gently, in the same way he had touched her daughter's face, and he wiped away her tears.

"Woman, you have great faith! Your request is granted, your daughter is healed, and her demons are gone," he stood and helped her to her feet. "Your mission has been successful. Like a warrior, you have stormed heaven's gate to be victorious. Go home, Bernice, and see your Fatoula. She is waiting for you, and she has something to say to you."

Bernice's hands flew to her mouth with a gasp of joy. Tears shimmered like pools in her eyes. She reached out and took his hand, kissing it with her deepest gratitude. Then she turned and ran to her home.

Yeshua watched her go with another jolting reminder that his death was quickly approaching. This was the first of many other signs that a new harvest season was beginning. It would not be long now before he would fall like a kernel of wheat into the earth.

**

Bernice flung open the door. Quickly, she scanned the room to find her daughter standing in a beam of sunlight streaming through the window. Fatoula spun around at the sound of her mother.

"Ummi!" Fatoula shouted. "Come, let me tell you about the man who is the Light of God. He saved me from the darkness. He told me I would never have to fear the darkness again."

Bernice yelped in awe to hear her daughter's voice for the first time and see her beaming with such delight. She knew her daughter was healed. How had the man been with her and with her daughter at the same time?

Bernice's mother began, "I thought sure Fatoula was dead, but then she came back to life and immediately began to tell me about the Man of Light."

"Just wait until I tell you what happened," Bernice told her mother. But first, she lifted her daughter into her arms and spun her around. Fatoula's laughter filled the room like the music of the tinkling bells on tambourines.

~ 8 ~

TREADING ON HIGH PLACES

"[The LORD] is your shield and helper
and your glorious sword.
Your enemies will cower before you,
and you will tread on their high places."
Deuteronomy 33:29

Eventually, the word began to spread that Yeshua was in the Tyre and Sidon region. Jews began to look for him in hopes of hearing his kingdom teachings, but some of the local Greeks and Syrians gathered as well. He spent several days teaching. But before the word of his location could spread, they left under the cover of night. He did not have the luxury of staying too long in one place.

As they traveled away from the cities and back out onto the inward roads of Lebanon, Rock said, "I have to tell you, I am glad to be leaving this area."

Yeshua winced at their unchanging attitudes towards the Gentiles, "Do you remember how you felt when the Pharisees began to complain about our lack of ritual cleansing and eating with defiled hands?"

Rock silently guessed he was about to get another lesson.

"Take care not to become a hypocrite. When a person becomes devoted to my Father, they become Corban—set apart—made Holy."

He glanced at Rock to look for evidence that he understood, "Let's take a break."

The group ventured into a grove of trees just off the path.

He began to teach, "Listen to me, all of you. Understand this: Nothing outside of you can defile you. Going to Sidon and Tyre did not defile you. It is not what you eat that defiles you. It simply goes in and comes out.

"No, it is 'the darkness within you' that defiles you. The darkness within your heart—your evil thoughts and impure desires. What defiles you is lust, envy, unfaithfulness, greed, covetousness, malice, deceit, lewdness, slander, arrogance, and folly. These evil behaviors pollute your motivations and make you unloving and unclean; they are what defile you. Thinking you are better than others just because you are a Jew defiles you. Since the fall, sin has been a poison within every man. Even you."

"When I sent you to the Jews on your missions, it was not because Jews are somehow better than other people, but because the promise was first given to them as the chosen people through whom the Messiah would come. It is only right that the promised kingdom should begin with them for having believed the promise and because Jews like yourselves still have a role to play in the coming harvest.

"There is a season for all things. Up to now, the season of salvation has been for the Jews, but now that season is coming to an end, a new generation or season for the Gentiles is about to begin. For now, during the transition of seasons, they will overlap. But you, my chosen people, you will help implement my kingdom among all peoples, Jews and Gentiles alike."

The men exchanged incredulous and confused glances. 'A season for the Gentiles? What was he saying?'

"You will be my seed bearers," Yeshua said. "You will go where I send you."

**

Having taken the northern route through the city of Sidon, Yeshua led them onto an interior road that eventually veered to the south. The terrain became rugged, with towering peaks to each side. They were grateful for the Roman roads laid over ancient paths that made their travel through this area easier.

"Where are we going, now?" His men wanted to know.

Yeshua kept his council to himself, "You will see."

The northern route took them further from the territories of Herod Antipas, but this was not the only reason he had taken this road. From the moment he had returned from his temptation, there had been something he had kept in mind to do. Now it was time. He had headed north, treading the ancient northern boundary of the promised land once given to the tribes of Jacob, Abraham's children.

Cresting the long and steady incline, they came upon a level plain where they first caught a view of the magnificent Hermon mountain range; its three peaks waited ahead. The tallest one was on the historic Amorite border, called Mount Hermon or Baal-Hermon. This was the place where Israelites first began Baal worship. It was sometimes called the Gray-Haired Mountain because of its snow coverage and rocky face. Its height had been widely known as "the Eyes of the Watchers."

Enoch had claimed that on the heights of Hermon, Satan had placed his throne. It was the headquarters from which the fallen ones served Lucifer and the Amorites worshipped. It was called 'the Mountain of the Sheikh' or 'King'. The word Hermon meant 'Taboo'. The watchers drew humans to this sight to worship Satan through sexual orgies and acts of abomination. They bred with the daughters of Adam there and produced a race of giants known as the Nephilim and the Rephaites, like Og and Goliath. Both Joshua and David fought against those remaining of this race who also consequently despised God and his people.

Hermon was the place where people did things that ought not to be done. The Mountain was banned for its total lack of acceptable morality. It was considered the 'highest' of all high places. On that mountain, the Canaanites and later the Israelites prostituted themselves to demonic spirits. The mountain was the ultimate ziggurat and a stumbling block to Israel and the world.

When Satan had transported Yeshua to Hermon's pinnacle far above the earth, it was to offer him all the kingdoms of the earth. He had said, "If only you would only join in and worship me, I will give you my power over the kingdoms of men."

Satan and all 'the gods', all of the evil and defiling things that were worshipped on this mountain, would be conquered. Yeshua was going up to its peak to lay siege against it by way of his prayers. This power of the sins represented on this mountain would soon be as destroyed as if it had cast into the depths of the sea.

The disciples had no idea of his intent. They wondered, 'Why is Yeshua taking us into the heart of such a pagan land?'

After taking the long way around the mountain, they arrived at Caesarea Philippi in the territory of Gaulanitis. The city was built to honor Caesar and garnish Roman favor. To the outward eye, the city was beautiful and otherworldly with its well-groomed gardens and the flowing waters, but the stone face above and around the pool was covered with vestibules bearing idols of the goat god Pan and various other gods and goddesses. The satanic rituals of bestiality were practiced regularly here. This city was more immoral than the disciples could imagine. Pan lorded over these demonic exploits that included sacrificing goats and tossing their bones into the abyss below.

The cliffs were of limestone, dolomite, and gypsum. Which had allowed for numerous demonic doorways and altars from which the gods could watch the perverse worship. A large pool flowed from the large and gaping cavern. Its depths dove below the mountain to connect to the black abyss. It is named 'the Gates of Hades.' The cavern was like the rotted mouth of the dead, open and ready to devour anyone who stepped upon the mountain. The carved antechambers of the gods were reflected in the waters of the large pool. The well-tended gardens, with their display of lush foliage, offered the illusion that it was the garden of Eden. Roman columns, porticos, and statues of mostly naked gods and goddesses were everywhere. Jupiter and Pan were more prominent than the rest. The disciples blushed at the idols' nakedness, seeing such things as pornography meant to stir their lust. They cast their eyes to the ground in an effort to avoid them.

Simon moved reluctantly along. The tawdry suggestiveness of this place raised his hackles.

"How can such an evil place be so lush?" he asked, "And, why did Yeshua lead us to this place," he asked with clear upset, "Why are we here?"

"I'm sure he has his reasons," Andrew tried to calm him.

Yohan agreed, though he looked as uncomfortable as Simon.

Simon felt they were ganging up on him for saying what everyone was thinking. "Then why hasn't he told us what it is?"

They walked through the whole garden. Yeshua spoke not one word. They took a path that led right up to the mouth of the grotto. There, they took in the massive size of the cavern. It looked like a rotting orifice, the stuff of nightmares.

"Do you know what this grotto is called?" Yeshua asked them.

"No," They said in unison. "Should we?"

"It is called the Gates of Hades. The gateway to the great Abyss."

Even though they were Jews, they had lived among the unclean Romans long enough to have heard a good number of their myths about gods and goddesses. They knew enough to know this was a place to be feared.

Yeshua leaned against the rock to look at the clear flowing waters below. Then he turned to his men. They expected him to make some insightful statement against this place or to deliver some sort of new teaching. Instead, he intently studied their faces as if gaging their thoughts. They felt unprepared when he asked them, "Who do people say that I am?"

They looked at one another as if for clues to a riddle.

Yeshua never asked a question without a purpose. It felt like a trick. They were sure that he knew what people said about him. People voiced all kinds of opinions around him all the time. Some were not kind. The rest called him the Son of David, the promised Messiah, a rebel against the kingdom of Caesar, the Baptizer resurrected from the dead, and a prophet; opinions were varied. His enemies called him a madman, a false teacher, Beelzebub, a blasphemer. Some said he was Elijah, a miracle worker, Moses, the list went on and on.

Yeshua watched their faces as a few spouted off a few of the safe assumptions. "Yohannan."

"Elijah."

"Jeremiah."

"Moses."

They waited.

Yeshua looked into the darkness of the cavern.

When he turned back to them, his eyes were searching and intense, as if he were looking into the depths of their souls in the very same way he had looked into the cavern.

"What about *you*?" His question was almost a whisper.

He let the question hang in the air over the waters.

He had wanted to ask them this question for a long time. Now, he needed to know. In this land of great darkness, did they recognize his light? He had come to stand beside this doorway to hell to challenge the devil himself.

"Who do *you* say I am?" His searching eyes traveled from face to face. His men could see that their answer was of the utmost importance to him.

No one rushed to answer.

He wondered, 'Despite all they have seen, after all I have done, do they still not know me? Do they still not know who I am?'

His chest constricted with a longing so strong that he suddenly felt asthmatic. He had chosen these very men. They had been constantly with him up to this moment, and he had put his confidence in them. Hadn't he brought them to this place for them to testify to him to the evil one for that very reason?

'Will not one of them proclaim my identity to the very depths of hell?' He searched their timid and unsure faces. No one spoke.

His gaze fell upon Rock.

Simon had been holding his breath, waiting to allow the others the chance to speak up since the others frequently scolded him for always stealing their thunder.

But when his eyes locked with Yeshua's, he saw a pain laid bare there. His words rushed out like a breath he had held in too long, "You are the Messiah, the Son of the living God!"

His loud and emphatic words echoed off of the rock face and bounced up from the water and walls of the cavern, amplified.

Yeshua beamed like a proud parent, "Blessed are you, Simon, son of Jonah," he said and took Simon's head in his hands. "Nothing of flesh and blood has revealed this to you. This knowledge is from my Father in heaven. And, now, I tell you that you are the Rock."

Yeshua looked into Simon's face, and he said, "On *this* rock, I will build my kingdom. Even the gates of Hades will not prevail against it. With these very words, my kingdom comes!" Yeshua's joyous proclamation echoed within the cavernous grotto.

Rock was overcome with Yeshua's words of praise, and tears of joy shimmered in his eyes.

Yeshua threw his arms around Rock, and he pounded his back. "I tell you, I will give you the keys to the kingdom of heaven; whatever you bind on earth will be bound in heaven, and whatever you loose on earth will be loosed in heaven."

Yeshua looked around at all the other watchful faces, seeing that one by one, they were experiencing this revelation of this truth. They nodded their agreement, ready for this kingdom to begin.

Becoming solemn once again, he added, "But for now, let's keep my identity to ourselves."

In the depths of the grotto, Satan gnashed his teeth, "How dare you come to the very place of my worship to speak those words! Be careful who you challenge. I will make you pay for this. Just watch and see. The day is coming very soon, Messiah, Son of the living God, when I will show you who is in charge!"

As they left that place, Yeshua said, "Let's go to find a place to set up camp. I plan to make the climb to the peak of this mountain. I will take the three of you along with me, he motioned to Rock, James, and Yohan."

"Why doesn't he take us all along?" Judas asked the others.

But looking up at the steep incline, the others didn't seem to mind that they were not invited to tag along. The journey had already been hard enough as it was. And who knew what trouble they might encounter along the way?

~ 9 ~

CONFRONTING EVIL

"Do not be afraid of him,
for I have delivered him into your hands,
along with his whole army and his land."
Deuteronomy 3:2

Come with me from Lebanon, my bride,
come with me from Lebanon.
Descend from the crest of Amana,
from the top of Senir, the summit of Hermon,
from the lions' dens and the mountain haunts of leopards.
Song 4:8

That night, having made camp, they were all happy to find their rest early. Exhausted, Rock and the others were glad that they had left Caesarea Philippi and traveled to a field with a rocky outcropping beyond the outskirts of the town. They had bathed and soaked their feet in the cooling waters of a tributary that ran through the area. Having caught a few fish, they had what they needed for a sufficient dinner.

As the fire died down to glowing coals, Yeshua physically felt the deep darkness pressing in around them all. He thought again of the gaping grotto. When he had peered into it, it had reminded him of a tomb. He didn't need to hear the scornful words spoken from the darkness to be certain that Lucifer would be coming for him, and his time was growing short indeed.

He thought, 'The upcoming festival season will play a critical role in my mission. Today's confrontation ensures what is to come.'

The day had shaken him when he had seen the blank stares when he had asked his men who they believed him to be. The fear had gripped him that despite everything he had done, was doing, and was yet to do, they might not know who he was. Even now, as he closed his eyes, a battle of emotions was being fought within him.

He wanted to be sure that his sacrifice would succeed, sure that the cross was the Father's plan, sure that Satan wasn't simply leading him into yet another temptation deceptively fueled by his desire to please his Father.

He needed to take time to review the words and the prophecies once again and know he would win the final victory just as it had been planned from the beginning. He needed assurance that some would come to believe and understand; and make his peace with his death and prepare for it. His men needed to be prepared as well.

What would they say when he told them the truth about what lay ahead? If he told them, perhaps they would all simply desert him. Trusting his Father's plan was his only way through his journey of faith.

He thought, 'I have to walk by faith, believing in what I have been given to do if I am to succeed. Only then can my disciples succeed. By being faithful to the plan, I will complete the work and rise again. And, I have to have faith in them too.'

He pondered this for some time, turning all of his concerns over to his Father. Finally, a peacefulness permeated him. Falling into a deep sleep, he dreamed, and in his dream, he heard a voice say, "Come up here to me on this mountain, and I will show you what must take place after this."

The next morning, in the light of day, Yeshua's steps felt more sure. He let his men sleep while he began to prepare the bread patties for their breakfast. After everyone had awakened, eaten, and was made ready for the day, he called them all to himself. It was the first of many times he explained to them what was going to happen.

"As you know, the time is coming for the fall festivals. Time is fleeting. I must go to Jerusalem and complete the work that I have begun there."

His men looked alarmed, and they noted their Master's was weighted with a heaviness.

"The day will come soon enough that I will be made to suffer many things at the hands of the elders, the chief priests, and the teachers of the law. There will come an appointed time when they will succeed in killing me."

Their eyes grew large, their faces grave with fear and concern. Their mouths hung open with silent questions. They did not know how to react to such a statement. He was serious. Was the pressure of that threat and conflict taking its toll on him? His statement made it obvious that he would not be recruiting armed defenders. His declaration made no sense at all!

Yeshua finished, "However, on the third day, I will be raised to life. I am telling you what is going to happen now before that time comes."

Everyone was so intent on his declaration of death that it was as if they didn't hear his final statement. No one said anything, unsure if this was some new test of their allegiance. Still, everyone understood how dangerous Jerusalem was for him.

"Why go to Jerusalem at all?" Thomas asked.

Yeshua got up and walked away to stand looking up the steep incline of Mt. Hermon. He thought, 'There, I have told them, Father. Whether they leave me now or not will depend solely upon you upholding their faith and strength. How can they have the strength otherwise to remain with me? Help them to stay the course and walk this difficult journey with me! Help them to come to understand Father."

A twig snapped behind him. He turned to find Simon standing a few feet behind him, his face pained.

"Lord, Thomas is not wrong. I heard your words back there, but this should not be! Never! This should never happen to you! There are measures we could take to protect you," he said persuasively. "This shall never happen to you!" He said an emphatic third time.

Yeshua saw Simon's earnest face and felt his loyalty to him. In truth, his words were what he wished he would hear from his Father. Simon's words were almost enough to undo him. But he knew better. Simon did not know he was being used to tempt his Master to disobey his Father's command. If only Simon understood the magnitude of his mission; if only they all did. Now, the evil one was using one of his strongest allies to undo him.

"Get behind me, Satan!" He shouted into the air, calling Satan at his game.

Simon looked into the air, not understanding, and jumped back in surprise at Yeshua's accusation. He shrunk as Yeshua turned his intense gaze upon him.

Apologetically, he began to explain and try to make a defense, but before he could say a word, Yeshua's direct and pained expression stopped him. His words were hot, "Your words are a stumbling block to me; you do not have in mind the concerns of God. You are looking at this through strictly human eyes. You cannot see or know what I know."

Rock was shocked and confused by his rebuke; he wondered, 'What did I say that was so wrong? Certainly, he does not want to suffer and die?'

Yeshua saw the confusion and defeat on Rock's face. Reading his thoughts, he shook his head in frustration. Of course, this had to be expected. Hadn't his own family thought he was mad? It would take time for his men to understand. In fact, he realized they might not understand until after it was all over. He patted Rock on the shoulder and put his arm around him to lead him back to the others. "You must not say that again!"

Everyone was quiet and thoughtful for the rest of that day. Yeshua's pronouncement was a lot to take in.

'No need to stop there!' he thought, 'They have to understand that this is not just about me. This includes each of them as well.'

After walking and surveying the base of Mount Hermon, they went back to their camp. That evening, Yeshua gathered them in yet again.

"Listen to me. I need to clarify the future for you all. Whoever wants to be my follower must deny themselves and take up their cross. You must be willing to sacrifice yourself for others, just as I will. To be clear, there will be suffering in following me. Surely, you have picked up on this?"

"We are to become like soldiers?" Thomas asked.

Yeshua smiled at him thinly, "Yes, there will be warfare, but it is not a battle against flesh and blood that we fight. Although, it is true people will be set against you. Our battle is one of the spirit. Whoever wants to save their life will lose it, but whoever loses their life for me will find it."

"He demands that we die with him," Thomas interpreted for emphasis.

If their faith in him should hold, each of these men would suffer and ultimately die an untimely death on account of him. He said, "No student is above his teacher. What good will it be to gain the whole world yet forfeit your soul? Or what can one give in exchange for one's soul?Remain faithful. When the Son of Man comes in his Father's glory with his angels, he will reward each of you according to what you have done. Truly, I tell you, some who are standing here will not taste death before they see the Son of Man coming with his kingdom."

**

For several days, they stayed in the vicinity, hiking around the base of Mount Hermon. A few people came to Yeshua and were healed. As they traveled, they sang one psalm of praise after an-other. Every evening, they returned to their base camp.

They questioned Yeshua, "Why do we linger here?"

"I am preparing to take this mountain."

His men remembered that Joshua had once marched his men around Jericho in preparation for the Lord to bring down the city walls and for them to take the city. They wondered if there was a correlation. That evening, while they ate their twilight dinner, the mountain loomed over them. Yeshua noticed them looking up at the mountain where the torches were being lit at the various temples of the Roman gods.

He said to them, "I tell you the truth, even if you have faith as small as a mustard seed, you can say to this mountain, 'Move from here and be cast into the sea,' and it will move. If you have faith, nothing will be impossible for you."

The men stared up at the mountain, wondering at what power it would take to move such a mountain.

On the seventh day, Yeshua took the three, Rock, James, and Yohan, and began the climb. The others remained at the base camp. With their ascent, Yeshua began to sing a song that his men didn't know: *"Come with me from Lebanon, my bride, come with me from Lebanon. Descend from the crest of Amana, from the top of Senir, the summit of Hermon, from the lions' dens and the mountain haunts of leopards. You have stolen my heart, my sister, my bride; you have stolen my heart...."*

His men listened to the words of his song, not knowing the words from the Song. They could not guess that it was even then being fulfilled.

They wondered, 'Who is he singing about as the bride? True, it had not escaped them that Yeshua had a close connection to Mari, but he had never acted in any way like anything more than a brother to her or to any of the other women who owed him their lives or served him. He treated them all the same, like mothers, sisters, and daughters, much like he treated them as sons or brothers. He even allowed those women to be instructed alongside them.

Yet, at the sound of his singing, the three men found their hearts strangely moved.

As the climb grew harder, between labored breaths, Yeshua told stories to entertain them with the history of this area.

"This is where Moses and Joshua destroyed the giants in the land. Here, my Father exhorted Israel, 'Never again fear the giants or their evil powers. For I have given them into your hands.' Just as he defeated the Rephaim, Joshua and his men were enabled to utterly defeat Og, the King of Bashan, and Sihon, the King of Hesbon. He gave this land into the hands of the children of Israel. The prophecy states the Messiah would come to subdue these powers of evil and utterly destroy them."

They passed over twenty shrines and temples to the foreign gods that their subsequent conquerors had built. Some were ancient and ram-shackled, almost hidden in the brambles. Some had been rebuilt or enlarged into temples more elaborate than the ancient temples of Baal. They were occupied by the Roman's contemporary gods of Jupiter and others. Some structures were quite beautiful and well-manicured. Charming in appearance. Still, Rock, James, and Yohan could not help but shiver at the deeds performed there.

Yeshua said, "The religions of men can be dangerous. This was where the bulls of Bashan dwelt. And later, the bulls of the Israelites. Old superstitions led the people astray."

He clarified, "People superstitiously attributed the fertility and fruitfulness of their land to Baal or the gods of the land. There have been many captors of this mountain, and they have all staked their claim to it by placing a temple to their god upon it. Now that Rome has conquered the land, they have placed their version of Baal here as if he will rule over this land. Thus, these temples are to Jupiter. But there is only one God."

"Then, why are we climbing this mountain?" James gathered the courage to ask, for Rock had remained tight-lipped since his last rebuke. He refused to ask the obvious question.

"We ascend so I may pray here and ultimately take back all that has been lost. This is where the fallen ones, whom Enoch called 'the watchers,' began to lead the people further away from my Father and into great sin."

They wondered, "Is he going to confront the evil spirits on this mountain and establish his throne from here with only the three of them."

At times, the climb became precarious when they stumbled over a tumbled rock or a lose stone tumbled from the heights above. Occasionally, they looked out over the rocky cliffs to see they were ascending higher and higher above the valley below. It was a beautiful sight. Even as fit as they were, their legs grew tired, and their muscles ached. It grew hard to keep going, and they had to rest before pushing onward. They stopped and looked out over the rough and wild terrain, called 'the haunt of lions and leopards.' They wondered what they would do should they be confronted by one. The landscape below seemed small and insignificant from these heights.

It was almost evening before they made their final approach toward the pinnacle. The sun glowed red at its setting, a breath-taking sight like they had never seen. The altitude made them feel even more tired and out of breath. It was late summer, but already, the evening was cool at such a height. The three huddled into their cloaks and found a comfortable place to sit down.

Yeshua went to stand on the highest point to look out over the land. He looked bronzed in the setting sun, like an epic hero with the wind whipping his hair and cloak. He remembered having been transported to this place during his desert temptations. Satan had laid the world before him, promising him an easier path than the one he faced now. He had overcome his temptation then, and he would pray to overcome it now. Looking out over the beautiful land, he knew it was up to him to win the victory over evil once and for all.

He began to pray, knowing prayer is where all human victory begins. He prayed the words of scripture, remembering how Moses fought and won his battle with God's people and how Elijah had stood against these same demonic forces over Israel. As he prayed, it was as if the two prophets came to stand with him in his prayer, encouraging him and pointing out all the things he needed to know.

"This is how you fight evil and defeat it until it is cast into the sea." Moses summarized, reiterating how Pharoah's army was swept away in the Red Sea.

Elijah reminded him, "Listen to the small, still voice inside of you; it will strengthen you to be able to finish your work."

The disciples had drifted into a dreamless sleep until a holy brightness awoke them. There, on the pinnacle, they saw Yeshua still praying, but now his face was transformed. It beamed with an incredible force of brightness. His ordinary garments became radiantly white. They were as bright as a streak of lightning. All three beheld this fearful sight.

They saw the two men standing within the light conversing with Yeshua. They, too, glowed with the brightness of his light. They intuitively knew who the two men were, though they had long since departed from Israel to become a part of its history.

The three men were struck down with awe, and they hid their faces on the ground. They heard the two prophets talking to Yeshua about his upcoming departure and all that must yet take place. They did not know they were seeing into the spiritual realm. They only knew they were overwhelmed by what they were witnessing.

Rock did not pause to think before he blurted out, "Master, it is so wonderful that we are here to see this. Let us build three temples, one for each of you!"

It wasn't until much later that Rock understood how insulting his offer must have sounded. Who was he to build a temple for God? Or that he, too, should have a temple on this profane mountain along with all of the other false gods.

A thick cloud enveloped them and the majesty of the scene before them, as if to say... "Hurry, draw the curtain. They are not worthy to witness his glory."

Each one feared they had been struck blind. They could see nothing but the cottony darkness. Within the darkness, a voice spoke a command, sounding as if it spoke right beside their ear, "This is my son, whom I have chosen; listen to him!"

At this command, the mountain shook beneath them. Fearfully, they held on with their faces to the ground.

When the cloud dissipated, their sight returned. The incredible vision was gone. Now, on the pinnacle stood the lone figure of their Master praying earnestly in the dark of the night, seemingly oblivious of anything else. Each wondered at the sight they had seen, and they wondered, 'Had the others seen it too? Meanwhile, Yeshua continued to pray through the watches of the night.

~ 10 ~

TURNING TOWARD JERUSALEM

He steadfastly set His face to go to Jerusalem.
Luke 9:51

The disciples awoke to Yeshua still standing on the pinnacle of Mt. Hermon, looking out over the land. A large dark buzzard circled above, protesting his presence with a blasphemous screech. Yeshua looked out over the land, strengthened by his night of prayer and meditation. The morning's rays warmed him. A light breeze ruffled his hair and pulled at his garments as if to urge him onward.

He remembered the words given to his predecessor Joshua, who had once conquered this mountain: *'Be strong and very courageous. Be careful to obey all of the law my servant Moses gave you; do not turn from it to the right or the left, that you may be successful wherever you go.Keep this Book of the Law always on your lips; meditate on it day and night so that you may be careful to do everything written in it. Then, you will be prosperous and successful.Have I not commanded you? Be strong and courageous. Do not be afraid; do not be discouraged, for the Lord your God will be with you wherever you go.'*

He had done what he had come to do. He would abolish Satan's power. He peered into the distant future to see all the Nations of the World gathering here on this mountain to make ready to destroy

88

his people forever, and then Satan's power would come to an end. But, for now, he had another mountain to conquer to the south.

He turned to look towards Jerusalem. His jaw tightened with determination. From this day, Jerusalem would be his goal and direction. It would not be easy. Constant conflict would face him all along the way. The large buzzard continued to circle overhead with a malicious eye.

During the descent, the men kept remembering their glimpse of his glory. They were uncharacteristically quiet. Yeshua could tell they did not know what to say to him.

"Don't tell anyone what has been revealed to you until after I am raised from the dead." The three exchanged glances. All three wondered, 'What does this rising from the dead mean? If he could rise from the dead, why die at all?'

Finally, having seen Elijah on the mountain with Yeshua, they asked, "The scribes claim that Elijah must come first. When will he come?"

"Elijah does indeed come first to restore the children to the Father's heart. Elijah has already come, but no one recognized him. They did to him whatever they pleased. It is also written about the Son of Man that he will go through many sufferings and be treated with contempt. So, as it is written, will the Son of Man also suffer at their hands."

Understanding dawned, Yeshua was talking about Yohannan as Elijah. And his death would be next. This news shook them.

At the foot of the mountain, a small group of people had arrived searching for Yeshua. They had remained waiting for him to descend the mountain. It was not going so well for the disciples in the camp. They felt ill-equipped and overwhelmed to minister to the Syrians. So, on arrival, the people clamored for his help. A man ran to Yeshua with a look of desperation on his face, "Teacher, I beg you to take a look at my son, my only child. A spirit seizes him, and he suddenly screams with convulsions and foams at the mouth. He can't find a moment of peace, and it is destroying him. I begged your disciples to drive the demon out, but they were not able."

Yeshua saw his disciples cowed in fear; their faith was so weak.

He wondered, 'Why do these people constantly fall to the occult as if it were a game that they could control? Too many have opened spiritual doorways that have caused such spiritual oppression. They make a sport of playing with darkness.' That darkness was the reason he had gone up on the mountain to pray.

"You are an unbelieving and perverse generation." Yeshua proclaimed in his loud prophet's voice. "How long must I remain among you and witness your depravity?"

The demons controlling the people raised their fists in outrage and grumbled at each other. But Yeshua stood his ground unmoved.

"Bring your son here," Yeshua told the father.

As soon as the man led his son forward, the demon slammed the boy to the ground to take hold of the boy's throat. The boy convulsed and pitched, fighting to breathe. The father paused, wondering if this man could heal his son.

Seeing this, Yeshua asked, "How long has this been happening to him?"

"From early childhood. If you are able, please help him."

"If?" Yeshua looked intently into the father's eyes while the son twisted and fought to breathe. "All things can be done for those who believe."

The man's face melted into panic, thinking this healer would not heal his son because of his doubts and poor choice of words.

He dropped to his knees, begging for his son. "I believe! I believe! Lord, help my unbelief!"

Yeshua spoke sternly to the spirit, "Let go of the boy! Leave him now! And never enter this boy again!"

Coming out of the boy, the spirit reared up and started towards Yeshua as if to attack him next. But Yeshua held up his hand, and the creature was stopped short. He hissed.

"Not yet," Yeshua spoke authoritatively, and the demon departed.

"Look, he is dead!" The people cried out. The father held his limp son in his arms.

Yeshua looked down at the boy. His face was still and blue. With a touch, the boy's chest rose with a quick gasp. Regaining consciousness, the boy was surprised to see Yeshua hovering over him. He sat up and saw the light emitting from Yeshua. Shyly, the boy hid behind his father, peeking out at the man who had rescued him, "Abba..."

"It is okay. This man healed you."

"Slowly, the boy came from his hiding place to search Yeshua's face."

The onlookers marveled, "Who is this man that even the demons obey him?"

**

Afterward, the people dispersed in groups, still processing what their eyes had seen.

Thomas asked Yeshua, "Why couldn't we drive this demon away?"

"A lack of faith. Remember what I said about being able to move a mountain? Faith is always the key; even the faith as small as a mustard seed. Still, the strongest demons will require a greater power. Those can only be removed by prayer."

That night, a presence hovered over Yeshua and whispered in his ear, "What we have done to the boy, in Jerusalem we will do to you. You will be handed over into the strong hands of the men from this region." It was so real. The hair on the back of his neck stood on end.

Shaken, he called together all twelve of his men, saying, "Listen to me, this is important! The Son of Man is going to be betrayed into the hands of men."

The words jarred the disciple once again. Yeshua was visibly trembling, quite violently. They were shocked, afraid, and confused.

Here was the man who had just driven out demons and set the boy free. Yet now, he trembled with fear of a coming abuse. Yeshua had confronted the Sanhedrin, but he had never trembled like this, or shown any such fear. This incongruity was not lost on them; it made it even more difficult to believe his words or understand them.

Nevertheless, from that day onward, Yeshua never stopped telling his disciples that death awaited him in Jerusalem, even as he preached day by day and reached out and healed the people.

His power was obvious to all. Despite the disciple's concern for his sanity, there was no one that they loved more; they refused to leave his side. They earnestly believed his words, even if they were confused by his trembling warnings.

<h1 style="text-align:center">~ 11 ~</h1>

THE PROBLEM OF GREATNESS

For those who exalt themselves will be humbled,
and those who humble themselves will be exalted.
Matthew 23-12

The rest of his Syrian mission was hard, but in the end, it bore some fruit. It was time to move on to the Decapolis.

While Yeshua had been on the mountain lost in prayer, his mission had once again seemed possible to endure. But now, having made the slippery descent back to his operation, Yeshua found himself immediately re-immersed into the crucible of human need. Attempts of his enemy's intimidation stuck to him like his clothes in the late summer heat. Leaving Mt. Hermon behind, the sun burned down upon them all, sucking any moisture up from the earth in steamy waves of intensity. Precious sweat trickled down the side of his face, and he felt his body's depletion.

They quickly drained their water supply and sought to resupply them by the river's edge. As they traveled, they swatted at the annoying biting flies that continuously buzzed them and flew at their faces like arrows. Everyone was irritable. They had hardly been prepared for the heat that rose from the sun-scorched hills as they traveled toward the Galilean Sea. They could not wait to reach

Capernaum, to plunge themselves into the water to bathe and cool off. That thought was all that kept them plodding along.

Yeshua walked ahead while his men lagged, divided into pairs and groups. They whispered in lower voices, which told him they did not want him to hear what they were talking about. At various points, a voice or two would rise, becoming erratic and emotional.

One asked, "What will happen to our group, to our movement, if what Yeshua says is true?"

Lacking confidence, another one asked, "Surely, he has not brought us this far for nothing?"

"We will become laughingstocks if he is killed and our mission will come to nothing. The Pharisees will have a field day with that," the voice sounded like Nathaniel.

"Someone must take the helm to keep the movement going, but who?" Judas asked, as if there was only one choice. "Simon thinks he is best suited, but he is too unpredictable, too impetuous. He is a doer, not a leader."

"It stands to reason that it would be James. He is the solid one. He is older than Yohan. And, he is one of the three."

"I don't know; he can be sort of accusatory, and he has a short fuse. He could be worse than Simon. At least you know where Simon is coming from," Andrew defended his brother.

"Maybe Yohan?"

"Yes, but Yohan is a hot head, just like James. And, he is little more than a kid."

"Why does it have to be one of the three? What about Judas? He seems smart enough, and he handles our finances and purchases."

No one replied, so Zel let that thought drop.

Someone spoke tentatively, trying not to be offensive, "He has not been a part of the three. It is clear, is it not, that Yeshua would choose one of the three."

Yeshua heard their furtive whispers and their reasonings. It grated on his raw nerves. His dehydration was giving him a headache, and his muscles ached from the previous mountain climb.

He held his tongue and thought, 'How should I handle this?'

He walked on acting none the wiser.

They converged on Simon's home after their swim in the lake, clean and refreshed. Deborah and her Ima fed them. They laid back with their stomachs full and glad for the comforts that felt like home.

Deborah was only too happy to have her husband safely returned. Stoically, she did not let on how upset she had been during the long weeks of having no idea where Simon was. When she heard of the rough places he had traveled, she was all the happier for his safe return.

Nonchalantly, Yeshua stretched his legs before him and made himself comfortable. When the conversation waned, he asked, "So, tell me, what were you all arguing about on the way?"

A guilty silence stretched before them. Each man wanted to divert the question but dared not try. They took to studying the callouses on their hands, staring at the ground, the wall, out the window, or anywhere rather than meet his seemingly all-seeing eyes.

A dog growled in the street, causing some to shiver at the ominous sound. Someone shouted at the dog, there was a sharp yelp, and it became quiet as if someone had sent the creature on his way.

Realizing that Yeshua had heard their words, a few tugged uncomfortably at their necklines. No one spoke.

Then, feeling confident that his brother was at the top of the list, Andrew thought, 'Why not have Yeshua settle this discussion once and for all.'

So, he mustered his courage and asked, "Lord, who is the greatest in the kingdom of heaven?"

The other men looked up, hopeful that Yeshua would provide a pecking order and let them off the hook.

Yeshua arched his eyebrow at Andrew's shrewdness, causing Andrew to drop his eyes aware that he had just incriminated himself.

Yeshua looked across the room, seeing Simon's little one resting in her father's arm.

"Ana! Come here." He held out his hands and gave a happy clap.

Ana all but leaped from her Abba's embrace and toddled across the floor to stand expectantly before her 'Yeshi.'

"See our little Ana? She comes when she is called. She looks expectantly at me, waiting to be told what she should do. I am telling you the truth: unless you men change and become like this little child, you will never enter the kingdom of heaven. Humility is key. Whoever becomes humble, like this little child, is the greatest in the kingdom of heaven. Then, whoever welcomes such a little one in my name welcomes me."

He patted his lap, and Ana all but jumped into it; Yeshua lifted her into the air high above him. She squealed with delight, and they laughed together. He lowered her and kissed her chubby little cheeks, tickling her with his beard, causing another fit of giggles. Then he lifted her once again to make googly eyes at her face-to-face.

The men watched him delighting in the child and she in him. But like thick-headed clods, they missed his message, hardly wondering what he meant.

"When you humble yourselves before the Lord," Yeshua said to them as he lowered Ana again to more kisses, "he will lift you up."

Again, he lifted Ana high over his head, beaming at her. She giggled uncontrollably, holding out her arms. "Look at me. I am flying like a birdie!"

Finally, he sat her back in his lap, and she wrapped her chubby arms around him. Resting her head against his heart, she looked up at him adoringly.

His expression became serious as he stroked Ana's curls, and then he looked up at his men. "The greatest in the Kingdom of Heaven is the one who humbles himself to be a servant of all. Whoever does not trust in the kingship of my Father, or obey his commands and acknowledge his authority over their lives with the same abandon as this little child, will never enter into the kingdom eternal."

They all felt admonished, even though he had said nothing to them at all. They took his parable to their sleeping mats. It was a while before exhaustion overcame them. Still not putting two plus two together, this issue of 'the greatest' was far from settled in their minds.

**

They had scarcely returned to Capernaum before a loud knock came at the door. Rock opened the door to find the Pharisaic business owners standing at the entrance and demanding to speak with Yeshua.

"We heard you were back in town. Look," they reasoned with him, "we don't want any trouble in Capernaum. We are telling you, leave this town and go somewhere else. Herod is still looking for you, and if he finds you here, we may all be found guilty of harboring a criminal. He wants to kill you, just like he killed Yohannan the Baptizer. We don't want any problems here. If you don't leave, we will be forced to tell him you are here."

Yeshua nodded, "I understand, but go and tell that fox, "I will drive out demons and heal people today, tomorrow, and the next day until my work is done and I reach my goal. No prophet will die outside of Jerusalem."

"You will go?" the men asked hopefully.

Yeshua nodded and waited patiently until they turned to leave.

**

The Fall Festivals were soon to begin. Devoted Jews were preparing for the yearly trek to Jerusalem. That afternoon, Yeshua's brothers were also motivated to come by for a visit.

"Herod has been anxiously searching to find you," James said as if he didn't know. "We told his men that we didn't know where you were. But they didn't believe us. They threatened us."

"I am sorry to hear this. But it is best that I keep you uninformed." Yeshua pursed his lips.

"Look, we were just worried about you," Jose said.

"As well, you should be worried for me, but I suspect you were more worried for yourselves."

Yeshua glanced over all of his brothers, "But look, you are all fine, and so am I for now."

"The fall festivals will begin soon. Aren't you preparing to attend?"

Yeshua felt sure his family was being pressured, "No."

"But why would you linger here in this backwater place? No one makes it big here. You should leave Galilee and go into Judea. There, you can become more well-known," James was way too friendly while offering him counsel to advance his mission, which they had patently denied.

Yeshua felt a flush of anger. He set his jaw at James' audacity, "Do you think fame is my goal?"

He recalled the taunts of Satan on the pinnacle of the temple during his desert temptations. What bothered him the most was that his brothers were pretending to care about him and his mission. But they were encouraging him so he could go and be killed. They hoped to be rid of him for good.

James mustered on with no clue he was speaking under Satan's authority, "If you show yourself to the people of Jerusalem, you will become great. Show your disciples how exalted you can become. Hiding out in fringe locations won't make you king."

Yeshua quietly listened to his brother's persuasion as if he were considering his wisdom.

"If you keep yourself hidden, how will you gain the people's support?" James continued. It was as if he couldn't stop, "Show your miracles and your true self to the world and to the powers that be."

Yeshua discerned it was not his brother speaking; rather, it was Satan's fear and intimidation that had been inflicted upon his family through the evil one. Even after all the testimonies of his miracles and works, his brother still did not believe in him.

He bowed his head to hide his smarting eyes, 'Even my brother is willing to offer me up to the Herodians to protect himself.'

With a tremulous expression, he placed his hand on James' shoulder, searching his face; intimately, he said, "James, my time is not yet here. For you, now is as good as any other time."

He held his brother's gaze.

James realized Yeshua understood what he was doing. He saw through him. And, for the first time, James understood that Yeshua was fully resolved to die.

Yeshua spoke haltingly, "The world cannot hate you because you follow its thoughts, but the world hates me because I testify that its works are evil." The firmness of his expression dared his brother to say otherwise.

He released his brother's gaze, then patted his shoulder encouragingly, "You go on to the festival; make your atonement; celebrate the law, and get your fresh start. As for me, I will not go up to this festival just now because my time has not yet fully come."

James left rebuked. Still, it was not easy to be the brother of the man that people were calling "the Messiah." James could not see how his brother's infamy could end in anything but execution. He lumbered away under the fear of the trouble Yeshua would surely bring upon them all.

**

"What will we do now if we aren't going to the festival?" asked Yohan. He had heard the conversation, and despite his youth, he understood all too well that Yeshua was as endangered in Capernaum as in Jerusalem.

"You don't think that James...," his question trailed off, seeing the distress on Yeshua's face.

Hearing Yohan's question, the others drew closer to hear his response. Yeshua motioned to his men. They all found a seat to listen, "Many think I have come to bring peace, but you know I have come to render much more than that. I'm telling you I have come to bring fire on the earth, and how I wish it were already kindled! But

I have a baptism to undergo first, just as I keep telling you. And how distressed I am until it is completed. My presence does not bring peace but division. Look at my own family. You can see the truth of this. If there are five siblings in a family, they will be divided four to one, three to two, or five to one. Because of me, fathers will be separated from their sons, sons from fathers, daughters from mothers. Likewise, the ones closest to you may also become your enemy and become willing to hand you over to the authorities because of me. This is what it means to be set apart unto God. It is part of the cost of being chosen by God to follow me."

"I also struggle with going to Jerusalem for the festival," Nathaniel said honestly. "Even more so after hearing what happened to our Galilean brothers and sisters at the last festival."

Zel nodded, "What a curse! To have your blood mixed with the wine and incense offered to pagan gods! Could there be anything worse?"

Yeshua wanted to set the record straight. "Do not think that these Galileans were somehow worse sinners than all the other Galileans because they suffered this way. I tell you, no! Satan is always on the prowl, looking for a way to take advantage, all the while searching for those he might destroy. Mourne for your brothers and sisters. They were in the wrong place at the wrong time. Such persecution could happen to anyone. When you hear of a story of such suffering, you should be driven to repentance, knowing it could just as easily have been you. The truth is, they were likely targeted simply because they were from Galilee, and it is known that the movement of God's kingdom is happening here."

He took a deep breath, exhaling slowly, "Let me tell you a story of what is to come."

"A man had a fig tree growing in his vineyard, and he went to look for fruit on it, but he did not find any good figs worthy of harvest."

Yeshua thought back to his Passover visit several years before his ministry began. He had been revolted by the corruption, the greed, and the impurity he had found inside the Temple. His eyes narrowed at the memory,"Greatly disappointed, the owner said to the man who took care of the vineyard, 'For three years now, I've been coming to look for fruit on this fig tree, but it has produced little to nothing. Just cut it down! Why should it use up the soil?'"

"'Sir,' the man replied, 'leave it alone for one more year. I will dig around it and fertilize it. If it bears fruit next year, fine! If not, then I will cut it down.'"

He looked around the circle, "I am telling you now, Yohannan was right in his teachings. The axe is already waiting at the base of the tree; the owner of the vineyard will not relent much longer."

As usual, they looked at one another, wondering at his strange metaphors and trying to make sense of them.

He rose to his feet to go out for a walk. Pulling his hood up to cover his head and face, he told them, "We will remain tomorrow for our sabbath rest. After that, we will set off. We will not yet travel to Jerusalem."

The men let out the collective breath they had been holding, glad not to be traveling the road with all of the other pilgrims. Herod's men would be watching for them along the roadways. They reasonably feared being handed over to Herod's men. It would be almost as bad as being handed over to the Romans, who would take them for a group of zealots. Most of all, they feared Yeshua's words about his death, feeling sure that it could very possibly include their own.

~ 12 ~

BE SET FREE

It is for freedom that Christ has set us free.
Stand firm, then, and do not allow yourselves
to be burdened again by the yoke of slavery.
Galatians 5:1

Sabbath morning, Yeshua and the Twelve went to the synagogue in Capernaum.

Jairus went to Yeshua with a warning, "Yeshua, I am glad to see that you are well, but it is not wise to remain in Capernaum. Herod has put a price on your head. Even now, there is likely word being sent to him."

Yeshua nodded his understanding. "So I have been told."

"Don't tell me where you have been or where you are going. Then I can speak truthfully that I know nothing."

Yeshua nodded, "Of course."

Despite Jairus' warning, he entered the synagogue. Many people were happy to see him. A group began to gather around him. But others grew fearful at his presence. When it came time for the teaching, Yeshua stepped forth to read the scroll. He read from the 66th and 67th Psalm of David, the LORD's Anointed:

'Shout for joy to God, all the earth! Sing the glory of his name; make his praise glorious. Say to God, How awesome are your deeds! So great is your

power that your enemies cringe before you. All the earth bows down to you; they sing praise to you; they sing the praises of your name. Come and see what God has done, his awesome deeds for mankind! He has preserved our lives and kept our feet from slipping.

'For you, God tested us; you refined us like silver. You brought us into prison and laid burdens on our backs. You let people ride over our heads; we went through fire and water, but you brought us to a place of abundance. Come and hear, all you who fear God; let me tell you what he has done for me. I cried out to him with my mouth; his praise was on my tongue.

'If I had cherished sin in my heart, the Lord would not have listened; but God has surely listened and has heard my prayer. Praise be to God, who has not rejected my prayer or withheld his love from me!'

He rolled the scroll and touched it to his forehead and then sat to teach.

"Why has Israel been brought under the heel of one oppressor after another?" Yeshua began with the question.

"Why have our people been forced to carry heavy loads upon their backs?

"Because our nation has forgotten who they were meant to serve. They have turned away from God to pursue other desires and priorities."

Yeshua's eyes were as unfathomable as night, and yet they shone with a perceivable light as he gazed challengingly from face to face.

"Does not the Father always hold his hands out to you? Does not the presence of your enemies test what is in your heart? Does the LORD not refine you as one refines silver? The enemy is all around us.

"Yet, here we are. We exist as a testimony to the Father's faithfulness.

"So why do you persist in carrying heavy burdens on your back? Why do you struggle to stand, falling with your face in the dust before your enemies? Could it be that your sins are too precious to you? I tell you, the time to repent is now.

"Repent for the kingdom of heaven has come near to you. Produce fruit in keeping with repentance.

"For I tell you, another fire is coming soon to burn all the dross away. Why should you perish when grace could be had? Don't let the men of Nineveh stand to testify against you. As evil as they were, they repented at the time of Jonah. Now, someone greater than Jonah is here.

"You cannot hide your guilt from God, who searches hearts and minds."

The congregation felt a stubborn resistance within their soul, even though they felt naked and exposed before him.

He continued, "Once David, who was the LORD's Anointed One, prayed to the God of Israel saying, 'Let those who seek the LORD not be put to shame because of me. For I endure scorn for your sake, and shame covers my face. I am a foreigner to my own family, a stranger to my own mother's children.'

Yeshua met the eyes of his brothers before he continued, "Because I am consumed with zeal for the house of the LORD."

He looked around at the room of questioning faces.

"The King prayed for God to deliver both him and God's people from their burden and afflictions. I tell you the truth: Those who reject the LORD's Anointed reject God, and they are doomed. They set their table of fellowship as a snare and a trap for him. Their eyes are so darkened that they cannot see the truth.

"Therefore, their backs will be bent low with affliction forever. The wrath of God has been kindled against them. The enemy of the Anointed one of God has no share in God's salvation nor his kingdom. Their names will be blotted out of the Book of Life."

His eyes seemed to see into their very minds, and they felt unaccountably frightened.

Yeshua stood and walked toward the people, holding out his hands to each one compassionately, beseechingly.

"But look, the Lord hears the needy. He does not despise his captive people. Come unto me, all you who are weary and burdened, and I will give you rest. For my yoke is easy, and my burden is light."

Now, there was a woman in the congregation. She was hidden toward the back. As he had been teaching, his eyes had been drawn to her time and again. Her back was bent so low with deformity that the woman could only stare at the ground before her. She looked utterly miserable as if weighted down with some unseen burden. She had angled herself sideways just to see this young Rabbi's face as he spoke. His words reached into the very depths of her soul. She began to weep; tears fell from her downturned face, and her nose was running, too. Self-consciously, she wiped at her face and craned her head to glimpse him once again.

Yeshua positioned himself near her. He could tell she had carried her affliction for a very long time. "Daughter. Come here," he held out his hand toward her.

Hope sprung to life within her chest. He was speaking to her. She touched her chest to calm her clamoring heart as she stood with great difficulty to come and stand before him. She waited before him, breathing heavily for her efforts. Her deformity compressed her chest cavity severely upon itself, making it hard for her to breathe. Yet, all the while, she kept trying to peer up at him.

"Woman, you are set free from your infirmity," Yeshua placed his gentle hands on her, and immediately she straightened. An expression of shock and awe filled her face. She felt a great lifting and release. The pain disappeared, and a renewed freedom of movement within her bones, ligaments, and sinew. It was as if a huge boulder, a heavy oppression, had been lifted from her.

Now, she could look directly into Yeshua's face and see his compassion. She was overwhelmed with joy and awe. Although she was now standing straight and tall, she melted gracefully to her knees before him to take hold of both his feet. She touched her head to them. She began to sing the Psalm of praise for God's deliverance. Yeshua lifted her to her feet. For some moments, their eyes were locked in a private moment of joyful understanding. She knew her pain had not been without purpose. But it had been for this testimony to the grace of God.

"Know the truth, for the truth has set you free," Yeshua told her.

She nodded enthusiastically, understanding that truth was not a concept but a person.

Jairus dared not move, for once again, he had witnessed Yeshua's miracle of healing. The memory of what Yeshua had done for his daughter filled him. He was revisited by the awe and joy he had felt. He began to sing the Psalm of Praise as well, and others joined to sing with him.

The congregation coursed forward to surround Yeshua and rejoice at the woman's healing.

On the fringes, the Pharisees waited. They whispered to one another. When the place of meeting was emptied, they made their approach, untouched by the indescribable miracle they had witnessed. Their leader stepped forward, angry and challenging, "Why do you continue to break the Sabbath? Isn't it true there are six days available for work? Allow the people to come and be healed on those days, not on the Sabbath."

Lingering people turned to listen; their brows knitted with concern.

Yeshua stepped back from the Pharisees as if their words were acid to him, "You hypocrites! Do not each of you on the Sabbath untie your ox or donkey from the stall and lead it out to give it water?Then why shouldn't this woman, a daughter of Abraham, whom Satan has kept bound for eighteen long years, be set free on the Sabbath day from the affliction that has oppressed her?"

The people who were praising God moved nearer toward Yeshua as if to flank him, daring anyone else to approach him with confrontation.

Seeing that everyone was watching with disapproval, the Pharisees left red-faced.

~ 13 ~

BE OPENED

"If anyone has ears to hear, let them hear."
Mark 4:23

They sailed early in the morning towards Decapolis, away from Herod's threat, away from Capernaum. They were headed toward Gerasa, the shore where Isair had found his right mind and the pigs had sunk into the abyss. But first, they stopped at the border town of Bethsaida. Several of his disciples had family there.

When Yeshua walked through the street, people laid their sick along his footpath, eager to be healed. The crowd began to grow with people coming from the Decapolis region hungry for the good news. Apparently, Isair had been busy.

Yeshua moved out onto an open plain to the east, and he taught there for three days. When his men had finished their visits, he was ready to move on to another town. But he realized the people had run out of food. Once again, he turned to his men and said, "They are hungry. I do not want to send them away like this less they faint on the way."

He was surprised when they said, "Where are we going to get enough bread for so many people out here in this deserted land?"

They had forgotten the meal he had produced only months before. Had they learned nothing? It was as if they had some mental disease or weakness that made them forget what their eyes had seen and their ears had heard. Their time together was growing as short as their memories. He was tempted to admonish them, but what good would it do? They were helpless and incapable. It seemed they would always need him to remind them of such things.

This was why he was praying for his father to send them an advocate, a teacher, to remind them of the words of God constantly when his time was done among them. Without the Holy Spirit, they would surely fail and fall away. He had to trust in the Father's plan.

So, with great patience, he said, "How many loaves do you have among you?"

They quickly checked their provisions. "Seven, and there are two fish."

Yeshua ordered the people to sit down and lifted the offering to his Father and prayed.

"Blessed are you, LORD our God, who brings forth bread from the earth. May this people be faithful and multiply like the loaves and the fish."

Everyone ate their fill until they could eat no more. Even after their stomachs were filled, there was an abundance left over. The disciples retrieved seven baskets back from the crowd of over 4000 people. Yeshua blessed the people. Then they left to re-enter the boat to move along. As they sailed away, Yeshua looked back at the people waving from the shore, knowing the Father would multiply his work there. Although this region was known for its pagan debaucheries, the people had received his words.

**

He directed Rock to sail to the region of Magadan on the other side. It was a place where Jews prided themselves on their holiness. There, he was met with a totally different reception. Instead of hopeful expectations, he was met with a troop of Pharisees and Sadducees seeking to entrap him and put him to the test.

"Give us a sign!" they demanded, as if they refused to believe the testimonies about him.

He sighed, "Why do you ask for a sign?"

If they had listened to the testimonies of others, they would know he was fulfilling the very scriptures that they claimed to know so well. For their rude demands, he refused to perform like a trick pony or offer further proof. They were not searching for him but looking for a way to deny him.

"Truly, I tell you, no sign will be given for you except for the sign of Jonah!"

"Jonah?" They looked at him with confusion and with derisive smiles. They waited for him to explain, but he did not. He would only be throwing good seeds on hardened soil.

He turned to walk back to the boat with his back against them. No one stood on the shore to wave him off as he left.

**

The shadows were lengthening now as the days began to shorten. The evening coolness was returning, and Israel's summer growing season was finished. It was the season for the people to enjoy their time of rest in the LORD and the fruits of their labors. People began to gather for their yearly journey of thanksgiving to Jerusalem. It was a time to deal with their wrongs, put the past behind them, and look forward to the promise of a new year and a new beginning.

Those yearly celebrations would not last much longer before coming to a climatic end. The people of Israel would be scattered to the four winds. Israel was entering its last days as a nation for this generation. The coming Gentile season loomed on the horizon with great promise. It was time to plant the seeds that would bring forth a new harvest.

Gaulandis was filled with the residual Greek and Roman cults of their latest conqueror. The region had several bustling points of commerce, and his followers from these areas would provide a strong outpost of protection against the earliest persecution of Jewish believers. Yeshua went now to preach among these people, so different from the devout.

It was late in the day when friends brought to him a man who was deaf and hardly able to communicate or understand. They begged Yeshua to place his hand on the man so he could hear. Not wanting the people to see what he was about to do, he led the man to a private place. The man was surprised when Yeshua took his head into his hands. He offered him a gentle smile. Then he put his fingers into the man's ears.

He prayed, 'Ears must hear before mouths can speak. Father, open the ears of these people. Open the doorway for your Spirit to come among them so that a movement can begin in this land.'

Then he spit on his finger and stuck out his tongue to indicate what he wanted the man to do. The man mimicked him. Yeshua touched the tip of the man's tongue as if he were placing his words on it. The man looked surprised.

Yeshua looked up to heaven, and with a heavy whooshing sigh, he said, "Be opened!"

The man's ears opened, and his tongue was loosened, so he was able to hear and speak plainly as if he had spoken all of his life.

"Oh my! Thank you, Lord," the astonished man exclaimed. His first words flowed right out. The man's laugh was deep and robust. He began to praise God, and he turned to his friends, "I can hear! I can talk!"

Having shared his joy, Yeshua told the man and his friends not to tell anyone.

They agreed, but they found they could not contain the news. They wound up telling everyone about the miracle. It seemed they could not stop themselves. The other people from that region were quick to listen, prompting many lost Jews to be found. Everyone told the story of the man who had healed and feds thousands.

"How is it that this man can do everything so well?" They shouted to anyone who would listen. "He even makes the deaf to hear and the mute to speak!"

Yeshua toured throughout Decapolis. In one town, he delivered another man from a legion of demons, and he preached there. He traveled through Pella and Philadelphia, then on towards Jericho along the trade route.

By this time, the Festival was already underway. His enemies were no longer guarding the incoming roads, thinking he had either come some other way or he was not coming. The Trumpet had sounded, and the days of Awe were well underway.

He prayed and asked his Father. "Should I go up to Jerusalem now?"

His answer was "Yes. Go."

His men were surprised when he said, "We are leaving for Jerusalem today."

"But Lord, by now, everyone will be there. It will be dangerous to travel through the deserted Jericho road."

Everyone knew ruthless men often lay in wait when the caravans had thinned during the festival times, intent on picking off stragglers to rob them of anything of value, even the clothes off their victims' backs.

Yeshua said, "We had to wait for everyone to arrive ahead of us. By now, even the thieves will be off celebrating their spoils."

Their expressions were doubtful. They much preferred the protection of a larger number of caravans on the road. There were fifteen in their party, and they were not armed for battle.

But the Lord's words proved true. They did not encounter thieves along the way. However, they did come upon a singular man who had been attacked and left in bad condition. He was stripped naked and had a nasty bump on his head.

"Shalom." Yeshua greeted the man. "Looks like you have taken a pretty bad beating. The man held his hand to his head and looked at Yeshua woozily.

"I never saw it coming. They must have dropped a stone from above."

Immediately, Yeshua thought of his Abba Yosef. He saw a large boulder lying nearby. Pointing to it, Yeshua said. "It must have narrowly glanced off of you. You are lucky to be alive."

Yeshua offered him his water pouch.

The man drank deeply. They provided him with a tunic and helped him to the nearest village.

"I am so grateful that you stopped for me," The man said humbly. "You were not the first to come my way. A religious man and a Pharisee passed me by before you came. Even though I called out to them, they hurried on, not wanting to be hampered by me."

After a bit, he asked, "Why? Why *did* you stop for me? I could have been a trap."

"Would any shepherd worth his salt leave one of his sheep, hurt and bleeding out in the hill country alone? No, he would anoint his sheep's wounds and put it upon his shoulder to carry it back to the flock."

"Thank you," the man's gratitude was sincere.

Later, when they had reached the nearest village, Yeshua instructed Judas. "We will need to pay for this man's stay here until he has healed."

"Why don't you just heal him instead?" Judas' question was pointed.

"Surely, by now, you know that is not the way it works. My power comes from the Father. I must do his will, not my own. Healing comes in different ways at different times; sometimes, afflictions serve to testify to my Father's purposes. So, instead, we will pay for this man's care."

Judas gave Yeshua a disgruntled look and started to object but thought better of it.

Catching his look, Yeshua said, "What? Isn't that why this money has been given to us? To do ministry? If anyone needs our help, isn't it this man? You act as though the money you manage belongs to you. My Father has given it to us to meet our needs, yes, but for much more than that."

They negotiated for a room with a man, then installed him safely before returning to the road again.

Yeshua motioned to Judas, "Open your pouch."

Reluctantly, he drew forth a coin.

Yeshua shook his head. "That is not enough."

Judas placed it back inside and grudgingly pulled out a larger coin.

Yeshua nodded and held up two fingers.

Judas extracted another to place in Yeshua's hand.

"Take this to provide for our friend's food and needs," Yeshua said to the caregiver. "Should this fail to cover this man's expense, I will cover the rest when we travel back this way. Take good care of our friend."

The man took the wayfarer into his home. But when he saw how much he had been given, he was astonished by the amount Yeshua had placed in his hand. He wondered at such generosity, "This is too much," the man objected.

But having seen his humble abode, Yeshua patted the man's shoulder appreciatively for his willingness to help, "If any is left over, please replenish your resources for yourself."

But even as he said it, Yeshua believed the man would likely give it to the wounded man when he was well enough to travel onward.

**

The disciples grew somber as they finished the last leg of their journey toward Jerusalem. They were full of questions they were too afraid to ask: 'Would this be the last of their journey together? Would Yeshua's prediction of death now come true? Would they all be caught in the crosshairs of conflict?'

Sensing their questions, he prayed that he would follow his Father's lead. He felt confident that the religious leaders would not succeed in their plan to kill him during this Festival. They would not kill him until the next Passover. Still, wisdom dictated precaution all the same.

~ 14 ~

PILATE

There were some present at that time who told Jesus
about the Galileans whose blood
Pilate had mixed with their sacrifices.
Luke 13:1

As Pontius Pilate began his procession through Jerusalem, he sorely missed the soothing salt breezes of Caesarea Maritima. Perspiration was beading on his brow and soaking his clothing under his Roman armor. He couldn't wait to bathe and don his toga, even though his parade had hardly begun. He wore a surly snarl like the mask of an ill-humored god. The dusty and sweaty pilgrims were flooding into the streets as if on cue. Pontius hated these festivals; they brought such unrest to this obstinate city.

"Patience, patience." He reminded himself under his breath, feeling the weight of Caesar's threat and pressure. He could not afford more trouble or make more mistakes. The horse he rode was as edgy as he was, obviously sensing his master's mood. The stallion reared up, dancing backward, then cantering sideways under Pilate's restraints on his bridle. Pilate reached down to soothe his horse as if he were really trying to soothe himself.

His presence in these parades struck fear in the hearts of everyone who saw him because he was followed by a regiment of over five hundred fighting men. The Roman militia was an impressive sight, meant to intimidate. The people picked up their pace when they heard them coming, moving to the sides of the walls, hoping the straining city streets could somehow make room for them and the quivering horse flesh and the advancing hooves.

In his mid-40s, Pilate sat ramrod straight, proud of his well-honed military physique. His detractors claimed he had no distinction worthy of a post such as governor beyond his abounding arrogance and ambition. Yet, fate had smiled upon Pontius and brought him somehow into Tiberias' favor. He had survived his former years of battle by sheer ruthlessness and cunning. Pilate had made a careful study of his superiors and learned how to pander impressively to those ranking well above him. He had made enough of an impression on those in high places to win him a prodigious marriage to Claudia Procula - the granddaughter of Caesar Augustus. Quite a coup!

Young Claudia was well-bred and favored with beauty, brains, and deeply rooted connections within Caesar's courts. He could hardly believe his good fortune that Claudia had returned his heartfelt affection for her. Claudia was the only soft spot in his otherwise heartless world. Unbelievably, his benefactor Sejanus convinced Caesar Tiberius to assign Pilate to the Jerusalem post as Procurator to Palestine because of his heavy hand.

His peers had been surprised by the choice, believing his governorship was too high an honor for such an uninspiring man. But no one dared to voice their opinion to Tiberius. Pontius lacked administrative diplomacy and acumen, but his military forcefulness made him formidable. Pilate had received the complete backing of Rome but with one condition: "Keep the Roman Peace."

Claudia happily accompanied her husband to Jerusalem when he traveled to the Antonia Fortress—once the stronghold of Herod the Great. Their apartment was luxuriously appointed, allowing Claudia to entertain as she pleased.

Some said Claudia hosted her events as if she were the queen of Palestine. This galled Herodias, and Herod was all too happy to snub Pilate's invitations. Why would they think they would attend? Pilate's rule, his home, and his fortress had once belonged to Antipas' father, King Herod. It should have been his. It didn't help that Pilate gloated over his newfound position of power and the luxuries that came with it. Pilate took Herod's rejections personally.

Antipas had aligned with Caiaphas to make Pilate's governance more difficult. He made every effort to make Pilate look inept. Both Herod and Caiaphas enjoyed finding ways to rebuff Pilate until they needed some favor.

To invoke more intimidation and power, Pilate entreated Caesar to allow him the sole right to render 'ius gladii' (the death penalty). It suited him for everyone to know he held their paltry lives in his hands. Tiberias was happy to grant Pilate this right, and he had been quick to use it. This authority set him above the two thorns in his flesh. Herod Antipas coveted the rule of all of Palestine. He wanted to be just like his father before him. As the high priest, Caiaphas only pretended a servile respect to maintain his assigned post. He privately longed to reign as both priest and king, just as the Hasmoneans had before him. Neither man could be trusted.

They were precariously dependent on one another despite their animosity. Pilate left Caiaphas to remain at his post rather than deal with the backlash from Annas and the Sanhedrin. And, even though Antipas had shaky ties with Tiberius as well, he was quick to tattle and play the loyal and obedient serf. Both Caiaphas and Antipas had tried to undermine Pilate's favor. Pilate had found himself having to answer his superior's pointed queries more than once because of them, and this infuriated him.

Still, he had no one to blame but himself for his latest faux pas.

In an act of arrogance, Pilate had made unilateral decisions concerning Jerusalem's most important resource—water. Failing to consult with the Jewish leaders concerning this precious and limited supply had brought him much trouble. The city was strained to meet the needs of the influx of people for the Festivals, to supply the mikvahs and pools, as well as drinking water for pilgrims and the whole Roman militia. When Pilate decided to install a number of Roman baths, a water crisis erupted.

Pilate took action without input from the city's leaders by ordering his engineers to build an aqueduct to reroute the springs of Bethlehem into the city. His utter disregard for the people of Bethlehem caused an outcry since they raised the sacrificial sheep and livestock for Jerusalem. They also grew much of Jerusalem's fresh food supply. Both Herod and Caiaphas were only too happy to intercede on behalf of their people by appealing to Tiberias.

Pilate added insult to injury when he demanded that the monetary offerings for the temple given by the pilgrims during Passover be rendered to him to pay for the building of the aqueduct. Thereby, he dared to undercut the priests, the Sanhedrin, and the temple's financial resources.

Jerusalem's leaders became riotous. In retaliation, Annas shrewdly hired zealot agitators to bring their deep-seated hatred of Pilate to Jerusalem in dissent. Propaganda was dispatched to Pilate that hinted at a possible Galilean plan to rise against Rome.

As Annas had planned, a few agitated zealots were sent into a large group of unsuspecting Galilean pilgrims who arrived to the wrong place at the wrong time. The innocent pilgrims were mistaken as being involved in an uprising against Rome. Pilate admitted it was a strategic stroke of genius. But he hadn't known that Annas had hoped to kill two birds with one stone. Annas had targeted the unsuspecting Galileans because so many had become followers of Yeshua. He had hoped that Yeshua and his followers might be among the pilgrims and perish in the confrontation.

Duped, Pilate had failed to recognize that there were really only a few loud demonstrators set as bait throughout the crowd of innocent pilgrims. He sent his militia disguised as Jews to infiltrate the crowd. Once dispersed within the crowd, they raised their hidden weapons and began systematically mowing down the unsuspecting pilgrims. That day, he filled the streets with bloodied bodies from the Court of the Gentiles to the Antonia Fortress. The people had cowered and begged for their lives. Having no weapons, the pilgrims never even fought back. Meanwhile, the zealot agitators had run for cover, leaving innocent people to die.

Afterward, Pilate celebrated his victory over the Galileans. Even though Pilate was an atheist, he made a great show of his contempt for the Jews by gathering up their pooled blood from the street and taking it to mix with his sacrifice of gratitude to the Roman gods. He had ground these people under the heel of his tyranny and thrown down their rebellion.

But, his celebration ended rather abruptly when he realized there was no outcry or demand for justice coming from the temple priests. The priests were eerily silent. Only then did he realize something was amiss. Questioning his men, he discovered the people he had ordered struck down in the streets had been only peaceful pilgrims, not insurrectionists at all. There were no weapons on any of them. There had been no casualties among the Roman soldiers.

When the word reached Herod that the people from his land had been murdered in cold blood, he went into a rage.

"How dare Pilate take the lives of my subjects without so much as a by your leave! He has gone too far, causing problems for me by his overreach." Quickly, Herod's demands for retribution were dispatched to Tiberius.

From Jerusalem, Caiaphas sent a dispatch as well. Neither man, cared about the people who had been slaughtered, but rather the boundaries that Pilate had crossed. They used his debacle to put him at a disadvantage.

All of this allowed Annas to leverage Herod's complaints to force Pilate to submit to a more agreeable alliance with him. Annas was greatly humored that Pilate knew he had orchestrated the whole affair, but he could do nothing. Pilate would learn not to underestimate him in the future. He chuckled to himself. He had put Pilate in his place.

Pilate was hard-pressed to account for his error, saying the Jews had tricked him. He was given a strong warning to stay in his lane, and the stakes concerning the peace of Jerusalem became his solemn priority. He ground his teeth every time he thought of it.

Now, only six months later, once again, as Pilate rode into Jerusalem on his unsettled warhorse, he wondered how much longer he might rule over Jerusalem and what traps they had set for him this time.

Swarms of people had already begun clogging the arteries. Seething with a bitter hatred, Pilate wanted to whip his horse and trample them all. But the people parted quickly before their oppressor; they pushed and shoved in their hurry to get out of his way. They turned their faces away, unwilling to look at him. They made themselves small.

Pilate was glad at their discomfort. He thought to himself, 'Fear is better than adoration.'

From his elevated position of authority, he looked down his nose with bitter disdain, finding Jerusalem's Festivals and its people to be deplorable. They gave him nothing but trouble.

~ 15 ~

BETHANY

You, God, are my God; earnestly, I seek you;
I thirst for you, my whole being longs for you,
In a dry and parched land where there is no water.
Psalm 63:1

Mari returned to Bethany at Yeshua's insistence when the men had fled up into the Syria-Phoenician regions. She had been waiting for word from him ever since. She returned from yet another day of sharing his teachings with women during the Fall Festival. While she did not enter into the women's court to teach, she taught in the common area at the foot of the steps.

She had positioned herself so she could watch for Yeshua, hoping to spot him as soon as he appeared. She had seen Joses, Yeshua's brother, who told her Yeshua was not coming to the Festival this year, but Mari still held out hope.

'Where is he?' she kept wondering. Little did she know that there were eyes on her, watching to see if anyone who looked like him should come to her. Caiaphas knew she had previously traveled with Yeshua and his disciples to Galilee. He felt sure that the Nazarene would make contact with her when he returned.

The Day of Atonement began this evening, so Mari ended her lessons with plenty of time to make her way back to Bethany before sunset. She and Susanna were followed outside the gates, but when no one met up with them, her spies let her go on unobserved.

Mari climbed the crest of Mount of Olives, leading to the Boethius compound just ahead. She was home early, while the sun was yet drifting toward the horizon. Coming into the courtyard, she could smell the delicious aroma of cooking. Martha's voice was heard from the kitchen, giving directions.

"Increase today's quantity by twenty people." She was calling out to her servants.

"Magdalene!" Young Yohan called out from the portico.

She quickly swept the perimeter to find Yohan with a broad smile, but her eyes did not stop until she found Yeshua. She dropped her pack and all but ran to his side, longing to throw her arms around him in welcome. Instead, she stopped short.

Yeshua uncoiled from his rest, standing to receive her. He held out his hands to her, taking her slender hands in his. They drank in the sight of each other.

"Lord, I just knew you would make it!" She said, slightly breathless. "Even though Joses said you were not going to attend this Festival."

"I wasn't sure if I would come or not. And we experienced a few delays along the way."

"It is so good to see you! To see you all!" She amended, as if noticing for the first time the other disciples.

"How I have missed being with you, and I have prayed earnestly for you…all. After my return, I have kept myself busy sharing your teachings with a small group of women from Jerusalem. Several have come to spend a significant amount of time here so they could share your teachings in the women's court."

"Sounds like you have been busy. I look forward to seeing those women in Jerusalem," his smile was sincere.

Mari saw that the Rabbi was tired; she motioned for him to sit and immediately took her place at his feet. "So tell me where you have been and what have I missed."

"We have been all over Syria. We returned to Capernaum. Then we made a few stops in the Decapolis."

"With the Gentiles?"

"Yes, with the scattered Jews, but a number of Gentiles as well."

"They have received you?" She asked, her eyes wide.

"Yes. Some have received better than our people."

"What does this mean?" She asked him, seeing this was disturbing to him.

"It means my time is drawing near. The end of my visitation here is all too rapidly approaching."

"Do the others know?"

"I keep telling them over and over, constantly, in fact, but ..."

"But...they don't want to believe it...," she finished for him.

He nodded.

"I can understand that. When will this happen?" she wanted to know.

"You know they are seeking to take my life even now."

"Yes, I know."

"But it won't happen until the appropriate time comes."

"When?"

"Don't worry, Magdalene, there is still work for me to do, and I will complete it. So, what about you? How has your time been here at home? Has your father softened towards you?"

"He doesn't know what to make of me, but I think so. He tolerates me, so that's something. He is so old now that I don't think he has the energy to worry about me. Eleazer has only asked me not to bring any other shames upon this household. And, I have enjoyed spending time with Lazarus and Martha. Of course, she has begun to try to order me around as if I were her servant girl once again," she rolled her eyes, "But I don't feel safe to move back to Jerusalem quite yet."

As if on cue, Martha came into the courtyard and spotted Magdalene instantly.

"There you are!" She piped. "I have been waiting for you. I could use your help in the kitchen!"

"I just arrived. I am just catching up with the Master!"

Martha narrowed her eyes, seeing how close Mari sat at his feet, chatting intimately.

"We only have a little bit of time left to finish the meal and clear it away before the sun sets and the fast begins."

Mari remained seated, unwilling to leave Yeshua's side. "Give me just another minute, and I will be there."

But jealousy reared within Martha's heart. She would have enjoyed having such a close relationship with Yeshua. She, too, longed for the freedom to sit close to him and to talk with him as her sister did, but she had a job to do by overseeing the house and the feasts. Everyone expected it of her. But she saw the special bond they shared. She thought, 'Why should I prepare and serve the feast while Mari socializes?'

Before she could recall Yeshua's last rebuke, she barked out sharply, "Mari, I need your help!"

Yeshua and Mari looked at her, surprised by her angry outburst. Only then did she remember the last time this happened. She tucked her head, pressing her lips together as if to catch the words and shove them back inside. Her ears burned with the embarrassed realization that she sounded like a bossy shew.

Yeshua saw her humiliation, but more he saw her heart. "Martha, we don't need a big feast! We could make do with just a few simple things."

Tears pooled in Martha's eyes, "I just...I would like..." She began awkwardly, unable to put words to the desires of her own heart to sit in Mari's seat.

"I know," Yeshua said tenderly.

Mari jumped up, tossing Yeshua a longing look, but she put her arm around her sister and said, "Let's go get this done so you can come and sit with us."

Together, they disappeared into the kitchen.

~ 16 ~

GOD WITH US

They will call him Immanuel.
(Which means, "God with us.")
Matthew 1:22

Yeshua sent disciples into the city to individually visit with their relatives who were at the festival. He traveled alone into Jerusalem wearing an unfamiliar cloak and head covering he had borrowed from one of the house servants. He kept his face hidden in shadow so as not to be recognized. He passed among the crowds of people listening to their conversations.

People were asking one another, "Where is the Galilean prophet? Isn't he coming?"

He picked up bits and pieces of conversations.

Some said, "He is a good man."

Some rebutted, "No, he deceives the people. He is an impostor."

"How did this man become filled with such wisdom and understanding? He has no credentials?"

"He is the Messiah."

"He is just the latest upstart playing upon a myth."

The people were divided about him. Still, whatever they said about him, whether good or bad, they whispered in private conversations. The threat had circulated that anyone speaking openly about Yeshua would be permanently removed from the temple and synagogues. It was dangerous to be identified as his follower or sympathizer. They feared losing their good standing within the community where they were once known, accepted, and admired. Only after he listened and understood the people's attitudes did Yeshua remove his disguise to address the people's concerns.

He stood on the steps and said, "I have come to tell you, my teaching is not my own. It comes from the One who has sent me. Examine the Scriptures against what I say, and you will find my teaching is from God. Didn't Moses give you the law? Yet, not one of you keeps the law. Case in point, here you are trying to kill me!"

"Who is trying to kill you?" some Pharisees laughed at him.

"You cannot be of God. You break the Sabbath by healing people on that day!" a scribe tried to shift the guilt to Yeshua.

"If a son is born on a day that causes the eighth day to fall on the Sabbath, don't you circumcise the child in keeping with the law? How is healing a person any less legitimate than marking and setting aside a child to God? How is it you are angry at me for this?"

The leaders began to whisper behind their cupped hands, "Isn't this the man the officials are looking for? Here he is, freely preaching publicly. Have they concluded that he really is the Messiah?"

Yeshua responded, "Yes, you know me, and you know where I am from. I am not here of my own accord. The One who has sent me is true.

"You do not know him. But I do know him because I am from him, and he has sent me."

Tempers flared at his insulting words. They tried to take hold of him. They reached out their hands to take him, but their hands kept failing and falling away before they could reach him. It was as if some power was swatting them away from him. He was able to walk among them without restraint. He walked right through the center of the crowd.

Seeing him untouched, many within the crowd believed in him, "When the Messiah comes, will he do more miraculous signs than this man?" his believers asked.

Hearing he was walking about, Caiaphas sent the temple guards to arrest him while he stood fearlessly among the people.

"Look, I am with you for only a short time. Then, I am going to return to the one who sent me. You will continue to watch for the Expected One, but you will be unable to find me, and where I am, you cannot come."

Every time he said the words "I am," it was as if a strange current traveled through the people who were seeking him, pulling them along. They felt his draw with every inch of their being. Those who denied he was God's Messiah felt his words grating on them more and more.

Someone whispered, "I bet he is going out to the Greeks!"

The temple guards arrived, but they, too, were inexplicably unable to act or move against him. Their feet became rooted in place to keep them from drawing any closer to him. They became trapped behind the people who were enjoying Yeshua's words.

**

Rock, James, and Yohan had happened upon the crowd surrounding their Rabbi while he publicly taught. Why was he ignoring the risks? Hearing his courageous and truthful words, they were surprised that his opposition did not move to touch him.

Later, they recounted the events of the day to the others, "There he was speaking openly to the people about his identity and the shortness of his time among them, hinting that he would soon be leaving," Yohan said.

"Yes, it appeared the guards had been told to take hold of him, but they could not move. No one even touched him." Rock added.

"How can that be?" James wondered.

"After all he has done, you would ask that?" Philip shot back.

The women invited Yeshua to take his meal with them that evening. His absence allowed his men to have conversations of their own.

"So…" Judas asked, "if he can keep them from taking hold of him, why does he keep speaking of them taking hold of him and killing him? He confuses me. Where is he going with all of this? If he said the word, thousands of people would come to his side to make him King."

"Just as if he says the word, thousands of angels would appear at his side," Rock added.

"Surely, by now, you know that war is not his plan," Yohan said.

"I am not sure; doesn't he speak of bringing a sword that divides? Are you sure? Is anyone?" Judas countered.

Rock shrugged, "Only Yeshua knows what he has planned. We just have to trust him."

**

During the remaining seven days, Yeshua made unexpected visits to different places to teach. He was here and there, found and not found, teaching then gone. He was ghosting the officials. When the Jewish leaders *were* able to find him, they tried to confront him and intimidate him in front of the crowds, "Tell us the truth now for the glory of God, aren't we right in saying that you are a Samaritan and demon-possessed?"

His challengers wore self-congratulatory grins at their latest scheme. Every Jew hated the Samaritans. If they could convince the people that he was a Samaritan, they would turn away from him.

Yeshua ignored their accusations completely. Instead, he answered. "A demon does not possess me. I honor my Father. But you dishonor me. I am not seeking glory for myself. But you should know, there is one who does seek it, and he is the judge. Very truly, I tell you, whoever obeys my word will never see death."

They laughed, "Now we know that you *are* demon-possessed!"

One Pharisee stepped forward to ask a sincere question, "Teacher, what must I do to inherit eternal life?"

"What is written in the Law? What does it say?"

The man answered, "'Love the Lord your God with all your heart and with all your soul and with all your strength and with all your mind'; and 'Love your neighbor as yourself.'"

"Correct," Yeshua beamed at the man. "Do this, and you will live."

The man said thoughtfully, "This is easy to say but not so easy to do. What if I have sinned unknowingly? How can I know I am justified? And, who is my neighbor?"

Yeshua looked up toward the taller buildings. He could see the shadows stretching toward the heights. The daylight was fleeing. But, he had just enough time to tell a story.

He motioned for everyone to take a seat.

He began, "A man was going down from Jerusalem to Jericho. On the way, he was attacked by robbers. They stripped him of his clothes, beat him, then went away to leave him half-dead.

"Now, a priest happened to be traveling the same road. But when he passed near, he saw the man lying in a broken heap. He passed by against the wall to avoid the man. Though the man called out to him, he did nothing. He left the wounded man in need and pain. Not long after that, a Levite came along to the place and saw the wounded man. But he was in a big hurry, so he, too, passed by on the other side and left the poor man for dead.

"Eventually, a Samaritan traveled the man's way. When the Samaritan saw him, he immediately took pity on him. He saw the man's brokenness and pain and his inability to save himself. So he went to him and poured wine and oil on his wounds and bandaged them. Then he put the man on his donkey and brought him to an inn to provide care of him.

"The next day, he took out two denarii and gave them to the innkeeper. 'Look after him,' he said, 'and when I return, I will reimburse you for any extra expense you may have.'"

Judas muttered under his breath to Rock, "Twenty. It was twenty denarii!"

Rock shushed him, giving him a fierce look.

Yeshua looked compassionately at the Pharisee, "Now, which of these three do you think was a neighbor to the man who fell into the hands of robbers?"

The expert in the law knew in his heart what was right, but he thought carefully before he replied, "The one who had mercy on him."

Yeshua told him, "Go and do likewise. For you are not far from the kingdom of heaven."

**

Later that evening, Yosef of Arimathea went to his friend, Nicodemus, and said, "You are right about the Galilean. He may have come from Nazareth, but I have never heard anyone speak of brotherly love in such a meaningful way. I felt compassion radiating from him. He is quite impressive, isn't he? If ever anyone would be Messiah, it would be a man like him. Could anyone have more wisdom than this man? And at such a young age!"

"I know!" Nicodemus clenched his hands before him, searching for the right words. "You feel cleansed, right? By his very presence and words, it is as if he were washing you clean."

Yosef nodded excitedly.

Nicodemus beamed at Yosef. "So, we both feel the same. His truth and love refresh the soul in a way that no one else ever has."

**

It was the last and greatest day of the Feast. People throughout Jerusalem were grumbling that the water supply was dangerously low and it was being rationed sparingly. Pilate was allowing only so much to be released at specifically scheduled times during the day. At the same time, Pilate and the fortress seemed to have no lack. The pilgrims resented the lack of Roman restraint.

"What does Pilate care if we have no water left?" they grumbled angrily. "In a few days, he will go back to Caesarea Maritima to his northern aqueducts!"

"Come, let us go to the temple and offer up prayers for the later fall rains to come speedily."

Yeshua blended into the crowd easily on this day of the festival because everyone attended this day dressed all in white. It was a day renewal, intended for the people to embrace a new beginning along a new year, to look forward, not back, to happily celebrate their newly found peace with God. It was a day of fresh starts. The temple grounds were filled with the sound of a multitude of voices; some were praying, others were singing with the cantor to the ancient Davidic psalms. The combination of sounds were like the sound of many waters.

This was Yeshua's favorite day of the Festivals. He closed his eyes to feel the prayers flowing over him, resonating within his being. It was almost as if the people were singing from within him.

At the assigned hour, the priests took up their golden vessels in a procession led by the musicians and choir to the pool of Siloam. Though the pool was not as full as it usually was, they were able to fill the pitchers from the huge immersion pool. The Levite choir sang salvation songs; the musicians played lyres, trumpets, cymbals, and harps. It was a visually moving sight, with all the priests, Levites, and people dressed in their robes of pure white like a bride prepared for her groom.

As the sun began its descent, the people clapped and cheered the priest on. Some people danced in unison to the music. Each adult held their oil lamps of flickering light. The Menorah blazed, casting light on every face, and danced upon the walls.

When the Priests reached the temple gates, the Levites raised and blew the ram's horn, announcing their return. The discordant sounds of the shofar blended with the light and joyful sound of the other instruments and the loud clanging of the cymbals, creating a backdrop of majesty and grandeur. The sounds were ancient and otherworldly, flowing together with the beautiful words of the psalms being sung. The shofars reminded everyone that YHWH was present, and he had promised to raise his own horn of salvation. At the shofar's call, everyone raised their lamps high to create a sea of dazzling light. Even old men danced in celebration. Everyone was caught up in the beauty of this evening. Yeshua's heart yearned, and tears sparkled in his eyes. Spellbound, he let the worship flow over him. This was the glory his Father so justly deserved.

For a moment, everything seemed to fall away, and he was temporarily transported to a future time and place. He saw the lavender sky being rolled up like a scroll; heaven and earth became one. Light and faces, words and blueprints were whirling all around him to the sound of the singing.

He heard the woeful cry, "Is there anyone worthy to open the scroll? Anyone?

His heart raced with passion. He shouted, "Here I am!"

But he blinked. He had returned to *this* eighth-day celebration.

The priests entered the courts and encircled the people on the floor, lost in prayer and song. This celebration was a prefiguring, a prelude, of all he would soon accomplish. Voices swirled around him:

'Now is the day of the LORD's salvation.
I lift up my eyes... where does my help come from...
To you whose throne is in heaven....
Our eyes look to the LORD our God until he shows us his mercy...
Our help is in the name of the LORD, the Maker of Heaven and Earth,
The scepter of the wicked will not remain ...
Unless the LORD builds the house, the builders labor in vain...
Blessed are all who fear the Lord....
With you, O Lord, there is forgiveness; therefore, you are feared.
Put your hope in the LORD, for with the LORD is unfailing love, and with him is full redemption.
For he will personally redeem Israel from all their sins.'

The priests circled the base of the altar of sacrifice seven times, playing their instruments and singing the songs of ascent.

Twelve priests ascended the stairs. They carried their silver pitchers of water for the cleansing away of old sins. They took up their assigned places between the four horns of the altar. The music stopped, and voices grew silent.

The High Priest read the words from Isaiah 12:2-3.

"I will praise you, Lord. Although you were angry with me, your anger has turned away, and you have comforted me. Surely, God is my salvation; I will trust and not be afraid. The Lord, the Lord himself, is my strength and my defense; he has become my salvation. With joy, we have drawn water from the wells of salvation."

Everyone waited, listening to blasts of the shofar.

Then, priests hoisted up their large pitchers to pour out the abundance of water over the altar. Water shot out of the four horns in sooty waterfalls. Without delay, the priest poured out seven bowls of the deep red wine from Bethlehem. When the wine mixed with the remaining waters, the altar became four rivers of blood flowing in four different directions.

To the people, the red wine drink offering meant the restored fellowship with Yahweh.

Only Yeshua understood the significance of these rituals, and momentarily, he swayed.

Meanwhile, the people around him shouted their praise in an apex of joy.

'*This,*' He thought. 'This is the promise of God to make all things new. All the sins of the past are washed away and forgiven by the water and the blood. The people receive a clean slate.'

Caiaphas held up the scroll and read the words of Isaiah 55, *"Come, all you who are thirsty, come to the waters; and you who have no money, come, buy and eat! Come, buy wine and milk without money and without cost."*

These were his Father's words. He listened.

"Give an ear and come to me; listen, that you may live. I will make an everlasting covenant with you, my faithful love promised to David. See, I have made David a witness to the peoples, a ruler and commander of the peoples. Surely you will summon nations you know not, and nations you do

not know will come running to you because of the Lord your God, the Holy One of Israel, for he has endowed you with splendor."

Tears stung Yeshua's eyes, and his voice became tight and filled with emotion.

Caiaphas continued: *"Seek the Lord while he may be found; call on him while he is near. Let the wicked forsake their ways and the unrighteous their thoughts. Let them turn to the Lord, and he will have mercy on them, and to our God, for he will freely pardon. As the rain and the snow come down from heaven and do not return to it without watering the earth and making it bud and flourish, so that it yields seed for the sower and bread for the eater, so it is with my Word that goes forth from my mouth."* Caiaphas had no understanding of the words he spoke.

Looking up towards heaven, Yeshua said to his Father. " With your help, I will not fail you."

Caiaphas continued, "For the LORD has spoken: *'My word will not return to me empty, but will accomplish what I desire and achieve the purpose for which I sent it.'*

Caiaphas ended the readings and left his station before the altar.

"Father, let me complete all your commands for this joy set before me." Yeshua prayed. He pushed through the crowd to ascend the empty stairs. The eyes of every person were upon him. The whole assembly waited. Standing before the altar, he motioned to himself and shouted in a very loud voice, "If anyone is thirsty, let him come to me and drink. Whoever believes in me, as the Scripture has said, 'Streams of living water will flow from within him.'"

The people realized he was boldly claiming to be the Messiah. He was saying he was the LORD's salvation. A charge of energy ripped through the crowd, and the people held up their hands and lamps toward him to joyful shouts and exclamations, "Here is the Christ! I knew it! Praises be to Yahweh, for he has kept his promise and sent us his salvation!"

Others grew angry, convinced he was a political hack simply taking advantage of the lack of drinkable water. Others thought he was a madman bent on disrupting the event. Some became so angry they tried to get to him, wanting to rip him from limb to limb. But they found their feet frozen in place as if they were held back and unable to move. Skeptics asked, "How can the Messiah come from anywhere but Bethlehem, where David lived?"

Caiaphas shouted angry commands to the temple guards, "Seize him!"

But their feet simply would not move. Some took stones up into their hands to pelt him but could not lift their arms to cast them. His enemies wanted to surge forward to overtake him, but they could not move.

Yeshua simply left, walking away from the volatile scene with no one following him. He disappeared into the night without a trace.

As he was descending the steps of the temple, he came face to face with a regiment of waiting Roman soldiers, readied to make sure no uprising would occur on such an emotional night as this. Their commander, Pilate, sat on his stallion, flanked by his bodyguard. Pilate saw Yeshua walk confidently down the steps alone. His white robe tugged back tautly in the breeze. He was impressed by how much this Jew favored a young god. Intrigued, Pilate leaned forward to get a better glimpse of his face.

Yeshua stopped, and the two simply stared at one another as if in an odd moment of recognition. Yeshua offered Pilate a grave nod before he continued down the remaining steps to move silently along into the falling darkness. Pilate leaned forward to watch his retreating form until he had disappeared. He couldn't say why, but he felt troubled in his spirit. Being pragmatic, Pilate shook off the warning, 'He is just another Jew. One is no different from another.'

Inside the temple grounds, the guards were being called forward to give an account of their lack of action to Caiaphas.

"Why didn't you obey my order to capture the man?"

With beseeching palms, they tried to explain knowing it sounded bizarre, they insisted, "We couldn't move our feet."

"That is ridiculous!" Caiaphas shouted, but he could tell the fear on their faces was not because of him.

"We couldn't move, I tell you!" Malchus shouted. "Who has ever spoken the way this man does!"

"You mean he has deceived you too! Look at us: do any of the rulers believe in him? No! And who are these people? They know nothing of the Law!"

Nicodemus came forward and tried to ask, "Does our law condemn any person without first hearing him to find out what he is doing?"

Caiaphas turned his harsh appraisal upon him, "Ah! Nicodemus! So, you are suddenly from Galilee, too? Don't be foolish! Search the Scriptures! No prophet comes from out of Galilee!" Menacingly, he stepped close and breathed into his face, "You should be careful, Nicodemus. Are you not one of the Sanhedrin?"

~ 17 ~

THE FIRST WILL BE LAST

"For my thoughts are not your thoughts,
neither are your ways my ways,"
declares the Lord.
"As the heavens are higher than the earth,
so are my ways higher than your ways
and my thoughts than your thoughts."
Isaiah 55:8-9

Yeshua made his final approach from Jerusalem to Bethany under a moonlit sky. It was late. Actually, very late. The others had arrived hours ago. Lazarus was holding a vigil, waiting for Yeshua to appear, knowing he had gone to spend time in prayer. Finding him on the path before him, Yeshua could see Lazarus clearly had something on his mind. He greeted his friend with a hug.

"Now that the festival is over, I suppose you will take to the road again?" Lazarus asked.

Yeshua nodded, "I have places yet to visit before winter descends upon us."

Lazarus nodded. After a pause, he added, "Martha, Mari, and I want to go with you."

Yeshua looked surprised. He studied his splendidly dressed friend, remembering their time together in Qumran. Back then,

Lazarus had submitted to the simple life of the brothers, anxious to learn the old ways and to be readied for the Messiah. But he never completed his commitment to the brotherhood or Yeshua. Instead, he had returned from his pious exploration to assume the mantle of his family's expectation. He was chastised to follow the path of his father and grandfather, to pursue wealth and prestige for the family name. Truthly, Lazarus enjoyed the privileges of his creature comforts. He wanted to be righteous, but his family placed their hopes on him, that he might one day become a high priest and resurrect their family's honor.

Meanwhile, Yeshua had hoped Lazarus might throw off his family's restraints and expectations to follow him as his disciple. Now, very little time remained of Yeshua's mission. He had only six months left. Even so, he would not discourage his friends. He loved Lazarus, as well as Martha and Mari. On the other hand, he did not need an untrained hot shot with dragging feet to slow him down.

Lazarus waited, watching Yeshua's face. He was expecting to find a hint of Yeshua's excitement that he wanted to join his team. But when Yeshua did not jump to reply, Lazarus offered, "We will follow you wherever you go."

"Will you?" Yeshua's look was doubtful.

"If Mari could make it in the mission field, why couldn't Martha and I?"

"Martha?" He simply queried, remembering the last time she had been Lazarus' excuse to return.

"If Mari goes, Martha will be jealous and determined to go, so yes."

"I have no time for petty jealousies. You had better make it clear to her how hard it is out there on the road."

"I will."

"You can't come looking like...that." He pointed at Lazarus's fine garments, "It will only make you a target. Also, if you are to come with me, you must leave your money here. You will live from our communal money bag as we do."

Lazarus looked tested by the mere thought of it.

Seeing his reluctance, Yeshua made the point he really wanted to make.

"In fact, if you are sincere in wanting to follow me, then sell everything you have and give it to the poor."

"What? Are you serious? Look, I am honest in all my business dealings…"

"I don't doubt it. But that is not the point. Look at the men who *really* follow me. They have literally given up *everything*. Mari left *everything* behind in her previous life to follow me as well. Material things just get in the way and bog you down."

Yeshua asked softly, "Isn't that what Elisha did when Elijah called him? He slaughtered the oxen of his livelihood and built a fire with his plow shares. Then, he followed Elijah. Why? Because he wanted to go with Elijah and serve God. He wanted to become a prophet and a servant of God. He was serious about it, not simply taking a field trip."

Lazarus felt rebuked. He tucked his head with hurt and confusion.

"But I am a businessman; this is my livelihood. Are you asking me to give up how I make my living?"

Yeshua shrugged, leaving the question hanging.

But after a few steps, he stopped and turned around to stand eye-to-eye with his friend. His face was intense and emotional when he asked, "Is it Lazarus? Is it your business that gives life to you?"

Lazarus was shaken and speechless, not knowing what Yeshua wanted him to say.

"I do want you to follow me," Yeshua assured him.

He left his invitation standing between them for several steps when he said, "I am just not sure you are ready to follow me."

Seeing the distress on Lazarus' face, Yeshua swiped at his eyes and said, "If you decide to come, bring no money. Bring nothing that shows you have wealth. Judas will handle our expenses. When the travel gets hard, I imagine you will want to come home. But I will still be spending myself on behalf of the people who will put their faith in me. I will have to keep moving. You will be on your own."

Lazarus nodded gratefully, even though he didn't know if he could live up to Yeshua's call.

Yeshua continued, "Before you make up your mind, you should know what I have told the others. A terrible suffering death waits for me in Jerusalem in the future. It won't be long now. The risk is real for anyone who follows me. People will hate and despise you because of me. They will want to kill you too. You must count the cost. If you follow me, you must be willing to take up your cross. Can you die to self so you can follow me and be my disciple?"

"I don't know," Lazarus said honestly. "I don't know. I need time before I can know what I am willing to do."

"Fair enough," Yeshua nodded. It was an honest answer. He would not snuff out Lazarus' smoldering wick. He could only hope it would, in time, flame to life once again.

"Well then, we are going out into the wilderness first, then eventually, we will travel on to Qumran as well. If you come with us, you will have to carry your load and work right along with the rest of my men."

Lazarus accepted his offer, "Deal. We will get ready to go with you."

But Lazarus wondered, "Can I do what Yeshua demands of me?"

Yeshua watched Lazarus head into his apartment. He saw all the potential Lazarus held. He prayed that this journey would set him free so he would use it.

Having heard the last bit of the conversation, Simon approached Yeshua, "So, Lazarus will join us on our journey?"

"Yes, for a time."

Simon didn't say anything else. His silence conveyed his dismay. What could he say? Still, a little niggling voice inside his head told him, 'Look at them. They are such old friends. Surely, Lazarus will gain Yeshua's favor. Here I have been with him almost from the very beginning, and now will all the rewards go to someone who previously refused to follow him. I don't have the same education, connections, or leadership training that Lazarus has. He beats me hands down.' His heart sunk, 'Will Yeshua set me aside to make Lazarus his right-hand man.'

He hated himself for thinking it because Lazarus had been very kind and hospitable to them all. He had sheltered them and fed them whenever they came to Jerusalem. Lazarus and Martha's home had been a haven to them. Simon had never dreamed that Lazarus would come and take his place. But now, he felt sure he would. Had his years of sacrifice been for nothing? He looked as despondent as he felt.

**

Later that night, when the men had heard the news that Lazarus would be traveling with them, Yeshua felt the heaviness of their concerns. They remained aloof and quiet towards both him and Lazarus. The joy from the festival had evaporated into thin air. Previously, a great many people had come and gone amongst their group. But they had never worried about it, sure their positions were secure. But tonight, for the first time, they all felt the threat of who is in and who is out.

As a group of headstrong men, their group already had enough relationship issues. But now, Lazarus sent all of their interpersonal issues scattering around like snow in a glass globe. With the status quo disturbed, they were forced to work out a whole new pecking order of living together, threatening the trust it had taken months, even years to build.

They thought, "We have been with him all along! Now Lazarus will just waltz right in and receive the kingdom rewards we've worked so hard to gain. Overhearing their furtive and jealous conversations, Yeshua called them together to hear a parable.

They came ready for a rebuke because they knew no 'story' was just a story.

"Listen," he said, "the kingdom of heaven is like a landowner who went out early in the morning to hire workers for his vineyard."

He noticed the exchange of uneasy glances, "Now the landowner agreed to pay each worker a denarius for the day, and he sent them off into his vineyard to work."

Andrew and Yohan glanced at one another, for they had been the first chosen. Yeshua looked at them, tipping his head to their seniority.

"About nine in the morning, he went out and saw others standing in the marketplace doing nothing. He told them, 'You also go and work in my vineyard, and I will pay you whatever is right.' He looked at Philip and Nathaniel. He nodded towards them, and he said, "So they went."

"He went out again about noon..." He looked at Rock and James.

"...and about three in the afternoon, he did the same thing. He took his time to look around, then at Simon, Thomas, Thaddeus, Judas, James, and Matthew, making sure they knew he knew their seniority and self-assigned pecking order.

"About five in the afternoon, he went out and found still others standing around. He asked them, 'Why have you been standing here all day long doing nothing?'

"'Because no one has hired us,' they answered.

"He said to them, 'You also go and work in my vineyard.' So, they also went into the vineyard to work.

"When evening came, the owner of the vineyard said to his foreman, 'Call the workers and pay them their wages, beginning with the last ones hired and going on to the first.'

"The workers who were hired about five in the afternoon came, and each received a denarius. So, those who were hired first suddenly expected to receive more. But each one of them also received a denarius."

It was as if he had lanced a boil. Yeshua could see their outraged faces, colored brightly by the fire's warm glow. It was priceless. How well did he know the thoughts of his sheep?

"When they received their denarius, they began to grumble against the landowner."

Now, Yeshua raised his fist and mimicked their outraged voices. "'These who were hired last worked only one hour,' they said, 'and you have made them equal to us who have borne the burden of the work and the heat of the day.'"

"But the landlord answered one of them," Yeshua looked toward Simon, 'How am I being unfair to you, friend? Didn't you agree to work for a denarius?Take your pay and go.

"I *want* to give the one who was hired last the same as I gave you. Don't I have the right to do what I want with my own money? Or are you envious because I am generous?'"

Shocked anger filled their faces.

Yeshua continued his story. He spoke as the landlord, but they felt like he was talking directly to them. His men wanted to object, but how could they? To do so would reveal the truth of their thoughts and their little understanding of the kingdom of God.

It was true that Yeshua could *include* whoever he wanted, whenever he wanted. And he could *elevate* whoever he wanted to elevate. He was in charge, but still, it just did not feel *fair*. Swallowing their angry words, they looked down at their hands.

Solemnly, Yeshua said, "So the last will be first, and the first will be last."

'Is this another riddle?' They asked him, thinking. 'Why doesn't he just say it? We are getting pushed aside.'

Sensing their confusion, Yeshua stood to his feet, "You men still do not know the thoughts or purposes of God."

Yeshua had just let them know he was in charge. And, they could either receive the positions he offered to them or not. He chose who got to come along on the journey with him. Now, they had to figure out where that left them.

~ 18 ~

WHEAT, WEEDS, PEARLS

The proverbs of Solomon, son of David, king of Israel:
for gaining wisdom and instruction;
for understanding words of insight;
for receiving instruction in
and doing what is right and just and fair;
For giving prudence to those who are simple,
knowledge and discretion to the young—
Let the wise listen and let the discerning get guidance—
Seek understanding through proverbs, parables,
and the riddles of the wise.
Proverbs 1:1-6

The late fall and early winter rains began right on time. Hard driving rains fell in sheets. The winds grew cool. Yeshua and his disciples had hardly arrived at their new mission field before muddy puddles made the byways unpassable and the wadis filled. As they traversed the Jericho road, they kept to the high grounds, fearing the rushing waters flowing below. Indeed, the torrent rushing from Jerusalem indicated that the harder rains were coming behind them. This kind of rain made it impossible for outdoor teaching. Instead, they visited from home to home, and he taught in the synagogues along the way. No one could complain because this outpouring of rain was the answer to the many prayers for the needed water that had been offered in Jerusalem.

Yeshua could not wait for the great outpouring that would come from the heavenly realm on that day when his kingdom through the Holy Spirit would be poured out upon the earth. Then, the seeds he had planted would begin to blossom and grow. Meanwhile, he continued to sow more seeds. Yeshua sent the disciples into the people's homes, where they sat by their fires to teach and drink hot tea. They hardly saw Yeshua except at the synagogues. This was not what Martha and Lazarus had imagined, but Mari had grown used to long separations and used that time to teach the women and children.

Every time the rain relented, they headed to yet another village and town, grateful to see the dim rays of the sun. The temperatures grew cooler, but they enjoyed the more temperate days of teaching outside as much as possible. Yeshua drew large crowds on those days. They bundled up to attend even as the cool air took on a biting nip. The 'darkness' followed him. It lurked amongst the people. Not everyone who pursued him was his friend. Many did not embrace 'The Way'. There were people everywhere who continued to search for a way to accuse him and cause conflict, infiltrators who tried to worm their way in, then purposefully make trouble. The larger the crowds, the more he felt their presence.

One day, he told the people a frequently told parable, "The kingdom of heaven is like a man who sowed good seed in his field. But while everyone was sleeping, his enemy came and sowed weeds among the wheat. Then he went away. When the wheat sprouted and formed heads, the weeds also appeared.

"The owner's servants came to him and said, 'Sir, didn't you sow good seed in your field? Where then did the weeds come from?'

"'My enemy did this,' he replied.

"The servants asked him, 'Do you want us to go and pull them up?'

"'No,' he answered, 'because while you are pulling out the weeds, you may uproot some of the wheat with them. Let both grow together until the harvest. At that time, I will tell the harvesters: First collect the weeds and tie them in bundles to be burned; then gather the wheat and bring it into my barn.'"

Everyone with gardens and fields understood the problem of weeds, but what was he really referring to? The disciples were accustomed to their Rabbi teaching with coded stories publicly. Even so, his stories often left them struggling to understand, right along with most of all the other people. His words were like arrows that targeted a particular audience and were meant to pierce their specific shell of resistance. He usually ended the parable by saying, "Let those who have ears hear." As if to say that some would not hear or understand. They were embarrassed to admit they seemed as deaf as anyone else.

That night, all his disciples were gathered with him around the warmth of the flickering flames, burrowed in their cloaks, and they sat close together for warmth.

"All of the people are coming to you, Master. What happens next?" Nathaniel asked. He hoped Yeshua would finally reveal his plan for the kingdom he spoke of so frequently.

Yeshua nodded and smiled wanly at Nathaniel's attempt.

Nathaniel pressed again, "The kingdom is expanding and growing. But if we do not throw off the Roman oppression, how can it ever work?"

Yeshua's face was solemn and brooding as if a heavy weight was pressed upon him. Still, he offered no words.

Finally, Thomas asked, "Who is the enemy sowing the weeds?"

"It is good for you to ask for clarification. Never be afraid to ask me anything that you do not understand." He spoke as a patient teacher would speak to a simple child.

"The one who sowed the good seed is the Son of Man." He touched his chest.

"The field is the world."

"The good seed stands for the people of the kingdom who receive my words and begin to grow and mature."

"The weeds are the followers of the evil one."

"The enemy who sows the weeds is the devil."

"The harvest is the end of the age, and the harvesters are angels." He looked at them closely to make sure they understood. It was an important truth.

"Just as the weeds are pulled up and burned in the fire, so it will be at the end of the age for the people who serve the evil one. The Son of Man will send out his angels. And they will weed out of his kingdom everything that causes sin, and all who are intent on evil. They will throw them into the blazing furnace, where there will be weeping and gnashing of teeth. Then the righteous will shine like the sun in the kingdom of their Father. Whoever has ears, let them hear."

There were THOSE words again.

He went on to explain, "There will always be bad seed among you wherever you are. Imposters who pretend to be someone they are not. They will be there trying to choke out the good seed, the true believers. Unfortunately, they will be attached or rooted with the believers, making their removal impossible without doing great harm to true believers. Don't try to weed them out because it also uproots those close to them who do believe. Remember, wheat and the darnel weed look very similar. A non-believer can learn to walk and talk just like a true believer. Only God knows if they believe or the evil hidden in their hearts."

"So then, we should not be overly impressed by the crowds of people following you because some are darnel?" James asked.

Yeshua nodded, "Not everyone who says to me, 'Lord, Lord,' will enter the kingdom of heaven. Only the ones who do the will of my Father who is in heaven. Many will say to me on that day, 'Lord, Lord, did we not prophesy in your name? And, in your name, drive out demons? And in your name perform many miracles?'

"Then I will tell them plainly, 'I never knew you. Away from me, you evildoers!'"

They gaped at him, wondering who among them was the darnel.

He said, "Surely, you know this from the Scriptures. Daniel wrote, 'Everyone whose name is found written in the book will be delivered. All who sleep in the dust of the earth will awake. Some will awaken to everlasting life, others to shame and everlasting contempt.' This is not a new idea. There will be an accounting for every person."

"How can we know who is wheat and who is weed?"

"Only by the Spirit can you discern rightly, for only the Holy Spirit knows. Pray for this kind of discernment."

"How will the kingdom advance if we are surrounded by so many who don't want the kingdom to succeed?" Yohan asked.

"Don't be discouraged. Didn't I tell you that if you had even the faith as small as a mustard seed, nothing could stop your faith? Faith, my friend, faith. The kingdom of heaven is like a mustard seed, which a man took and planted in his field. Just one small seed.

"Although it is the smallest of all seeds, when it grows, it becomes a small tree. The birds of the air come and perch in its branches to enjoy its shade, hoping to gobble up all the seeds. Yet, in their foraging, the birds knock many other tiny seeds to the ground. They take root and sprout, and a new plant begins. Soon, the whole field is filled with mustard shrubs, glorious with all of their beautiful yellow flowers.

"As you know, it is hard to stop the proliferation or the perseverance of the mustard seed once it has truly taken root and has begun to grow. It is hard to pull out. This, also, is like the kingdom of heaven. And the whole field can become full of mustard plants that begin with just one seed because mustard plants are tenacious, and they are hard to destroy."

"Look, here is another example. The kingdom of heaven is like yeast that a woman took and mixed into about sixty pounds of flour. She worked it until it was worked all through the dough. The tiny filaments of yeast permeate the whole loaf to transform a small lump into many loaves. In the same way, the faith and knowledge of God will fill the whole earth."

Yeshua spread his hands toward his disciples, "I am telling you of things hidden since the creation of the world just as the prophets foretold. Things that will slowly come to light in your lives. And yet, they will crucify the one who speaks these words to you."

Yeshua did not stop there. He looked toward Lazarus. "The kingdom of heaven is like a treasure hidden in a field. When a man found it, he hid it again, and then in his joy went and sold all he had to buy the field."

Lazarus looked sheepish. He had resisted Yeshua's challenge to do this. He loved Yeshua and wanted to be faithful, but he often felt he asked too much.

He wondered, 'Why is this so important to Yeshua? Can't he understand my father Eliezer expects this of me?'

Lazarus thought back to his father's happiness when he came home from Qumran. He had pounded his back, saying, "Son, your time of free thinking is past. It is time for you to take your place, join the family business, and become a part of the Sanhedrin. Where will this Yeshua fellow get you? Nowhere. He is radical and dangerous. You will become an outcast from your people. You endanger everything our family has worked for by inviting him to stay here at your house. Do you want to be cast out of your faith? Don't you realize you are playing a dangerous game with your very soul?"

And now, Yeshua seemed to be saying the same thing. Lazarus felt torn, or like he was walking a tightrope.

Yeshua saw the battle going on within Lazarus. He would not give up on his dear friend. Still, he would prod him at every opportunity.

Yeshua turned his gaze toward Mari, Martha, Susanna, and Joanna, who had joined them along the way, then to each of his men, including Lazarus. He was filled with such love for them all. It made his heart hurt.

He told one last story for the evening, "Again, the kingdom of heaven is like a merchant looking for fine pearls. When he found one of great value, he went away and sold everything he had, then bought it, paying the price for it in full."

Everyone wondered, 'What is he talking about now? What is the pearl?'

But not Mari. She understood what he was saying. He could see it in her eyes.

"You are all very precious to me." He all but whispered. His eyes lingered on her for several heartbeats.

Mari took great pleasure in knowing that she was treasured, even though he was speaking of them all. But for her, after all her experiences of abandonment, misuse, and loss, she knew she needed his unchanging love more than anything else. His love was precious to her. She was confident that Yeshua would give his all and pay whatever the price to keep her and the others for himself forever. How could she not do likewise to have him?

~ 19 ~

SALT AND LIGHT

For now, we see only a reflection as if in a mirror;
then we shall see face to face.
Now I know in part;
then I shall know fully, even as I am fully known.
1 Corinthians 13:12

They made their way to their final stop—Qumran. It didn't seem so long ago since Yeshua had left the enclaves of these sparse and lofty shelters. Six years before, he had come to study the sacred texts. Here, his plan for redemption had been formed by Scripture. Here, he had prepared for the work he was finishing now. The words had excited him, even knowing where they would ultimately lead him. He was so grateful for his Father's instruction. Scripture was a supernatural document that had been written down and preserved for him to find and follow. He was his Father's word made flesh. He was the "yes and amen" to all of his Father's promises.

Those holy words from his Father had been carefully preserved, like dormant seeds once planted in the soil of Israel, so that, someday, they would be embodied within him. Those ancient words of truth were spoken down through the ages and preserved for thousands of years.

Their small caravan came to the flats of the Dead Sea before making the way up to Qumran. The waters on the Dead Sea sparkled like an aquamarine in crystal settings, a jewel against Jordanian heights on the other side. White mounds of salt lined the shoreline as a testament to its deadly strength. No fish or other wildlife exists within it. People traveled to this place to gather the salt to use for its healing properties, exported in bath salts and skin lotions.

They turned aside to take a break.

"These waters are so unusual!" Zel said, taking in the vista.

They marveled, for this was one of the most arid and unusual places in the world.

"How did this come to be?" Matthew asked.

When no one answered, Yeshua looked at them with surprise. "You do not know?"

"No." They said and shrugged. "How would we?"

"Surely you know the story of Sodom and Gomorrah?" Yeshua asked.

"Yes, but what does it have to do with this sea?"

"Well...everything! You have read of the perversion and violence that once was found in these cities, right?"

The disciples shook their heads.

"Evil had possessed the people so completely that the two cities and everything around them had to be destroyed. The spiritual corruption had to end. People of this region had become completely possessed by it. Even Lot, whom Abram begged to be rescued, had sunk to such a low standard in such a short period that he tried to compromise by offering up his daughters as an acceptable sacrifice to the mayhem of the cities. He was willing to do something totally evil to keep the people from committing an even greater sin of forced perversion. Compromise or concessions with evil never works with the demonically possessed. It only serves to make matters worse. The story is written in the Torah as a warning to everyone.

"Lot had been reluctant to leave the land behind because the river valley was beautiful. At that time, it flowed with living waters. The land was fertile and productive, temperate, and near to the sea. The land was beautiful. But when my Father sent his angels to investigate, Lot and his family hesitated. Because of Abraham's prayers, two angels grasped the hands of Lot, his wife, and his two daughters to lead them out of the city to safety.

"As soon as they were brought out, the angels told them, 'Flee for your lives! Don't look back, and don't stop anywhere in the plain! Flee to the mountains, or you will be swept away!'

"On that terrible day, the wrath of God came against this place from the heavens. The meteor came in hot, with a burning tail, striking in the middle of this plain large enough to take out four of the five cities. It struck with such force that it rocked the earth's foundations, pushing tar and combustible gases to the surface. It turned this valley into a fiery pit, a hell, much like the sea of fire that will be kindled in the second death.

"Lot's family was told to run for their lives and never look back. In remorse and disobedience, Lot's wife looked back, sorrowing for all she was leaving behind. She was instantly turned into a pillar of salt. Who knows how many people became pillars of salt that day, disintegrated, their souls taken into the fiery pits?"

He looked around at all of the astounded faces, seeing that they had really not known.

Some of them had begun to peel off their cloaks, bags, and shoes upon arrival, preparing to go for a swim. But having heard these words, they slid their cloaks back on and stared with amazement at this body of water, seeing the reality of it for the first time.

"The land was salted, and razed, purified, but it remains a place of death. This water cannot sustain life. Until the day of the earth's redemption and renewal comes, and the way to the sea is closed. Only when my father opens its gate will life ever exist in this place.

"Speaking of salt... it purifies and heals; I have chosen you to be salt and light to this world. You can only do this if you keep my word. My words are a purifying fire that will save your brothers and sisters of their sins, bringing healing to them and preserving their lives...I am making you to be the salt of the earth.

"But if salt loses its saltiness, how can it be made salty again? It is no longer good for anything except to be thrown out and trampled underfoot. Don't look back and long for your old life, or you will become a pillar of salt." He pointed to a mound of crystals standing on the water's edge.

"Keep my salt among yourselves while also being filled with my grace. Hold one another accountable, but keep peace with each other."

"But you said this salt kills everything? What do you mean?"

Yeshua answered, "Keep the balance between salt and grace. Too much of even a good thing, like salt, can kill."

Yeshua looked teasingly at them, "Well, aren't you going swimming?"

They all looked at one another, unsure of what to do.

Rock said, "No, I'm good. I will just use the mikvah when we get to Qumran."

Yohan nodded his agreement.

And Yeshua laughingly ruffled the youth's hair and laid his arm around his shoulder affectionately. They moved onward to make the final climb to Qumran.

**

They were welcomed into the compound with a joyful gladness. Yeshua's old friend Malachi came out to meet him, along with all of the brothers who had heard of Yeshua's exploits. Some brothers had even traveled to hear his preaching, surprised that the one they had been searching for had been with them all the time. For some, their previous fraternity became a stumbling block to them. Would the Messiah be such a simple man, the son of a carpenter? Hadn't he dwelt among them, doing the same work as them? These contrarians refused to hear what he had come to say, and they argued against those who had.

"Why didn't he tell us who he was when he was with us?" Some wanted to know, feeling foolish.

'He is simply an opportunist. That is why he poured over the texts. He is a fraud, for surely we would have known him to be the Messiah when he lived among us.'

Others said, "Yeshua has always been a humble man of peace. He is not a Messiah who can overcome the Romans. How will such a peaceable man regain for us our kingdom?"

The more zealously inclined had heard what he had done at the temple and could not believe that Yeshua had turned over the tables and opened the animal pens.

'Why did we not see his zeal when he was here with us?' they wondered.

The camp was divided in their opinions. Tension ran high because of it. And, of course, they had heard about Yohannan's brutal death. Many of the Essene camps, including Qumran, had been visited with inquisitions concerning their affiliations with Yohannan and Yeshua. They knew Antipas had been looking for him. Rumors had also reached them that the Sanhedrin had put a price on his head. They welcomed him now, primarily because Yeshua's enemies were their enemies.

With his arrival, groups gathered with a variety of motivations. Some sought to test him, some to hear his teachings, some with resentment, some with inquiry, some hoping to see him do a miracle, some with skepticism, and a few with real excitement. Most of them were upset that Yeshua had brought women to their compound. All of this made for lively conversations. It reminded Yeshua of why he had kept his own counsel during his studious years.

Those who had once worked with him remembered Yeshua affectionately. They quickly brought food and refreshments to him and his disciples. Some could not resist asking about the awful news of the Galileans, whose blood Pilate had mixed with his sacrifices since Yeshua had preached in Galilee.

"We wondered at first if you were a part of them, but then we were told you were still teaching."

One of them asked, "Was it anyone you knew or some random zealot group?"

Yeshua gave his head a brief shake, "Whether I knew them or not, it was terrible news. They were just ordinary people headed to worship. Do you think that these Galileans were worse sinners than everyone else because they suffered this way? I tell you, no. Death is after us all."

Some in the group sniffed as if they disagreed.

He continued, "But unless you repent, you too will all perish. And, it was the same with those eighteen who died when the tower in Siloam fell on them—do you think they were more guilty than all the others living in Jerusalem on that day? They were just people in the wrong place at the wrong time. But I will tell you all that unless you repent, you, too, will perish."

A stunned silence hung heavy in the air. His friends and the skeptics both looked at him with disbelief and confusion, for there was no one who strove harder for holiness than them, not even the Pharisees. They had known Yeshua was related to Yohannan, but when had this prophet's fire been kindled within Yeshua? When had his voice carried such authority? They understood that they had not known the man who had lived among them, quietly doing his work. He knew them. There would be no pretense. This would not be the friendly banter they had expected. Yeshua had no time for banter now. His message was far too important. Hadn't everyone at Qumran claimed to be waiting and watching for the Messiah? Hadn't they watched hopefully for him in a time when others no longer held such hope? Hadn't they done everything possible to live up to the Scriptures they treasured and scribed daily? Hadn't they sacrificed all the comforts of wives and families to live lives devoted solely to God's work?

Still, here they were holed up in this compound. They were still waiting.

He knew what they were thinking. But now, they needed a savior just as much as anyone else. Their Savior did not conform to the expectations of men, and they were surprised. That was good because he needed them to join forces with God's coming kingdom. His fiery words set the tone for their days together. Over the next few weeks, the brothers questioned him about many things.

They were frank when they challenged him, "We can see that you have taken on Galilean men of various trades, one even being a tax collector. We have also heard you have shared table fellowship with prostitutes! And, here you are traveling with women in your party. This is not what we expected."

Their comments made disciples feel scrutinized and unworthy, and the women feel unwelcome.

"Why do you heal on the Sabbath?" Another asked.

"By what power are you healing the people?" They wanted to know.

"We have heard you have even gone to the Samaritans and into the unclean lands of the Gentiles. This makes no sense. Why would you defile yourself?"

"Isn't the Messiah the King of Israel? Not the Gentiles."

"What will you do about the Herodians?"

"Is your power from God or some other spirit?"

"Why was Yohannan, a prophet for God -- who purified the people, killed by Herod?"

"If you are the Messiah, why didn't you lift your hand to save him?"

Their questions were hard-hitting, pointed, and painful. Yeshua answered them patiently, seeking to impart new insights through the Scriptures. Yet, many were skeptical and found it hard to believe that he was "The Awaited One" they had been waiting for.

Finally, Yeshua brought out the scroll of the suffering servant. He read it before all of the brethren of Qumran, saying, "Listen to the words of the prophet Isaiah in his fifty-third writing: *'Who has believed our message, and to whom has the arm of the Lord been revealed?*

He grew up before him like a tender shoot and like a root out of dry ground. He had no beauty or majesty to attract us to him, nothing in his appearance that we should desire him. He was despised and rejected by mankind, a man of suffering and familiar with pain. Like one from whom people hide their faces. He was despised, and we held him in low esteem.Surely he took up our pain and bore our suffering, yet we considered him punished by God, stricken by him, and afflicted. But he was pierced for our transgressions. He was crushed for our iniquities. The punishment that brought us peace was on him, and by his wounds, we are healed.

'We all, like sheep, have gone astray; each of us has turned to our own way, and the Lord has laid on him the iniquity of us all. He was oppressed and afflicted, yet he did not open his mouth; he was led like a lamb to the slaughter. And, as a sheep before its shearers is silent, so he did not open his mouth.

'By oppression and judgment, he was taken away. Yet, who of his generation protested? For he was cut off from the land of the living; for the transgression of my people, he was punished. He was assigned a grave with the wicked and with the rich in his death, though he had done no violence, nor was any deceit in his mouth. Yet it was the Lord's will to crush him and cause him to suffer, and though the Lord makes his life an offering for sin, he will see his offspring and prolong his days, and the will of the Lord will prosper in his hand. After he has suffered, he will see the light of life and be satisfied; by his knowledge, my righteous servant will justify many, and he will bear their iniquities. Therefore I will give him a portion among the great, and he will divide the spoils with the strong because he poured out his life unto death and was numbered with the transgressors. For he bore the sin of many and made intercession for the transgressors.'"
He searched their faces, hoping for them to understand that *this* was their Messiah.

"Yes, we know this writing," one of the scribes said.

"Who is this righteous servant that Isaiah writes about?" Yeshua asked.

They stared at him uncomprehendingly.

He answered for them, "He is writing about a servant that will become the ultimate sacrifice for the sins of all; one who is willing to suffer for his people. He is writing about a savior who will save mankind from their sins. When you see these things happen, you will discover God's Messiah."

They stared at him, not comprehending.

"Everything about me has been written in the Scriptures. You search them, believing they are the key to your salvation, but I am the living Word that has been written; I am the key. I stand before you, ready to fulfill everything the Father has written about me. I go to Jerusalem soon to fulfill these words. When I do, then you will know this is how all who believe in me will be saved. The kingdom comes by way of the one sent to suffer."

A sea of blank faces lay before him. They were void of all understanding about what he had just read or said. He looked at his disciples, and their faces seemed to be just as blank. He thought, *'Ever hearing but not hearing, ever seeing but not seeing.'*

He searched the sea of faces. His eyes fell on Malachi.

A light wavered dimly in his eyes, as Malachi dimly remembered when he had first wondered if there was more to Yeshua than met the eye. Now he saw he had been right. He remembered when he and Yeshua had discussed Psalm Twenty-two. Yeshua had seen the Messiah in every obscure passage, and he understood all the words that confused him. Now, it made sense.

Awe illuminated his face. He stood to his feet and came to bow before Yeshua with his head lowered and tears dripping from his downturned face. Malachi looked up and said simply, "*I* believe you. I *believe* you, Lord."

~ 20 ~

DEDICATION OF THE TEMPLE

Be careful, and watch yourselves closely
so that you do not forget the things your eyes have seen
or let them fade from your heart as long as you live.
Deuteronomy 4:9

"Son of man, you are living among a rebellious people.
They have eyes to see but do not see
and ears to hear but do not hear,
for they are a rebellious people."
Ezekiel 12:2

Winter had come, dusting the highlands with several inches of fresh powder. A damp chill was in the air. The Festival of Dedication at Jerusalem was at hand. It was not a required feast. Only the most zealous and devout came to celebrate this happy Festival. The Festival commemorated the rededication of God's temple and the miracle of the light that burned from the lampstand for eight days, although they had only found enough oil to light the lampstand for one day. Yet, the lamp had continued to burn until they could prepare more oil to fill the lamp. This had been a sign to God's people that God was with them and he was ready to bless them by being their spiritual light.

Yeshua went to the Festival of Light not only to provide God's light for those eight days but, more importantly, to dedicate the temple of his body for the service of what lay ahead.

As soon as they returned to Bethany, Eleazar descended upon Lazarus and Martha, demanding that they uphold their positions of responsibility to the household. He reprimanded them for being away so long. Mari looked for ways to assist Martha in preparing for the family feast for the eight days of the celebration. They made fresh candles, then turned to the baking of sweet bread, filling the air with the smell of beeswax and sweet spices.

Yeshua once again covertly traveled into Jerusalem to take measure of those attending the Festival. Though there was lively bustle about the city, it lacked the intensity of the fall festival. On every street corner, the air was filled with the scent of baking sweet bread, roasting nuts, and the strains of the joyous Hallel Psalms. People sang and hummed the joyous songs of praise for the LORD, the God of Israel, as they worked.

Colorful robes from distant nations filled the streets. People greeted each other, united by warm blessings for their native land, Jerusalem, and the temple. Their memory songs were of the ordinances of God and his acts of salvation. They sang songs of longing and thanksgiving for the righteous king that was sure to come.

When Yeshua entered Solomon's colonnade, the Jews of Jerusalem spotted him and came to gather around him, saying, "How long will you keep us in suspense? Speak up! If you are the Messiah, just tell us plainly and stop with your strange riddles."

It was hard to believe that even in the midst of all of the joyous festivities, they still wanted to kill him, "I have told you, but you do not believe. The works I do in my Father's name testify about my identity, but you do not believe me because you are not of my flock."

Everyone knew he was making references to Ezekiel's prophecy of the good shepherd, another messianic prophecy. The Sanhedrin leaders bristled.

Yeshua continued, "My sheep listen to my voice; I know them, and they know me. They follow me. I give them eternal life. Because they believe they will never perish. Who can snatch them out of my hand? My Father has given them to me. And he is above all authority; no one can snatch them out of my Father's hand."

Before they could think of a worthy retort, he said, "I and the Father are One." He couldn't state his identity more clearly than that.

The listening crowd ignited with anger as if he had thrown kerosene on a fire. His opponents picked up stones and readied their arms to stone him. But their uplifted arms became as heavy as lead. They could hardly hold them aloft. He saw the strain on their determined faces.

He said, "I have shown you many good works from the Father. For which of these are you stoning me?"

They scowled, pressing against the unseen forces that held their arms at bay as if they were arm wrestling against the wind.

"We are not stoning you for your good work," they replied, "but for blasphemy because you, a mere man, claim to be God."

"Have you forgotten that it is written in God's Law, 'I have said you are gods'? If Moses called them 'gods,' to whom the word of God came. Then what about the one the Father set apart as his very own Word and sent into the world?" His question hung in the air. "Why then do you accuse me of blasphemy because I said, 'I am God's Son'? Do not believe me unless I do the works of my Father. But if I do the works of my Father, even if you do not believe me, then believe the works I have done. Through my works, you may know and understand that the Father is in me, and I am in the Father."

Once again, they strained furiously, trying to rush toward him to seize him. But it was as if their feet were cemented to the ground.

He remained untouched. He turned to leave them, staring at their disobedient hands and feet.

He called out over his shoulder as he took his leave, "Listen to the words of the Psalms being sung. Even they testify to my coming."

**

The next morning, Yeshua entered the temple grounds. He watched one of the younger priests scamper up the ladder to hoist the container of oil used to light the first of the nine lamps. The oil was for the lighting of the Shamash, which was the central, elevated, and preeminent lamp from which the eight other lamps would receive oil to become ignited. Each day, a new chamber would be opened to release the oil of the Shamash to another lamp. Another channel was opened on each day of the eight-day festival. The Shamash lamp was lit early on the first morning to remind everyone that the first of the eight candles would be lit at sunset. Only the Shamash would shine forth its light that day.

After the young man had descended, Yeshua pointed up to the lamp, directing those listening to him to the brightly flickering flame. "I am the Shamash among all of you. I am the Light of The World. Whoever follows me will never walk in darkness but will have the light of life. Everyone receives their light from me."

From the periphery, the Pharisees were quick to challenge him, "Ha! Here you are, appearing as your own witness; your testimony is not valid."

Yeshua said to them, "Didn't Isaiah tell your ancestors, 'You look for light, but all is darkness; for brightness, but you walk in deep shadows. Like the blind, you grope along the wall, feeling your way along like people without eyes.'

"But remember, he also testified, 'to the people walking in darkness, a great light would come. Today, in this land of deep darkness, a light has dawned for you. And soon, my Father will enlarge his nation," his voice echoed with authority.

Hatred twisted the faces of the Pharisees. They did not understand what he was saying. They only knew 'he' would not be their light. They stormed away to plot against him.

**

Late that afternoon, Yeshua was walking through the streets of the city. Sunset was drawing near, and the Sabbath would come to an end. Just then, he encountered a blind man who had been born with no eyes begging for alms on the side of the road. His footsteps slowed, and he came to a standstill. The disciples behind him saw the man as well.

Nathaniel asked, "Teacher, who sinned, this man or his parents, that he was born blind?"

"You misunderstand the situation," Yeshua replied, his voice low. "His blindness has happened so that the works of God might be displayed in this man. He was afflicted so he could bring glory to God."

The disciples looked confused.

"Remember what I said this morning? While I am in the world, I am 'the Light of The World?'" He went to the man and squatted down. The man's face seemed to be searching the darkness before him with surprise, as if he recognized something or someone that he could not see. Uriah's hand shot out in front of him, and he caught hold of Yeshua's hand.

"You! You have come!" Uriah declared with excitement.

"Yes. I am here," Yeshua replied. He took Uriah's hand in his and patted it.

"Will you trust me with what I am about to do to your eyes?" He asked the man.

"Yes, I do!"

Yeshua spit upon the ground several times, making a pool of saliva to make a mud plaster. After scraping and mixing it around, Yeshua plucked up two plugs of mud to place a cake on each of the man's eyes. He rubbed it into place so the mud could stick, making an obvious mess.

When he had finished, he said, "There, now. Go and wash in the pool of Siloam."

The man knew he was not far from the pool. He stood and took up his walking stick. He moved forward, feeling with his stick for his way.

As he went, numerous people stopped to watch him shuffle by with the mud covering his eyes. They wondered, "Who would do such a thing?"

Uriah felt as if a light led the way before him. When he reached the pool, he went quickly into the waters to submerge himself. He scrubbed at his eyes to rinse all of the mud away. Once they were clean, while he was still under the waters he opened his eyes. He saw the light dancing within the murky depths. He came up out of the waters and lifted his head to find a whole new world of light. He blinked with wonder and excitement.

Strange and wonderful sights were everywhere, shapes and colors that he could have never imagined. He bent over to look into the waters where he still stood. He saw for the first time his reflection staring back at him. He laughed, joyous and awestruck, "I have eyes!"

A block away, Yeshua smiled with satisfaction.

Uriah looked at everything around him, astonished by all he saw. Looking up, he caught the brilliant glow reflected on the clouds above. His eyes followed the light to see the brilliant golden light glowing warmly upon the stone walls and the tree tops. Although it was the end of the day, and soon the sky would fade into gray, there would be no more darkness for him. Even the growing darkness seemed bright to a man who had been born with no eyes.

Finally, the trumpet sounded out the setting of the sun. A new day had begun. Yeshua had done what he had come to do; the Shamash had lit the first of the eight lamps. It was time to go to Bethany to rest.

**

The next morning, Uriah was up and out early to see everything he had only imagined.

His neighbors and those who had formerly seen him begging in the streets were baffled, "Isn't this the same man who used to sit and beg?"

Some said, "No, he only looks like him."

But Uriah testified, "Yes! I am that man."

They stared at his eyes. How could they not? They were an unusual shade of gray-blue, sparkling and otherworldly, bringing such life to his face.

"How then were your eyes opened?" they asked.

He held out his hands in wonder, "The man they call 'The Master' made some mud and put it on my eyes. He told me to go to Siloam and wash. After I went and washed, then I could see."

"Where is this man?" they asked him.

"I don't know, it was late last evening," he said. "But, I am hoping to find him."

"Let us take you to the synagogue so you can give glory to God and offer him a proper thanksgiving. Maybe the people there can help you find this man."

At the synagogue, the Pharisees took charge of Uriah when they heard that Yeshua had healed him.

Uriah couldn't understand why their voices were so angry and accusatory, "Yesterday was the Sabbath. This man profaned the Sabbath with his work."

Uriah cringed in confusion.

"How did he do this?" They asked him.

"He asked if I trusted him, and then he put mud on my eyes. He sent me to the pool to wash my eyes." the man replied, "I went and washed my eyes clean, and now I see."

The oldest Pharisee shouted at Uriah, "This man is not from God; he does not keep the Sabbath."

But the other man was more pragmatic. "Then, how is a sinner able to perform such signs?"

More Pharisees joined the conversation, and an argument ensued. Uriah watched these men, incredulous at their anger. Some turned to look at him as if he would break the tie. The others looked at him as if he were the guilty party. All eyes were on Uriah, demanding, "What have you to say about this man? It was your eyes he opened."

"I would say he is a prophet, at the very least," Uriah said. "Only a person with God's authority could do such a thing."

"Why are we asking you?" One of the men shouted, "Clearly you are lying!"

The others joined in, "Look at this man! He must be a fake!"

"Yes, a pretender! Surely, this man was not born blind."

One of the more rational said, "Who can speak for you? Who is your family?"

Uriah told them, and they sent for his family, refusing to let him go his own way as if he were a criminal. When his parents arrived, they realized they could easily lose their standing in the synagogue.

They looked at their son as if to say, 'We won't be implicated with you.' They asked him, "What kind of trouble are you bringing down upon us."

Uriah shrugged in confusion and held out his hands to them in appeal.

"Is this your son?" the older Pharisee asked, smoothing his robe. "What do you have to say about him? Was he really born blind?"

His mother nodded, "It is true. He was born with no eyes."

"How is it then that now he has eyes, and now he can see?" The Old Pharisee leaned towards her threateningly.

Uriah's father answered, "Look! All I know is that this *is* our son. He lives with us. And he *was* most certainly born blind! But how he can see now, or who opened his eyes, we cannot testify. We were not there. Ask him. He is of age; he can speak for himself." He knew any Jew in Jerusalem who acknowledged Yeshua as the Messiah would be put out of the synagogue.

His mother spoke up, "Tobias is right! Our son is of age. Ask him."

The old Pharisee turned on Uriah once again in frustration, "Give glory to God by telling the truth."

He prodded him for an acceptable answer, "We know this man, Yeshua, is a sinner."

Uriah's parents stepped back, refusing to give any further response. But Uriah stepped closer to the old Pharisee, speaking directly to him in a loud voice as if the Pharisee had hearing problems, "Look! I have already told you. I know nothing about this man. I do not know whether he is a sinner or not. Who am I? But there is one thing I do know. I was born blind, but now I see!"

In frustration, the group of leaders demanded, "What did he do to you? How did he open your eyes?"

"You are unbelievable! I have already told you over and over again, and you refuse to listen. Why do you want to hear it all again? Do you want to become his disciples, too?"

Their anger erupted, "I knew it! You are this fellow's disciple! We are disciples of Moses! We know that God spoke to Moses, but as for this fellow, we don't even know where he comes from."

Uriah scoffed at the lot of them, "Now *that* is remarkable! *You* don't know where he comes from, yet he opened my eyes. Even *I* know God does not listen to sinners. He listens to the godly person who does his will.Look! I can see. Nobody has ever heard of such a thing. Who has ever opened the eyes of a man born blind? If this man were not from God, how could he do such a good and miraculous thing for me."

"Who are you to lecture us? You..., you were steeped in sin at birth. How dare you preach about this man to us!"

They took Uriah by the arms and threw him out into the street.

When word reached Yeshua of what had transpired, he went looking for Uriah. He found him near Solomon's Porch, searching for his healer.

Yeshua went up to him and took his hand. Looking into Uriah's new heavenly blue eyes, he asked him, "Do you believe in the Son of Man?"

Uriah cocked his head, recognizing the distinct timber of Yeshua's voice and remembering the touch of his hands.

"Who is he, sir?" the man asked. "Tell me so that I may believe in him."

Yeshua said, "You are looking at him. He is the one speaking with you."

Uriah stood speechless for some long moment, taking in every curve and plane of Yeshua's face. He noticed his heavily lashed eyes were luminous even in their darkness. They were soft and yet sure. He took note of the gentle curve of Yeshua's lips and the silky smoothness of his beard.

He bent at his waist and said, "Lord, I believe."

He dropped down at his feet to worship him.

He said, "I always believed you would come. I always believed that someday, I would see your face. I always believed that my blindness was for some good reason that I didn't understand. Today, my faith has become sight."

Yeshua lifted him to his feet. Then he turned to those watching, "For judgment, for clarification of what is right and to condemn what is wrong, I have come into this world so that the blind will see. And for those who see, to become blind."

The Pharisees replied, "What are you saying? Are you insinuating that we are the blind ones?"

They turned on Uriah, "Why do you bow before this man and worship him? Worship belongs to God alone!"

Yeshua met their defiant stares, "If you *were* blind, you would not be guilty of sin, but since you *claim* you can see, your guilt remains. There will be no excuse; there will be no other recourse."

When the people saw the Pharisees were challenging Yeshua once again, they gathered near to hear the exchange.

Turning from the Pharisees, he turned his attention to the people, "I tell you the truth, anyone who does not enter the sheep pen by the gate but tries to climb in by some other way is a thief and a robber. When the shepherd enters through the sheep gate, he brings his own sheep in with him.The gatekeeper opens the gate to the shepherd. And the sheep listen to their shepherd's voice. He calls out to his sheep and calls them by name. They follow him because they know his voice. They refuse to follow a stranger. In fact, they run away from him because they do not recognize the stranger's voice."

The Pharisees looked at one another stupidly, "Why are you talking about sheep?"

Some in the audience perfectly understood what Yeshua was saying. He offered those people a tired smile and, touching his chest and said, "Very truly I tell you, I am the gate for the sheep. All who have come before me are thieves and robbers, but my sheep have not listened to them. I am the gate; whoever enters the keep through me will be saved. They will come in and go out and find good pasture and be nurtured.The thief comes only to steal and kill and destroy; I have come that my sheep may have life and have it completely."

He raised his hands to the people. Then, once again, he motioned to himself, "I am the Good Shepherd. The good shepherd lays down his life for his sheep. The hired hand is not the shepherd."

He glanced toward the Pharisees, "They do not own the sheep. That is why, when the wolf comes, the hired hand will simply abandon the sheep and run away, allowing the wolf to attack the flock and scatter it.The hired man runs away because he does not care about the sheep."

The people recognized the truth in his words. The Pharisees had no concern for them.

Yeshua looked around the wide circle of people, "I am the Good Shepherd."

His voice was filled with conviction, "*I* know my sheep, and my sheep know me, just as the Father knows me, *I* know the Father. *I* lay down my life for the sheep. I have other sheep that are not of this sheep pen. I must bring them in also. They, too, will listen to my voice, and they will merge as one flock with one shepherd."

"Why are you listening to him?" the Pharisees shouted at the people. "He makes no sense."

But Yeshua continued talking to the people, ignoring the Pharisees. His words carried more authority than theirs.

"My Father loves me because I freely lay down my life, only to take it up again. No one takes my life from me, but I lay it down of my own accord. I have the authority to lay it down and the authority to take it up again. This is the command I received from my Father."

Some within the crowd began to weep because they understood that their Messiah was saying he was going to give his life for theirs.

One man shouted, "He is demon-possessed, raving mad. The Pharisees are right. Why are we listening to him?"

Another answered, "This is not the ravings of a man possessed by a demon. Have you ever heard of a demon that opened the eyes of the blind? Now, *that* makes no sense."

It was as if a sword had dropped between the people within the crowd, and they became deeply divided. "If you will only give us a sign that would prove your words...," the wily old Pharisee prodded. "We need proof. Surely you understand this."

"It a wicked and adulterous generation that asks for a sign! But none will be given to you except the sign of the prophet Jonah. It was three days and three nights that Jonah was hidden in the belly of a huge fish. In the same way, the Son of Man will be buried three days and three nights in the heart of the earth."

"Man, make yourself clear!" The Pharisee shouted.

Yeshua stepped near to the man and lowered his voice. Laying his hand on his own chest, he said, "Destroy this temple, and I will raise it again in three days."

The Pharisee scoffed, remembering what Caiaphas had said to that previously, 'It has taken forty-six years to build this temple.' He gestured grandly as if one could take in the Temple with a simple glance.

"And, if it were leveled, are you saying you are going to raise it in three days?" They laughed in unison, throwing up their hands at the absurdity.

But the temple Yeshua had indicated and declared to destruction was the temple of his own body. But since they had no ears to hear and no eyes to see what was plainly before them, they remained blind and deaf. They did not understand that he was dedicating his body to destruction.

~ 21 ~

BLESSING OF THE LIGHT

The Lord is my light and my salvation. - Psalm 27:1

He pours contempt on nobles,
And disarms the mighty.
He reveals the deep things of darkness,
And brings utter darkness into the light. - Job 12:21-22

See to it, then,
that the light within you is not darkness. - Luke 11:35

Leaving the grandeur of the temple late in the day, Yeshua and his men tracked their way up the Mount of Olives toward Bethany. As they often did, they paused a little over halfway to enjoy a moment of rest before taking the rest of the incline towards Bethany. Their stomachs were growling, and they dipped into their snacks of nuts and dried fruit.

It had been a clear and pleasant day, but clouds were building in the west. Even so, the sun beamed brightly on the backside of the city. Its beams shot like a diadem from behind its cloak of clouds momentarily, putting on a dazzling display. The whole city seemed to glow golden. The angled planes of the towers and spires throughout the city made it a study of shadow and light. Like Janus—the

Roman god, Jerusalem presented a sunny face while its shadows hid its alter ego.

As the sun sank lower over the city, it was blanketed in a soft amber. Its spires sparkled like topaz. The eastern wall was shadowed with variations of lapis lazuli, mother of pearl, and lavender. The shadowed base appeared in tones of purple. The golden hour was quick to come and quick to pass away. But when the right moment appeared, the sight of this city on a hill could steal one's breath away.

Yohan said, "Look how beautifully the light plays upon the city."

"Yes," Yeshua took in the sight. "It is beautiful...," he paused. Then he added, "But soon, the city will be cast into darkness."

The way he said it made Yohan ask, "What do you mean?"

"Light comes and lights the day, but once the light goes, little light can be found."

Again, there was something in his voice that made Yohan turn to search his face.

Rock stood beside them, also enjoying the sight that never failed to impress him. But, he had also heard the undertones of ...what? Doom? He took his seat on the other side of Yeshua. Together, the three appreciated the view.

"The stones of the city walls are huge," Rock said, trying for a little levity. He was reminded of his nickname. "How would you like to be the stone mason working on those big boys?" He nudged Yeshua with a low whistle.

When there was no response, Rock looked to find the Lord was pensive and brooding.

"Look at them now," Yeshua said. "The day will come when they will lay in a heap of ruins. The city will become the haunt of jackals. Not one stone will be left upon another."

As he spoke these words, the sharp cry of an eagle pierced the air above them. Its shadow passed over them. They looked up to see the impressive and mighty wing span pump into a glide toward the city wall. Their eyes tracked its flight until it had disappeared.

They shivered at the portent of such a disaster yet to come. Both men turned to him, waiting for an explanation.

Yeshua dropped his snack back to his pouch, "The temple is set for a coming destruction."

As he said this, his face suddenly blanched as if in pain. His voice became filled with a breathless dread, "I tell you the day is coming when the Son of Man will be delivered into the hands of the chief priest and the teachers of the law. They will condemn him to deathand hand him over to the Gentiles to be mocked, flogged, and crucified. On the third day, he will be raised to life."

They noticed that as he said this, his hands were trembling. Fear and foreboding flooded the air around them at Yeshua's words of warning.

This was not the first time he had mentioned his coming death. For months now, it had become an unnerving and reoccurring theme. They never knew what to say to him or do to offer relief.

Now, they leaned forward. Their eyes searched his as if they were assessing his mental health. Death was constantly on his mind. They struggled, not wanting to believe his words. But what could they say? A battle seemed to be at work within him. His resolve indicated there could be no other recourse.

Their routine response had become to simply forget his words almost as soon as he said it. It was as if the very thought was too uncomfortable, too demanding to consider. By pretending Yeshua would work everything out allowed them to move on and keep trusting him.

But this time, Rock asked him, "When will this happen, Master?"

The sky was already drifting into darkness; Yeshua stared toward the flames of the large menorah displayed in the distance. "The next festival. When we enter Jerusalem, it will begin."

"Passover?" Yohan asked

Yeshua turned to look at Yohan. He thought of him like a son his physical body could not yield to him. They had shared a special bond of affection from the start. Yohan looked up to Yeshua and leaned on him as his spiritual father. He had remained one step behind him since that first day by the Jordan. Like Mari, he hardly left his side. Yohan was also Cohen by bloodline. Though Zebedee had fled with his family from Jerusalem long ago, both he and Salome had family that still served at the temple in Jerusalem. Their two boys were raised to be devoted in the way of holiness. Even at a young age, Yohan had been given wisdom beyond his years. He was a deep and sensitive thinker.

As Yeshua and Yohan stared at one another, Yohan remembered what Yohannan had said about Yeshua. "The Lamb of God who takes away the sins of the world."

A single tear formed and brimmed in Yohan's eye, then broke its banks to rush down the length of his face, coming to rest in his sparsely sprouted beard. He swallowed hard. For the first time, he understood what Yeshua was saying, even though he hated to think about it. He placed his hand on Yeshua's shoulder and bowed his head with sadness.

**

It was the Feast Day before the Sabbath in the Boethius compound. The indoor fireplaces had been filled, lit, and stoked to a festive blaze to stave away the cold nip. Zel and one of the household servants set the mood by playing a simple stringed instrument and a flute to the tune of the Hallel Psalms. It was a sizable gathering of family, a few close associates, some women from Jerusalem, and a few good neighbors. Yeshua and his disciples joined around the bountiful table spread with sweet delicacies, conversing before the meal began.

Eliezer sat at the head of the table next to his father and brother. He had invited a few of his associates to the feast. His guests had been more than a little curious about the Galilean guest. They had come to hear Yeshua's words for themselves. This private setting allowed for this away from the eyes of Caiaphas. They had surmised that Caiaphas feared the Nazarene, and that was enough for Eliezer to offer him hospitality.

Eliezer had grumbled to his children about their constant hospitality to the Nazarene and his men. But his adult children adored Yeshua. They were convinced he was the Messiah. Eliezer was still unconvinced. He couldn't help but wonder, 'What will the Nazarene say or do today?' Though he had to admit, his riddles made for interesting debates.

That night, Eliezer's pharisaic friends had entered the banquet hall elegantly attired. They were fastidious in their ritual of hand and foot washing. They showered one another with the honorifics due to their elite status. They took the seats of honor closest to Eleazar as befitting their position. Reclining on pillows, they discussed their latest financial successes and congratulated Eliezer on his latest windfalls. Their conversation was peppered with a jovial and 'good-natured' competition. They swapped stories to highlight their wit and wisdom in turning denarii.

Finally, as if to provide entertainment, Eleazar asked, "Yeshua bar Yosef, do you have words of wisdom to share before the banquet is served?"

Having just observed the parody of the pharisaical wealthy, he tailored his words to the moment, he began, "Whenever one is invited to a wedding feast, there are certain etiquettes to observe. If there are no placards, the wise person is careful not to take the seats of honor but take a lower seat.

"After all, one never knows when a person of more distinction than may have been invited. It would be embarrassing for the host to have to say, 'Friend, I need your seat for my honored guest. Please move to another.' Of course, once everyone has arrived, all the mediocre seats might be taken. Then, one would be forced to settle for the seat of least importance.

"But if one takes the lowest seat, and they are esteemed by their host, when he sees a person of renown in the lowest seat, he will say, 'Friend, move up here to a better place at the table.'

"Then that person will be honored in the presence of all the other guests. For all those who exalt themselves will be humbled, and those who humble themselves will be exalted."

The Pharisees nodded their agreement, "Quite right! Great advice!" They did not consider that even at that moment, another person should have been more highly esteemed than themselves. But Lazarus and his men shifted uncomfortably, understanding his implication. Had Eliezar believed they were indeed sitting at the table with Israel's long-awaited Messiah, shouldn't he be given the seat of honor?

Yeshua continued his banquet theme in his teaching, knowing Eliezar resented the frequent times he and his men filled his table and enjoyed the families fare, "When you give a banquet, don't just invite your friends, your brothers or sisters, your relatives, or your rich neighbors; if you do, they will simply invite you back. Then, your good deeds will be repaid.

"Instead, invite the poor, the crippled, the lame, the blind, and *then* you will be blessed. Although they cannot repay you, you will be repaid at the resurrection of the righteous."

Eliezer and his friends tried to imagine such a meal, but offered pinched smiles that lacked understanding. They wondered, 'What is wrong with inviting friends and family?'

Yeshua began to speak to his disciples in a low voice as if his storytelling were over. The whole table grew quiet eavesdrop on his words.

"There was a rich man," he told his disciples. "His manager was accused of wasting the rich man's possessions. So, he had the manager brought to him. He asked him, 'What is this I hear about you? Give an account of your management. Because I cannot trust you to be a manager any longer.'"

Yeshua looked around to make eye contact with each of his disciples, "The manager said to himself, 'What shall I do now? My master is taking my job from me. I'm not strong enough to dig, and I'm ashamed to beg. I know what I'll do, so people will still feel goodwill towards me. Perhaps they will still welcome me into their houses after I lose my job.'

"So the rich man went out and began to call on each of his master's debtors.

"He asked the first, 'How much do you owe my master?'

"'Nine hundred gallons of olive oil,' he replied.

"The manager told him, 'Take your bill, sit down quickly, and make it four hundred and fifty.'

"Then he went to the second and asked, 'And how much do you owe?'

"'A thousand bushels of wheat,' he replied.

"He told him, 'Take your bill and make it eight hundred.'" Yeshua paused, letting them reflect.

His next words were unexpected, "The master commended the dishonest manager for his shrewdness because he had found a way to make money for himself and to earn the goodwill of the people."

Judas nodded; he understood that kind of shrewdness. But the other disciples looked confused.

One said, "Clearly what the manager did was wrong; who could commend such an underhanded action?"

Judas said, "But the manager was only looking out for himself and his future. He sold that, which was not his, to gain a future for himself."

The money-loving Pharisees listening from the head of the table also understood the manager's tactic. No one was more crafty at making a denarius off of their master than they were.

Yeshua looked at his disciples and quoted a proverb, "For *the people of this world* are more shrewd in dealing with their kind than are *the people of the light*."

Silence stretched around the table. Privately, everyone replayed his words, sensing there was a judgement or rebuke among them, but they couldn't say what it was.

His men stared at him, waiting for him to offer an explanation.

Seeing their expressions, he was glad to explain, "Use worldly wealth to gain friends for yourselves. Then, when your money is gone, you will be welcomed into eternal dwellings."

Lazarus shifted uncomfortably beside him. The contrast between taking and giving was not lost on Judas, Eleazar, or the Pharisees. Judas could see that his words *were shrewd.* He looked with disdain, 'He would give everything away to the poor.'

Yeshua took a drink, "Whoever can be trusted with little will be trusted with more, and whoever is dishonest with little will also be dishonest when given more."

Judas felt his master's eyes upon him, but Judas maintained his eye contact, without remorse he refused to flinch.

Yeshua looked toward the Pharisees, "If you have not been trustworthy in handling worldly wealth, who will trust you with true riches? Heavenly riches? If you have not been trustworthy with someone else's property, who will give you property of your own?"

He paused, regathering everyone's attention, before he said, "I am telling you the truth: No one can serve two masters. Either you will hate the one and love the other, or you will be devoted to the one and despise the other. You cannot serve both God and mammon."

Judas sighed. He had heard this before. But now the wealthy Pharisees heard his contempt. As wealthy businessmen, their sole goal was to increase their income in any way possible. They turned to Eliezer and said, "No wonder people want to kill him."

"Look, you asked for an audience with him. Please don't blame me if he offends you. I tried to warn you. Young people are idealistic. They have little experience with the real world."

Yeshua asked Eliezer, "Why do you feel you have to justify yourself in the eyes of these men? Seek God's approval instead. My Father knows what is in your heart. People value wealth and power, as well as the praise of their peers, but these things are detestable in God's sight."

Eliezer wanted to refute him, but words eluded him.

The meal was ready, so Martha came and stood by the family menorah, preparing to light the last final candle. She took hold of the lit Shamash candle and prayed, *"Blessed are You, Lord, our God, King of the Universe, who has made us holy with your commandments and kindles the light within us with the light of your presence to remind us of all your truth, good works, and miraculous deeds. You have sustained us that we may share this feast.*

She lit all eight candles. The lamp blazed. Everyone joined her to say, "We praise the greatness of your name, your wonders, and your salvation."

The flames flickered.

Yeshua prayed privately, 'Father, kindle our light within them.'

And, the Feast of the Light began.

~ 22 ~

CALL TO ARMS

"Everyone who calls on the name of the Lord will be saved."
How, then, can they call on the one they have not believed in?
And how can they believe in the one of whom they have not
heard? And how can they hear without someone preaching to
them? And how can anyone preach unless they are sent?
As it is written:
"How beautiful are the feet of those who bring good news!
Romans 10:13-15

Once again, Yeshua left Bethany for Qumran. Lazarus acquiesced with Eliezer's demands for him to remain in Bethany.

Simon noticed that Yeshua was disappointed that Lazarus remained behind. Previously, Simon had feared being replaced by Lazarus' giftedness and personality. But now he understood why Yeshua had predicted Lazarus would be with them 'for a while.' Family was a strong deterrent to one fulfilling one's calling. Rock felt unexpectantly sorry that Lazarus would not be coming with them. He had grown to enjoy his affable company. Finding a moment of privacy, he asked Yeshua, "Did you know Lazarus would not make this trip with us?"

He answered, "How hard it is for men of substance to enter the kingdom of God! Indeed, it is easier for a rope, indeed even a camel, to go through the eye of a needle than the wealthy to enter the kingdom of God."

Simon pondered Lazarus' devotion, hospitality, and his obvious love for Yeshua. He felt a moment of alarm, "Who then can be saved, Lord?"

"No one is perfect. Not Lazarus, not you, not even Yohannan, who gave his very life for the way of truth," he paused to let that thought sink in.

"Then why all this hardship and mission? Why have we left all we had to follow you!" His voice rose in confusion and fear.

Yeshua stopped walking to turn toward Simon and to those who had come closer, "What is impossible with man *is* possible with God. Do not despair. I am telling you the truth, no one who has left home or wife or brothers or sisters or parents or children for the sake of the kingdom of God will fail to receive many times more than they have in this age."

He turned to continue down the path, assuming the disciples followed behind him. Truth was, he *was* sad to leave his good friends Lazarus, Martha, and Mari. His time was almost over. He had to keep reminding himself that what was coming would not be the end but a new beginning. He had been pained by the disappointment in Mari's eyes when he told her he needed her to remain behind with her family. She understood what was coming. Anxiously, she wanted to be with him. He couldn't tell her that she had to remain for a reason.

A seismic event was soon to unfold. It would be an effect that would set many things in motion, but it also would prepare Lazarus, Martha, and Mari for what was to follow. No king could afford to be ruled by his own desires or comforts, and a righteous king had to sacrifice his own comfort for the well-being of his people. In the end, his Father's plan would work all things for the good of all his people.

With resolve, he turned his mind toward his last visits to Qumran and the villages in the wilderness. 'This is my final chance to change and prepare their minds and to impart the needed words of instruction. Whatever I have left to say, now is the time.'

**

The men of Qumran dropped everything to welcome him back again. He had come to reiterate his teachings with a hard-hitting message:

"Be on your guard against the yeast of the Pharisees, which is hypocrisy. A man, after God's heart, must be humble and willing to listen to the words of God. Rest assured, there is nothing concealed in your lives that will not be disclosed, nothing hidden that will not be made known. Whatever you have said in the dark will be heard in the daylight, and what you have whispered in the inner rooms will be proclaimed from the roofs. Nothing is hidden from God!

"Therefore, now is the time to come clean with God, to confess, repent, seek forgiveness, and to purify yourselves for the work that lies ahead. My friends, do not be afraid of those who kill the body and after that can do no more. No, instead, fear the One who has authority over you even after your body has been killed. He has the authority to throw you into hell. Yes, I tell you, fear him. No messenger is greater than the one who sends him. So, gird yourselves with my Father's words and prepare to take them out to our nation and beyond."

"But Lord, look what happened to Yohannan!" one man called out.

"Yes, we have all grieved over Yohannan and many others who have earnestly sought to serve God. There is a multitude of evil in this dark world. Five sparrows are sold for almost nothing. But how much more valuable are you? But I promise you, not even one little sparrow is forgotten. All life is precious to my Father. As for you, the very hairs of your head are numbered. You are worth much more than many sparrows. Therefore, I tell you, do not fear the evil around you. Do not remain hidden here in the wilderness huddled together, for evil will find you wherever you are. Salt that clumps up together is not helpful. It becomes frozen."

Yeshua moved around the large room filled with devout men. He held out his hands to them and laid his hands on those who were receptive. Looking around, he asked, "Haven't you consecrated yourself and set yourself apart as holy unto the Lord? I tell you, whoever goes out and publicly acknowledges me before others, the Son of Man, will also acknowledge before the angels of God. You are the salt of the earth. You are to be light bearers to the world, purveyors of the Kingdom of God.

"What good will it be if I give you my light and you hide it away in these caves? It must be placed on a stand to offer light to every person. Shine brightly with the kingdom message; others will see your good deeds and glorify your Father in heaven. Spread the light—the truth—that you treasure.

"Do not be fooled into thinking that I have come to abolish the Law or the Prophets; I have not come to abolish them but to fulfill them. Therefore, do not set aside even the least of my Father's commands. You are called to a higher righteousness, far above that of the Pharisees and the teachers of the law. My Father's commands spell out the law of love, of the Kingdom of Heaven. So be holy just as your Father in heaven is holy."

The fire of the Spirit was kindled in Yeshua's eyes as he offered them his encouragements and admonitions.

His countenance became serious and fierce, "But whoever disowns me before others will be disowned before the angels of God.If you have spoken against the Son of Man, I stand ready to forgive you. But if anyone blasphemes the Holy Spirit, they will not be forgiven. Be careful, for you decide your own fate.

"When the day of distress comes, you will be brought before synagogues, rulers, and authorities. Do not worry about how you will defend yourselves or what you will say,for the Holy Spirit will teach you at that time what you should say. Do not be afraid. Be strong and courageous in the Lord."

As he looked around the circle of faces, his eyes fell on one upturned face of a man named Stephen. He stared at Yeshua with wide-eyed adoration. For a moment, Yeshua faltered, understanding the sorrow Elijah had felt when he had spread his own prophetic cloak over Elisha's shoulders, recognizing the battle that lay ahead for him. Yeshua's face softened, and he reached out his hand to place it on the young man's head to endow him with a special blessing.

On the sidelines, James whispered to Rock, "Look! Our master is like a consuming fire, like a king rallying his troops for war. I have never seen him so forceful or direct."

"Clearly, he is calling us all to a movement. He is calling our brothers to arise and join him."

"Is he calling them to follow him now or in the future?"

"I'm not sure. But I think the Lion of Judah has awakened. There is something in his expression, his words... I can't quite put my finger on it. He has always been bold in his call for repentance and action, but now his passion burns brighter than ever. His message is from his heart, and he no longer fears any repercussions. And, have you not noticed how no one has any power to stand against him? Even in Jerusalem, Caiaphas hid himself away from him, unwilling to fall to the sword of his words. Instead, he sent his lackeys. But they were all powerless in his presence. Who has ever seen a man speak with greater authority or conviction?"

Yohan agreed, "Yes, he is fierce and filled with a righteous resolve. He is like a lion."

"Yes, and now he roars," Rock agreed.

**

For the duration of his visit, Qumran was overwhelmed by the power of Yeshua's message to them. As he prepared to move on, he stood before them once more to speak his parting words, "I have come to bring fire on the earth; very soon, it will be kindled! But first, I have a baptism to undergo, and I am resolved to complete it!Do you think I came to bring peace to the earth? No, I tell you, but a division. Because of me, every family, every group, every organization, and even the world itself will be shaken and divided, including this place.

"You who remain faithful through the coming tribulations will receive a great reward. Some of you have believed my words. But some have not. Even in coming to you, I have divided this compound, leaving conflict in my wake.

"When the Son of Man comes in his glory, with all the angels with him, he will sit on his glorious throne. All the nations, every person, will be gathered before him.

"On that day, he will separate the people one from another as a shepherd separates the sheep from the goats. He will put the sheep on his right and the goats on his left."

Once again, he walked among them as the general of a holy army, taking measure of each man. They trembled as he passed by them.

Yeshua promised, "Then the King will say to those on his right, 'Come, you who are blessed by my Father; take your inheritance, the kingdom prepared for you since the creation of the world. For I was hungry, and you gave me something to eat; I was thirsty, and you gave me something to drink; I was a stranger, and you invited me in; I needed clothes, and you clothed me; I was sick, and you looked after me; I was in prison, and you came to visit me.'

"The righteous will answer him, 'Lord, when did we see you hungry and feed you, or thirsty and give you something to drink?When did we see you a stranger and invite you in, or needing clothes and clothe you? When did we see you sick or in prison and go to visit you?'

"The King will reply, 'Truly I tell you, whatever you did for the least of these, my brothers and sisters of mine, you did for me.'

"Then he will say to those on his left, 'Depart from me you who are cursed into the eternal fire prepared for the devil and his angels. For I was hungry, and you gave me nothing to eat; I was thirsty, and you gave me nothing to drink; I was a stranger, and you did not invite me in; I needed clothes, and you did not clothe me; I was sick and in prison, and you did not look after me.'

"They will answer, 'Lord, when did we see you hungry or thirsty or a stranger or needing clothes or sick or in prison, and did not help you?'

"The King will reply, 'Truly I tell you, whatever you did not do for one of the least of these, you did not do for me.'

"Then they will go away to eternal punishment, but the righteous to eternal life."

Everyone flinched at the threat of his pronouncement. It felt surreal to them that this was the same man who had once dwelt amongst them, by all accounts lowly and humble. They realized they had not really recognized his holiness. It had been hidden from their eyes. Now, they saw Yeshua for who he was. Many lowered their eyes under his gaze and bowed their head in submission to him. Malachi thought to himself, 'Yeshua makes Yohannan look tame.'

Winding up his sermon, Yeshua asked them, "So who is the faithful and wise manager? The one the master puts in charge of his servants to give them their food allowance at the proper time."

Yeshua stood next to Rock and placed his hand on the back of his neck. Rock felt the weightiness of his hand claiming him once again before he moved on to the others who had been with him so long. He looked intently at each of his twelve.

"And, it will go well for that servant whom the master finds doing his bidding when he returns. Truly, I tell you, he will put that servant in charge of all his possessions," his eyes lingered on Simon, causing a multitude of overwhelming emotions to swell within him. He was making it clear that his disciples would be left in charge of his mission.

He stepped away and then turned to look at them all, "But suppose the servant says to himself, 'My master is taking a long time in coming.' He starts to think his master's servants belong to him; then, he begins to beat the other servants, both the men and the women. He has them *serve* him. He eats, drinks, and gets drunk. He becomes lazy and lets the master's house fall into dereliction.

He scanned the disciples and then the whole room. His eyes fell on Judas, on James, on Yohan, and then he swung back to Rock yet again, "The master of that servant will come on a day at an hour when he does not expect him. He will cut him to pieces and assign him a place with the unbelievers."

Fear filled Simon's face, and his ears flamed as he thought back to the man he had once been: Loud, braggadocios, brawling, with a perverse mouth, given to the turn of an eye, and indulging in too much wine or beer.

Yeshua turned his gaze away from his disciples and back to the men of Qumran, "The servant who knows the master's will and does not get ready or do what the master wants will be beaten with many blows.But the one who does not know and does things deserving punishment will be beaten with few blows. To everyone who has received much, much more will be demanded." Again, he scanned the faces with discernment.

Turning to the Twelve, he said, "From the ones who have been entrusted with more, far more will be demanded."

He began to close out his message, "You have heard it taught, 'Love your neighborand hate your enemy.'" Some of the politically zealous nodded their heads in agreement, knowing that hate well.

Yeshua met their nods with a shake of his head, "No." With soft affection, he told them, "I am telling you, love your enemies and pray for those who persecute you, that you may be children of your Father in heaven."

He touched the head of one surly-looking man, "Your Father causes his sun to rise on both the evil and the good and sends rain on both the righteous and the unrighteous. If you love only those who love you, what reward will you get? Even the tax collectors are capable of that?" He stopped to chuck Matthew under the chin with a good-humored smile. Matthew smiled back.

"And if you greet only the people you like, what good are you doing more than others? Even pagans do that. Be perfect, therefore, as your heavenly Father is perfect. Show love to everyone, knowing that your Father values them. This will hold you together and sustain you in all the days ahead."

**

Yeshua carried his final teachings from town to town. Large crowds gathered around him in places where he had previously performed signs and wonders and spoke the truth. He continued to call people to himself. But, he also admonished those who had seen his miracles but failed to heed his words. His words were no longer gentle but delivered with fire and force that left the people in his wake with a decision: Did they believe him or not? Would they change or not? Or would they continue as stiff-necked people?

Yeshua had no time to worry about this; he knew it was the fear of the Lord that was the beginning of wisdom. Everyone had to be warned that they would give an account to God when their last day appeared.

~ 23 ~

ALL ROADS LEAD HOME

(Return to) him—before the silver cord is severed,
And the golden bowl is broken;
Before the pitcher is shattered at the spring,
And the wheel is broken at the well.
Ecclesiastes 12:6

Time was speeding by now. The very first signs of a coming spring were evident. The buds on the trees became noticeably fattened. For Yeshua, every minute was carefully planned. They had completed their tour in the Decapolis cities and the eastern reaches of Galilee. Now, they were headed to their hometowns and villages for a short visit with their families. His men were ready to take a break. He understood their restless impatience. They had spent the best part of the last three years traveling abroad with him. And it wasn't just his men who were becoming restless. The people were as well, as if they sensed the increasing opposition and danger. The Pharisees constantly pressed him publicly, demanding to know when the Kingdom would appear. But how could *they* see it? They did not understand the things of the Spirit. They thought in terms of their flesh.

He told them, "My Father's Kingdom will not become visible in the way you are thinking. His kingdom is not something that can be observed. No one can say, 'Look, here it is,' or 'there it is,' the Kingdom of God is already in your midst and is waiting to be made manifest *within* you."

They rolled their eyes, "I told you, this kingdom is a figment in his mind. He is delusional!"

When they sailed away from the eastern reaches of Galilee, Judas told him, "Master, you have so many people eager for you to take action, to do more than provide them lip service. They want proof; they want something tangible. How can the kingdom come if people have nothing to get behind, nothing tangible to believe in?"

Yeshua inhaled sharply at Judas' words, feeling his ire rise. He caught himself and let his breath out slowly. He looked at his hands, forcing his fists to uncoil. He stared up into the sky for several moments before he answered Judas. His intensity transformed. He spoke with an eery calm, "The time is coming when you will long to see one of the days of the Son of Man, but you will not see it."

He turned his gaze toward the horizon, then toward the others. He told them loudly, "People will tell you, 'There he is!' or 'Here he is!'

"Don't bother to go running from place to place. Because when the Son of Man appears in the future, he will come like lightning, which flashes and lights up the sky from one end to the other. Who knows where lightning will strike or when?"

His eyes remained on the horizon to the north. They followed his gaze and saw the dark cloud head building; they saw the lightning flash swiftly to the ground. They wondered how long before the storm would come upon them. In the spring, those storms moved quickly south to claim lives.

Yeshua faced them with a heavy heart. "But first, I must suffer many things and be rejected by this generation."

"Will there be any clues before it comes upon us?" Thomas wanted to know.

"The warning has already gone out, but few are taking it seriously. It will be just as it was in the days of Noah. On that day, people were eating, drinking, marrying, and being given in marriage right up to the day Noah entered the ark. Then, the flood came and destroyed them all. It will be like that on the day of the Son of Man. So what should you do?"

He offered another example, "It was the same in the days of Lot. People were eating and drinking, buying and selling, planting, building, and making big plans.But the day Lot left Sodom, fire and sulfur rained down from heaven to destroy them all. It will be just the same on the day the Son of Man is revealed."

"On that day of destruction, don't be the fool who tries to hold on to this life. If you are standing on your rooftop, don't worry about your possessions, don't reach to take anything with you, or go down to get your belongings. Likewise, no one in the field should go back for anything. Instead, lift up your hands to be carried away. Remember Lot's wife! She didn't want to leave her life behind. I am telling you, whoever tries to keep their life will lose it, and whoever hands their life over freely will preserve it.

"I tell you, it will be like this: On that night, two people will be in one bed; one will be taken and the other left.Two women will be grinding grain together; one will be taken and the other left."

"Where, Lord?" Their voices were full of alarm.

Yeshua replied solemnly, "Think! Wherever there is a dead body, there the vultures will gather."

His men stared at him, trying to decipher what seemed to them like a cryptic message, even though he was speaking plainly to them.

Yeshua stood up in the stern and looked toward each of the key areas in northern Galilee, to the places where he had performed his greatest signs. He asked them, "What has been the response in Galilee? What evidence do you see that anything has ultimately changed? Didn't they demand a king to feed them as if he were their servant? Even after all they have seen me do, they are unwilling to change even the smallest of their wayward actions."

His men couldn't refute him. When push came to shove, only a few had remained to hear Yeshua's words. What could they say?

They felt his pain when suddenly he cried out in a ragged voice full of sorrow and indignation, "Woe to you, Chorazin! Woe to you, Bethsaida! For if the miracles that were performed in you had been performed in Tyre and Sidon, they would have repented long ago in sackcloth and ashes! As it is, it will be more bearable for Tyre and Sidon on the day of judgment than for you."

Turning towards their destination, he shouted, "And you, Capernaum, where is the evidence of your repentance?"

Now, he clenched his fist in the air, "Will you be lifted to the heavens because of the miracles done among you? No, you will also go down into the depths of Hades. For if the miracles that were performed in you had been performed in Sodom, it would have remained to this day. I tell you, it would be more bearable for Sodom on the day of judgment than for you."

His men leaped to their feet, looking towards their homes, half expecting to see fire fall from heaven. These were the homes where their families lived and people they had known all their lives. The menacing flash that split the darkness of the cloud over the seashore did not make them tremble. Rather, they trembled at the power within Yeshua's loud and indignant words.

**

The boat landed at Capernaum. Yeshua waded over the smooth pebbles to the shore. This was where his signs and works had begun. Everything was business as usual. Some of the other fishermen were at work sorting their fish. They looked up to see his crew, and they made sideways remarks to one another. His presence was an interference with their business.

Rock pulled his boat ashore. With a wave, he left, running to his home. The other men had been deposited to their family homes with a plan to meet up a few days later. Yeshua headed towards the home of his family in Capernaum. He was looking forward to a visit with his mother. Although he had missed Miriam and his brothers, this visit was more about preparing her for what lay ahead in the month to come.

A variety of emotions passed over Joses' and Si's faces when Yeshua was suddenly found at their door. As if only then did they realize how long Yeshua had been gone.

"Yeshua!" They shouted in unison. Si moved quickly to inform the others. Jude appeared to embrace his brother awkwardly. James sauntered out at a leisurely pace with his hand perched on his belt. He casually slapped Yeshua's on his arm as his welcome. Then he stood back to study him.

Miriam broke past him to land in Yeshua's arms with a joyous and upturned face.

"Yeshua! Why have you stayed away so long? I have been so worried about you!" she admonished him as only a mother could.

He took her by her shoulders and hauled her back into his embrace. With her head tucked under his chin, he said softly, "Ima, you know why I have been gone so long."

She held him a little closer, for all the ways her imagination had run wild with concern for him, "Come and tell me everything."

She pulled him behind her into the house. His brothers left through the door he had just entered, and they shut the door behind them. He watched them go.

Miriam sat out a basin for him to wash his feet. She scurried about to set some refreshment before him. Restraining herself before she let loose her stream of questions. Most of her questions he simply could not answer. He knew his brothers were listening just outside. He could not trust them. He would not endanger the communities he had visited. If he were going to implicate anyone, it would be himself.

"Why isn't Mariamne and the others with you?" she asked, revealing her great affection for her and her family. She was sure Magdalene would never remain behind by choice. Miriam understood Mari's devotion to her son. She wore her heart upon her sleeve. Her eyes were ever adoring and worshipful whenever they were turned toward him.

"Magdalene remained behind with her family...at my request."

Miriam saw the pained look that crossed his face.

"It is for the best. Lazarus remained for the family business...and Martha remained to run the compound. Mari is helping her, and she has a small number of women who frequently visit her away from the prying eyes of Caiaphas."

Miriam had seen how Mari gave him support and offered him an intimately shared understanding. Now, Miriam sat close to her son, knowing she was a poor substitute for his adoring disciple. He smiled at her attempt to comfort him all the same. He sighed deeply, and she noticed his expression of determined resolve.

To relax him, Miriam took up a pleasant chatter, telling him of all the local news. Two-year-old Yosef burst into the room to be immediately drawn to Yeshua to play. He leaped into his outstretched arms. Then, scrambling back down, he ran around the room, only to return and throw himself back into his uncle's arms.

Yeshua relaxed, enjoying the toddler's giggles. All the while, he listened as his mother filled him in concerning his Uncle Cleopas and Aunt Mary; she told him of a recent visit of her cousin Salome, about his brothers and their work, and about the news of Deborah and Abigail, and Jairus and his family—the synagogue official, who had recently become friendly. She continued until she recognized the exhaustion in his eyes. "Why don't you go and take a nap before dinner? It will do you good."

**

He had slept through dinner. Miriam let him sleep. When he got up, Miriam was waiting for him with a covered meal. She heated it before she sat it before him to eat. Everyone else was outside by the evening fire, allowing him to have rest and quiet.

Yeshua put off the news he had come to share. He took a bite of the savory stew she sat before him, "Umm, so good. When you travel with a bunch of fishermen, you find you hardly eat anything but fish. I am not complaining. I am grateful for the food. But I have always loved this dish."

She flashed him a smile and waited.

Yeshua asked her, "Have you had any royal visitors lately?"

She knew he meant Herod's militia.

She playfully replied, "Not until today. Herod seems to have given up since you have been gone from Capernaum for so long. He has turned his attention elsewhere, but I am always watching for his officials."

He nodded, "Yes, that is why after tonight, I won't be staying with you. Once word gets out that we have returned and I am near, I don't want to cause problems for you all."

He chewed a crunchy piece of bread, then used the last of it to sop up the savory broth from the bowl.

Miriam's face fell, "Then I will come and stay with you where you are."

She waited in fear that he would make her remain behind, just as he had Mariamne. But he did not refuse her.

She realized there was more, "So, what is so heavy on your heart?"

He shook his head, "Ima, I will only be here for a few days, then I must continue onward. The time is near..." and his voice cracked. He offered her the same doleful expression she had sometimes glimpsed ever since he was a boy. 'A man of sorrows,' she realized.

She leaned toward him, pressing her forehead to his. "Oh, my precious boy!"

She whispered, "Let me come with you." She couldn't imagine letting him go on alone.

He shook his head. "No. The trip I have planned would be too hard on you, and I have much yet to accomplish along the way. It would be easier if you could meet me in Bethany prior to Passover." He looked hopeful.

"Passover..." Her brows gave became two sad question marks, "But that is only what...a few weeks away."

Silently, she admonished herself that she had not known this. Hadn't he told her he would be sacrificed as God's intended Passover Lamb?

"Ima, they are going to capture me in Jerusalem, like a ram caught in a thicket."

His hands started to shake, and his lip trembled, and tears began to fall, "I knew my work would be hard to do, but now it is terrifying..."

"Then, don't...," she began.

Yeshua put his fingers to her lips to stop her, "No. You know I must do this. The decision was made long ago, longer than time itself. It has to be just as my Father and I planned."

What could she say? She knew he was right. Even so, the taste of bitter bile rose in her throat. Her heart fluttered with hysteria. She looked down silently, but her soul cried out to Yahweh, 'How can you demand my son from me?'

From the beginning, without knowing the end, she had trusted the Almighty God of Israel and of all Creation. He had given her the honor above every other woman. But now, Miriam wanted to vent her hurt and pain upon him, just as a wife might vent her scorn. But she knew she could not afford that luxury, if only for her son's sake.

She resolved herself, 'If Yeshua must be strong and courageous, then I must be strong and courageous for his sake.' Miriam swallowed her bitterness like a pill.

Seeing his mother's distress, Yeshua squeezed her hands, but his eyes were solemn and pleading, "Ima, I will need you there. I know I am asking a lot of you. I know it will be hard for you to witness, but if I can just see your face or hear your voice, I know it will strengthen me."

His trembling hand clasped hers tightly. "When the cross comes, I am not sure there will be even one person who will pray for me, be on my side, or understand what I am doing. I just need one friendly face there on my behalf."

"Surely there will be others. Your family, your followers."

"I am not so sure. You must be strong for me, Ima, just as you were in the beginning, so I can be strong for you and for everyone else who will come to believe!"

Looking into his beseeching eyes, she felt sure this was what Simeon had meant so long ago about a sword piercing her own heart, too. But because her son needed her, she nodded and kissed both of his hands as if to take all his fear away.

"Yes! I will be there! I am your mother. How could I not? If you must go through this, then I must go through it with you."

Miriam thought of the unbearable ripping pain she experienced when Yeshua was born. She had thought she might be torn in two.

But now, she knew she was less than a month away from a much worse ripping pain that just might destroy her completely.

~ 24 ~

BROTHERS

For even his own brothers did not believe in him.
John 7:5

Yeshua went out into the small courtyard to visit with his brothers, who lounged around the outside fire pit, making a point to avoid him. They straightened when he came out of the door, acting as if a threat had entered their camp. Their tension was palpable when he sat down with them as if he had not noticed. After greeting them, he waited in amiable silence for one of them to speak. But no one offered him even a polite small talk. Loyalties to James were strong. Even those who had previously greeted him said nothing at all to him. Yeshua once again felt the pain of the divide. Since James functioned as the head of the household, his younger brothers were co-dependent on James for a home. Even Si remained silent. 'Clearly, my absence had not made their hearts grow fonder,' Yeshua realized.

So he tried to fill the gap. He asked about their work, their day-to-day lives, their plans for a chosen trade and marriage... but it all came to little of nothing.

Finally, James asked him, "Why are you here, Yeshua?"

He dropped his head when he heard the harsh edge in his brother's voice, "You will know soon enough." He looked into his brother's eyes, making James squirm a little.

"We can't have you here. You will incriminate us all. Do you want to wipe out the house of Yosef?" James asked him.

Yeshua held up his hands in surrender, "I have already made other plans. I am only here for tonight. Others would gladly welcome me into their homes, even if my brothers would not. I plan to leave tomorrow. Allow me this one night's rest, this visit with Ima and with you all. You are, after all, my family. But since our conversations have worn thin, let me tell you a story..."

James looked vexed, but his other brothers looked relieved.

He launched into his story, "As you know, Father Jacob had twelve sons. However, he loved Yosef more than any of his other sons because Yosef was the answer to Jacob's prayers. He had waited and prayed for Rachel to conceive for years.

"As the boy became a young man, Jacob set Yosef apart from his brothers. He even had a very colorful and ornate robe made for Yosef to distinguished him and set him apart from his brothers. To his brothers, the coat was a glaring reminder of Yosef's favor as his chosen heir. Of course, they were filled with jealousy. They couldn't understand why their father had loved this one son more than the rest of them. Judah hated Yosef most of all. He treated him with harsh resentment, refusing to speak a kind word to him."

His brothers squirmed uncomfortably, and James glared at him. But he went on as if he were totally unaware of their discomfort, "Then, one night, Yosef had a vivid dream. It was a dream given to him by God. He shared his dream with his family, 'Listen to this dream I had: We were binding sheaves of grain out in the field when suddenly my sheaf stood upright. Your sheaves gathered around mine and bowed down to it.'

"His brothers said to him, 'Ah, so you think you are going to reign over us.' They grew angry and mocked him, hating him all the more.

"Then Yosef had a second dream. This one was even more detailed, and it seemed to give credence to the first one. He couldn't resist telling his brothers this dream as well. 'Listen,' he said, 'I had another dream, and this time the sun and moon and the eleven stars were bowing down to me.'"

"This time, when he told his family this dream, his father heard him and rebuked him, 'What is this dream you had? Are you saying that your mother and I and your brothers will all bow down to the ground before you?'

"Jacob decided that his favor had given Yosef a lofty opinion of himself. He rebuked him for making trouble with his brothers. But privately, Jacob wondered about Yosef's dream because he knew God had also visited him in a dream when he was a young man and his ancestors as well. Still, his brothers' jealousy and resentment grew all the more.

"Sometime later, his brothers had taken the flocks away to graze. They remained in the distant land for far too long. Jacob grew worried that something had happened to them. He sent for Yosef, saying, 'I am concerned for your brothers who have lingered too long in the fields. I am sending you out in search of them. They were going to graze the flocks near Shechem. Go to them to see if all is well with them and the flocks. Then return and bring word back to me so I can rest easy.'

"When Yosef arrived at Shechem, he did not find his brothers. But a man found Yosef wandering around in his field and asked him, "What are you looking for?"

"He replied, 'I'm looking for my brothers. Can you tell me where they are?' The man nodded and directed him to his brothers. But when Yosef found them, they saw him coming in the distance.

"They said, 'Look, here comes that dreamer!'

"Judah said to the others. 'Here we are out in the wild. Come now, let's kill him and throw him into one of these cisterns. We can say a ferocious animal devoured him. Then, we will see what comes of his big dreams.'

"But when Reuben heard Judah say this, he wanted to rescue Yosef from his brothers' hands. 'Let's not take his life,' he said. 'Don't shed his blood. Let's just imprison him in this cistern.'

Reuben said this because he knew Yosef's death would break his father's heart, and he loved his father, and he planned to return and rescue him later.

"So, when Yosef arrived, they stripped him of his ornate robe and threw him naked into the dark pit.

"Later, a caravan passed by from a foreign land on their way to Egypt. Judah and the others sold their brother for 20 shekels. He was to be sold as a slave in Egypt.

"Before they returned home, they took Yosef's regal robe and dipped it in the blood of a slaughtered goat.

They took it back to their father, saying, 'Look, here we found your son's robe.'

"Jacob was devastated. They were unprepared for his terrible grief. He could not be consoled. Only then did they realize that they had done a truly abominable thing. Day after day, their Father's grief was evident as he wasted away and blamed himself for sending Yosef to his brothers. Even years later, their Father was only a shell of his former self. They believed that every affliction that came upon them was because of what they had done to their brother. When the famine came, they knew God was punishing them because of their unconfessed sin. Their secret separated them away from both God and man.

"Meanwhile, in Egypt, Yosef was suffering, attacked by accusations, jealousies, hardships, afflictions, and imprisonment during his slavery. His life was not even his own. However, the LORD remained with him and gave him wisdom and favor in every situation. Years passed, and God raised Yosef time and again to rule over his peers. Even in his slavery, he was a prince among his peers. Yosef was careful to be a man of integrity, to work hard, and to carry out all his assigned responsibilities.

"One day, Yosef was called forth from the tomb of his prison cell. He was taken to Pharoah because of his gift of insight into divine dreams. He was asked to interpret a dream that was frightening Pharoah! Through prayer, the LORD showed Yosef the meaning of Pharoah's dream and the result of what was to come. Pharoah realized God's power was with Yosef, and he had given him a special gift of wisdom and insight from his God. He believed Yosef had it within him to provide what was needed to save the lives of the people of Egypt and the other nations. So he took off his signet ring and gave it to Yosef, giving him authority to rule over the land. That was how Yosef became the only one who could dole out the measured portions of the bread of life and ensure that there would be enough food for everyone.

"In the end, Yosef's brothers did come to him and bow at his feet just as he had dreamed. They looked to him to receive what they and all people needed to be saved. Yosef recognized them when they came to him. He also painfully remembered how they had abused him. They became terrified when they realized this was their brother because he held their lives in his hands. Yet, despite his terrible mistreatment, he was able, with God's guidance and grace, to offer them the grain they needed. He forgave them and showed them mercy, and he brought them to Egypt to live under his protection. When he was reunited with his brothers, he chose to forget their rejections and the treacheries of the past. His grief was turned to joy. His family received the gift of peace and reconciliation. Yosef threw his arms around his brothers' necks and received them back as his brothers. He had them tell their destructive secret to their Father and bring Jacob back with them to also live under his protection and provision. So Jacob got his son back."

Yeshua ended the story there and wiped away his tears from his cheeks and beard. A heavy sadness sat upon his chest. His brothers would not meet his eyes. But he took heart, believing that one day his brothers would see him for who he was, remember his retelling of this story, and understand what he had done for them.

No one said anything. Finally, Yeshua said, "I think I will turn in now. Shalom."

His brothers remained and glanced surreptitiously at one another to gauge each other's reactions. The story had cut with its truth. Hadn't James even told them he would hand Yeshua over to Herod if it would save the rest of them? Only, Yeshua had disappeared to parts unknown before James had the opportunity to do the deed.

The brothers waited for James to speak.

He growled at them, "What are you looking at? Yeshua is not Yosef."

Despite his rebuke, their accusing expressions were not lost on him.

~ 25 ~

THE KING'S MEN

"[*Who*] has stirred up one from the east,
Calling him in righteousness to his service?
[*Who*] hands nations over to him
And subdues kings before him...
[*Who*] has done this and carried it through,
Calling forth the generations from the beginning?
I, the Lord—with the first of them and with the last—I am he."
Isaiah 41:2-4

The Twelve regathered in Capernaum after they had traveled to their homes to share Yeshua's dismal prophecies of what would transpire in Jerusalem. Some of the parents tried to persuade their sons to refrain from going to Jerusalem with him.

Simon told Deborah, "Don't worry, I will keep the Lord from harm and myself as well." But this did not comfort her. She was too young to become a widow. But there would be no stopping her husband when he had made up his mind. Suddenly, all the fear she had first felt came rushing back to taunt and threaten her.

Salome, the mother of James and Yohan, returned with her sons to have a 'visit' with Miriam. She was armed with a willful boldness, determined she would shamelessly make her requests known concerning her sons. She prepared her convincing argument, thinking:

'Who is more devoted than my sons? Kings needed godly men beside them whom they could trust. And, we are your closest relatives besides your brothers who have shunned you. If you restore Israel, my sons should be by your side.'

James told her, 'Yeshua plans to do a miracle that no one has ever done before.

Yohan added, "He has promised to rise from the dead. Surely, after this, he will assume his rightful kingdom."

That evening, the disciples and the families gathered at Matthew's home. After the meal, Yeshua stood before them all to announce, "You have all heard we are going up to Jerusalem, and the Son of Man will be delivered into the hands of the chief priests and the teachers of the law. They will condemn him to death and will hand him over to the Gentiles to be mocked, flogged, and crucified. On the third day, he will be raised to life! Remember, I have told you this even before it happened."

Salome saw her opportunity to intercede on behalf of her sons. She called forth her sons. Together, they came to kneel before Yeshua to make their appeal, as one would a king.

Graciously, he watched her, knowing her heart and loving her loyalty to her sons. "What is it you want?" His voice held no trace of sarcasm.

"Lord, you know how devoted my two sons are to you and your teachings. If it would please you, I would ask that you grant that one of these two sons of mine may sit at your right and the other at your left when you establish your kingdom."

Yeshua heard her earnest prayer while she shared with him the desire of her heart. It was a noble desire, and he realized that if the shoe had been on the other foot, his own mother might have done the same thing on his behalf. But poor Salome had absolutely no idea of the implications. He looked at her sadly, not wanting to dash her hopes and dreams for her sons. They would indeed have very important places in the coming kingdom. In reality, his kingdom would not go the way she imagined. His kingdom would remain under fire, and his disciples would become ready targets.

"You don't know what you are asking," Yeshua said to her.

He looked at the eager and waiting faces of James and Yohan as if he were weighing them. Yohan's Adam's apple worked up and down several times. James shifted from knee to knee uncomfortably with his hands on the ground before him with his lips pursed tight.

Yeshua thought of the coronation ceremony that awaited him on the cross. His words came out raw and brusque, "Do you honestly believe you can drink the cup I am going to drink?"

"We can," they answered, as unknowing babes.

He stared into the distant future and said to them, "You will indeed drink from my cup..."

Stirring from his vision, he reached out to lift their chins, "However, to sit at my right or left is not for me to grant. These positions have already been prepared by my Father."

When Rock saw what was happening, he drew the attention of the other nine to Salome, James, and Yohan down on bent knee, making their appeal. The other disciples were outraged at their request. Yeshua saw the trouble brewing on the faces of the men, and he motioned them to him, "Rock, all of you, come here."

They eagerly came, ready to debate and make their own appeals. Their mouths were already open with accusations and rebuttals. But he put up his hand to stay their words and bid them to sit, "Are you all really this competitive?"

He raked his hands through his hair and smoothed his beard, pacing in a circle of momentary frustration. When he stopped, he lowered his voice to speak in measured tones, "My Father's kingdom is not a game of one-upmanship! Why do you make it about which of *you* will rule? Whose kingdom is it? God's or man's. It will take everything each of you has to shepherd your assigned flocks into the kingdom. You are not thinking clearly. You know that the rulers of the Gentiles love to lord their power over the people, and their higher officials exercise authority over them. But it must not be this way with you. I would have hoped that by now, you would have understood this."

His men stared, struck by his words and longing to understand exactly how and where each of them would fit into the coming kingdom. They wanted details, not nebulous words of promise.

Yeshua lowered his voice even more, "Whoever wants to become great among you must be your servant. Whoever wants to be first must be a slave to others. Look at me! Do you see a golden crown upon my head or an ornate scepter in my hand? Am I rich? Do I sit on cushions and simply point my finger? No. I go out to be with the people. I am giving my life to them.

"Just as the Son of Man did not come to be served, neither should you be served. The Son of Man came to serve and to give his life as a ransom for many." He flung his hand in the air, "Reverse everything you know about the kingdoms of man. That would be the kingdom of my Father. Can you understand this?"

His men blinked, trying to imagine such a kingdom. It seemed counterintuitive.

"Quit worrying about if Rock, or Yohan, or James will lead, or who will take my place, or wield power. My Father has already assigned you places. You are called to love one another and serve in this kingdom together as one." He brought his two hands together as one. He begged them to understand this strange kind of leadership.

"Haven't I told you already that you will be seated upon twelve thrones so as to judge the twelve tribes of Israel? But the first will be last."

"What does that mean?" Nathaniel asked since the last part seemed to be a riddle that was key to the timing of things.

Yeshua pursed his lips and sat down, silent.

**

Yeshua was looking forward to seeing his sister and nephew in Cana. How quickly the boy was growing. He had just received the recent news that he was walking and babbling words, and now a second child was on its way.

The terrain to Cana was open and wide, giving views of orderly fields of barley still a bit green but softly feathering and swaying with the spring winds. The wheat fields were starting to put forth heads, and in the distance, he saw the fresh shoots and leaves of the vineyards lined out in neat rows. An almond orchard was entering its blooming season, and it reminded him of their former trip. Everything looked perfect, pastoral, and peaceful. In the distance, Mount Tabor stood like a sentinel, watching over everything below.

Six years had passed since he had taken his retreat to that mountain to discover his mission from his heavenly Father. He had prayed for his purpose to be revealed. So quickly, his purpose was drawing to its completion. Only Yosef had known of his dream. Yeshua still missed his earthly Abba. Yosef had supported his journey Qumran, knowing it would prepare him for finding his way. It was like only yesterday.

Almost to Cana, they encountered a blockade; ten men converged on the road ahead of them, looking like waifs and goblins. They appeared to be waiting for his approach.

They called out, "Yeshua, Master, have pity on us!"

"Lepers!" came his men's shouts of alarm.

Some reasoned, "Perhaps they had heard of Jahleel's healing."

They waited, pleading like a flock of needy sheep.

Yeshua paused; he did not indiscriminately heal on demand. His healings were signs and miracles for those who were sincerely seeking God and were led by the Holy Spirit—who knows all things. The men began to approach, but he held up his hand to stop them.

He called out to them, "Go, show yourselves to the priests."

He made no promise, nor did he touch or approach them. And, he gave no further instruction.

For a moment, the ten men looked at one another, clearly discussing what they should do.

One man said, "Look, he has told us what to do. When you are healed, you are to be examined by a priest. I say, let's go to the priest, just as he said."

So, the group turned and began to walk towards Cana to find the nearest priest. Miraculously, as they went, they were cleansed, and they rejoiced to see their healed skin and to examine one another's renewed faces.

But when the one man who had reasoned with the others saw he was healed, he stopped abruptly in his tracks. He was overwhelmed with wonder. He realized his healing was from God; God had done this for him!

His friends turned to see him standing there. "Aren't you coming with us to the priest for his blessing?" One man asked him.

He waved to his companions and said, "I will come along shortly. First, I must return to the man who healed me! For it is clear to me that God is with that man."

They stared after him as he hurried off, wasting no time to make his return.

Yeshua was not that far behind him, making his approach towards Cana. He picked up his robe and sprinted to Yeshua, shouting praises to God in a loud voice. He threw himself prostrate at his feet, completely face down and flat upon the ground. The man was shouting with praise and gratitude. Satisfied that this man was seeking God, Yeshua lifted him to his feet. He recognized the man's attire to be a Samaritan. The man could not stop saying thank you or staring at Yeshua with awe.

Yeshua glanced down the road but found it empty. He asked the healed man, "Were not all ten of you cleansed? Where are the other nine?Has no one else returned to give praise to God except for you?"

The man looked down the road from which he came. He was surprised to see that no one had followed him.

"I guess they have gone to the priest," he said with confusion.

Yeshua placed his hand on the man's shoulder and looked him in the eye, "Today, your faith has made you well."

So the man fell in step with the others and traveled on with them to Cana.

**

Cana did not go as well as Yeshua had hoped.

While he visited his sister and her new family, he could tell that Zerah and his family were on edge. During his early popularity, they had been eager to have him. Now, they considered him dangerous.

Few people ventured out to see him in the wide-open spaces, but they did not welcome him into their homes for fear of the repercussions of being closely connected to him. To keep from drawing attention in Cana, he sent most of his men on ahead toward Samaria. It was less of a burden to Zerah's family.

Before he moved on, Yeshua took his sister aside, "Hannah, the hard things I have warned you about are about to come upon me. This Passover, I will be taken captive by the religious leaders, and I will be killed on the cross. On the third day, I will rise again."

She stared at him as if he were a stranger. Words failed her in the face of his decision. She shook her head. "Don't tell me such things! Why are you doing this? You don't have to do this."

"But I do," he responded. "I just wanted to tell you that it will all work out for good in the end. Afterward, things will be different. I want you to know I will still be with you."

He made to leave, but she held on to him, sobbing with great emotion. She begged him not to go to Jerusalem. He tried to comfort her by reminding her that this was his purpose and that the result would be for the good of all people.

Zerah pulled her from her brother's neck, holding her back tenderly. He reminded her that she should not get so upset because of the baby. He angled his glare towards Yeshua as if to reprimand him for her agitation.

Yeshua spoke softly to Hannah. "I love you. No matter what you hear, you must know I will be fine in the long run. You know I never break my promises." He smiled and winked at her.

She calmed a little with those words, tears dripping off her nose and chin. She sniffled and took a swipe to her face, "Yes, it is true; you always keep your promises, though not always as quickly as I would like." She still had not forgiven his delay when he had visited Yohannan. But hope shone in her lovely eyes.

~ 26 ~

SOUR GRAPES

There is a time for everything,
and a season for every activity under the heavens:
A time to be born and a time to die,
A time to plant and a time to uproot,
A time to kill and a time to heal,
A time to tear down and a time to build,
A time to weep and a time to laugh,
A time to mourn and a time to dance,
A time to scatter stones and a time to gather them,
A time to embrace and a time to refrain from embracing,
A time to search and a time to give up,
A time to keep and a time to throw away,
A time to tear and a time to mend,
A time to be silent and a time to speak,
A time to love and a time to hate,
A time for war and a time for peace.
Ecclesiastes 3:1-8

Yeshua came to share the good news with the Samaritan people one more time. The last time he had preached in Samaria, the whole town had come out to meet with him. He was really looking forward to a favorable reception and a chance to reach more people. The seeds of his last visit had incubated and should be ready to sprout. Samaria would be a good way to take his mind off of what lay ahead and bolster him for what was to come. But when he arrived, the people did not come out to meet him with the grand reception he expected; in fact, only a few came out to hear him talk.

"I don't understand, what has happened?" He asked his disciples, "Where are the people?"

He had even sent his disciples ahead to prepare the people for his visit. He looked at Philip expectantly. But Philip shifted uncomfortably on his feet, not wanting to betray the others.

"Where are the people?" He was clearly upset.

When no one else answered him, Judas finally spoke up with a challenging tilt of his chin, "They are upset that you are going to Jerusalem."

"But clearly, I am a Jew. They have known this. What does that matter now?"

"They are upset because you told them the time is coming when there would be no need to worship in Jerusalem. They said, 'If that is true, then why are you going to Jerusalem?'" Thomas explained reasonably.

Philip looked at his feet, "Yes, well...someone, I am not saying who, may have told them that you are talking about being put to death there."

"They don't understand that at all," Judas said, "And they are not the only ones. You should be taking Israel by storm."

It all became clear to him that his men were trying to sway him through the Samaritans.

When Yeshua attempted to enter the village to clarify his purposes, the people refused to listen to him. "Go on, go to your precious Jerusalem! Go on and let them kill you! And for what? They have rejected you as if you were one of us! What kind of Messiah are you to walk right into a coup," they shouted. "We would gladly have made you our king. We would have joined forces with you, but not when you surrender yourself to those who despise you, and who despise us! How can we?" They were so angry at him that they drove him out of their village.

James and Yohan had been with Yeshua in Cana, but now they were outraged at the Samaritans on Yeshua's behalf.

"What do you expect from these pagan people?" James shouted. "Who are they to run you out of their town?"

Yohan looked wild-eyed, like he was itching for a confrontation with the people, "Lord! They are no different than they were from Elijah's day! They deserve the very same treatment he offered them when he was here. Let us call down fire from the heavens like Elijah! Maybe then they will listen to you?"

"No, no, no!" Yeshua shouted.

"There will be no fire to fall here today. The people have been confused. And I can see that someone was all too happy to offer up news that was not theirs to tell."

He looked at each of the nine men who had set this conflict in motion. Judas had separated himself by walking on ahead as if none of this had anything at all to do with him. Once he was a good distance out, he stood looking nonchalantly out into the evening sky as if trying to judge the weather. The other eight fell in with the other three and walked doggedly behind their master, knowing he was not pleased with the result of their mission. Now, there was nothing more to do than move on to another village. The evening was descending.

Yeshua stopped when he came upon an open field on the side of the road. "Let's camp here," he pointed to the field.

Later, while lying on his bed roll, he looked up at the stars and noticed only a sliver of the moon for light. Yeshua recalled this was how he had spent his first night on the run right in this same area, knowing that Caiaphas was searching for him. It had been very dark then, too. It felt like a bookend of sorts to his story. He remembered the taunts of the evil one that night. Now, once again under the darkened sky, he felt his old foe nearby, ready to taunt him once again and try to convince him that everything he had done was all for nothing. He was going to suffer and die for nothing but fools. And, tonight, it did feel like little to nothing had changed. Yeshua felt the temptation to doubt his work and his intent.

He whispered to the shadows, "No, it will not be long now. Our standoff will come to an end."

When morning came, the men were all hungry and unprepared because they had anticipated breakfast in the village that was well behind them. The men examined the vines along the side of the field, hoping to find any sort of fruit. Regretfully, they found the vines still flowering, and only a few tiny hard green pods had formed. Yohan brought a few of them to Yeshua.

He ruffled Yohan's hair, knowing he was trying to make amends, "Yohan, it is not the season for grapes."

Yohan looked at the tiny green knobs in his hands and understood that Yeshua had spoken a prophetic word to him. He let the small pods fall through his fingers. He answered him with the words of Jeremiah: "Yes, sour grapes leave a man's teeth on edge, and in the end, every man must be responsible for his own sin."

Yeshua nodded, pleased that Yohan remembered Jeremiah's words. Still, he was sad to know a day of harvest would eventually come to this land, and the crushing would be horrible.

Hungry, they struck out down the road, already anticipating what lay ahead in the next village. Yeshua talked as they went to divert their thoughts from their growling stomachs. "Don't worry about your life, what you will eat, or about your body, or what you will wear.Life is more than food. Consider the ravens: They do not sow or reap; they have no storeroom or barn, yet God feeds them. And how much more valuable are you than the birds? Do not worry. You will receive what you need. Do you honestly think *you* can add a single hour to your life?Look at these wildflowers growing; he motioned to the brightly colored poppies and lupine accenting the fields of fresh, bright green." He paused for a moment to gaze out over the vibrant landscape. It was a feast for the eyes. The others gathered around him to look out over the field as well.

"Do you see them laboring or spinning for what they need? Yet I tell you, not even Solomon in all his splendor was dressed like one of these." His admiration for his Father's handiwork reflected on his face. He motioned and turned to see their appreciative faces.

"If this is how God clothes the grass of the field, which is here today, and tomorrow is thrown into the fire, how much more will he feed and clothe you—you of little faith!Do not set your heart on what you will eat or drink.Those who do not trust God are frantic for such things. Your Father knows that you need them. Seek first his kingdom and his righteousness, and he will give you these things as well."

They offered brief nods. But the groaning returned when they came to the next hill, feeling their hunger all the more as their legs carried them up the incline. They were still reflecting on Yeshua's words as they made the crest of the hill and rounded a bend. When they looked up, from obsessing over their grumbling stomachs, they found a small village just off the road.

Yeshua laughed at their relief, "See, little flock, your Father is pleased to give you just what you need as you need it. And, he will give you the kingdom, too."

~ 27 ~

SALVATION COMES TO JERICHO

> I trust in your unfailing love;
> My heart rejoices in your salvation.
> I will sing the Lord's praise,
> for he has been good to me.
> Psalm 13:5-6

Yeshua entered Jericho with the plan to pass through the city and move on. But upon his approach, people began to be drawn to him. This was totally unexpected, but it indicated his Father was at work there.

Word spread throughout the town: "The Nazarene Rabbi, which the people are calling 'the Messiah,' has come to our town."

Zacchaeus heard this news in the conversations around him, even though no one shared this news directly with him. Why would they? They despised him. To them, he had everything money could buy and more.

'Surely,' they thought, 'he does not need or want a savior.'

They were wrong. Zacchaeus lived a very lonely life. The only people who talked with him were Romans and businessmen interested in commerce and making money. Privately, he longed for a relationship with Yahweh.

Recently, he had heard good news, 'The Nazarene Rabbi took a tax collector as one of his students'! He was assured, 'This Holy Man eats at the table with tax collectors and their guests.' Who had ever heard of such a thing?

He thought, 'I want to meet that Holy Man.'

Zacchaeus was despised more than all the other tax collectors because he was the *chief* tax collector. Jericho was at the crossroads of trade coming from the north, east, and south. All trade was taxed when it was conveyed through Jericho. He exercised authority over the trade that passed through to Jerusalem and to merchants who served the Eastern world. He maintained strong working relationships with the merchants of Jerusalem, who also wished to export their goods. But they would never greet him on the street.

As the overseer of all trade, Zacchaeus had become a very wealthy man. And he worked long hours. Since he was a Jew, the religious leaders were most happy to receive his generous offerings, but they shunned his hospitality. Only Romans and pagans considered an invitation to his home. They brought prostitutes to his feasts, still he took careful pride in being the gracious host. Whenever he traveled to Jerusalem, his business associates feigned indifference towards him. He was still just a tax collector. They could never share their table with him.

Zacchaeus had decided that today he would see Yeshua for himself, he wondered, 'What kind of man draws such large crowds?'

He made his way down a side street to get ahead of the procession. As he approached, he saw how crowded the street had become. There was already a press of bodies with people stacked ten deep in front of the alley byway. Since Zacchaeus was a short man, he would never be able to see him over the crowd.

He became panicked that his only chance might pass him by. But Zacchaeus was resourceful, especially when he was determined. He ran to the street entrance and pressed his way through the crowd. He made his way to a sizable fig tree that spread out to shade the street below. He jumped as high as his short legs would boost him, trying to grab hold of one of the larger branches. When he could not reach it, he abandoned all his pride. He turned to the closest sturdy-looking man and begged him, "Would you help me? I cannot see the Lord. I must see him. Please, give me a leg up to the tree."

The man laughed good-naturedly and stooped to provide him a foothold to heft him up. A few people jumped in to help him. Zacchaeus barely caught the limb. It took everything he had to haul himself onto the branch. Once he was secured, he stood and scrambled higher to a better vantage point. He found his footing and braced himself to watch and listen. When Yeshua came into view, the clogged street pressed to a quiet standstill.

The Rabbi was younger than he had expected, but the teacher's confidence and authority were seen even from his view within the flowering tree branches. He listened intently, feeling the power of his words. He had never heard anything quite like him.

Yeshua said, "I tell you, whoever publicly acknowledges me before others, the Son of Man will also acknowledge before the angels of God. But whoever disowns me before others will be disowned before the angels of God.And everyone who speaks a word against the Son of Man will be forgiven, but anyone who blasphemes the Holy Spirit will not be forgiven."

Someone in the crowd called out to him, "Teacher, what should I do since my brother will not divide our inheritance with me?"

Yeshua said, "Ah, you wish to appoint me to be a judge or an arbiter between you?"

He shook his head as if to himself, then said, "Watch out! Be on your guard against all kinds of greed; life does not consist of an abundance of possessions. There are more important things to seek."

As shared by his fame, he launched into a story, "The field of a certain rich man yielded him an abundant harvest.

"The man thought to himself, 'What shall I do? I have no place to store the bounty of my crops.'

"He decided, 'I will just tear down my barns and build bigger ones so that I can store all of my surplus grain.

"Once his barn was built, he thought to himself, 'Now, I have plenty of grain laid up for many years. Why work? I can take life easy and eat, drink, and be merry.'"

"But God said to him, 'You fool! This very night, your life will be demanded from you. Who, then, will get what you have prepared for yourself?'

"This is how it will be with whoever stores up things for themselves but is not rich toward God."

Zacchaeus realized he was like the rich man in the story. Indeed, wasn't he giving his whole life to the work of building himself a huge barn, and though he gave to God, wasn't there something more that he needed? He didn't know what that was exactly, but he felt the Rabbi could tell him. He wished with all his heart that he could have a private conversation with this holy man. His heart was hammering; he wanted to call out to the teacher to invite him to his house, but how could the man take him seriously—a grown man calling out to him from the tree?

Just then, Yeshua looked up to see his winsome face hidden in the foliage, filled with questions and longings. Concerned for the man standing on the limb, he shouted, "Zacchaeus, come down immediately. I must stay at your house today."

Zacchaeus was so startled that he almost fell from the limb, catching himself just in time. He hung dangling in the tree. Yeshua hurried over to help catch the stout little man. Before he could get there, Zacchaeus slipped. Both feet hit the ground with such force that he teetered backward, trying to catch his balance. He was about to slam to the ground, but before he took the hard hit, Yeshua caught hold of his hand and caught him under his arm.

He stood him to his feet with a laugh, "Okay! That was pretty immediate!"

Zacchaeus emitted a loud bubble of surprised laughter, something his pride would normally have never allowed him to do. His face beamed.

The crowd surrounding them, however, scratched their heads, asking each other, "Will the Rabbi really go to stay at this tax collector's house? Why would he choose to be the guest of that sinner?"

Hearing what the people were saying, Zacchaeus stepped forward and said to Yeshua, "Look, Lord! Here and now, I give half of my possessions to the poor, and if anyone can show proof of where I have cheated them, I will pay them back four times the amount."

Yeshua beamed at Zacchaeus, saying, "Today, salvation has come to the house of Zacchaeus. Who can doubt that this man is a son of Abraham? The Son of Man came to seek and save the lost. Today, a lost son is restored."

Yeshua and his men went with Zacchaeus to his large home on the hill, and became his house guests.

~ 28 ~

THE ONE YOU LOVE

Surely it is you who love the people;
All the holy ones are in your hand.
At your feet, they all bow down,
And from you receive instruction.
Deuteronomy 33:3

Yeshua and his disciples had been in Jericho for several days when a messenger appeared at Zacchaeus' door.

"I have a message for Rabbi Yeshua of Nazareth. Please tell me that he is still here?"

Zacchaeus's manservant held out his hand to receive the message.

The man shook his head, "No, since this is urgent, I was told to place this note in his hands alone."

Rebuffed, the doorkeeper looked the man up and down, deciding whether to get Yeshua or to refuse him. There were certain protocols; he knew he could not trust the motive of every person who came to his master's door.

To convince him, the messenger showed him the letter's seal. Again, the servant reached to take it, but the messenger drew it back with a patient smile.

"Wait here." The doorman said gruffly and closed the door.

Some moments later, Yeshua came to the door, "You have a message for me?"

He recognized the servant from Martha's home. He understood the implications. His lips tightened into a grimace, then a weak smile. Martha's manservant handed the message immediately to Yeshua. "Lord, it is an urgent personal message from the one… from the House of Boethius."

He waited expectantly.

Looking down, Yeshua saw the seal of Mariamne. A watch tower was impressed in the red wax. Mari. He tapped the papyrus in his hand and motioned the messenger in for rest and refreshment.

His men waited expectantly for Yeshua to read the sealed scroll.

Instead, he went out on the terrace and stood staring off into the distance as if he could see something there that they could not. This was one of those moments when their Master seemed to be listening to hear an invisible voice or looking to see things they could not see. They had learned not to disturb him. They waited until he turned and seemed to be present to them again.

"Lord, is it from home?" Rock asked with concern and drew near, worried for his family.

"It is Lazarus," Yeshua said, even though he had not yet broken the seal of the scroll. "He is ill."

"It must be serious if they have sent for you. When shall we leave?"

"We are not going …yet. This sickness will not end in death."

No one batted an eye, for they had seen Yeshua heal people from far away. They assumed that was his plan. Perhaps he already had. They resumed their conversations without concern.

Yeshua withdrew to the upper portico and remained there for several hours. Alone, he paced and prayed, staring out towards Bethany.

Later, when the topic was raised again, Yeshua told them. "This illness will be for God's glory so that God's Son may be glorified through it."

They took his words to heart, confident that Yeshua would provide healing to Mari, Martha, and Lazarus as needed. They thought no more about it.

Later that evening, Yeshua opened the scroll to find Mari's neat writing. "Yeshua, we need you. The one that you love is sick."

Mari had written him a simple note, but it was loaded with a code of intimacy, sending a message she knew he would understand. He closed his eyes, and tears seeped out at the edges. He wiped his eyes and sat the scroll aside. Mari was waiting for him to come and save the day. It was all he could do not to get up and run to her. But he did not.

**

It was not until two days later that Yeshua roused his men early, "Let us prepare to go up to Bethany."

Thomas said, "But Rabbi, why would you do that? It hasn't been that long since the Jews in Jerusalem tried to stone you. It is too dangerous!"

"Thomas is right,' Philip agreed, "why would you want to go back now?"

Yeshua was resolute, "Are there not twelve hours of daylight? It is early. Anyone who walks in the daytime will not stumble, for they can see.When a person walks at night, they cannot see, and they stumble."

Sometimes, his archaic riddles were simply frustrating. So they prepared to go and reluctantly said goodbye to Zacchaeus, thanking him for his fine hospitality. They vaguely remembered he had spoken of daylight previously; it was usually in reference to his Father's work. But they couldn't help but grumble about heading back to Jerusalem.

They did not want to be exposed to the family's illness, they wanted to avoid conflict with the religious authorities, and they feared their leader would be captured and killed. Nor did they want to be caught in the crosshairs and die with him. They could see nothing good coming out of it.

But when Yeshua showed no sign of relenting, Thomas slapped his knees and stood up wearily, "All right, our Lord wants to go up to Jerusalem. Let us all go with him—so we might all die with him." He dramatically flung his arms towards the west as if he were hurling them all toward Jerusalem to speed things along. His voice was loud; it dripped with sarcasm and pent-up frustration.

Yeshua stared at Thomas. A hint of a smile played at his lips but didn't quite reach his eyes. Finally, he said, "Our friend Lazarus has fallen asleep, but I am going there to wake him up."

Thomas, the literalist, gave Yeshua a challenging look, "Well, that is just great. If he is resting, he will soon get better." He thought Yeshua meant a natural sleep.

When Thomas did not pick up on nuance, Yeshua let out a frustrated sigh. He had not wanted their journey to Bethany to be laden with grief and confusion over Lazarus' death. But it became apparent that to overcome their reluctance, he needed to tell them the cold, hard truth.

He rubbed his forehead before he said bluntly, "Lazarus is dead."

Everyone's head snapped up, filled with confusion.

"But you said…"

"I said, 'It will not *end* in death.' And for your sake, I am glad I was not there, so you may come to more fully believe."

As they often did, they looked from one to the other, with shock, wondering what he meant.

"Come on, go grab your things. Let us go to Lazarus," Yeshua urged them.

The circle of faces reflected their morbid shock.

"Dead?" Rock asked, shaking his head as if this could not be real. Was Yeshua losing his touch? Questions arose in their minds. Why hadn't he healed Lazarus from Jericho? Why had he delayed? Why had he allowed this to happen? Doubt swamped their minds. Accusing eyes pierced him, but Yeshua offered them no explanation. What made it worse, he showed no remorse for it. Their minds scattered back over the last few days, trying to make sense of it.

Thomas turned to the others. "Okay then... Let us also go back with Yeshua, so we may all die along with Lazarus!"

His sarcasm was not lost on Yeshua. He knew what they were thinking, but he also knew that faith-building often required confusion and doubt to help their faith grow stronger. This had been just as true for him. Faith was forged through pain and intended to help the person become even more resilient. He needed his men to be immovable even in the face of confusion and doubt.

Yeshua speared Thomas with a fierce look, "That is enough!"

**

Even from a distance, Yeshua could see a large crowd had converged upon their compound to mourn the family's loss.

"Lord, look! Half of Jerusalem is here," his men said with alarm.

It was true; many had come to pay their respect to the family of Lazarus, Simon, Eleazar, Martha, and Mari. It was no surprise, given the family's position in the temple, their service, business, teaching, and community.

"Lord, you cannot just walk in there. It would be too....dangerous," Rock appealed to him.

"I am not afraid. But I *do* prefer to talk with Martha and Mari apart from the crowds and confusion. Yohan go to Martha and let her know I am here and waiting at the city gate."

Yeshua waited for Martha under a spreading tree. He was expecting the two sisters' pain and disappointment in him, given how the family was taking Lazarus' death hard.

Martha's servant came immediately with water for them all. The servant confirmed that Lazarus had already been in the tomb itself for four days. In fact, Lazarus had died the same day he had been dispatched to Jericho.

When Martha saw Yohan, she hurried towards him, leading him away from Mari. Yohan took Martha's extended hands. "The Lord is waiting for you at the gate."

She gave a curt nod, signaling to her friends to remain with Mari. They understood that she was taking care of some business as the mistress of the house. Martha went with Yohan, deliberately walking with dignified steps, but anger burned in her eyes. She had words she wanted to say to Yeshua alone.

As he had guessed, Martha had been the strong one since Lazarus' death, but she and Lazarus were close. The household had looked to her to prepare for the thongs of people. Martha had done what Martha did best. Work and planning helped her to block out her own overwhelming emotions. She had been in a hyper-responsible mode from the moment of her brother's death. But her eyes were large and ringed with shock and grief, emotional exhaustion, and, yes, the intensity of anger.

But when she arrived and Yeshua stood before her, her emotions swept over their jettied banks. She wilted before him, all her pretense gone. Yeshua hurried forward, taking hold of her hands, fearing she might faint.

"Lord," Martha whispered, her voice weak and ragged. A great sob released as she leaned her head into his shoulder, "If you had been here, my brother would not have died…"

She pushed back to look at him with pleading eyes. Her throat caught, painful and tight, she said, "But… I know… that … even *now*, God will give you whatever you ask."

Yeshua knew what she was asking.

Tenderly, he assured her, "Your brother will rise again."

Martha held on to him, letting her tears fall unchecked on the front of his robe. She struggled to believe what he said.

She wondered, 'Does he understand what I am asking?'

She took a step back and wiped at her dripping nose. Pitifully, she said, "I know he will rise again in the resurrection on the last day."

'Ah!' He thought with surprise, 'she has been listening.' He felt pleased. Staring into her pleading eyes, he gave her a compassionate smile.

He stepped closer and whispered intimately, "I *am* the resurrection and the life. The one who believes in me will *live*, even though they *die*, and whoever *lives* by believing in me will never die."

His smile faded, becoming utterly serious, "Do you believe this?"

He searched her reddened and tear-soaked face.

Martha hung her head a moment, knowing she was selfishly demanding too much of Yeshua. She knew how much trouble the last miracle had cost him in Jerusalem when he had made the blind man see.

'I am selfishly borrowing more trouble for him,' she thought. Yet she desperately wanted her brother back, alive and well. He was, after all, her closest relative.

With a sad apology, she searched his face, "Yes, Lord, I believe that you are the Messiah, the Son of God, who is to come into the world."

They stared at one another with understanding.

Then, he looked around her towards the house, "Where is Mari?"

"I didn't tell her you were here. She is taking this hard. I selfishly needed to see you alone before telling her." She looked down at her hands and offered him a thin and apologetic smile.

She knew Mari held a special place in his heart, "I'm sorry. I will go and get her."

She released his strong hands and stepped back, "You should know Mari has been slowly coming undone. Well, she is not...doing well. She has been watching for you and....well.... when you didn't come right away..."

"Would you go and bring her to me?" He asked.

Martha went to find Mari where she had left her, still listlessly sitting by herself, totally unaware. In the beginning, Mari had been strong when the illness beset Lazarus, confident their brother would recover. She had poured herself into prayer. As it grew worse, she had sent word to Yeshua, having received word that he was near. But as soon as the messenger had taken to the road, Lazarus' breathing had become more and more distressed. She had gone to the upstairs window and stared out towards Jericho, praying, willing her thoughts and prayers to the Lord.

When Lazarus died, Martha began the proceedings of the funeral, but Mari stood still in the window praying, watching, and waiting. Even after he had died, she had waited and watched, believing he would arrive at any moment and he would rectify everything. The messenger returned, but Yeshua was not with him. That was when her composure began to crumble.

"It will not end in death," the messenger told her. But he was wrong. Lazarus was already dead. She walked away from the window, her faith overcome with grief and confusion. Didn't Yeshua care for her after all? Where was he? Hadn't she told him they needed him—*she* needed him? She had thought that *she* was somehow special to him. How could he not know how much she loved him? Hadn't she professed it all? He was her Rock. She felt suddenly unanchored, a drift on a sea of nothingness and pain, abandoned—just as she had been time and again since her childhood.

All of the demons of her childhood seemed to be dancing in the shadows around her, whispering, "Who are you? You are nothing to him!"

Days, hours, and moments passed as the light in her eyes was slowly dimmed. She had taken on the appearance of a pitiful waif. Her wide eyes were staring at nothing, surrounded by dark circles. When Martha bent down to whisper in her sister's ear that the Lord had come, Mari stared at her blankly as if she had no idea who Martha meant.

Martha bent down low in front of her sister's face and said, "Look at me! The Rabbi is here, and he is waiting for you by the city gate. He is anxious to see you."

Mari stared at her sister, blinking several times. Then, suddenly, it was as if those words broke the spell. She grabbed at the words as if they were a lifeline. She arose quickly and took off running to him.

When the women who had been sitting with Mari noticed how quickly she sprang up and departed, they quickly found their feet to follow after her.

"Where is she going? To the tomb?" Susanna asked Martha.

"No, the Master is here," Martha told her.

They, too, ran following Mari.

When Mari reached the gate, she found Yeshua there waiting for her. She stumbled the last remaining steps, falling to her hands and knees before him. Her scrambled emotions were plain on her face. She crawled towards him the last bit of the way and broke down sobbing hysterically. She took hold of his feet, crying like a wounded animal. Then, in a shrill voice, she said accusingly, "Lord, if you had been here, my brother would not have died. Where were you? I thought you would not come....I, I, I thought...."

Yeshua bent down, seeing how her heart was broken. His own heart was also broken in two, knowing that to make her stronger, he had caused Mari this pain. He lifted her face towards his. As he wiped the tears from her face, it seemed as if they were beginning to stream down his own face.

"Sh, sh, sh," he whispered, "I am here. I am here. I will always be here."

She lifted her fevered eyes to his, searching as if for something she had feared she had lost.

Seeing her crumbled face, a sob caught in Yeshua's throat, choking him and blurring her face. He could only hope that she would come to understand why this had happened after everything had passed. He had taken no pleasure in her terrible momentary pain. But, he hoped this painful experience would strengthen her faith for what was coming.

He stood, lifting Mari to her feet. She grasped his robe, unwilling to let him go. He ran his hand over her hair and made shushing sounds like soothing a frightened child.

With tears still hanging in his lashes, he gratefully acknowledged each of the women who had come out to support Mari. A circle of familiar faces, Susanna, Joanna, and many others who had traveled out to sit at his feet with Mari. His heart went out to each of them, his love for them shining in his eyes.

When the disciples saw his wet eyes and felt the rays of his affection for the women, they lowered their eyes with embarrassment. Not for his show of emotion but because they had miscalculated the depth of Yeshua's concern in this situation. Why had they been so blind to what he was feeling?

Yeshua took a few deep breaths to steady his heart. This was just the precursor to the pain that was going to crush these, his children, on account of him. Obedience was not without suffering. He wiped his eyes and cleared his throat, "Where have you laid him?"

"Come and see Lord," Susanna spoke up, taking the lead.

As they moved along to the tomb, Yeshua's tears continued because of their pain. By that time, other mourners had come to join them on their way. When the people heard his sobs, they said, "See how he loved Lazarus!"

But some mourners grumbled to one another, "Why this charade? If he was able to open the eyes of the blind man, then why couldn't he keep this man from dying?"

Standing in front of the freshly decorated family tomb, Yeshua was once again overcome with emotion and dread. Now, in his mind's eye, he was facing 'Death' personified. His emotions morphed with an intensity of sorrow, dread, and rage. Yeshua hated death so much that he felt the temptation to shatter the stone that covered Lazarus' grave.

His rage dated back through the ages to the very first death of righteous Abel. He stared at the tomb for a long moment. He did not move or speak. The fierceness in his face was enough to make one tremble. A battle seemed to be raging inside of him.

He understood that by completing this last sign, he was setting the precalculated wheels of his approaching death in motion. This miracle would show his disciples that he had the power to overcome death with life. By raising Lazarus (his third resurrection to date), he was challenging Death to a duel. One in which he would die, but Death would be defeated.

The tomb was cut out of an already existing cave. A large stone was set across the entrance. It was a tomb for a rich man. Yeshua stepped forward and braced his legs as one readied for the battle. He took a deep breath. His nostrils flared with determination, anger, and disgust. He gave a loud snort of derision. He would destroy Death.

"Take away the stone," he commanded so loudly that it reverberated off of the stones. A loose stone broke free and fell to the ground.

"Lord," Martha cried out, "he has been there four days."

Yeshua brows knitted fiercely together; he glanced her way, "Martha, did I not tell you that if you believe, you will see the glory of God?"

Martha covered her mouth, her eyes wide, "Yes, Lord."

A few of Yeshua's men hoisted the stone from the opening. The smell of the already rotting flesh poured out from within. James doubled over as if to retch at the putrid scent. They fled from the opening and covered their noses, trying not to breathe it in.

Yeshua looked up towards heaven and lifted his hands in appeal, "Father, I thank you that you have heard me. You always hear me. So the people standing here might believe that you sent me...."

He paused and then called out in a loud voice, "Lazarus, come out!"

A hush fell upon the people. They waited. Moments passed. The gaping darkness taunted them all. But then, there came a shuffling sound from within. His wrapped head appeared, leaning forward, searching for the light through the cloth. Bound by his wrappings, Lazarus took stiff, little steps forward. Everything, including his hands and feet, was wrapped with strips of linen. A cloth still covering his head and face. Lazarus made muffled grunts. A cool breeze swept in and carried the remaining smell of death away. The crowd stood rooted with fear and fascination, watching what had been a corpse creep forward.

Yeshua shouted to them, "What are you waiting for? Go and unwrap him. Take off the grave bindings and let him go."

Martha ran to Lazarus and unwrapped his face. And, there he was alive—her brother Lazarus. His handsome face was now revealed. He was confused but beaming with wonder. Martha's hands flew to her mouth, and then she threw her arms around her brother and reached up to kiss his face. He stood there waiting patiently, and then he said, "Hey, Martha, could you unwrap me first!'

Everyone stood speechless, their hands over their mouths. Their eyes were wide with amazement and wonder. They watched the siblings unwrap their brother.

Then they all turned to Yeshua. He offered them a victorious smile. Everyone present knew he was not like any other man. Truly, only Yeshua could be the LORD's anointed.

The family, disciples, and guests from Jerusalem were overwhelmed with so many emotions. The Lord had been faithful, after all. Now, they knew he had the power to raise a man four days dead from the grave. They hung their heads with embarrassment, feeling slow, confused, and wondering, 'Why did we ever doubt him?' Obviously, this was why he had been slow to come to Bethany. For this reason.

Even the Jews who had come from Jerusalem to comfort Mari and Martha had seen what Yeshua had done, so they put their faith in him.

News of this feat traveled quickly to Jerusalem and the Pharisees. Horror and fear distorted the leaders' faces. More people would go after Yeshua after hearing he could save them from death. The Chief Priests wasted no time before calling a meeting of the Sanhedrin. Gathered, they sounded like a loud and irate hive of hornets. It was hard to bring the meeting to order.

Annas sat in the seat of highest honor. He stood to his feet and lifted his hands. The voices slowly quieted. He spoke with an unnatural calm as if he was the very voice of reason. "This must not be allowed to continue. How has it come to this? For three years, we have been trying to be rid of this carpenter from Nazareth. Yet, what have we accomplished? If we let him go on like this, performing these signs, everyone will believe in him. Then the Romans will come and take away both our temple and our nation."

A voice called out, "But what about the signs?"

"Who is speaking?" Annas looked around.

One of the younger Pharisees lifted his hand.

Yosef of Arimathea stood and stepped forward with boldness, "I agree with him. Look, this man has raised a man from the dead. How can any *mere man* do that? Surely, the LORD is speaking to us through these signs. Shouldn't we examine or try to understand what they mean?"

A few other men nodded their heads.

This caused Caiaphas to jump to his feet, seething with anger, "How can you say that? You know nothing at all! Do you not realize that it is better for you that one man should die for the people than for the whole nation to perish?"

Everyone shrunk back with uncertainty, hearing the truth in his words. Caiaphas had hated this miracle man from the moment he had driven the money changers out of the temple. But what they didn't know was that at that moment, as high priest, Caiaphas had actually prophesied God's truth to them. Yeshua would die for the sake of the Jewish nation,and not only for that nation but also for all the nations and the scattered children of God.

One of Caiaphas' followers said, "Imagine what will happen when he brings the believers together and makes them one! We must act soon."

With fear of his growing power and popularity, the Sanhedrin made it their sole goal to find a way to take Yeshua's life. They gave orders that anyone who knew where Yeshua was should report it immediately so they might go and arrest him.

Word traveled back quickly to Eleazar of their decision. Going to his son Lazarus, Eleazar warned him that it was not safe for Yeshua to remain in Bethany. The beginning of the Passover Festival was only a little over a week away. Yeshua left, traveling through the harsh wilderness of the Jordan Rift Valley to a small and remote village named Ephraim. There, he remained hidden with his disciples until Passover approached. Ephraim was on the edge of the plateau, and it overlooked the broad valley below. Believers there had offered their hospitality the year before, and now it became a refuge.

Meanwhile, the Pharisees came several times to the compound to question Lazarus and demanded to know where the Nazarene had fled. When Lazarus offered them nothing to use against Yeshua, they grew irrational. They grew even angry with Lazarus. He was living proof of Yeshua's power. When the leaders implied they should seize Lazarus in his place, Eleazar came and stood with his son with threats of his own. When they left, he posted guards and locked the gates.

When they were gone, he turned to Lazarus and said, "I knew your messiah would land you in trouble."

But Lazarus replied, "Really? Father, because of Yeshua, I am alive and not dead."

Eleazar could not argue, for he had grieved at his son's death, and he had rejoiced when Yeshua had called him out of the tomb. "I know. But it would seem you have lost your life to gain your life."

That day, Eleazar sent a legal document and a letter to Caiaphas saying, "Back off. Do not place my son in the middle of your fight with Yeshua. Call your dog's off of Lazarus. My son has done nothing wrong. Your behavior makes no sense at all. If anything happens to him, I will split your administration and make it a misery for you."

~ 29 ~

UNHOLY ALLIANCES

Why do the nations conspire,and their people plot in vain?
The kings of the earth rise up, and the rulers band together
against the Lord and against his anointed.
Psalm 2:1-2

Satan witnessed Yeshua's actions at the tomb of Lazarus with an odd delight. "Does he really think he can overcome the grave?"

His reptilian eyes narrowed, foreseeing the ways this latest miracle would inflame those he had carefully positioned in the halls of power in Jerusalem. He had personally been restrained from touching the flesh of the "Son of God," this Human One. But now Yeshua was walking step by step into the trap he had set for him—the cross.

Few men could withstand such physical suffering without losing faith. Touch the body with pain, and even the best failed. Briefly, he remembered Job. It had not worked with him, but he hadn't encountered the cross.

Still, Satan couldn't wait for his revenge. Yeshua's defeat would give him complete control over the sons of man. How easy it was to plant thoughts and plans into their godless minds. He despised humanity because they were so precious to God. He looked forward to destroying the whole lot. But humanity was only useful to the extent that their suffering pained God. And without God, they were all too willing to destroy one another and then themselves with little effort on his part. They became like a pack of wolves that turned on one another.

'Soon, there will be no limit to my power,' he smiled wickedly.

Even though he had wielded power over humans for a long time, he was still only a dog on a long leash, who could be jerked back into his place. 'Soon,' he thought, 'that leash will be cut.'

**

For the past three years, Caiaphas had found no rest because of Yeshua. When at first the Nazarene had appeared, he had failed to recognize him. Something about the eyes seemed familiar. Eventually, he remembered the know-it-all kid from Galilee, and he put two and two together. That had been over twenty years ago earlier while he was still establishing himself. The kid had entered the yearly competition of the Bet Midrash in Jerusalem.

Normally, a twelve-year-old would not have been allowed to enter. The age to be tested in the oral law was fifteen. But the Rabbi from his village had friends on the council. He had convinced them, quite sure the boy could hold his own. Caiaphas led the questioning, and other teachers in the law joined in for the challenge. They had been amazed at his knowledge. But Caiaphas had made it his goal to cause the boy to stumble. The competition was meant to humble 'the weak' and strengthen 'the strong.'

This youth, however, had gazed serenely at Caiaphas and his cohorts, completely unrattled. He gave confident answers. The ease with which he answered, had made Caiaphas' questions look weak as if *he* were the student. What was worse, the boy was only a carpenter's son. And, he had only studied under the country rabbi.

At the time, his mentor Annas had laughed at his comeuppance, teasing him that a twelve-year-old boy had parlayed him all too well. It had been humiliating for him. Caiaphas took pride in his own intelligence. Few could converse in the law better than him.

He also remembered that when he had given him unto Annas to put in his place, even Annas could not stump him.

Caiaphas had studied under some of the best teachers. And as a teacher, he had been privy to some of the brightest student minds. One of them had been the son of the priest Zachariah. Yohannan, though young, was to become a priest, a descendant of Aaron and Zadok. He had also understood the Scripture better than Caiaphas, light radiated from Yohannan's interpretation. Even then, the boy had zealously believed the Messiah was coming. Indeed, he was already there. He couldn't wait to serve him.

In fact, when Yohannan attended studies in the law, the boy had carefully outlined the scriptures that pointed to the Messiah. Even Caiaphas as his teacher had been intrigued with his insights. But when there came a change in the position of high priest. Yohannan's family defected to the wilderness to avoid the dangers.

In the new political climate, Caiaphas' mind took a strange turn. He thought, 'If I could become High Priest, perhaps I could gain the opportunity to become the King as well. Just like the Hasmonaeans were king and priest, I could become a Messiah for the people.' It began as a silly fantasy about becoming the savior of Israel, but quickly morphed into the desire to make a name for himself. He had kept his thoughts to himself.

His teacher, Annas, was a very powerful Sadducee. Caiaphas made himself Annas' righthand man and became aligned as a Sadducee. He gained the trust of both the Pharisees and Sadducees alike, and even some of the independent elders because of his knowledge of the law and his brilliant business mind. Caiaphas made sure everyone prospered.

His marriage to Annas' daughter had officially made him a member of Annas' family. After Annas aged out, his sons had each taken a turn as High Priest to keep the position in the family and firmly under Annas' direction. Only recently had Caiaphas finally gained his turn. He understood he had to defer to the old man by allowing him to believe he was still calling all the shots. Why not?

Annas was politically potent, and he was an effective shield and sounding board in all controversial matters.

Now was Caiaphas' time! He had made it to High Priest by being religiously tolerant and an ally to Herod Antipas. Pilate, however, could be a problem. Unfortunately, he would need Pilate's help to dispose of this Galilean who was stuck in his crawl like a piece of bony fish.

He sat down to script a missive to Pilate to set the stage, *"Since you are the governor of Judea, I wanted to alert you that trouble is brewing in Jerusalem due to a roque Galilean rabbi named Yeshua of Nazareth. I am sure you have heard of him. He is beginning to draw large crowds and announce that he is the rightful king of the Jews, the Messiah, the Son of God. Together, we should be able to put down his uprising against Caesar and the Republic. I hope we can be allies in this."*

Placing his seal, Caiaphas regretted his previous power plays that had drawn lines against Pilate. He could only hope that Pilate would see this warning as a peace offering and an opportunity to work together.

To hedge his bets, he also sent a note to Herod Antipas, *"Friend, I look forward to seeing you in Jerusalem for the Pesach. I am working on a plan to remove the latest blight against Judah and Jerusalem. He claims to be 'the King of the Jews'. I believe you have taken some interest in this Yeshua of Nazareth as well. He has been rallying much of Jerusalem and Galilee to his false teachings and must be dealt with immediately. I am sure that I can count on your support in this matter. Please give my warmest regards to your queen, Salome. I still remember performing your marriage with great affection."*

After years of trying to collect some offense on Yeshua, Caiaphas still had nothing of substance. The man was totally selfless; he had no vices at all. In fact, what he did learn about him should have given him pause. Had he looked at the evidence, he might have realized that Yeshua fulfilled all of the prophecies.

Indeed, he had the prescribed pedigree, although he never flaunted his familial lineage. He spoke with the fire of a prophet. He was a healer who gave sight to the blind, made the lame walk, and healed the insane, among other things. He zealously challenged the religious system. He had been born in Bethlehem. He could read the hearts of men. He had a supernatural authority in his teachings, and, oh yes… he had raised the dead to life. It is funny what people do not see—when they do not want to see.

For the past year, Yeshua had been elusive, impossible to find. When the Festivals came, suddenly he would show up to stand in the temple and make 'blasphemous' proclamations about himself. Yet the people believed him, and the crowds swelled around him. He had even appeared on the temple grounds. He could not account for the ways Yeshua had evaded his guards or the traps he had set before him.

Caiaphas had learned not to challenge Yeshua publicly; it was humiliating. He remained in the shadows and sent his followers to do his bidding. Every time he thought he had him, Yeshua simply slipped away untouched. But what bothered him most of all was the fact that Yeshua had no respect or fear of him, and that undid him.

Now that Yeshua had raised Lazarus from the dead, the people of Jerusalem could talk of nothing else. And Caiaphas could think of nothing else except how badly he wanted him dead.

Caiaphas called in the best scholars of the law to create a consortium to craft questions layered with sticking points. His goal was to corner Yeshua and make his theology look faulty or to entrap him. The teachers of the law went to work searching for difficult issues they might use against Yeshua. They divided into debate teams to practice their rhetoric. Their goal was to be totally prepared to obliterate any answer Yeshua might give.

Caiaphas even called in Gamaliel's best young disciple from Tarsus, who was full of fire and promise. There was no one more zealous for the law than young Saul.

He would make sure the Nazarene would never embarrass him again, and he would stop his encroachment upon his kingdom.

Caiaphas never drew the correlation that he was behaving like Ahab, who had killed a righteous man to steal his vineyard. As a man of the law, he never thought to fear what might happen to those who plot against God.

**

A letter was brought into Herod's throne room on its silver tray, "Your Majesty, you have received a letter from the High Priest. Nervously, Antipas took up the letter and broke the seal.

"What is it?" Herodias asked him, leaning forward with interest.

He breathed a sigh of relief to learn Caiaphas was chasing this rabbit in Jerusalem. "Oh, nothing that we need to concern ourselves about."

He did not want to make this 'messiah' his next problem. The death of the Baptist had cost him sorely in popularity amongst his people. His dispute with Nabataea had caused Rome to turn a critical eye toward his position as tetrarch. Herod felt he was skidding on the edge with Caesar. He needed the people to accept him as their Jewish King. But even more important, he *had* to be in the good graces of Rome, where he had been favored for his present position.

The thought of this Yeshua of Nazareth unnerved him because of the Messianic rumors. Antipas had spent his whole life dodging political bullets, the intrigue of his Father and his siblings from his father's house. He refused to be dethroned now. Up to this point, he was still alive and wanted to keep it that way.

Now, Pilate ruled from Antipas' father's former stronghold—the Antonia Fortress in Jerusalem. It was all too clear who really called the shots in Jerusalem. A thin smile curled his lips. Yes, he would support Caiaphas' efforts to get rid of this latest upstart dubbed "king of the Jews". He hoped he was successful, and he wanted nothing to do with it.

**

When Pilate received Caiaphas' warning, he broke the seal and read the missive. He sighed, muttering a crude string of curses.

Turning toward his wife, he said, "Great! Just great! Caiaphas writes of a new problem in Jerusalem."

Claudia raised her head from the chaise where she was watching her husband don his military attire in preparation for travel.

"And, what problem is that?" she asked, sitting up and paying close attention.

Pilate was grateful that he had at least one trusted confidante, "Some Jewish carpenter from Nazareth. It seems he has been gathering large crowds of people around him. Caiaphas didn't say much except that he may need my assistance. I don't know anything about the man beyond that. Still ... Caiaphas does not scare easily. I dare not disregard the warning. But as you know, after the last debacle Caiaphas caused me, I do not trust him. I have to wonder what he is plotting against me this time."

His full lips disappeared into a grim line, "I have never been so humiliated, all because of him and that degenerate old man whose skirt he hides behind."

Claudia came to Pilate with a sympathetic smile, going up on tip-toe to kiss his well-shaved cheek. "Pontius, you are smarter than Caiaphas. You can judge the situation on your own when you get there. It is interesting that even though he entrapped you the last time, now he suddenly needs your assistance. You are the man with the power at the end of the day."

Her words bolstered him. Pilate kissed Claudia on the top of her head, "This is why I keep you around." he smiled, looking deeply into her eyes. She was the best thing in his life.

He gave her buttocks an intimate squeeze and buried his head in her neck.

He asked her, "Are all your things packed and ready to go?"

"Of course," she said, waving her hand nonchalantly. She pressed herself to him, "Everything is ready, and the servants have taken our luggage. Jerusalem, here we come." Her eyes gleamed with excitement.

"I don't know why you like going to that awful place."

She rolled her eyes, "Because silly, it is the center of the world, that is why. Open your eyes and see it for what it is. All the nations come to gather there. And you are the ruler of *that* important and ancient city."

~ 30 ~

A TRAITOR REASONS

Even my close friend, someone I trusted,
One who shared my bread has lifted up his heel against me.
Psalm 41:9

Judas, son of Iscariot, was growing increasingly impatient with Yeshua. When the crew left their hiding place in the wilderness, they returned to Jerusalem for the Festival of Passover.

Yeshua told them, "This is it. Time to fulfill my purpose. The chief priests and the Sanhedrin will send me to the cross."

They all wondered, 'Why is he so determined to be crucified? It doesn't have to be that way.' But no one argued with him.

Judas had tried to subtly offer Yeshua other possibilities for handling his conflict for months now, but Yeshua was as resolute as ever. He was sick of hearing his warnings.

He thought, 'I have strapped myself to a sinking ship. If Yeshua is crucified, then what will that leave me? We will all be hung on a cross of our own.' It nagged at him that Yeshua had even said as much almost from the very beginning. *"Take up your cross and follow me,"* he had said. At the time, it had seemed like hyperbole or a metaphor, a strange philosophy."

But now, he realized for the first time, he had really called him to follow him to a painful death. 'I didn't think he meant it literally.'

Judas had stopped trying to talk to the other disciples about it; they preferred to ignore his words. He glanced up at the others trouping ahead before him.

'Look at them, walking so trustingly behind him like sheep being led to the slaughter. What will death accomplish? Yeshua claimed he would be resurrected from the dead, but how can a dead man raise his self? It is crazy talk, even for a miracle man. He will just be dead.'

'And speaking of that, what was the deal with Lazarus' death and resurrection? Could it be that Yeshua really is the biggest charlatan of all? Obviously, Lazarus was in on it... along with Mari. Perhaps she slipped some Egyptian elixir to Lazarus. His family came from Egypt. So perhaps Mari was Yeshua's assistant in the biggest scam of all time? That would account for him leaving her behind. Mari would do anything for him." His nose was crinkled, like one confronted by an unpleasant smell.

'And, if he really did raise Lazarus from the dead, then he allowed him to die in the first place. Lazarus is one of his very best friends. Would he demand such a feat from me? To go to my death so he could raise me up?'

As he mused, the others left him alone to brood. They didn't ask; they didn't want to know what he was thinking. Judas could be overly dramatic and full of negative scenarios. How many times had his drama caused trouble for them? They left him to trail behind.

Judas had not noticed he was becoming separated from the group while lost in his thoughts, 'Yes, it is time for me to find a way out of this mess before it is too late. It has been semi-lucrative, but now I need to think about my future. I am not going to hang from some tree just because Yeshua is set on it. I don't need Yeshua to make a good living! I have ciphered off enough money from donations to live quite well for a while.

'But now that the High Priest has actually put out a warrant for his arrest, there will most certainly be trouble. I don't want to be caught in it. What can I tell people if I default? After all, I have been testifying that Yeshua is the Messiah—the Holy One of God. My credibility will disappear. But if I helped them to find him? No one else would ever need to know about it. I imagine the High Priest would be willing to pay anything to get him. I could name my price. Maybe I could even sweeten the deal by negotiating for a booth of my own in the temple. That would provide me a good income," His eyes took on an unnatural gleam at the thought of it.

'But what about Yeshua?' Judas stared ahead to his righteous form, leading the pack. He felt a slight stab of conscience. 'I would really hate for anyone to hurt him or for anything evil to come upon him. He has truly been my friend. A good friend. He has trusted me in ways no one else ever has. He is, perhaps, the best friend I have ever had. And what do they have on him that could stick?

'On the other hand, even if they had something, it is Yeshua's fault that I am in this position, isn't it? If he would only listen to me and just follow my advice. But he has made this choice himself; he has set his course for death. I would be a fool if I just blindly followed him without thinking of myself. What good is our friendship if we are both dead?' Judas reasoned.

'Besides, this may prove to be the little shove of reality he needs to wake up from his surreal fascination with death. Perhaps he will arise and become the real Messiah he is supposed to be, the One everyone is waiting for. Then, that would be a win-win for him and me. Then, wouldn't he be grateful to me and depend on me to keep the coffers? He would be happy that I had forced him out of his comfort zone.'

Yeshua's spiritual antennae had gone up, and he could feel the force of an active evil in their midst. Satan's presence was like a dark cloud obscuring the sun, leaving a stench like that of an over-used latrine or a cavern of death in its wake.

He dropped back watchful and silent, searching through the ranks of his disciples until he had come alongside the solitary and sullen Judas. He noticed, out of the corner of his eye, that Judas had given him a long and hard sideways perusal as if he were assessing him. Judas continued down the dark trail of his self-justification and, ultimately, his self-destruction.

Judas didn't acknowledge is presence, or speak a word to him, Yeshua knew Judas' decision had been made.

~ 31 ~

CONFESSIONS

If we confess our sins, he is faithful and just
and will forgive us our sins
and purify us from all unrighteousness.
1 John 1:9

When her house servant announced that Miriam, the Lord's mother, was there and waiting in the courtyard, Mari put down what she was doing and immediately went to her. Miriam had never come to her home. She usually stayed in the city with relatives when she made her festival trips, but Mari had grown close to Miriam while she was in Galilee. As soon as she saw her face, Mari knew she had come with serious intent.

Anxiously, she invited Miriam into her apartment and sent for refreshments.

Once the preliminary hospitalities were out of the way, Mari asked, "You have come because of Yeshua? How is he?"

Miriam looked down at her clasped hands, hating to bear such bad news, "Actually, I have not seen him yet. I am following his instructions from several weeks ago. He was home, and he asked me to come here just prior to Passover to wait for him. He should be arriving soon. I am sure you are expecting him," she tried to smile.

Mari said, "Then, let me have a room opened for you, and let's get you settled in."

After Miriam was settled, she found Mari working in the courtyard. She went to her and asked, "Mari, we have important things to discuss before Yeshua arrives. Are you free to talk now?"

Mari stood and dusted herself off, then went to wash her hands. She led Miriam to a shaded corner of the portico. They took their seats, and she waited for Miriam to share her thoughts.

"Recently, when Yeshua visited us in Capernaum. He shared with me what will take place this Passover."

Mari leaned forward, her eyes narrowed and searching. She frowned with dread, "So, it is time."

Miriam was not really surprised that Mari was aware of what was coming, "What do you know?"

Mari took a deep breath, "What little I know, I have known since Yohannan's death. I had a vision, insight, or intuition... I had dropped a pitcher of wine, and it made quite a mess. We have hardly had any time to talk about it.

"The last time we met, Yeshua came to raise Lazarus from the dead. So...there was little time to talk before he was gone again." She wrapped her arms around her thin shoulders and shuttered.

"From death?" Miriam asked. "What do you mean?"

"Lazarus was dead four days before he came and called him out of the tomb. It was a dreadful event that had our heads spinning."

Miriam remembered his words when they had last spoke. How would either of them witness the violence of the death Yeshua had prophesied?

She said, "I am glad that you know, at least some part of it. We both need to be prepared. I don't know when exactly, but he said it would be during this Passover that he would be crucified. It is almost upon us." Miriam's fist went to her lips as if she wanted to press the words back in.

Mari bowed her head, and tears sprang to her eyes. "He says he was born to be the Lamb of God who will forever remove our sins."

"Yes, I know. He has asked me to be present at the crucifixion for him. He knows this is a hard ask. But, he fears there won't be another friendly face to focus on when the time comes. I am sure there is more to it than this. Still, I promised I would be there for him. But...I don't know if I am strong enough to go it alone."

Mari understood what she was trying to ask. She grasped Miriam's hand tightly in her own, trying to imagine such a feat, "I will go with you. He has called me to stand by his cross." She bowed her head, recalling how horrible her grief had been when Lazarus died. But this she feared would be her undoing. The grief of his suffering death would crush them both.

She opened her mouth, but no words came out. Miriam understood what Mari could not say, and she enfolded her with shared empathy. Together, they swayed back and forth and sobbed, allowing their tears to drip onto one another's shoulders.

Finally, Miriam stepped back to gauge Mari's strength, "Magdalene, I am not asking for me. I wouldn't do that to you, but I am asking for Yeshua's sake. He needs both of us."

Hearing Yeshua's nickname for her 'Magdalene', Mari was reminded that he had given her that name from the very beginning. He had chosen her to stand in the gap and witness his death.

She asked, "Where else could we be, you and I? Yeshua stood in the gap for me when the high priest threatened to throw me over the precipice and stone me to death. I would do anything for Yeshua. Anything."

"Magdalene, together we will be strong for him, you and I. Perhaps some of the other women, too? Do you think?"

Mari nodded her head, making the pain-filled pact.

Miriam said. "This won't be easy."

Mari whispered the prayer, "May God give us both the strength we need to do this."

**

On the afternoon of the ninth day of Nisan, Yeshua returned to Bethany. After hugs and greetings, Lazarus took his seat, anxious to talk with Yeshua about all that had happened since he had raised him.

Lazarus said, "It was so surreal when I heard your voice calling to me, and I awoke in the darkness. It should have been terrifying, but because it was your voice, I was not afraid. I simply got up and traveled towards the light, towards your voice."

Yeshua lips curved into a satisfied smile, "Yes, the light will always lead you to where you need to go. If you will, but follow it." He looked up meaningfully at Lazarus.

"It is good that you went away into the wilderness," Lazarus frowned. "The Pharisees from Jerusalem came every day for a week looking for you and questioning me. It is strange; some of the men had been good friends to me before my resurrection. They kept grilling me over and over about how my death and resurrection transpired. They demanded to know by what dark power you raised me to life. They insinuated all sorts of things. Some said it was a ruse. It was as if suddenly I was an evil person. Even after they heard my answers, they refused to believe me. They were not concerned about me at all. They were hoping I would give them some sort of information to use against you."

"There were plenty of witnesses of what happened," Yeshua said. "Still, this is how it will be. People will hate you because of me. Just remember they hated me first."

"I know that now. Since then, many of my friends and associates have turned on me. They have accused me of all sorts of things. We had to close the gates and post guards because of the death threats. My resurrection has obviously frightened the leaders of Jerusalem."

Yeshua sighed heavily and shook his head. "It is me they want, not you. Soon, they will forget about you when I am found on the temple grounds. Later on, they will turn their focus on you and the others. Be ready for that."

"Abba says everyone is watching for you and asking, 'Isn't he coming to the Passover?' They are eager to find you. The city is already overflowing with people, and now the word is filling the streets that you have raised a man to life after four days."

"People fear death."

"Yes, but they fear that you have brought me back to life perhaps more. It may cost you your life. I am sorry, Lord." Lazarus said with deep remorse.

Yeshua laid his hand on Lazarus' shoulder. Eye to eye, Lazarus saw the weight of Yeshua's sorrow, "It is time for the Son of Man to be raised up before the people. You are no more guilty than all the others I will die for. You simply played a needed role in a much larger and very ancient story. You are not alone in this. There are more people than you can imagine who have also played their parts in the events of these days."

"I am so sorry that I did not go with you much earlier when you first asked me to go. I know I have been a disappointment to you. I have been selfish and weak..." Lazarus didn't understand why Yeshua had even bothered with him since he had forsaken the chance to be his disciple so he could conduct business and play politics. Yet here he was, still his friend, and he had brought him back from the dead.

"Lazarus, yesterday is past. Today, you must do your best, and tomorrow will continue to challenge you. I forgive you that you did not follow me yesterday. Be my disciple today, and in the days ahead, follow me," he said without bitterness.

"But you have said you will be lifted up this Pesach, so how can I follow you? Do you want me to follow you with my own cross?" Lazarus asked, all too familiar with crucifixions. Even on that day, Roman crosses surrounded the city.

"Will you?" Yeshua pointedly asked him.

Lazarus looked down, pained and confused, "If that is what you wish."

A moan escaped him. Yeshua wished he could promise a different outcome, but he could not. "Let us just worry about this moment. Tomorrow will have troubles enough as it is."

Lazarus gave him a tremulous smile, "I will try to do that, but can you?"

Yeshua pulled some dates and nuts from the dish before him and filled his mouth, knowing he needed to eat and be strong for the days ahead. He gave a brief nod.

After an awkward silence, Lazarus changed the subject, "The festival will formally begin tomorrow. It is the tenth day of Nisan. Bethlehem's lambs are encamped just outside the city, being readied for tomorrow's markets along the road to the sheep gate. The streets will be clogged with the shepherds and their flocks so that people may purchase and register their offerings."

Yeshua stared at his second handful of nuts, "Yes, 'The Lamb' is standing outside the gate. Tomorrow it will all begin."

**

When Mari heard Yeshua had arrived, she did not come out to greet him straightway. Instead, she went to observe him talking with her brother from an upstairs alcove. She freely took this opportunity to look upon the one she loved. She pressed the sight of him into her heart like a flower set to dry. So that later, she could replay this memory of him on a later date, and enjoy the lingering fragrance of his beauty.

Truthfully, Mari still felt awkward and embarrassed concerning her previous actions when he had raised Lazarus. His sudden departure afterward had left no time to settle things between them. She watched, waiting for his conversation with Lazarus to end. She needed to beg him for his forgiveness. However, Lazarus' conversation ran lengthy. She could see he was troubled by Lazarus' words. No doubt it had to do with the death threats Lazarus had received. And for what reason? Because he had been raised to life?

Since Lazarus' illness, death, and resurrection, Mari's thoughts and emotions had been tossed upon a sea of confusion and regret, 'How could I have ever doubted him? He has never let me down. He must think me pitifully weak. How was I so easily fooled into thinking he did not care about me or my family? Even so, why didn't he bother to send me word or explain his delay?'

But as she asked this question, the answer jolted her, 'Because he shouldn't need to.'

After days of self-recriminations and wrestling with herself, Mari realized that raising Lazarus to life would catapult Yeshua to the cross.

'Had he known?' She closed her eyes, 'Of course he did.'

Now, the one he teasingly called "the Watch Tower" felt incredibly small and unworthy. She was ashamed of her doubts, her anger towards him, and her loss of faith. Now she understood that by her actions, her begging at his feet and demanding a miracle, she had brought disaster upon him. Her heart felt sick with this knowledge. Of course, Lazarus would not be with them now had Yeshua *not* raised him from death. But now she could see, he would give his life in the place of Lazarus.

While watching him, she acknowledged her love for him. Through it all, she had been like his sister, mother, aunt, student, or friend to him. But her love for him was no secret. She wore it on her sleeve. Yeshua had brought her heart to life, connecting her to him with more intimacy than she had ever known with anyone else. She couldn't imagine her life without him. Although Mari had long suspected Yeshua would face a violent death, now it was utterly unthinkable.

She had promised Miriam, but even more, she had promised Yeshua.

Even from her distanced perch, she saw the sadness in his soulful eyes. The plains of his face appeared gaunt and colorless despite his sun-darkened skin. He had lost weight. His strong shoulders seemed hunched as if he were carrying the weight of the world. Her heart ached for him.

She thought, 'Though he looks ordinary and weak, I know better. I have seen his miracles firsthand, I have heard Miriam's stories surrounding his birth, and I have read the prophecies. I have sat under his teachings and walked with him. I know that the glory of God lives within him. He is the Son of God, the redeemer of Israel and the world. Who am I to have gained such wealth? I am but a sinful and foolish woman.'

Mari screwed up her courage. She would go to him and admit her faults, ask for his forgiveness, and set their relationship right once again. Only then could she find peace. She knew Yeshua would forgive her for doubting him when Lazarus grew sick and died. He had never failed to forgive an earnest request.

She went downstairs and picked up a servant's pitcher. She went out to the table to refill his cup. His face lit up the moment he saw her. She blushed with pleasure and felt encouraged. She found her place at his feet, ready to make her confession. Lazarus saw Mari had business to discuss, so he excused himself to go and talk with the other disciples.

"I have to make my confession," Mari said plainly.

Yeshua leaned forward to hear them, "I am listening."

She recounted all of her overwhelming thoughts and her crazy emotions over the last few weeks. She confessed her doubts, her anger, and her lack of faith. He listened, allowing her to get all of her thoughts poured out before him.

"I, too, am sorry that you have been so distressed. I felt your pain even from a distance. I was praying for you. What happened here with Lazarus was necessary for what is to come in Jerusalem, for Lazarus, and for you."

Her brows drew together as she considered his meaning.

"What have you learned?" he asked her. "Where are your emotions now?"

She reached out and took his hand, examining its size and strength. She ran her fingers over the veins, sinew, and bones of his strong hand. She looked up at his face, "That you are trustworthy and true, even when I do not see you, even when you are not here in the flesh, even when you have not yet responded, you are still there, and you have not deserted me. And I have learned that only you can save us from death."

He smiled a grateful smile and whispered a fierce command, "Remember these things in the days ahead, Magdalene."

She smiled at his use of her nickname, feeling all had been set right between them. Suddenly, a breeze tossed her head covering away like the weight of her guilt. The sun shone down warmly upon her head, and for the first time, Mari actually realized it was spring. She took a deep breath, inhaling the sweet scent of jasmine.

She looked up at Yeshua with total adoration and thought, 'There has to be some fitting way to show my love for him.'

Then it came to her. She knew just what she would do.

~ 32 ~

CHOOSING THE LAMB

...on the tenth day of [the first month]
each man is to take a lamb for his family,
one for each household.
Exodus 12:2

As the pilgrims gathered in the city of Jerusalem, only one name was on everyone's lips: Yeshua of Nazareth. The people from Jerusalem, who had seen him raise Lazarus from the dead, could not stop speaking of it, "One minute, we were overcome with the stench of death. The next minute, the stench was gone, and Lazarus was stumbling out of the grave, still wearing his grave clothes! Surely, this is the sign we have all been waiting for. The Messiah! He is here."

People were watching for him, not wanting to miss this momentous occasion of proclaiming and celebrating Israel's saving King.

"Where is he?" They whispered behind their hands, "Surely he will come for the Passover."

Word had spread that he would come from the Mount of Olives. That day, the masses went out to line the road and wait for his appearance. The crowd kept building, and they waited. As the shadows began to lengthen, they wondered, "Will he not appear? Were the messengers wrong?"

**

Midday, Yeshua sent Philip and Andrew into the village to search for a young donkey. Just as he had indicated, they found a donkey and a younger colt standing together. They moved to untie the tethered animals.

A man rushed out to challenge them, "Hey, what are you doing with my donkeys?"

They stepped back and calmly told the man what Yeshua had told them to say, "The Lord has need of them." They blinked innocently at the man, waiting for his reply.

A strange expression appeared on the man's face as if he was remembering something that surprised him.

He whispered to himself, "This morning, I did ask God to give me some way to serve him."

The disciples waited until the man nodded, "Yes, yes, then, you may take them. But I must warn you, the colt has never been ridden, though we have been working with him. And he still resists separation from his mother, so you must take them both."

The disciples sighed with relief, "Of course, we will take care of them and return them when the Lord is finished with them."

The man waved them off but quickly finished his current task. He was unsure of why he felt such a hurry.

**

When the disciples returned to the Lord with the animals, he smiled and came to meet them. He bent to touch the colt's leg joints, then straightened, satisfied. "Yes, you will be able to do it."

He looked soothingly into the face of the young jack, saying, "I will need you to be strong for me today my friend. I have an important job for you. Can you do that?"

The donkey's ears leaned toward his voice, listening intently. His head bobbed, and he stepped forward to nuzzle Yeshua. They gazed into one another's eyes as if they were speaking.

Then, Yeshua reached out to rub the face of the mother as well, "And what about you?"

The mare stepped closer, her head beside her colt.

He laughed again, "Okay then! This will require both of you."

Philip laid Yeshua's cloak over the back of the colt, and with a slight boost, he was gently seated. The jack stumbled awkwardly sideways, unaccustomed to this heavier weight.

Yeshua's feet dangled loosely, not so far from the ground. He patted the jack, "You can do this. We will take it slow," he said reassuringly, and the colt's ears twitched.

"Let's go, Philip; lead the mare. We will follow by her side."

As they rode through the town, a crowd began to gather. They recognized the man who had raised Lazarus. They understood the significance of this moment. They ran to grab palm fronds to wave around him, and people cast their cloaks on the ground before him to indicate their support, submission, and reverent respect. They were filled with the excitement of the Messianic procession.

"The Rabbi is openly declaring he is the rightful king!"

Recalling the prophecy of Zechariah, some took up the shout, "See your king comes to you, gentle and riding on a donkey, on a colt, the foal of a donkey."

The man who owned the two donkeys looked up with surprise to see his animals were playing a part in this historical moment. He dropped his tools and ran to join in, walking along with the crowd. He was proud that his donkeys were bearing the promised king. As he went, Yeshua was met by the masses waiting on the decline below, shouting their praise and waving their branches to cheers of excitement.

The crowd sang a Hallel, a song of salvation, Psalm 118, that had been sung at every Passover since the people began to travel up to the house of the LORD.

'Let shouts of joy and victory resound
in the tents of the righteous:
"The Lord's right hand has done mighty things!
The Lord's right hand is lifted high;

the Lord's right hand has done mighty things!"
I will not die but live,
and I will proclaim what the Lord has done.
The Lord has chastened me severely,
but he has not given me over to death.
Open for me the gates of the righteous;
I will enter and give thanks to the Lord.
This is the gate of the Lord
through which the righteous may enter.
I will give you thanks, for you answered me;
you have become my salvation.
The stone the builders rejected
has become the cornerstone;
the Lord has done this,
and it is marvelous in our eyes.
The Lord has done it this very day;
let us rejoice today and be glad.
Lord, save us!
Lord, grant us success!
Blessed is he who comes in the name of the Lord.
Hosanna! Blessed is the King of Israel!
Hosanna to the Son of David!

Yeshua's eyes burned, and hot and glistening tears tracked down his face into his beard upon hearing these particular words proclaiming him as the LORD's Anointed, the King of Salvation. They sang this song and called out with shouts. The people were actually begging him to see his work of salvation through to completion. He looked around at all the excited faces, knowing that everyone who calls upon the name of the LORD will be saved.

His disciples were jubilant, caught up with the excitement of the crowd. They were so proud that he was their Rabbi—their Lord and Master.

Even Judas thought, 'Perhaps things will work out after all.'

The road curved, and there before his eyes stretched the panorama of the whole city of Jerusalem, 'the City of God's Peace.'

"But where, where is your peace?" Yeshua whispered. "If only you would hear my words and not harden your hearts. Oh Jerusalem, Jerusalem, you who kill the prophets and stone those my Father has sent to you, how many times have I longed to gather your children to myself, just as a hen gathers her chicks under her wings, but you were not willing!"

Matthew heard his murmured words and took note of his tears and sorrowful frustration.

They came to the second dip toward the valley and the gate. The crowd of people swelled, ready and waiting for him to appear. The singing and shouting took on a life of its own. The path was barely passable. Yeshua leaned down to whisper into the ear of the young donkey prodding slowly behind his mother. His muzzle was touching her haunch. He was skittish and alert.

**

The day had been abnormally slow. Caiaphas wondered, 'Where are the people?'

Usually, by now, the road to the Sheep Gate was clogged with people eager to present and register their lamb as their choice. Having registered, they would be provided a reservation for slaughter on the fifth day. But today, the sheep gate was eerily quiet, barely a trickle.

Finally, he ascended the tower to the pinnacle of the temple—to survey the roadways for blockades. Whenever he stood on this spot, he always enjoyed a brief moment of exaltation, thinking, "THIS is my temple. I rule this temple and city." He looked around as if he, a mere man, could rule this place."

Remembering why he was there, he cut short his moment of self-gratification. He looked toward the sheep gate, searching for the pilgrims with their lambs, but nothing. He began to look in all directions. He clucked his tongue, "Where are they? Well, maybe it simply means more men and money tomorrow." He wondered if perhaps the Roman troops were blocking the way, but he saw nothing, and that made no sense. They used the entrance gate designated for them.

He looked towards the Antonia Fortress that housed the majority of the Roman-Syrian Legion during the Passover. But judging by the large number of Roman standards displayed in front, it appeared most of the troops were in. He thought, "Surely they have already arrived."

He glanced toward the Fish Gate coming from Caesarea and Shechem. There, he saw an elite garrison of legionaries approaching from Caesarea, "Ah, yes! Pontius Pilate, that Roman pig, is sitting his stallion like a king at the helm." The man rankled Caiaphas. "Still, it does not appear that the Romans have withheld the people."

He looked toward the Gennath Gate, pretty much empty. 'No surprise. Herod's retinue means little to the people, but he can be invaluable at times.' Looking towards Herod's diminutive palace, he saw Herod's guards were already at their post. The large torches around the estate were already lit well before evening fell. Clearly, Herod was arriving shortly. He scanned past his own large home and through the Sanhedrin quarter. Nothing amiss there.

Hinnom wasn't worth a glance. A dense haze lay over the burning refuse. He scanned past the Mount of Offense and the Kidron Valley, but nothing. He was about to turn back towards the steps, but a flash of an undulating movement caught the corner of his eye.

"There!"

A large mass of people lined the small road descending from the Mount of Olives. It was jammed with people lining each side of the road, surging around and behind someone.

He spoke an explicative, then shouted to himself, "Who-What is that?" He peered closely, squinting his weakened eyes to make it out.

'It is a man... riding? But riding what?' The man on a small donkey was approaching the Eastern Gate. He strained his ears to listen to the distant hum of excitement.

"Is that singing or shouting?"

He saw the people waving their arms and holding palm fronds, the national sign of Israel's government. This appeared to be an all-out rebellion against Rome and Caesar.

He all but stopped breathing in his shock, "Who would be so absurd as to do something like this on this of all days?" He swallowed hard, considering the consequences of such an action. His eyes narrowed dangerously.

"It can only be that Nazarene. This is exactly what I warned everyone about!"

It was undignified to run, but he could ill afford to wait a moment. Down the steps, he hurried, tossing out a litany of commands to the guards below. They scattered at his command to do his bidding.

**

When they were almost to the bottom of the Mount and approaching the gate, Yeshua looked up to find malevolent eyes upon him, looking down from the same pinnacle where Satan had tried to tempt him to prove himself. There, he saw a lone figure standing and watching. Even from a distance, he recognized the distinctive official garments of the High Priest, 'Caiaphas.'

During his last two festivals, Caiaphas remained careful to keep a measured distance from him and to avoid any public confrontations.

Yeshua spoke into the void between them, "There you are, just as you were meant to be."

A few moments later, a large group of Pharisees converged on the path to block the roadway, looking like a gathering of crows. As they hurried towards him, their billowing sleeves looked like black wings. They stood directly in the path of the procession despite all the songs and celebrations.

Shouts rang out around them, "Blessed is the king who comes in the name of the Lord!" and "Peace in heaven and glory in the highest!"

The Pharisees covered their ears with pained expressions as if the words would injure them.

"Teacher, rebuke your disciples!" they called out to him.

Yeshua did not halt his approach but kept going. All the while, they shouted their rebukes. When they saw he was not stopping, they all slid to his left while the animals advanced. When Yeshua came beside them, he leaned towards the huddle of men, his voice caught and cracked in his throat, his tears burned, his eyes filled with sorrow too deep for words, "I tell you the truth, if these people were to keep quiet, the very stones of this mountain would cry out."

The Pharisees covered their ears and spit on the ground, refusing to look upon him.

He halted the colt so he could speak to them. His words were hot and salty, "If you, especially you, had only known on this day what would bring you peace—instead now it is hidden from your eyes."

"What are you speaking about?" They shouted. "We see perfectly what you are doing!"

He told them, "The days will come upon you when your enemies will build an embankment against you and encircle this place. They will hem you in on every side.They will dash you to the ground from these very walls, you and your children who dwell within. I am telling you that your enemies will not leave one stone upon another *because* you did not recognize the time of God coming to you."

He motioned to his men to continue.

The Pharisees remained suddenly rooted in confusion and morbid fear. Yet, they rejected every word he had said.

The procession came to the entrance of the Golden Gate. Yeshua slid off the colt to many cheers. Before he turned towards the temple, he leaned in close to the colt he had just ridden. Taking two apples out of his satchel, he offered an apple to each animal. He leaned close to murmur words of praise to the colt and to rub the length of his nose. His ears pitched forward to listen to every word,

"You did well, my young friend. You delivered me right to the gate just as you were meant to do." He gave a quick scratch behind the ears of both animals.

Just then, their owner stepped forward from out of the crowd. "I will take care of them, Lord," the man said with a bow.

Yeshua nodded his head and touched his heart.

Then he reached out and touched the man with a blessing. "See? You have fulfilled your obligation to God today."

The man's mouth dropped open in wonder.

Yeshua turned towards the gateway of the Temple. With only Yohan at his side, they entered. He stepped over the portal and disappeared against the wall to his right. He stood there facing the sheep gate to watch each sheep led forth to be given a cursory glance and marked for sacrifice. The people were given a number and a time to return to have each sheep inspected for unnoticed flaws. A good number of sheep would be found lacking, replacement sheep would be offered, and the prices would be haggled to receive an acceptable lamb.

As he waited, many of the people who had been a part of the procession streamed in to fill the courts, looking around to find him. They had fully expected to find Yeshua proclaiming himself as the Messiah before the priest.

Instead, he was hidden from them as they walked right past him without a second glance.

When the crowd stopped coursing into the inner courts, his men realized that they had been holding their breath and shifting on their feet. They, too, had thought Yeshua would take some action. Before they could utter a word, a trumpet sounded. Suddenly, Yeshua joined with Yohan and the other men. He said, "It is done; the Lamb has been chosen."

They looked confused. "What do you mean?"

"It means we did what we came here to do for today. Let's go. We will be back early tomorrow." And with that, he turned to leave. Yohan hurried along beside Yeshua, thinking about what he had just witnessed. The other disciples, as they often did, shrugged. They were content that there had been no trouble that day. No one asked any questions. They did not want to look ignorant of the things that perhaps they should have known.

Once they had descended the temple steps, they breathed a collective sigh of relief. For as they had drawn closer and closer to the city gate, the air had become supercharged. They had worried about the confrontation that was sure to come.

~ 33 ~

A LONG DAY

"At that time, Michael,
the great prince who protects your people, will arise.
There will be a time of distress such as has not happened
from the beginning of nations until then.
But at that time, your people—everyone
whose name is found written in the book—will be delivered.
Multitudes who sleep in the dust of the earth will awake:
Some to everlasting life,
others to shame and everlasting contempt.
Those who are wise will shine
like the brightness of the heavens,
and those who lead many to righteousness,
will be like the stars forever and ever.
Daniel 12:1-4

The last moments of Yeshua's life were now quickly fleeting. The anxiety was already building like a pressure in his chest, so bad at times that he could hardly breathe. The horrors of what lay ahead taunted him. Words of the law and the prophets flowed through his thoughts, instructing him. Every illness or agony he had healed would come upon him. When the terror seized him, his hands trembled, his legs grew weak, and his stomach cramped.

Then, his Father's words would come to calm him once again. He fought not to show his ambivalence or fear for the sake of those who followed him. They, too, would face the same trials in their lives, and they would need the strength of his conviction to do what they had to do.

An inward voice kept repeating, "Yeshua, be strong and courageous. Do not be afraid. You are the promise of my salvation, and I will be with you."

Even so, he did not feel at all strong, and his Father's presence seemed to be distanced as if this was something he must do on his own.

He found a precious few moments of sleep, but only after hours of prayers. Every night, he awoke to the darkness with a start. His first waking thought was of the coming cross, of death, of the tomb, leaving his cheeks wet from his tears.

This morning, he'd awoke after a heart-wrenching dream about Rock.

In his dream, Simon was trembling in fear and saying repeatedly, "I don't even know that man." Would not even Simon stand by him? The stench of evil remained near him. He knew his foe was constantly watching him and was at work underfoot.

Satan mocked him, "Stand if you must. But who will you save out of all of this pain and effort? Look at them. They are just weak-willed men steeped in selfishness. They belong to me, loyal in their sin. They will never persevere to serve you after all is said and done."

He battled a frightening sense of desolation but continuously pushed it away, not allowing those negative thoughts to stay with him.

His Father's words became his mantra, "Only you can save them."

Looking around in the darkness, he saw the others were sleeping deeply and peacefully, unaware of the evil stalking them. For a second, he envied their lack of knowledge. He got up and went outside to stretch his tense and aching limbs and clear his pounding head. He found a private spot and sat down to pray. Eventually, as he prayed, his hands stopped shaking. He began to pray for his disciples, especially Simon, "Father, I have to believe you will help them to stand. After all, you have given them to me. Together, we can strengthen them to overcome all the wiles of the evil one by the power of the Holy Spirit. After Satan has done his worst to them, help them to stand, to never give up on what you have prepared for them."

He prayed for some time, ending with the needed provisions for this day. On this day of the Festival, the priests would do their detailed examination of each chosen lamb and scrutinize them for any imperfection.

"Father, give me your wisdom and words," he prayed. "Do not let your chosen one be put to shame."

**

The horizon had barely tinted pink before he and his disciples were making their way to Jerusalem. Today would be a day of confrontation. They had only grabbed a few handfuls of nuts before setting out, planning to get food in Jerusalem. But as they traveled, Yeshua began to feel inordinately hungry. His restless night was catching up with him. His body was demanding nourishment.

He saw a fig tree ahead full of greenery. He approached it wistfully, searching for edible fruit. But it was not the time for figs; Jerusalem was not Jericho. He gave a huff of frustration as he stared into the tree.

"So, you simply refuse to bear me fruit!" He accused the tree. "Okay then, may no one ever eat fruit from you again."

The disciples were surprised to hear his uncharacteristically harsh words over the tree. The curse sounded ominous on his lips. He was clearly upset. Rock remembered another time in Galilee when Yeshua had told them a parable about about another fig tree. It had been planted in the vineyard three years earlier, but when no sign of fruit had been found on it, and the owner had decided to cut it down. But his servant begged for yet one more year, saying,

"If there is still no fruit, then I will cut it down." He wondered now if the two stories might be related.

The fig tree had long been the symbol of Israel. By law, any fruit that grew on a tree under the age of three was not to be consumed. When it bore fruit in its fourth year, no one was allowed to eat of the fruit of the tree because that year's crop was holy unto the LORD. Had this tree refused to produce fruit for the LORD? No, it was simply not the season for this tree to produce its fruit. Still, Yeshua had condemned the tree. Was this a sign that Jerusalem was unwilling to bear any fruit to the Lord because it was not yet its season, and his curse was a sign of the things yet to come? He wanted to ask the Lord, but he could see he looked stressed, so he held his question.

In Jerusalem, Yeshua walked with purposeful determination to the temple—the business of sheep examination and haggling was underway. Nothing had changed from the Passover three years earlier when he had come to prophesy to the religious leaders. Once again, there were all kinds of animals defecating in the temple courts, and monies being exchanged. Expecting this, Yeshua pulled the homemade whip from his satchel. Once again, he put to driving the out livestock and freeing birds from their cages. He drove the money changers out of the temple grounds. One man reached out to take his money, and Yeshua struck his hand, not allowing anyone to take the money with them.

"Why do you do this thing?" He asked them. "Do you not understand the scripture that says, 'My house will be called a house of prayer.' You have turned it into a den of robbers!"

A delegation of the chief priests, teachers of the law, and elders appeared quickly. They had been waiting for his arrival, ready to question him.

"By what authority are you doing this?"

Yeshua approached the man, and everyone grew silent so they could hear.

"That is a good question, but first, I will ask you a question. Tell me: Yohannan bar Zachariah's baptism—was it from heaven or of human origin?"

The delegation turned to one another, discussing Yohannan in hushed whispers.

One priest said, "If we say, 'From heaven,' he will ask, 'Why didn't you believe him?'"

Another said, "But if we say, 'Of human origin,' all of the people will stone us because they are persuaded that the Baptizer was a prophet."

His question left them cornered and defeated. The delegation turned back to him and answered, "We don't know where it was from."

Yeshua saw their collusion and cowardice. "Neither will I *tell you* by what authority I am doing these things."

The men looked desperately to one another, seeing that already their inquisition was falling apart; how quickly the table had been turned against them.

Yeshua turned to the gathered people who had witnessed his exchange, and he began to speak a parable to them, "A man planted a vineyard. But then, he rented it to some farmers and went away for a long time. When the time for harvest had come, he sent his servant to the tenants so they would give him some of the fruit of the vineyard."

His eyes bore into the religious delegation, "But the tenants beat him and sent him away empty-handed."

He turned back towards the people, "He sent another servant, but that one also they beat and treated shamefully and sent away empty-handed. He sent still a third, and they wounded him and threw him out."

The people shook their heads to show their disapproval.

He spun on his feet, holding up his finger to make his point, "Finally, the owner of the vineyard said, 'What shall I do?' I know I will send my son, whom I love; perhaps they will respect him.'"

He turned back towards the delegation, "But when the tenants saw the son, they talked the matter over. 'This is the heir,' they said. 'Let's kill him, and his inheritance will be ours.'

"Hence, they threw him out of the vineyard and killed him."

Yeshua walked in a wide circle before the gathering of people like an attorney preparing for his closing argument before a court gallery. He paused to look each listener briefly in the eye, "So, I ask you...What then will the owner of the vineyard do to these tenants?"

He let the question hang in the air, demanding the appropriate sentence of justice.

He turned towards the delegation and held out his hands, "Anyone?"

But every person remained silent; no one said anything because they feared God's justice would fall on them.

His voice became a low growl, "I will tell you...The owner will come and kill those tenants. He will give their vineyard to others."

When the people heard this verdict, they were alarmed, saying, "God forbid!" For they all clearly understood he was speaking of Jerusalem.

Yeshua turned to face the delegation; his eyes flashed like lightning from one face to the other. He posed them another question, "You are scholars, now tell me, what is the meaning of the Hallel psalm sang at Passover, which says, '"The stone the builders rejected has become the cornerstone."'

He saw in their eyes that they understood he was questioning the prophetic song about God's salvation and the Messiah. They did not answer but tilted their chins with a surly sneer.

Yeshua continued, "Everyone who falls on that stone may be broken, but anyone on whom that stone falls will be crushed."

The delegation turned and walked away, licking their wounds from his encounter, "He has made us look like buffoons in front of the people! We cannot let him get away with this!" They imagined his murder as if they had not heard his parable of warning at all.

They left eager to find another way to arrest him. But they had to be shrewd because it seemed that all of Jerusalem hung on his every word.

Caiaphas called up his second team to send them out as spies amongst the common people. Yeshua went to find a quiet corner inside the women's court. Again, a large crowd of both men and women gathered around him. The spies dispersed themselves amongst the crowd, hoping to catch Jesus in something he said. Their hands were itching to deliver him over to the governor.

One spoke beguilingly to Yeshua, but his smile was coy, "Teacher, we know that you speak and teach what is right. You show no partiality. You teach the way of God in accordance with the truth." Yeshua never trusted flattery. Solomon wrote, 'Flattering tongues spread nets for the feet.'

Earnestly, the beguiler asked him a loaded question, one meant to divid the people from him, "Is it right for us to pay taxes to Caesar or not?"

Yeshua looked at the finely dressed man assessing him, he said. "Show me a denarius."

Eager for the capture, the man produced a variety of coins from his money bag and quickly plucked out a denarius, handing it to Yeshua.

Yeshua stepped back as if it were a thing of offense and shook his hand at the coin as if at a disgusting thing. His reaction reminded the people of the injunction that there were to be no unclean pagan monies within the temple grounds. Too late, the man realized his error. But Yeshua motioned to the embarrassed man holding the coin, "Whose image and inscription are on it? Would you show the people?" The humiliated man held up the coin.

"Caesar's," the people replied in unison.

He turned back to the man with a grim shrug, "So, I say to you, give back to Caesar what is Caesar's, and to God what is God's."

Astonished by his easy answer, the man slowly dropped his coin back into his money bag. Feeling like a chump, he moved to the back of the crowd. Caiaphas' consortium had been so sure that this question would put Yeshua away. Instead, the man had looked like the lawbreaker and Yeshua, like the wise and benevolent holy man. The others who had come with him sank back into the crowd, afraid to open their mouth against him.

**

All afternoon, in the women's court, Yeshua had been facing the offering boxes that lined the wall. Throughout the course of the day, the trumpets had been sounding as large offerings were placed into the boxes. There were thirteen boxes, each with designations. Some were the required yearly temple tax, some were sin offerings or guilt offerings, but the rarest of all were the benevolent or fellowship offerings, which were not required.

One poorly dressed elderly woman visited the mandatory boxes to give her temple tax and sin offering, but she continued to the fellowship/benevolence box with the little she had left. Yeshua could tell the woman was very poor. Yet, she walked eagerly to the box with a smile. He had not seen such a cheerful giver the whole day. He stopped teaching to come his feet watching the woman empty her money bag of its remaining contents. Two very small common copper mites fell into her hand, and with an expression of pure delight, she dropped them into the fluted opening above the box. But, because her offering was so small, the trumpet did not sound. She was so pleased in her giving that she had not even noticed; when she turned from the box, she was beaming. She glanced up to see Yeshua was watching her. Her eyes dropped meekly, but she glanced back up in time to see his approval. Her heart swelled, and she clasped her hands to her heart. He smiled and nodded.

Before she had completely left the court, Yeshua drew his men's attention to her.

"Look at that woman. Did you see what she did?" he asked them. "She has given more than anyone else."

They watched her retreating form with only a mild interest.

"She doesn't look particularly wealthy," Judas observed.

"Oh! But don't you see it? She is! She is rich beyond measure with a treasure you cannot see. Look at all of these other people—they have given their gifts out of obligation. Others have given their gifts of goodwill, but they were out of their wealth. This woman, however, voluntarily gave a fellowship offering out of her poverty, giving all she had. She emptied her money bag into the keep, and she rejoiced to do it!" His face glowed with pleasure.

They were incredulous that he could rejoice over such a small sacrifice from such an old and impoverished woman. No one else would have even noticed. If they had, they would have shaken their head to scoff at her offering. But here was the Lord, enlivened by it in a way that he could hardly explain.

"She trusts the Father with her life to give all she has, every last drop. So, I can, too. I can, too!"

They shook their head, not understanding what he was trying to say.

**

That evening, while leaving the temple gates behind, Yeshua felt weighted down with exhaustion; his steps were lagging.

His men, however, were in jovial spirits, glad for all of Yeshua's successes during the trials of the day. They were proud that he was their Rabbi. He had put all the scholars to shame. As it happened each time they left the temple, the disciples looked around with admiration at its impressive structure.

Yohan asked, "You indicated this would all be destroyed. When will this happen?"

The others heard his question and moved in closer to hear his answer, "Yes, teacher, what will be the sign of when this will take place?"

He replied: "Watch out that you are not deceived. For many will come in my name, claiming to be me and saying, 'The time is near.' Do not follow them. No one knows the day or the hour, not even me. You will hear of wars and uprisings, but do not be frightened. These things must happen first. Even then, the end will not come right away. Many things will come to pass. Nation will rise against nation and kingdom against kingdom. There will be great earthquakes, famines, and pestilences in various places, and fearful events and great signs from heaven when the end is near."

He paused in the path and turned to them all, "But before all this happens, they will seize you and persecute you. They will hand you over to synagogues and put you in prison, and you will be brought before kings and governors, and all on account of my name.Through it all, you will bear testimony to me. You must make up your mind not to worry beforehand about how you will defend yourselves."

He turned and began to walk once again, giving time for his words to soak in. They followed, suddenly solemn.

"When you are confronted like I was today, I will give you words and wisdom that none of your adversaries will be able to resist or contradict. You will not be alone; I will be with you. Make no mistake; you will be betrayed by even your own parents, brothers, sisters, relatives, and friends. They will cut you off. They will put some of you to death. Everyone will hate you because of me. Despite these conflicts, not a hair on your head will perish. Stand firm, and you will obtain life."

"So, how will Jerusalem fall?" Rock asked, wondering if they were to have a hand in that.

"When you see Jerusalem being surrounded by armies, you will know that its desolation is near. Those who are in Judea must flee to the mountains, those in the city must get out, and those who dwell in the country must not enter the city. For this time of punishment must be fulfilled just as it has been written. How dreadful it will be in those days for the young women! Such distress. This city will be no more."

"A strong sword will come against this land, and some will be taken as prisoners and scattered amongst the nations." He stopped and looked back towards the city, foreseeing a desolate, fallen city there and, eventually, the vision of another/gentile temple to a different god. He looked back to his men and said, "Jerusalem will be trampled on by the Gentiles until the time of the Gentiles is fulfilled."

"Time of the Gentiles?" Rock asked with a controlled outrage.

"Yes, the time of the Gentiles approaches."

Everyone was quiet, trying to take this all in, trying to understand. There would be no overthrowing of the Roman government...not for a long time. Then what could they hope for? What were they striving towards? As they approached the crest of the Mount of Olives, they came upon the fig tree Yeshua had rebuked that morning. Now, it hung limply. It's beautiful, vibrant green leaves were withered and scattered across the ground.

"Look! Rabbi, the tree you cursed has lost its leaves in one day."

"What? Did you doubt it?" Yeshua asked. "Strengthen your belief. When you ask me, I will do whatever you ask. You can tell this tree to be moved, and it will be moved. You can tell that mountain to be thrown into the sea, and it will be done for you."

They took a moment of rest to sit upon a low-lying wall. They watched with fascination as the lights were being lit against a darkening periwinkle sky. The distant torches glittered like diamonds; their fire was dancing.

Looking down upon the city, it was as if Yeshua saw the whole of the earth at the same time. He said, "Then when the end comes, there will be signs in the sun, moon, and stars. Throughout the earth, nations will be in anguish. Everyone will be perplexed by the roaring and tossing of the sea." He paused, drawing a heavy breath, "So much will be going on that people will faint from terror, apprehensive of what is coming upon the world, for the heavenly bodies will be shaken."

His men swallowed hard at such words, wondering, 'What hope can there possibly be for humankind? Perhaps we don't really want to know.'

But Yeshua was looking into the future, prophesying, and no one spoke but him, "Then, at that time, the nations will see the Son of Man coming in a cloud—with power and great glory."

He spoke into the void as if he was talking to the people of the future—to people living throughout the earth, throughout all space and time, "When these things begin to take place, stand up and lift your heads to the heavens because your redemption is drawing near."

He motioned to the tree that he had cursed: "Take a fig tree or any of the trees. When they sprout leaves, you know that summer is near. Just so, when you see these things happening, you will know that the kingdom of God is near. Truly, I tell you, this generation will certainly not pass away until all these things have happened. So be careful how you live. Don't be weighed down with worry or distracted by drunkenness. You will be caught like a mouse in a trap. For these things will come upon all who live throughout the face of the whole earth."

Yeshua seemed to return to the present, looking around the broad circle of men, his eyes bearing a mixture of sorrow and joy at this vision. "Always be ready and watchful and filled with prayer so you may be able to escape all that will soon begin to happen. Most of all, pray that you may be able to stand before the Son of Man when this time comes."

He looked back toward Jerusalem once more. Then said, "But come now, it has been a long day. It is time to rest, eat and sleep." He stood to climb the rest of the way towards the Bethany compound.

~ 34 ~

DAY OF WOES

For the LORD gives wisdom;
From his mouth comes knowledge and understanding.
The LORD is a shield to those whose walk is blameless,
For he guards the course of the just...
For wisdom will enter your heart,
And knowledge will be pleasant to your soul...
Wisdom will save you from the ways of wicked men,
Whose words are perverse,
Who have left the straight paths to walk in dark ways,
Who delight in doing wrong,
And rejoice in the perverseness of evil,
Whose paths are crooked
and who are devious in their ways.
Proverbs 2:6-15

Again, Yeshua entered the temple the next day, knowing the religious leaders would be waiting for him with their arsenal reloaded. He had been teaching only a short time when some of the Sadducees—who say there is no resurrection, came to pose their first question.

"Teacher," they postured, "Moses wrote for us that if a man's brother dies and leaves a wife but no children, the brother must marry the widow and bring forth an offspring for his brother.

"There were seven brothers. The first one married a woman, and he died childless.So the second brother married her next, but he died. So, the third brother married her. In the same way, all seven brothers died. None left her with any children. Then, finally, the woman died too.

"Now then, at the resurrection, whose wife will she be, since all seven were married to her?"

He stared at them long enough to let everyone know how foolish their question truly was. Everyone knew they held no belief in the resurrection. In fact, the Sadducees have always insisted that people died and were no more. Only now, after Lazarus' resurrection, were they taking this tact.

Yeshua shook his head at their ignorance and thinly veiled assault, "The people of *this age* marry and are given in marriage. But those who are considered worthy of taking part in the age to come and in the resurrection from the dead will neither marry nor be given in marriage.Neither can they any longer die, for they have become as the angels. The children of the resurrection are God's children."

The presenting Sadducee grimaced, realizing that now he had trapped himself. He could hardly argue against the resurrection now that he had posed his foolish resurrection question. He was quiet in their chagrin.

But Yeshua pressed on to share more about the resurrection and eternal life with the audience at large, "Let me remind you of the account of the burning bush, even Moses understood the dead rise. Didn't Yahweh tell him that he *is* 'the God of Abraham, and the God of Isaac, and the God of Jacob.' Moses makes it clear that Yahweh is not the God of the dead, but of the living, for to the LORD all of his people are alive."

The Sadducees strained to think of an argument, but they could find none. Their lips pressed into grim lines, but their outrage burned in their eyes.

Someone started to clap their hands, rejoicing at Yeshua's winning words.

Even one of the teachers of the law shouted out his hardy approval, "Well said, teacher!"

The people shout their approval of Yeshua's wisdom. None of the Sadducee's dared to ask him more questions. The floor was completely his, and he took it with purpose, posing a pointed question to the crowd, "Whose son is the Messiah?"

The people waited, afraid to say anything.

"Most people would say he is the son of David, but for all of David's many sons, where are they now?" His searching look reminded them all of the lineage that was literally cut off to become only a dead stump.

He continued, "Here is an even better question: why is it said that the Messiah is the son of David? Look at the Psalms. David himself was presented with a vision, and he declared this: 'The LORD said to my Lord: Sit at my right hand until I make your enemies a footstool for your feet.'"

He spread his hands in query and looked pointedly to the Sadducees, Pharisees, Priests, Teachers of the Law, and finally to the people.

When no one responded, he continued. "David calls the one that was to come 'Lord.' How, then, can he be his son? Does a father ever call his son 'Lord'?"

Everyone whispered in amazement, for the case he was making was airtight.

Yeshua turned and came to stand before his disciples to warn them and those listening, "Beware the teachers of the law. They sit in Moses' seat. You must carry out the law as they tell you, but do not do what they do, for they do not practice what they preach.

They are happy to load people down with a burden of guilt, but they sit back doing nothing to remove it."

He turned narrowed eyes on them, "They love to parade around in long and flowing robes. They expect to be greeted with respect in the marketplaces. They demand the most important seats of honor in public feasts and at banquets. They rejoice in devouring widows' houses. They stand before the people and make a great show with their lengthy prayers." He pointed his finger at the religious lot, saying, "These men will be punished most severely for their hypocrisy."

His words were like a punch to their gut, but the gloves had only just come off. And collectively, they all reared back like a basket full of uncharmed cobras, ready to strike. Again, to his disciples, he spoke, "But I am telling you that you are not to be called 'Rabbi,' for you have but one Teacher, and you are all brothers." The disciples nodded.

"From now on, do not call anyone on earth 'father,' for you have one Father, and he is in heaven. The greatest among you will be your servant, just as I have told you." The disciples nodded once again, understanding that they were not to be like the religious elite.

Yeshua was not finished; he turned to the delegation of silenced leaders gathered around him. He stepped towards them so he was eye to eye with them. He pointed his finger toward them with an expression of disgust. The disciples had rarely seen such a fierce look of judgment on Yeshua's face. It was one he reserved for the demons.

"Woe to you, teachers of the law and Pharisees, you hypocrites! You shut the door to the kingdom of heaven in people's faces. You yourselves refuse to enter, and you block the way for those who are diligently searching for the door to enter.

"Woe to you, teachers of the law and Pharisees, you hypocrites! You travel great distances, searching to win over a single convert for your ranks. When you find them, you make them twice as much a child of hell as you are.

"Woe to you, blind guides! You say, 'If anyone swears by the temple, the vow means nothing. But, I tell you, anyone who swears by even 'the gold of this temple' *is* bound by that oath. Which is greater: the gold or the temple that makes the gold sacred? You are blind fools! You have no regard for that which *is* holy. Anyone who swears by this temple swears by the one who dwells in it. You are worse than the pagans, swearing by things you do not understand.

"Woe to you, teachers of the law and Pharisees, you hypocrites! You measure out your sacrifices, offering nothing more than required. But you have neglected the more important matters of the law—justice, mercy, and faithfulness. You strain out a gnat, but you swallow a camel.

"Woe to you, teachers of the law and Pharisees, you hypocrites! You clean the outside of the cup and dish, but inside of you, you are full of greed and self-indulgence. Blind Pharisee! First, clean the inside of the cup and dish, and then the outside also will be clean.

"Woe to you, teachers of the law and Pharisees, you hypocrites! You are like whitewashed tombs, which look regal and stately on the outside, but inside, you are full of dead men's bones and of everything unclean, of hypocrisy and wickedness.

"Woe to you, teachers of the law and Pharisees, you hypocrites! You build tombs for the prophets and decorate the graves of the righteous to honor them as if you ever cared for them. You say, 'Unlike our ancestors, we would not have taken part with them in shedding the blood of the prophets.' Yet, by your own testimony, you are the descendants of those who murdered the prophets. So now, go ahead then, and complete what your ancestors started!

"You snakes! You brood of vipers! How will you escape being condemned to hell? Even so, I have sent to you prophets and sages and teachers. More will come. Some of them you will kill and crucify; others you will flog in your synagogues and pursue from town to town. In this way, you will become the scapegoat so that all of the righteous blood that has ever been shed on earth, from the blood of righteous Abel right up to the blood of Zechariah, son of Berekiah, whom you murdered between the temple and the altar. Truly, I tell you, all the consequences of your violence will come upon this generation."

The gathering of people surrounding them were shocked and stood in utter silence. Their opened mouths worked, searching for words, but no one spoke, for they were struck mute by the power of the truth that had just been spoken. Horror clenched each man in his gut while each devious heart tried hard to deny his words. The words of woe hung over the delegation like the closing of a final curtain.

Yeshua departed. Eleven of his apostles followed him, but the twelfth did not.

Judas was so upset that he could not move. All he could think was, 'There is no way Yeshua will ever become the king! He has just alienated every power broker in Jerusalem. If he has set his course for crucifixion as he says, well, today he achieved his goal.' Judas thought, 'It is time for me to save my own skin.' He had placed his bets on a dark horse, but now he could see he would never pay off. He had to find a way to cut his losses before it was too late.

~ 35 ~

BITTER-SWEET

While the king was at his table,
my perfume spread its fragrance.
My beloved is to me a sachet of myrrh,
resting between my breasts.
My beloved is to me a cluster of henna blossoms,
from the vineyards of En Gedi.
Song of Songs 1:12-14

The compound of Bethany was a welcomed sight. Tonight, as they had climbed the Mount Olives, Yeshua had not even paused to glance back toward Jerusalem. The tension of the day still pressed heavily upon him. He was welcomed to the complex by the delicious scents of a feast and the women bustling around as they put the finishing touches in place. Lamplight flickered, and flowers adorned Martha's long table. Some of the women who had traveled with Mariamne had also come for the meal. Salome was there, and his mother's sister had come also. When he entered the hall, they turned expectantly, making efforts at bright smiles. He could see by their practiced smiles that the women were aware pf what was coming. Ima and Mari had spread the word to this fellowship of sisters, and they had come to be with him and comfort him. Martha was doing what she knew best to do, hustling around, calling out orders to the other women and servants, determined to give him all his favorite foods.

Since the weather was so pleasant, she had set the feast out in the courtyard. The smell of roasting meat scented the air, adding to the festive flair.

"Lord, we have made a feast in your honor..." Martha told him.

Showing his pleasure, he said, "Yes! And it smells so good."

"We wanted to celebrate what you did by raising Lazarus from the grave. We can hardly believe he is alive again and no worse for the experience."

He smiled and leaned in to kiss the top of Martha's head. This was how she showed her devotion.

She released the breath she had been holding, "Go and refresh yourself so you can take a seat with Lazarus and the others; the food will soon be on the tables. She shooed him away like a child sent to play. The servants made their way around to each disciple to cleanse hands and feet before the meal.

Throughout the banquet, everyone tried to keep their conversation light and cheery. They ate, laughed, reminisced, and swapped stories, enjoying the grand gesture of Martha and Lazarus' generosity. The men and women alike devoured everything on the table, leaving it to look like a plague of locusts had passed through. The men even competed for the last pieces of the flat loaves of unleavened bread so they could scrape the bowls empty of the various spreads. The table became a sad skeleton of emptied bowls and platters. A few of the men sheepishly licked from their fingers before the bowls were removed. A sweet-smelling dessert was soon delivered, and everyone was happy to indulge. His friends toasted him while they shared their favorite stories about him.

There was much laughter and a lot of serious stories that left eyes wet but hearts warm. But for the most part, Yeshua remained quiet and appreciative of this happy distraction. The evening light had faded, and the torchlights were lit, and the smell of night jasmine filled the air. With the setting of the sun, a new day had begun; it was now the Preparation of the Lamb Day.

Mari had been watching Yeshua. She could tell that despite all the merriment, a pall hung over him. He had not eaten as much as she would have hoped. His smiles and laughter were tinged with sadness. Those who knew his moods tried their best to lighten his heart. Their eyes had met numerous times during the meal. As everyone finished their desserts, Mari decided that it was time. She got up and disappeared into the house.

Yeshua watched her as she went. Privately praying for her and his Ima, willing them a strength to carry them through the days ahead, just as he done with his friends and followers. He looked around the table from face to face, privately praying for strength and trust through what was to come. Everyone was so busy talking that they did not notice his prayerful scrutiny.

Then, as she had done once before, Mari entered the room carrying an ornately carved alabaster bottle filled with an ancient and sacred mixture of nard. The recipe dated back to times of old. His chin lifted expectantly when he saw her with her eyes fixed boldly on his. This perfume was the ancient combination of nard and spices esspecially created for those who those consecrated unto the LORD. This holy anointing oil was meant only for God's ordained purposes. She bowed down before him.

"Lord." She raised her head to look at him waiting.

When she saw his approval, she opened the container. Before anyone could say anything to her, she leaned up to pour some part of the nard upon his head. The rich warm oil ran down his curls, into his beard, and onto his robes. The perfume's unique scent was all at once woodsy, spicy, sweet, pungent, and medicinal. The scent was strangely comforting to him, speaking strength and peace to his soul. He closed his eyes and leaned his head back, breathing in its power. The fragrance of myrrh, cinnamon, calamus, and cassia wafted through the courtyard, so potent that everyone was filled with the effects of the scent.

When Yeshua opened his eyes; his look reassured Mari that she had done well.

She reposition herself to leaning down over his feet. She poured the rest of the oil on Yeshua's callused and careworn bare feet. Tentatively and gently, she touched them, lifting each foot to cover them completely. She couldn't help but think, of the many miles his feet had walked to find the lost, including her. She carefully covered every scar and callus, and she coated his lower calves. She kept her eyes on his, bold in her adoration. All the while, her tears ran down her face to fall upon his feet to be blended with the oil.

When words failed her in her grief, simply moaned. Finally, she said, "I'm so sorry! So sorry for my doubts, for my demands, my sins, my part in this, ...for the many things I have done."

He could see that her remorse was heart felt and her shame was real.

She whispered, "Lord, I know who you are. I know what you are doing for me, for us all." He reached out his hand to caress her cheek, "Mari..." His voice was tender, and forgiving.

She smiled a wobbly smile; then, she bowed low to caress his weary feet with her cheek. She turned her face to them and pressed her small wet kisses along the arch, covering them with her sobs. It was as if an artisan well had opened. All of her emotions became a waterfall upon his feet and mixed with the oil. She unwrapped her freshly washed and shiny long hair. She began to use it to rub away the unneeded oil from his calves, ankles, and feet, just as she had done on that first night.

When she had finished her ministrations, she sat back on her heels, with her head still bowed. She sniffled and dried her eyes on the sleeves of her tunic. He looked on her with the tenderness of a father, with the concern of a brother, with the sorrow of a husband, with the unquestionable authority of her sovereign, and the absolution of her high priest. His expression offered her peace and confidence. They stared at one another, while he communicatied all these things.

Mari whispered, "I will always be your servant."

The table watched, mesmerized. Something holy and beautiful had just transpired between them. Mari's acts of devotion seemed to give voice to what everyone around the table was felt; all, except for one.

Mari's devotion had angered Judas. Catching the heady scent, Judas smelled money. She had spent a fortune and for what? To be poured out like cheap wine? Wanting to put Mari in her place, Judas arose to sauntered over to stand over the two of them. With a jarring insolence, he intruded into their space. His attitude was surly and indifferent to the preciousness of this moment. He leaned down between them to lift the beautiful container. Sniffing the perfume, he made a churlish face. He examined the container to estimate its considerable worth. He was in a dark mood. Without looking at either Yeshua or Mari, he bit out a sharp and menacing question that offended everyone who heard it, "Where did you get this?"

At his impertinence, Yeshua's eyebrows shot together like swift lightning bolts. But with his accusing eyes on Mari, he did not notice.

"Why wasn't this perfume sold and the money given to the poor? It is worth a year's wages!"

Yeshua's face shapeshifted to one of a ferocious lion. His low, fierce growl sounded out so real that it caused Judas to stumble backward, and drop the bottle.

Mari reached out to grab the lovely container before it shattered on the stone pavement.

Yeshua stood to his full height, leaning ominously toward Judas, "Leave her alone." Although he gave his command quietly, the strength in his words sounded to Judas like a roar. Judas lifted his hands as if shielding himself.

Yeshua drew in face to face, "She has anointed me for the day of my burial. Don't you realize this? The poor will always be among you, but your opportunity to serve and honor me is coming to an end.... If only you really did care about the poor or anyone else at all."

Judas stepped back, taking measure of the situation. He quickly turned to escape further scrutiny. He returned to the shadows.

Yeshua offered his hand to lift Mari to her feet. She meekly held the container to her chest. Then she reached out and placed her slender hand lightly upon his arm. Locking eyes with his, she said, "I will be there."

Understanding her intent, Yeshua's face softened.

"I will be there for you," she whispered the promise again. "along with Miriam, no matter how hard it will be."

They shared a sad smile that did not reach their eyes. He nodded, saying what was needed with no words. Mari saw he was bolstered by her worship. She dropped her hand and took her place with the others.

Later, she lovingly put the container away; while bringing out the old one knowing his burial was not far away. Mari would treasure these jars for the rest of her life as her sacred and treasured keepsakes, not because of the cost involved. But rather, the cherished memories they would evoke everytime she undid the stopper. She would never forget all her savior had done for her or how she had felt that first night when she had exalted Yeshua to the highest place in her life, forever.

She would be forever grateful for the special bond that exist between them.

~ 36 ~

PREPARATION OF THE LAMB

"I will also make you a light for the Gentiles,
that my salvation may reach to the ends of the earth."
Isaiah 49:6

Yeshua left the shelter of Bethany for the final time to go to Jerusalem. There, he would spend his last day with the people and then share a Passover meal with his disciples.

Magdalene, Miriam, Salome, and the other women traveled with him, unwilling on this day to leave his side. They had heard how Yeshua had fiercely spoken words of warning over the religious leaders the day before.

The disciples asked him, "Lord, where do you want us to make the preparations to eat the Passover?"

"The Father is providing a place for us away from the public eye. Rock and Yohan, I am sending you to prepare our meal. Listen carefully to me. Go into the city. There, you will see a man carrying a jar of water. You will have no doubt, for it will be as if he is there to meet with you. Follow him. He will go to one of the larger houses in town and enter it. Go to the door and ask to speak with the owner. Say to the owner of the house, the Rabbi asks, 'Where is my guest room, where I may eat the Passover with my disciples?'

He will show you a large room upstairs, furnished and ready. Make preparations for us there."

The two disciples hurried on ahead with their detailed instructions, leaving the group behind.

"The Master never fails to surprise me with his resourcefulness, provision, and his relationships, even amongst the wealthy," Rock said.

They traveled into the city, where they found the man just as Yeshua had said. They followed him, and everything proceeded as promised. The owner of the house was honored to offer his upstairs room with its separate entrance. It had been prepared just as they had been told. They went to gather everything he had requested for their Passover Meal.

"I don't like being away from him this long," Simon complained. "I don't trust the religious leaders. I can't believe he would go right back to the teaching steps. How dangerous is that?"

"I agree. If it is going to happen during this Passover, then it could happen at any moment," Yohan cast Rock his own look of concern.

"Everyone else is with him!" Rock huffed, jealously longing to be at his master's side.

When they finally finished their preparation, they hurried to the teaching steps to join the others. They glanced around to survey the situation.

"Where is Judas?" Rock asked.

"We haven't seen him all morning," came the terse answer.

Yeshua was sitting on the highest step, unbelievably calm and speaking a parable to his followers. He was saying, "When a man believes in me, he is not only believing in me but also in the one who sent me. When you look at me, you also see the one who has sent me into the world to be a light capable of delivering you from the darkness.

"When the Son of Man comes in his glory bringing all his angels with him, he will sit on his glorious throne. People from every nation will be gathered before him. Then *he* will separate the people one from another just in the same way a shepherd separates his sheep from the goats. He will put the sheep on his right and the goats on his left.

"Then the King will say to those he placed on his right side, 'Come, you who are blessed by my Father; take your inheritance, the kingdom prepared for you since the creation of the world."

Yeshua paused to lift his chin with a nod of appreciation toward Rock and Yohan, acknowledging their return. A group of Greeks came to stand on the periphery of the crowd, watching and listening with great interest. He motioned to Philip to meet with them. Philip got up and went to the men dressed in elegant togas. He turned his gaze back to the large crowd gathered around him, "For I was hungry, and you gave me something to eat; I was thirsty, and you gave me something to drink; I was a stranger, and you invited me in. I needed clothes, and you clothed me. I was sick, and you looked after me. I was in prison, and you came to visit me.'"

He looked around at those searching themselves within, "Then the righteous will say, 'Lord, when did we see you hungry and feed you, or thirsty and give you something to drink?When did we see you a stranger and invite you in, or needing clothes and clothe you? When did we see you sick or in prison or go to visit you?'" Again, he paused to allow them to think.

"The King will reply, 'Truly I tell you, whatever you did for one of the least of these brothers and sisters of mine, you did for me.' Then, he will proclaim to those he divided off to his left, 'Depart from me, you who are cursed, into the eternal fire prepared for the devil and his angels. For I was hungry, and you gave me nothing to eat. I was thirsty, and you gave me nothing to drink. I was a stranger, and you did not invite me in. I needed clothes, and you did not clothe me. I was sick and in prison, but you did not look after me.'

"They will give him a simpering or surly answer, 'Lord, when did we see you hungry or thirsty or a stranger or needing clothes or sick or in prison, and did not help you?'

"But the king will reply, 'Truly I tell you, whatever you did not do for one of the least of these, you did not do for me.'" Some of the faces amongst the people looked distressed, but some became hardened and angry.

"Then, those will be drug away to eternal punishment, but the righteous will be led along the way to eternal life."

Having ended his story, Yeshua stood to look towards Rock and Yohan, "So, has everything been made ready?"

They nodded.

"It is time then, my brothers and sisters, for me to go," he began to make his way down the steps.

Philip called out to him, "Lord," he motioned to the Greeks waiting on the sidelines, "they asked if they could meet with you?"

Upon hearing this request, Yeshua stumbled backward to sink weakly onto the step. Yohan reached out to grab him and sat down beside him, still holding up his wobblily head in his hands.

"Are you all right?" he searched his ashen face. He saw his distress as he struggled to breathe. In his eyes, Yohan saw his terror, "Lord, what is it? What is it?" He leaned in to look intently into his eyes.

"Lord, I am here. Breathe, just breathe. This will soon pass." Familiar with these bouts of weakness, it seemed he was having a panic attack.

Yeshua grasped Yohan's arms, trying his best to steady his breaths. He stared into Yohan's eyes to ground himself. Finally, the wild beating of his heart slowed, and his strength began to flow back into him. When he finally stood, he said to Yohan, "Stay with me."

Yohan swallowed hard and said, "Don't worry. I won't leave your side."

Part of the crowd dispersed before realizing this had happened. Some had seen him fall and remained, concerned that he was all right. After the tremor had passed, Yeshua stood back to his feet. He looked around at all of the concerned faces standing around him.

They were surprised when he spoke up once more, in a loud and deeply distressed voice, "The hour has come for the Son of Man to be glorified.Very truly, I tell you, unless a kernel of wheat falls to the ground and dies, it remains only a single seed. But if it dies, it produces many seeds. I am telling you the truth; anyone who loves their life will lose it. Whoever hates their life in this world will keep it for eternal life."

He explained, "Whoever serves me must follow me, and where I am, my servant will also be. My Father will honor the one who serves me.

"As for today, my soul is troubled, and what shall I say? *'Father, save me from this hour?'* No, it was for this very reason I have made it to this very hour."

The people looked at him with confusion, 'What is going to happen this very hour?' They saw no threats nearby.

"Father, glorify your name!" Yeshua shouted up into the heavens.

At those words, a bright light flashed above in response. The people cried out and threw their hands protectively over their heads and dove for safety. A voice rumbled from the heavens above. "I have glorified it, and I will glorify it again."

Rock, Yohan, and James heard the words the light spoke, and they remembered they had heard this voice not so long ago upon the peak of Mt. Hermon.

The crowd peered up into the cloudless sky. Some thought perhaps the sound was thunder. But those who heard the words believed the angel of his Father had spoke his promise to his Son.

Once the crowd quieted down, Yeshua said, "The voice you heard was for your benefit, not mine. Now is the time for judgment in this world! The prince of this world will be driven out! And I, when I am lifted up from the earth, will draw all people to myself."

People fearfully looked towards the skies, wondering what the Rabbi meant. Was he going to be taken up into heaven? They looked up and saw nothing to indicate this would happen. No one was lifting him up into the skies. They didn't understand.

Some wondered, "Is he the Savior we are waiting for? Is the kingdom coming now?" But some wondered, "Is he a lunatic?" But no one could miss the divine authority of his words.

~ 37 ~

A DEAL WITH THE DEVIL

But if you have come to betray me to my enemies
when my hands are free from violence,
may the God of our ancestors see it and judge you.
1 Chronicles 12:17

Judas' tension with Yeshua had been building for some time. In his estimation, if Yeshua truly wanted to build a kingdom, he had gone about it completely the wrong way. What's more, Judas had never been able to persuade or influence him in the least little bit. Now, after having watched him shout woes at Jerusalem's leadership, followed by Mari's simpering display of wasting the nard that was worth a year's wages, followed by Yeshua's subsequent fury when he had called her on it, Judas' last string of goodwill had snapped. He was seething inside. Magdalene had always got under his skin with all her bowing and scraping before Yeshua. She heaped honor and praise upon him. It was more than he could stand. It was time to cut his losses. He would make his move today. Sullenly, he had entered Jerusalem with the rest of the group, only to slip away without a word. He went searching for a way to gain direct access to the chief priests.

Last night, he had lain on his bed, allowing grandiose fantasies to fill his imagination, 'Perhaps I can make a deal with Caiaphas to give me a money-changing booth. I would be rich. Not like the priest, but quite respectable. It would be a good start. You have to make money to make money.'

He imagined the possibilities, "I could ask for a small fortune to hand him over. Wouldn't they pay anything to be rid of him clogging their temple steps? Yosef ben Caiaphas and I have one thing in common. Yeshua makes us both look bad. I could become a hero to the High Priest and be freed from any incrimination. Who knows what offering him up might gain me?"

He talked his way around until he had found the chief guard, "I understand Caiaphas wants Yeshua--the Galilean. I have been with him as one of his followers. I could lead Caiaphas to him, but I must talk with Caiaphas directly."

The guard's eyes lit up; they had never been able to overtake the man because there were so many loyal fans around him, but if they could catch him away from the crowds...

He offered a discomforting smile and commanded Judas, "Come with me." Malchus was not about to let this 'disciple' go now that he had him.

**

When Caiaphas heard one of the Nazarene's own had turned traitor, he was beyond ecstatic. Just that morning, he had been berated by Annas because the Nazarene was still actively preaching at the temple. Also, some of the Sanhedrin had convened to put together a list of scriptural proofs detailing the ways Yeshua fit the messianic expectation, indicating the tides were turning.

Stone cold with fury, Annas had reminded him, "Rome is all too eager to discard the high priest who cannot control the people. They have done so many times, casting them away like dirty rags.'

Though Annas was now an old man, his influence was still powerful. His rebuke concerning his failure felt like the slice of a sword. Annas had wielded the Sanhedrin for well over forty years, and he was determined he would not lose his control now. He had smiled thinly at him and said, "I am fond of you, Caiaphas, and I have always believed you have the ambition to hold this post of High Priest with my help and council. I am counting on you."

Caiaphas was furious at Annas' veiled threat. But now, seeing a way through his dilemma, he called together Annas and his five sons. He was savvy enough to know it was best to have everyone play a part in this conspiracy. He would *not* become Annas' scapegoat.

**

Judas found himself suddenly taken by the arm and roughly led by the guard into the presence of the priests. It was a high holy day; therefore, the priests were impressively dressed in their full regalia; the same scent Mari had poured out the night before scented the air of their chambers as if to cover the dark overtone of their spiritual impurity. Judas held his hand to his nose to block the scent. Each man was seated upon an ornate chair as if they were kings rather than servants of God.

He felt the icy fingers of their collective power stretching toward him as if to grasp him by his throat. No one rose or greeted him. No one smiled or nodded their head. They offered no pretense of approval or comradery of any sort. Rather, he was speared by seven pairs of unfavorable eyes. They did not speak but waited. The guard goaded Judas forward.

Judas was not sure of how to address this body appropriately. For a moment, he froze. Awkwardly, he clenched his fists in front of him as if sensing an unseen battle.

"Well?" Caiaphas demanded impatiently. "What have you got?"

Judas tried to speak, but his words were a self-conscious croak. "I think perhaps I have made a mistake."

He turned as if to go, but the guard stepped in his path, staring him down with a cruel smile. He was unwittingly wedged into a snare of his own doing.

He turned back toward the men seated before him, desperate to find a way out of his predicament. When the way did not appear, he plunged ahead. "I am a follower of Yeshua of Nazareth. I can hand him over to you." He spread open his hands as if he were making an offering.

"Your name?"

"My name?" He stalled. He didn't want to give his name.

Malchus moved to his side and pressed his hand upon him.

He swallowed heavily to wet his dry throat, "Judas bar Iscariot."

"Why should we trust you—a traitor?"

"I am not a traitor, at least not to Jerusalem. I want to help you, but for a decent price."

"Ah, so you are selling your master!" Annas accused him, looking upon him full of disgust and scorn. "He is most popular among the people. Why would you do that?"

Judas stared at them, "He's an insurrectionist. He means to be the Messiah."

"What makes you think we want anything to do with him? Why would you say such a thing?"

"He is dangerous, is he not? When I followed him, I didn't know how dangerous he was. That is why I have come to you as a patriot." Judas assured them, his eyes narrowed like two swiveled red grapes.

"Why should we trust you?" Annas repeated.

Annas the Younger gave a wicked laugh, "Look at him; he would steal the coins from a dead man's eyes."

"So you are sure you can deliver this man to us?"

Judas nodded convincingly.

Well, the price for a slave is thirty pieces of silver. We will pay this to you, but you must never speak of it... as a patriot, of course." Caiaphas said with a wicked grin.

Judas was shocked by the audacity of such a low offer. This was not what he had imagined. He started to object but realized they could easily arrest him as well. So he closed his mouth.

"One stipulation: this must be done privately, preferably under the cover of night. We do not want to endanger the masses who do not know their right hand from their left. Can you deliver him tonight?" Caiaphas probed forcefully, ready to be done with this unpleasant business. This was not his first intrigue. Once this was done, few people would ever challenge him again.

"I was hoping I could..."

"You could what? Keep your life and not die with him?" Annas asked pointedly. "This secret must die with you."

His threat sounded a warning. Judas had no choice but to concede. He clamped his jaws tightly, hoping to keep his own life.

"One more thing, we need you to go with our men to identify him. We do not want the guards to confuse him or get the wrong man. Also, you will be required to testify at the hearing against your teacher. Blasphemy should do the trick. So, make sure you complete your work. Who knows, there might be a small bonus for you in all of this," Caiaphas cut his eyes at the other men with a delight that caused a tentacle of morbid fear to travel the length of Judas' spine.

"Now, remove him," a noxious look filled Caiaphas' face. He held a handkerchief under his nose while he looked away and dismissed him with a wave of his hand.

"Oh, and Malchus, make yourself and your men available to him tonight. Plan the time and place so you can follow through on your assignment. Keep me informed. When you are finished, bring the Nazarene to me."

Annas interrupted, "No, bring him to me first so I can question him." His arrogance insinuated that he could not trust the interrogation solely to Caiaphas.

~ 38 ~

PASSOVER OF THE LORD

When I see the blood, I will pass over you.
Exodus 12:12

I am bowed down and brought very low;
I am feeble and utterly crushed;
I groan in anguish of heart.
All my longings lie open before you, Lord;
My sighing is not hidden from you.
My heart pounds, my strength fails me;
Even the light has gone from my eyes.
My friends and companions avoid me...
Those who want to kill me set their traps,
Those who would harm me talk of my ruin;
All day long, they scheme and lie.
Psalm 38:6-12

Everything for the Passover dinner had been prepared and was set in place. The brass sconces held torches that lit the space, casting a warm and flickering glow. Yeshua stood by the door, waiting for his men to wash their feet in the provided basin to purify themselves before taking their seats for this sacred meal. It was not only a matter of good manners, but this was a special night—Passover.

But apparently, the guys had grown too used to being on the road. Instead of taking the time to prepare themselves, they all bolted in to take their places at the table.

The Passover meal was a sacred family event filled with traditions and rituals. Around the table, families spent hours recounting the story of the Passover, seated in a certain arrangement of honor and for the youngest child.

Rock and Yohan led the way to take a place on either side of Yeshua place as the Patriarch at the head of the table.

Yeshua grimaced; perhaps he had been too lenient with them. He went to the large jar of water and drew some out to wash his own feet. His men did not even take notice; their minds were already hungrily anticipating the meal laid out before them. Yeshua moved to the head of the table, "Rock, tonight I am inviting Judas to sit in the seat of honor on the left of me. Yohan will remain where he is because he is the youngest."

Simon looked hurt and confused. He wondered what he had done to warrant such a banishment and what Judas had done to deserve this great honor. Hadn't he been the one incharge of preparing the meal? Looking around, he saw that only the very last and lowest seat was left unoccupied. Self-consciously, he moved to the lowly seat and plopped down with a visible pout. Only then was he reminded of the parable Yeshua had once told the Sadducees who had thought too highly of themselves. Was that why he was humbling him?

In the corner, the women sat together at a separate small, low-lying table of their own, just glad to be included and to be with the Lord.

When everyone was seated, Yeshua stood and took off his outer garment. He tied the long-drying cloth of a servant around his waist for ease of use. He hauled the large water jar and a large bowl to the table.

Everyone watched him, wondering, "What is he doing now?"

He began at the head of the table, kneeling like a slave before first Yohan, then Judas, causing everyone to recall what Mari had done for *him* just the night before.

Yeshua continued to wash, rinse, and dry each person's feet around the tables as if tending to his children.

Yohan looked ashamed that he had forgotten to wash his feet. Judas stared straight ahead, intolerant and impatient, waiting for Yeshua to finish. Only when Yeshua had moved on did he cast his look of aversion his way.

No one offered to take Yeshua's place. Instead, they stared mesmerized, impatient, eager, or ashamed. It was humbling to have their Rabbi kneel at their feet to serve them in such a lowly manner. They were all painfully aware of their social faux pas. They struggled and searched for someone to place their blame. Eventually, all eyes fell on Rock. After all, wasn't he put in charge of this feast?

Finally, Yeshua stooped down before Rock's feet.

But Simon moved his feet quickly away, "No, Lord, it is not right that you should wash my feet." He said, his face aflame with humiliation.

Yeshua leaned toward Rock eye to eye with the ultimatum, "Simon, if I don't wash you, you can have no part with me."

Simon's eyes grew large with fear and confusion. He thrust out both his feet and his hands.

"Then, not just my feet, but my hands and head as well," Simon begged. He didn't know what he had done, but Simon was determined to be right with his Lord.

Yeshua smiled at Rock with great affection as he reached out to take hold of Rock's rather large and harry foot. Pouring the water over his feet, he said with amusement, "Rock, you have had a bath. If you have had your bath, you only need to wash your feet; the rest of the whole body is clean."

He finished his task and dried Rock's feet with the towel. He let them go with a small flourish of the towel as he stood, "You, my friend, are clean." His smile sent a ray of comfort into Simon's heart.

But Simon noticed his face became grim as he looked across the table.

Yeshua added, "But not everyone here tonight is clean."

Rock heard his words and wondered at the culprit.

Yeshua removed the towel from his waist and hung it on its stand. He redonned his outer garment so he could be ready to move out at a moment's notice. He suppressed a shiver and took the patriarch's seat. Some of the men were older than him, but in the last few months, he had sprouted silver streaks. Tonight, he appeared much older.

All eyes rested on him, waiting to hear his words.

"Do you understand what I have done for you?" he asked his men.

They stared back, clearly puzzled.

"You call me 'Teacher' and 'Lord'. And rightly so, for that is what I am. But tonight I, your Lord and Teacher, have become your servant to wash your feet." He looked around the table.

"In this same way, *you* should also wash one another's feet. Tonight, I have set you an example of what it is to be a servant leader. This is the way I want you to live with one another." He studied their obtuse faces, "Is any servant greater than his master?"

His question was met with silence.

"No. Nor is any messenger greater than the one who sent him. Now that you know these things, remember them and do them so you will be blessed. For a long time now, I have been waiting for this night. Now it is here."

He closed his eyes and prayed the prayer of thanksgiving over the bread. When he looked up, he said, "This is the same bread our fathers hurriedly ate in the land of Egypt. Tonight, we keep the Pascha. This is how you are to eat it, with your cloak tucked into your belt, your sandals on your feet, and your staff in your hand. This is the same way we will eat this meal tonight. We will eat it in haste; for it is the Lord's Passover."

He made his point by strapping his sandals onto his feet.

Seeing he was serious, his disciples did likewise.

As soon as his sandals were fastened, a spasm of heartbreak overtook him. He began to hyperventilate. Yohan turned to speak quietly to him and he worked to bring his breathing back under control. When he was able, he said to the group, "Truly I tell you, one of you will betray me."

Hearing this prophecy, the disciples were shaken. What was he saying? Hadn't everything Yeshua had ever told them came true.

"What?"

"Who is it?"

"How?" Came the exclaimations from around the table.

Their reaction was visceral, "Who would do such a thing?"

They scrutinized each other wildly for a sign of the guilty party. But they were all just as shocked to see their friends were examining them too, as if they were the guilty ones. The room became supercharged with tension and accusation. They looked to Yeshua to absolve them of that guilt, "Surely you don't mean me, Lord?"

Meanwhile, Judas did not meet anyone's eyes.

Yeshua told them, "I am telling you the truth; his hand is on this table, and he is dipping his bread with mine. The Son of Man will die just as it has been written about him. But woe to that man who betrays the Son of Man! It would be better for him if he had never been born."

Judas decided it was best to play along with the others, so he leaned in feigning innocence, "Surely you don't mean me, Rabbi?"

Yeshua turned to look at him squarely, "It is just as you have said."

Across the way, at the end of u-shaped the table, Rock was motioning to Yohan and mouthing, "Ask him who it is!

Yohan leaned back awkwardly against Yeshua's chest to whisper, "Who is it, Lord?"

"The one I hand this piece of bread," Yeshua took a piece from the bread of bitterness and dipped it into the bitter herbs. He loaded it full of the burning and bitter dip, then handed it to Judas.

It was not uncommon to offer a prepared morsel to a friend as a sign of ones favor. But when Judas took the sop and put it in his mouth. His eyes began to water, and his mouth burned at the load of it's hot bitterness. A sudden anger overtook him. At that moment, Satan entered Judas to take control of his thoughts. He grabbed for a water glass, but when he did not find one, he mumbled, "I need to go."

Yeshua leaned towards him, and gave the command, "Go quickly then, and do what you intend to do. Do not delay."

Judas sprung from his seat and hurriedly left the room. Through the opened door, Yeshua saw that it had grown dark. It was now Passover.

He drew in a shaky breath, 'The day of God's vengeance has begun, and what a terrifying day it will be.'

He regathered from his thoughts, only to hear the same whispered argument he had been hearing for months now concerning who would take charge once the worst had come to pass.

He pounded the table before him, "Are you really going do this again?"

His incensed stare of disbelief snapped every mouth shut.

He was living on borrowed time now. But he needed just a little more time...

Yeshua unwrapped another loaf and held it aloft for it to be acknowledged. Then he tore it in two to be distributed between the tables.

"This is my body; take and eat of it, for I am giving my body up for you tonight."

They looked around solemnly. Each person broke off a piece of the large flattened bread. They chewed the bread hurriedly, just as Yeshua had said.

"Remember, I am the true Bread that gives life to you whenever you eat of me."

He filled a large cup and held it aloft, speaking a blessing upon it, and then he passed it around to everyone, saying, "This is the cup of my redemption, poured out for the forgiveness of sins. Tonight, I institute a new covenant for you through my blood; drink it and remember my covenant of blood I have made with you. Whenever you eat the bread of my bitter suffering and drink the cup of my redemption, remember what I have done for you on this day."

Yeshua ended the meal. He led the group out of this upper room towards the Kidron Valley, headed toward the Mount of Olives. They sang the traditional Psalm 118 as they went. The full Passover moon rose red, coloring the landscape with an ominous combination of darkness vs. light. A brooding pathway lay before them, as well as shadowed versions of one another's faces. A wild dog howled in the distance, and another one answered. Otherwise, things seemed eerily quiet. Tonight, every Jew was ingathered with their families because it was the night of the LORD's Passover.

Yeshua began to talk to his disciples as they went, "Listen to me now, all of you. My hour is almost here, but I still have things to say to you. First, do not let your hearts be troubled. You believe in God; now believe also in me. My Father's house has many rooms; I am going there to prepare a place for you.And when the time is right, I will come back and take you to be with me so that you may be with me where I am. You know the way."

Thomas panicked, "But Lord, we don't know the way! We don't know where you are going, so how can we know the way?"

Yeshua answered him, laying his hand on his chest, "*I* am the way and the truth and the life. You can't return to the Father except through me. When you really know me, you will knowmy Father as well. From now on, because of me, you do know him, and you have seen him."

Now, Philip said, "Lord, just show us the Father, and that will be enough for us."

Yeshua stopped walking; he turned to look at Philip with tortured and searching eyes, "Don't you know me, Philip, even after I have been with you for such a long time? Anyone who sees me has seen the Father."

Philip dropped his head in confusion.

His voice was filled with sadness,"How can you say, 'Show us the Father'?"

Yeshua wondered, 'Have they come this far and still not know me? And Philip of all people?" He looked around, trying to gauge the understanding of the others, all he saw was confusion. He felt it like a crushing blow. He held out his hands to them, "What? Do none of you believe that I am in the Father, and the Father is in me? Even after I have told you? The words I say, I do not speak by my authority. Who do you think is speaking those words? It is the Father, living in me, who is doing his work through me. Believe me when I say that I am in the Father, and the Father is in me. At the very least, believe in the evidence of the works you have witnessed."

His beseeching hands dropped in disappointment, "I am telling you the truth. Whoever believes in me will do the works I have been doing. They will do even greater things than these because I am returning to the Father. Remember what I have told you, 'I will do whatever you ask in my name so that the Father may be glorified in the Son.' You may ask for anything in my name, and I will do it."

He paused, "Show your love for me by keeping my commands. That is the proof of your love for me.

"And, never doubt my love for you. I will not leave you as orphans," He said confidently, looking at each face; he paused a double beat on Mari before continuing. "I will ask the Father to give you another counselor who will help you and be with you forever—the Spirit of Truth. The world cannot receive his counsel because it neither sees him nor knows him. But *you, you* know him, for he has been living with you, and he will come to live in you. I." He patted his chest, "I will come to you."

Thaddeus spoke up, "Lord, why will you not show yourself to the world?"

He looked affectionately at Thaddeus, "When the world hates you, you will understand. Just remember, the world hated me first. You do not belong to this world, but I have chosen you out of this world.

"Don't forget what I have told you. The Advocate, the Holy Spirit, whom the Father will send in my name, will teach you all manner of things. He will remind you of all the things I have said to you. So be at peace. My peace I give you, not as the world gives; I give you a different kind of peace. Again, do not let your hearts be troubled, and do not be afraid. Be glad for me now that I am returning to the Father, for the Father is greater than I. When I return, be found believing in what I have told you.

"I cannot say much more now, for the prince of this world is on his way. But know this: He has no hold over me. He comes now so the world may know how much I love the Father and see that I do exactly what my Father commands of me."

They had reached the outcropping of the olive trees. He stopped to hug each of the women and Lazarus as well and blessed them all with a holy kiss. His mother held on to him, not wanting to let him go; she was trembling. He handed her off to Magdalene, saying, "Take care of her."

Mari's eyes glittered, wet with tears. She tried to imprint his face on her memory one more time. She nodded, then obediently turned Miriam and the others towards Bethany.

He and his apostles continued to the place of the olive press. The olive garden was deserted at night. In times past, he had spent time in prayer there at night. Tonight, it would become his prayer closet one final time.

Rock came alongside him, "Lord, though everyone may desert you, I will never desert you. Wherever you go, I will go with you."

"Rock, you can't go with me now where I am going."

"Why, why not, Lord? I will lay down my life for you," he vowed.

Yeshua turned to him, "Will you? Will you really die for me?"

Simon swallowed hard, suddenly unsure. He really wanted to be that person for Yeshua. He blinked hard at the sting of tears in his eyes. He didn't know what to say.

Yeshua spoke softly, "I am telling you the truth; before the rooster crows in the morning, you will say you do not even know me, not just once, but three different times."

Appalled, Rock began to object, but Yeshua held up his hand.

"Simon, listen to me Simon," he whispered intimately, "Satan has demanded to sift all of you like wheat, but he wants to sift you most of all."

Simon stared at him with large, confused eyes, wanting to object but feeling a sudden dread. Why him? Then, he remembered his pronouncement at the gates of hell.

Yeshua spoke soothingly to him, "But I have prayed for you that your faith in me will not fail. Once you have turned back to me, you will strengthen your brothers. I am counting on you for this."

Yeshua pressed his hand upon Simon's strong shoulder like a commander conveying his confidence.

He turned to them all, "Tonight, you will *all* become deserters' for it is written, 'I will strike the shepherd, and the sheep will be scattered. But when I have been raised from the dead, I will go before you all up to Galilee."

When they reached the inner wall of the grove, Yeshua told them, "Now, remain here and keep watch. Pray that none of you will fail in this coming time of trial. I will go over there to pray."

"Rock, James, and Yohan come with me." He stationed them a short stone's throw away.

"Stay here ... with me, ...stay awake, and watch with me!" He said, his voice trembling with emotion and desperation. Approaching the large stone of the press, he grew very agitated. Shaking and weeping, he climbed onto the large stone as if he were placing himself upon an altar. He fell to his hands and knees, then stretched out on the ground before his Father.

Everything within his flesh was screaming, "Run, run! It is not too late. You could still escape this."

Instead, he cried out, "Here I am, Father! I have come to do your will. Help me!"

He felt faint and collapsed upon the stone as one dead. It was as if all of his divine power had suddenly been removed from him. An angel from heaven bent down to restrengthen him so he could continue in his prayers.

"Abba, Father, for you all things are possible, please remove this cup from me. But only in accordance with your will, not mine."

He knew this desire was his flesh talking. He floundered as if his flesh and spirit were locked in a battle against one another. He felt all too weak and helpless at this crucial moment. He began by remembering the faces of all those he loved, rescued, healed, and renewed. Their joy was his joy, just as their pain was his pain. He bore their sins, and they were there with him now. He could not bear to lose them. The covenant had long ago been sealed, and since the baptism, their sins and diseases had come to rest upon him."

He made a primal, almost animal sound, a cross between a cry and a heavy sigh. "Yes, Father, the hour has come. Glorify your Son, that your Son may glorify you, for you granted him authority over all people so he could give eternal life to those you have given to him. Help me to glorify you on earth by finishing the work you gave me to do. Give me the strength to complete it. I give myself over to your will. Glorify me, Father, in your presence with the same glory I had with you before the world began."

He breathed heavily, knowing he would complete his work. There would be no rescue. Still, the loneliness of this moment overwhelmed him. He needed spiritual reinforcement, but none appeared. This battle was his alone. He returned to his closest friends only to find them sleeping.

"Please, could you not stay awake with me for just one hour? Wake up and pray! For me and you. The spirit is willing, but the flesh is weak!"

It was as if they were overspent from *his effort*. They could hardly lift their heads to look at him. Even as he turned back to the pressing stone, they drifted back into their stupor as if they were under some spell. He saw they were too weak to pray even for themselves, much less him. He was glad for all the many prayers that he had poured out for them over the years but even now he felt his work of prayer was not done and might never be done. He had to intercede on their behalf.

Climbing back upon the stone, he began to pray not only for himself but also for his disciples and their protection and for future generations of believers yet to come through their messages.

"Father, I have revealed you to those you gave me out of the world. They were yours; you gave them to me, and they have obeyed your word. I gave them the words you gave me, and they accepted them. They have believed that I came from you, that you sent me.Now, I pray for them. I am not praying for the world but for the ones you have given me, for they are yours.

"All I have is yours, and all you have is mine. They are my glory. My journey is ending here, but they will remain in this world. So, I am asking you to protect them by the power of your name, by the name you gave me, so that they may be one, just as we are one. I have protected them and kept them safe by the name you gave me. None has been lost except the one who was doomed to destruction, just as it has been written.

"I ask that the full measure of my joy will dwell within them. The world will hate them because of my word, but they are not of the world any more than I am of the world. Don't take them out of the world, but protect them from the evil one while they remain.Sanctify them, and make them holy, set them apart by your word of truth. Your word is truth. I have sent them into the world equipped with your word. So that just as I have sanctified myself by your word, they may be truly sanctified.

"My prayer is not for them alone, but also for all who will believe in me through their message. Bring them into perfect unity with one another in you and Me, just as we are one. May the world believe that you have sent me because of their unity.I give them the glory that you gave me, that they may be one as we are one— I in them and you in me—so that they may be brought to complete unity. Then the world will know that it was you who sent me, and you have loved them even as you have loved me. Father, let them be with me where I am. Let them see my glory, the glory you have given me because you loved me before the creation of the world.

"Righteous Father, though the world does not know you,I have made you known to those who belong to you, and I will continue to make you known in order that the love you have for me may also be in them and that I may be in them."

Anguish overtook him once again; time was running out, but he pressed forward, praying even more earnestly; with sobs, he pleaded, "Father, if you are willing, remove this cup from me. You withheld Abram's hand when Isaac was on this stone. But if I am the ram caught in the thicket, I bow to your will."

He stood and went to his disciples, once more hoping for the solace of their prayers, to know there was someone on his side. But once again, he found his disciples in what seemed to be a deep sleep. He didn't even bother to rouse them.

His heart was hammering in his chest and ears, and he felt dizzy. Pressed under the weight of his people, under the weight of this night, he staggered back to the stone a third time. He prayed with everything within him. From his efforts, sweat was pouring from every pore and every part of his body, enlivening the scent of the priestly oil Mari had poured out on him the night before. And, though the night was cool, he was drenched by the exertion of his struggle, as was the stone beneath him. Shivering, he looked at his sticky forearm and saw it bore the strange color of freshly pressed grape juice. Blood and water stained the linen of his tunic. He stared at it, realizing the scriptures were being fulfilled. He was being crushed for the transgressions of all mankind.

His only way forward was through the crushing.

An angel from heaven reached down to restrengthen him once again. He staggered to his feet, knowing his time of prayer had ended. His men were still asleep and hiding from the grief and terror of the night, but now the terror was upon them.

"Father, help me to do what I alone must do," he whispered.

He walked to Rock, James, and Yohan. They were utterly help-less. After all their proud proclamations, there they lay, unable to do even this small thing for him. He heard the approaching voices and saw the torches held aloft.

He spoke loudly, "Are you still sleeping and taking your rest? The hour is here. The Son of Man is being betrayed into the hands of sinners. Now, get up. Here they come."

As if a spell was suddenly broken, they all came awake and found themselves totally unprepared for the chaos that was about to ensue.

~ 39 ~

INTO THE HANDS OF SINNERS

Now, the betrayer had arranged a signal with them:
"The one I kiss is the man;
arrest him and lead him away under guard."
Matthew 14:44

Annas toasted Caiaphas, "Congratulations! It looks like you will finally get your Messiah."

"He is not my Messiah," Caiaphas replied, lacking any good humor. "But yes. I've all but got him now."

"I know the Sanhedrin can trust you to handle this, Yosef. But you must be shrewd."

Whenever the old man called him by his given name, Caiaphas knew to tread carefully. He understood that while they were family by marriage, Annas' would be happy to make him the scapegoat if this intrigue should go badly. He had long enjoyed his father-in-law's favor, but he was well aware that one could never fully trust a man like Annas.

Annas continued, "When the snitch brings you word of the Nazarene's whereabouts, it will be up to you to have everything readied to take action, including Pilate. You need the Romans to go with you to take him captive; that way, you cannot be blamed for any resulting uprising. You want to place the blame on Pilate. You want to say you are an innocent bystander forced to cooperate with Rome. Because people won't be happy when their hero is taken to the Roman cross, therefore, make sure your case is convincing that Rome needs this more than we do. Otherwise..."

Caiaphas heard the warning. He grimaced at Annas' use of the pronoun "you" as if he had no part in this. Annas was crafty; he would not allow himself to be held responsible. Caiaphas did, however, appreciate Annas' words of wise counsel; Annas was never wrong in his political assessments. And Caiaphas knew that as high priest, he would be cast onto the front lines. Public relations came with the territory.

He thought, 'As much as I despise that arrogant Roman, Annas is right; I must convince Pilate to lend his help. And to gain that, Pilate will expect me to come to him and grovel.'

"I will take care of it," Caiaphas said, tasting the bitter gall of it.

"See that you do and...and make sure the Sanhedrin and Pilate are ready to take action quickly." Annas advised him, adding with a chuckle, "You have been obsessed with this man and waiting for this since the first day he arrived. You may not get this chance again."

Caiaphas knew it would be a long day, but a day that had to count nevertheless.

**

On that night of Passover, when Judas came to the captain of the temple guard, Caiaphas had readied the guard and the Sanhedrin, but he still had to go and convince Pilate. Pilate had been out parading the street earlier that afternoon when he had tried to see him at the Antonia Fortress. He told Malchus to detain Judas while he hurried to Pilate's palace. It seemed to have more guards than the Antonia Fortress. He asked quickly for the head guard.

"I am Yosef ben Caiaphas; I am here to speak with Pilate. I left a message earlier at the fortress. He should be expecting me. It is about a matter of urgent concern."

The Syrian guard coughed up a wad of flehm from the back of his throat and spat it at Caiaphas' feet. "Is that so?" Enjoying this moment of authority, he stepped intimidatingly close, staring down at the priest.

Caiaphas fought to conceal his disgust while stepping back two steps so the Roman would not graze his robe.' Standing to his full height, he said, "This is of urgent and utmost importance to both Rome and Jerusalem. You must not delay."

The Syrian narrowed his eyes at the strangely dressed Jew whose finery rivaled Caesar. "Who may I tell the governor has come, Annas' catamite?" he chortled crudely. The other guards joined in.

With self-righteous indignation, Caiaphas' face flamed at their inference. It was not the first time someone had hinted at an immoral connection to Annas. Nothing infuriated him more than to be mocked. He coughed and stood straighter to speak more forcefully as he stared the guard in the eye, "Tell Pilate the High Priest is here to see him."

The guard wanted to play more cat and mouse, but not knowing the stakes, he feared the wrath of Pilate. Still, he was not about to rush at this man's bidding. They eyed one another grimly.

"Wait here," he commanded Caiaphas, leaving him standing uncomfortably at the gate, exposed to the eyes of passersby.

**

When the announcement was made that he had an untimely guest, Pilate was in his lavishly appointed dining hall with Claudia, enjoying the view of the hills around Jerusalem and celebrating their moment of Passover peacefulness. When his manservant entered to announce the head guard, Pilate tossed his fork onto the table with a clatter.

Looking at Claudia, he said, "Well, so much for that. I knew our moment of peace was too good to be true."

The servant stood, awaiting instructions.

"Well, don't just stand there. Bring the guard in," Pilate prodded him testily.

The guard appeared, gave his salute, and then remained standing at attention.

"Well, what is it now?" Pilate asked with an irritated sigh.

"You have a visitor, sir," covertly, the guard's eyes shifted to rake over the beautiful Claudia. Quickly catching himself, he cut his gaze back to his commander.

"Well?" The guard's glance made Pilate even more irritable.

"Sir, Caiaphas, the High Priest, is standing at the gate. Shall I send him away, Sir?"

"One could only hope," Pilate replied. Then, raising his craggy brows in question, he demanded, "Well, what does he say?"

"Apparently, sir, there is a situation that warrants your assistance... 'for the good of Rome,' and a letter he had sent to you," his tone dripped sarcasm.

A shadow of a smile played around Pilate's lips. "Ah, so Caiaphas needs a favor."

The Jews never did anything for Rome that didn't benefit them more in the long run. Still, this request made Pilate feel vindicated. It was immensely satisfying.

But his smile melted into a scowl almost as quickly as it came. If there is one thing he had learned the hard way, 'A Jew could never be trusted. There was always an ulterior motive.'

Buying some time to think, he said, "Let Caiaphas wait until I have finished my dinner. I will send for him after I am finished," his smile was grim.

In the past, Caiaphas had piously refused to enter a pagan building. He was far too holy for that. To come to his home was to admit he was desperate to have Pilate's favor.

Chewing his meat, Pilate thought, 'Yes, let Caiaphas come to me. Let him enter into the courts of the glory of Rome and swoon with envy while grieving for his precious purity at the same time. Caiaphas must be desperate if he is willing to break his rules to meet with me.' This thought lifted Pilate's spirits tremendously. He finished his meal and a second glass of wine before he allowed the priest to enter into his *pagan* home to ask for his mercy.

Claudia placed her bejeweled hand on his, "Now, what is that mischievous grin about?"

"Nothing. It is simply payback time." He grasped her fingers to his lips.

"May I stay for your meeting?" Claudia was curious about these Jewish priests and this turn of events. She wanted to judge Caiaphas' purposes for herself.

Normally, Pilate would have said no, unwilling to involve Claudia in his business.

But this time, he said, "If you wish." He was well aware that Claudia's presence would rankle the Jew all the more.

**

Caiaphas huffed impatiently while suffering the indignity of being made to wait. He hated Pilate with his every breath.

The guard returned to tell him. "Pilate will see you when he is available."

So he waited some more. When the servant finally came to the guard, the guard bid him to enter with a smirk. Caiaphas began to object. "We are not allowed to enter into a pa...."

But the guard held up his hand, "Shall I tell the Procurator that you have changed your mind?"

Caiaphas glanced up and down the street and into the shadows before he turned and entered Pilate's home. He would do whatever was required to take the Nazarene's life, even defile himself by entering a pagan's home.

He was led through the grand entry hall and up a flight of steps into Pilate's richly appointed dining hall, which was more grand than his own. Pilate nor his wife stood when he entered.

"So....what can I do for you, your holiness?" Pilate dripped sarcasm.

Caiaphas was left standing awkwardly before them while Pilate leaned back in his seat like a king.

"I am here about the man I wrote to you about."

"Refresh my memory," Pilate played coy.

"Yeshua the Nazarene. He is an insurrectionist who plans to make himself the king of the Jews."

"No, Barabbas is the insurrectionist, and I have already captured him. I think you are confused."

Claudia interrupted, "I have heard incredible things about this man, Yeshua of Nazareth. But he doesn't appear to be the kind of man that would stage an uprising".

Without acknowledging her comment, Caiaphas stared at Pilate, "The Nazarene has entered the city as if he were the Messiah, that is to say—'a king'. He carried out a coup this week by parading right into Jerusalem surrounded by adoring supporters who were celebrating him as their 'saving king.' He has broken our laws and threatened the temple, which you gain a share from…"

Pilate narrowed his eyes, "…and he has challenged you."

Caiaphas stopped, "You don't seem to understand what this means. The people are deceived."

"Yes, but by whom?" Pilate reproached him. He was well-informed about Yeshua. It was his business to know everything that went on under his jurisdiction. He knew about his little parade from Bethany that dispersed at the gate. Nothing came of it. In fact, the teacher had disappeared. He had rode in on only a small donkey, not a war horse. That is not an insurrection. Besides, if anyone tweaked Caiaphas' nose, they were okay with him. His sources told him this Nazarene only spoke of 'loving one's neighbor,' though it was a foreign idea to Pilate to be sure. That was no threat. He was known as a wisdom teacher, a storyteller, a bard of riddles, and a healer. The people were quite enamored with him and found him to be enormously inspiring and entertaining.

"He has blasphemed our God," Caiaphas spat out with disdain as if this should convince Pilate. "This requires the death penalty."

"Then take care of it. What is your religion to me," Pilate waved his hand.

"Are you not charged with the peace of Jerusalem? Isn't the death penalty solely your responsibility now as far as Rome is concerned? This can and will become explosive. It must be stopped now. All I am asking is that you send a few of your men with us to make sure no riot breaks out."

Pilate looked bored, "I don't need you to tell me what my responsibilities are. And I don't see a protest breaking out tonight. Every Jew is sequestered in his home, besides you. It is the quietest night of the Passover Festival."

"I am just asking for a few men. Otherwise, if trouble breaks out, it will be on you."

Pilate could see Caiaphas was zealous to punish this man. It was enough to make him want to champion the Nazarene. Still, what did this Jew ultimately matter to him? If he did Caiaphas this favor, both he and Annas would be indebted to him. This would help erect 'honor among thieves' as they put it. And, he would be glad to remind him.

Besides, Caiaphas had no teeth to put the man to death. He could have the man released tomorrow.

Rubbing the place between his eyes, Pilate acquiesced, dismissing Caiaphas with a threat, "I will provide support. But you had better not be messing with me. I will provide a few men. They will meet you on the upper road. But, remember, you will owe me big for this."

Caiaphas offered a curt nod before he was quickly escorted from the palace.

Pilate called for a centurion, "Get your men ready and go help Caiaphas with an arrest."

"Very well, how many will be required, sir?"

"Take your whole regiment," Pilate said grimly, knowing it was overkill.

The more manpower, the more the debt. It was his way of mocking Caiaphas for requesting his help to take this one man into custody. Such a large number would remind Caiaphas of who really had the power around here.

Claudia stood and draped her arm across Pilate's shoulders after Caiaphas had left, "Well, the High Priest is not what I expected. What do you make of it?"

"If Caiaphas is involved, it has to be foul. He has been nothing but a thorn, but perhaps by doing him this favor, I can turn the tables a bit."

"I just feel bad for the man he is hunting..." Claudia said. "What kind of crime is blasphemy anyway, that it should require death? I have a bad feeling about this."

Pilate stood and kissed her forehead, "You worry too much. Leave the worry to me."

**

Caiaphas sent Malchus to lead the charge, "Take that weasel Iscariot with you to lead you to him and to identify him, along with the chief priests, Pharisees, scribes, and our best temple guards." Taking his cue from Annas, he wanted all of the main leaders to be involved to hedge his bets. It would prove useful if things went badly; they would be implicated and forced to support him.

Malchus gathered his troops and the leaders and set out on the high road as planned to wait for the small Roman regiment to join him. But when the Centurion and his whole regiment of soldiers appeared on the street, Malchus suddenly felt more than a little uncomfortable in his mission. He had never been dispatched with a Roman before, and there was no love between them.

When Judas saw the show of force Caiaphas had gathered, he became overwhelmed with fear, realizing he was far out of his depth. These men were serious, and this was all his doing. This was nothing like the fantasy he entertained. This situation was all too real and dangerous.

'What have I done?' he wondered. 'It is too late to back out now.'

He trudged along between the guards; the money bag swung heavily at his side, causing the forty coins to clank and jingle with each step as if mocking him at his sparse reward.

When they arrived at the upper room, they found it darkened, deserted, empty, cleaned, with no trace of any recent use. Downstairs, they pounded on the door, but a servant answered to say they knew nothing about any meal upstairs; their Master was away at his family's home for the Passover meal.

"I thought you said he was here," Malchus questioned Judas, casting him a suspicious eye.

"It took so long to get here. I guess they have left," he stammered.

"Have you bothered the High Priest and Pilate tonight for nothing? What game are you playing?"

"No—I..."

"Look! This *is* happening tonight, so you better think fast. Or you will find yourself staked to a Roman cross."

"Perhaps they have gone to Bethany..."

"Bethany?"

"I'm not sure...perhaps he has gone to the Olive Grove..."

He shoved Judas forward, purposefully wrenching his shoulder, "Then, lead on. You better hope we find him there."

~ 40 ~

WHEN THE ROOSTER CROWS

> "Awake, sword, against my shepherd,
> Against the man who is close to me!"
> Declares the Lord Almighty.
> "Strike the shepherd,
> And the sheep will be scattered..."
> Zechariah 13:7

Judas panicked when they came to the olive grove. A morbid sweat of fear ran down his brow. How had he ever thought turning his Rabbi in would be a good idea? All his dreams and schemes had come to nothing. He had underestimated the Sanhedrin. For once, he understood how doing things one's own way led down the path of destruction. He felt sure he would never make it out alive. He faltered, wanting to run, thinking, 'What will they do to me if he is not here?'

Yeshua's words echoed in his ears, *'Whoever finds their life will lose it, and whoever loses their life for my sake will find it.'* The butt of a spear pushed him forward from behind.

The landscape before him looked eerie and surreal. He felt the heat of the bright torches flaming behind him and was smothered by their sickening and oily plumes. At the gate, he searched the shadows of the grove, looking past the twisted old tree toward the olive press. There, Yeshua stood unmoving, as if he had been waiting for *him* to come and rejoin the group. A terrifying guilt gripped him, proving against all odds that he did have some shred of a conscience. He shrunk back under Yeshua's watchful gaze, now fearing him as much as the men surrounding him.

"Is that him? Is he here?" Malchus wanted to know, spotting the man in the distance.

All at once, the other eleven disciples came to their feet. The mob looked toward them. Judas suddenly foresaw a terrible slaughter of them all, including himself.

"Wait," Judas said, "Wait. The deal was only the Rabbi. Allow me to approach him as we planned. I will identify him with a sign."

But then, he saw the other disciples stand and gather close around Yeshua as if *they* intended to protect him with their own lives. Hadn't these men been like brothers to Judas? He had not given a thought to them previously. And seeing him, their faces held nothing but disbelief and contempt for him.

"It is Judas! He is the betrayer." Nathanael shouted.

Judas turned quickly to Malchus, "The deal was only for Yeshua, not the others. They are nothing without him. He will be the one I approach and give a holy kiss."

The words sounded ridiculous even to his ears. 'A holy kiss?' The 'holy kiss' had become customary amongst those who believed in him as the Christ, a sign of love. But there was nothing 'holy' about his betrayal. Feeling the spear at his back, he moved to walk tentatively toward the Master. Malchus had given no heed to his words, when he looked back, he saw the armed men were only steps behind him. They stopped about ten feet away to allow Judas room to step forward and identify their target.

"Greetings, Rabbi," Judas offered a loud and lively greeting as if he were greeting a long-lost friend on the street. It sounded false even in his ears. His hands came together as if in an awkward prayer of sorts. He stepped forward, then leaned in to kiss his Teacher's cheek.

Yeshua waited and received his kiss, then drew back to look into the distressed depths of Judas' eyes. His gaze was a strange combination of judgment, compassion, pain, and sadness, knowing things would not end as Judas had thought.

"So, friend," Yeshua spoke hoarsely, "has this been your purpose? To betray the Anointed One with a kiss?"

Those words were like a slap of cold reality. Judas stepped back into the mob to hide himself from Yeshua's holiness and pain.

Yeshua looked around at the strange mixture of people holding torches and weapons. All of his enemies were represented, both the Jews and the Gentiles of the surrounding nations.

"Who is it you want?" He asked, his voice seeming far too reasonable in its authority.

"Yeshua of Nazareth," Malchus answered, and the guards moved forward, ready to apprehend.

Yeshua answered, "I am he."

As the words left his mouth, the force of them reverberated off the solar plexus of every member of the mob. Each man was thrown backward by the potency of those words, and they found themselves with their faces cast down to the ground. They did not know what had just hit them. Unbalanced by shock and fear, they struggled to regain their next breath, and the whole mob bowed helplessly before him.

Slowly, one by one, they wheezed a thin breath and tried to regain their feet.

Seeing that their pursuers were cast down, the disciples cried, "Lord, run! We will fight for you."

Instead, he stood rooted and waiting for his captors to stand while they tugged at their collars.

"Who are you looking for?" Yeshua asked them again, a little louder this time.

Malchus braced himself and rasped, "We are looking for Yeshua of Nazareth."

"I told you, I am he. If you are looking for me, then let these men go. I am the one Caiaphas wants. Why have you come for me with swords and clubs as though I were some criminal? Day after day, I have sat among you in the temple teaching, yet you did not arrest me."

No one answered. The answer was obvious.

Without warning, Simon leaped forward, discharging his sword. With a quick slice, Malchus' right ear fell to the ground, and blood poured from the side of his head.

"What are you doing?" Yeshua admonished him, halting Simon's arm in midair as he prepared a second swing. He held Simon's arm aloft. His eyes bore into his in rebuke, "Put your sword away! Shall I not drink the cup my Father has given me to drink?"

Confused and reprimanded, Rock dropped his small sword to the ground.

Yeshua whispered, "Simon, if I wanted to end this, the ten legions of angels that are surrounding us would strike at my word, but as it is, I will be taken."

Rock gulped, tears blurring his eyes, and his burst of bravado disappeared. In its place, terror overwhelmed him. Simon turned and ran, causing mayhem to break out suddenly. One by one, each disciple turned and fled, scattering in different directions.

Meanwhile, in the midst of the melee, Yeshua stepped forward to retrieve Malchus' severed ear. He turned to him and positioned the ear carefully into its rightful place. It found its fit, and Malchus' pain evaporated. Malchus touched his restored ear with confusion. He stared uncomprehendingly at the miracle man standing before him. He came undone and found he was unable to act. "Who are you?" Malchus whispered, touching his perfectly intact ear. Only the damp blood stains on his neck and tunic were evidence of the wound. He wanted to turn and run along with the others, but this was *his* mission and responsibility. A shame-filled quandary overtook him, and he found he could not move. Hadn't this paralysis happened to him once before in this man's presence?

The Roman Centurion behind him pushed Malchus aside and stepped forward to take charge. At the same time, his soldiers grabbed for the last straggler. One caught hold of the outer garment of one young disciple, and they began to haul him in. But with one desperate look towards Yeshua, suddenly his tightly woven garment tore in two, allowing him to break free, to bolt away like a frightened deer, leaving his dangling garment in the legionary's hands.

Yeshua, however, was taken hold of and thrown roughly to the ground. His captor enjoyed grinding his face in the dirt while he fell upon his shoulders, pressing his knee roughly between his shoulder blades while he bound him. His shin guard cut into his flesh, causing excruciating pain. He couldn't catch his breath and began to feel faint, but the next second, the brute stood and jerked him back to his feet. Pain ripped through his shoulder as he did, causing a sharp intake of air. He swayed on his feet dizzily, but pain exploded across his face. Adrenaline brought him back to consciousness.

Having blown off a little steam, the soldier brought near a wicked grin as if to say. "Look at me. You are mine now."

Yeshua recognized the spirit hidden behind the mask of the Roman's face; it was the evil one—his ancient nemesis. The Roman laughed again as if he was glad to have been identified before he gave Yeshua a rough shove forward. Thus began their obscene parade. This procession was quite different from the happy convoy that had begun the week. Tonight, the people's chosen Passover lamb was being led to the slaughter for the sins of his people.

They took him to Annas' home just as Annas had directed. The Centurion and several of his regiment were happy to invade the precious Jewish boundary and trample the courtyard in a show of having fulfilled their mission, "Pilate commanded we deliver this man to the *real* high priest—Annas," the Centurion was inferring that Pilate knew who was really in charge at the temple.

Annas was waiting and readied for the privilege of questioning the prophet before sending him on to Caiaphas.

**

Once the mob left the grove, Yohan found Simon, and he went to a relative's to be appropriately dressed to go to Annas' house. It was not something he was particularly proud of, but it turned out to be convenient that Yohan was related to Annas through his father, Zebedee. Boldly, Yohan went to Annas' door and, after giving his name, was invited in. But Simon was not allowed to enter. Simon leaned forward to whisper, "I will stay in the courtyard. Don't say a word, or you could be tried with him."

Simon felt immediately uncomfortable waiting in the courtyard among the temple and Roman guards. He could only hope they had failed to get a good look at him in the olive grove. He pulled his scarf up to partially cover his face and clung to the shadows. The night was growing cold. A number of men warmed themselves beside the outside charcoal fire pit. When it seemed no one had taken notice of him, he dared to draw near, stationing himself behind the others. He could see and hear most of what was happening from his vantage point.

The hour drug on, and he was preoccupied and brooding over what might happen. He failed to notice when the guards thinned out from in front of him, leaving his face exposed to the firelight. One of the servant girls happened by, irritable because of the crude attentions of the guards. When she caught a good look at Simon, she recognized him as a follower. To distract the men, she pointed her finger and said, "Look, that man there! Isn't he one of them? I've seen him with that rabbi in the women's court."

Simon hoped no one would listen to just a servant girl. So, he denied it with an affected and gruff voice, "Woman, I don't know what you are talking about."

It worked. The Romans believed him and turned away.

Glancing around for a more shadowed place to wait, he noticed a large number of priests and Pharisees pouring into the adjacent courtyard. He casually moved toward the gate.

**

Annas was officially dressed for the evening's events in his luxurious robes and turban. To the undiscerning eye, his white hair and beard gave him the fatherly appearance of wisdom and benevolence. However, Yeshua recognized the coiled viper that was within. Annas was pompous, calculating, and ruthless. He began his interrogation with a benevolent pretense as if he was interested in Yeshua's well-being. He planned to play 'the good priest,' leaving the bad priest role to Caiaphas. It was his personal belief that 'You gain more information with honey.'

"So, you have preached out in the wilds of Galilee?" he smiles benignly.

Yeshua kept his eyes on the floor as if he hadn't heard him.

Annas felt the flinch of irritation, but his smile wavered only briefly as if he was adjusting his mask. He allowed the silence to drag on, expecting the man to make some sort of appeal in the vacuum of his muteness. But his ploy had no effect. He shifted on his ornate couch, stroking the length of his beard, squinting to assess the man better. There were few that he could not charm.

"I remember you from your youth when you came before the elders to be tested. As I recall, you were quite precocious in your knowledge of the law, even then," he offered a favorable smile, waiting for a remark.

Still, no answer.

"Come now, won't you talk to me? I simply want to know more about you, your side of the story, your identity."

He paused, "Tell me about your ministry, your goals, your disciples. I would love to know more about you so I may speak up on your behalf to the council."

To put an end to the awkward charade, Yeshua looked up and asked Annas, "Why do you ask these questions as if you do not know me? Haven't I spoke openly to the world? Haven't I taught publicly in the synagogues and the temple, wherever our people have joined together? I have said nothing in secret. Why question me? Ask those who heard me. Surely, they know what I said."

Annas' pretense slid away to reveal his obvious displeasure. A man who was being paid to bear witness against Yeshua stepped forward to backhand Yeshua.

A new line of blood oozed from the corner of his already swollen lip.

The man got up in his face and shouted, "How dare you answer the High Priest this way!" He threatened to hit him again.

Yeshua said to him, "If what I said is untrue, then testify. But if I have spoken the truth, why do you strike me?"

The man had no rebuttal, so he dropped his uplifted hand.

Annas rose out of his seat with a cold glare, "Get him out of here. Take him to Caiaphas. Let him deal with him."

The guard jerked Yeshua roughly towards the portico between the two houses.

**

Simon saw the sudden movement on the portico. The guards were taking Yeshua across the portico to Caiaphas' home. A number of men traveled behind them. Yohan was among the number. He searched below to find Simon, motioning him toward Caiaphas' courtyard.

Simon followed the guards through the gate. Once he was there, another servant girl accosted him, "This man is one of them, I am sure of it. Look at him; isn't he a Galilean? He is a follower of the man on trial."

This time, the guards turned to look closely at Simon but was unsure.

He lifted his hands defensively and spoke loudly to appear more convincing, "Look! I don't even know the man!"

They stared at him suspiciously, but Simon pretended unconcern.

In Caiaphas' well-manicured courtyard, Simon avoided the inviting fire. He remained near the connecting gate, in the shadows, far from the others. From there, he continued his watch.

**

Caiaphas stood from his exalted seat as they led Yeshua into his makeshift courtroom. The room was filled with some of the most powerful religious leaders in Jerusalem. Caiaphas took command. Certainly, he knew it was illegal to make an official judgment under the cloak of darkness. To divert justice, however, he would hold the hearing of the testimonies at night but render the decision at the break of dawn. It was a slight technical legality.

Once the Sanhedrin agreed, God help anyone who stood against them. The room was riotous with excitement. With great satisfaction, Caiaphas held up his hands to signal for silence. Everyone quickly took their seat. Without delay, he called the trial to session without naming a crime.

Caiaphas called the first witness forward anyway, "What crime have you witnessed concerning Yeshua of Nazareth?"

"He circumvented the law of Moses in the matter of the woman caught in adultery. He refused to issue the command to stone her to death. And now, she follows him."

Another man stood and testified, "It is true; he did not order the stoning of the woman according to the law. Instead, he said, "Whoever is without sin should be the one to cast the first stone. No one was willing to cast the first stone...""

So, the first man's testimony (that he failed to give the order) fell apart. Caiaphas ground his teeth.

One after another, people stepped forward to testify against Yeshua, but each time, their testimonies disagreed, and the allegation fell apart.

Finally, a man stood up and said, "What are we doing here? Do we have no solid crime against him?" Confusion erupted.

Caiaphas leaned over, asking a distracted Malchus, "What is wrong with you? Where is Iscariot?"

The head guard looked around absently, as if he were somewhere else himself. He shrugged as if in confusion.

"You were supposed to bring him back with the Galilean to testify against him," Caiaphas growled.

"I haven't seen him," Malchus looked uncomfortable.

Impatient for a verdict, Caiaphas sent an ally out to meet with the next set of witnesses, "Make sure they have their stories straight before they enter!"

**

All this time, Yeshua stood silently with his head down. His eyes were closed as if he hoped for some sleep. He was acutely aware that Yohan was present, along with several other allies. But he purposefully did not look their way. Instead, he prayed for them to remain silent for their safety. This battle was not theirs to fight on his behalf.

A Levite, who maintained the Temple, entered to give his testimony as an eyewitness, "I heard this fellow say, 'I will destroy the temple of God and rebuild it in three days.'"

Nervously, the man waited to be dismissed.

Another eye-witness entered the meeting, repeating the same words, adding more to himself, "These are words of a madman."

"Well? What do you say to this?" Caiaphas demanded a response from the accused.

Yeshua opened his eyes and looked at Caiaphas, but he made no reply.

Anger and outrage drove Caiaphas to his feet. "Are you not going to answer? What is this testimony that these men are bringing against you?"

Yeshua looked at him as if to say, 'What matter would it make what I say?'

Caiaphas stomped his foot like a bull readied to charge. He looked around the room, "Enough of this!"

Turning his attention back toward Yeshua, he said, "I charge you under oath by the living God: Tell us if you are the Messiah, the Son of God."

"Haven't you said so?" Yeshua asked him.

The two men stared at each other.

"However, I say to all of you: After today and from this day forth, you will only see the Son of Man sitting at the right hand of the Mighty One and coming on the clouds of heaven."

At these words, Caiaphas stood up and tore the holy ephod from his chest, completely forgetting God's Levitical injunction that a priest must never tear his holy clothing. Caiaphas was too furious to remember the ancient law.

Unwittingly, by his own hands, he had torn away his ordination.

With a purple-faced rage, he shouted, "Blasphemy! He has spoken blasphemy! Why ask any more questions? You are all witnesses; do we need anything more? Tell me! What do you say, now?"

Seeing Caiaphas' rage, no one dared to quarrel with him or give any defense.

"He is worthy of death!" A few began to shout and kept shouting until others joined into the fray. Those who opposed them suddenly became fearful and weak-willed. Some even joined their voices to the others to avoid the conflict.

Yohan tried to stop some of the men near him. He covered his ears and hid his face from their malicious intent. An evil spirit seemed enraged by the Sanhedrin. Hatred possessed the room, taking captive holy men and turning them into cruel brutes. Guards, priests, and teachers of the law fought one another for turns to slap his Lord. Each one tried to strike him harder than the one before them. Some took turns pulling out chunks of his beard. His face became so swollen and bloodied that it was no longer recognizable.

Despising him, they spit into his face over and over. They covered his face with globs of slime, so it hung and dripped grotesquely from his features and his beard. In little time, they had made a ghoulish spectacle of him as if he was the most loathsome of creatures. Having destroyed his face, they turned abruptly to beating his body. It was as if they could not stop themselves.

"Here!" A Pharisee shouted, "Here is a blindfold! He accused us of being blind. Now let him be blind!" They tied a foul handkerchief around his eyes and head.

They beat him over the head, demanding in their delirious commands, "Prophesy to us, Anointed One! Who hit you?"

Yohan felt sickened, but he could only stare in horror, holding his hands on his head in disbelief. From the courtyard, Simon watched helplessly. He became so agitated that he began to pace, moving closer, wringing his hands. This caught the attention of one of the guards.

"Surely, you are one of them," the temple guard indicted him. "Didn't I see you in the olive grove with him? Weren't you the one with the sword that struck our relative Malchus?"

Simon froze in terror, seeing that the large man had him semi-trapped. To convince him otherwise, he swore a curse, "**** it, man! I told you I don't know that man!"

At that moment, a rooster began to sound its trumpet--morning was about to dawn.

At its sound, Yeshua's words rebuked him, "Before the rooster crows today, you will deny me three times....asked to sift you...stay awake and pray..."

He looked towards the portico. Yeshua had turned to stare through swollen eyes down on him. His once-loving face had become a mass of destruction, but Simon read his mind all the same.

"You, too? Didn't I warn you?"

Remembering his boastful bluster, Simon was dumbstruck by how miserably he had failed his master. His face crumpled, looking almost as pain-filled and distorted as his Lord's. He broke and ran out of the courtyard, unable to endure his Master's gaze. With the sun coming up, the light refused to hide him. Simon wept and stumbled along aimlessly, pressed low under the appalling weight of what he had done.

~ 41 ~

A DEFERENCE OF POWER

Fierce men conspire against me
for no offense or sin of mine, Lord.
I have done no wrong, yet they are ready to attack me.
Psalm 59:3-4

When the rooster crowed, Caiaphas knew the sun was beginning its ascent. He and his assembly prepared to go to the temple. He had Yeshua imprisoned in a dark underground dungeon, hidden under the palatial beauty of his home.

Sure of the decision, the Sanhedrin could not legally complete the final judgment until first light. Those conveniently excluded from the clandestine meetings of the night were preparing for their day and performing their devout acts of worship. They were not yet aware of what had transpired during the evening.

The trumpet had sounded at daybreak, and those present completed the business of the sentencing with minimal words, "Death for blasphemy."

Elsewhere in the temple, morning prayers and songs were rising to the Father, along with the sweet scent of incense. Many were already anticipating Yeshua's teachings for that day. They didn't know that Yeshua was about to be transported to the Antonia Fortress like a hardened criminal. Had anyone encountered him

338

along the way, they would have hardly known it was him, so disfigured were his features, so bloodied were his clothes. He shuffled, weighted in shackles that made every step difficult. Already, every part of his body was in pain, swollen, and bruised, but the worst was yet to come.

Pilate had not slept well after his evening conversation with Caiaphas. Now, he wondered if sending a regiment had been so wise after all. When the rooster crowed that morning, Pilate was already awake. He shivered with premonition and dressed quickly to leave for his headquarters, steeling himself for what he could feel was coming. Heavy in the air was the smell of a putrid evil that he could not quite put his finger on. He told himself, *'You are not a superstitious man.'*

He had hardly arrived when it was announced that a Jewish garrison had gathered at his door.

An army of the Sanhedrin flanked Caiaphas, all filled with bloody intent.

Pilate thought wearily, 'Oh, I see this is the mob he had warned me about. He just didn't tell me that he would be leading it!'

"By the name of the gods, man, what is so urgent that you assault my door at daybreak," he queried.

Now, Caiaphas' demeanor had changed. He was demanding, "This cannot wait. As you know, the Passover is today, and a Holy Sabbath is quickly upon us."

"I am not a Jew! Your sabbath means nothing to me."

"The Sanhedrin tried the man we were seeking last evening. This morning, he has been found guilty of breaking our laws and found worthy of death."

Pilate was aghast at how quickly the Sanhedrin had acted, "Then take him and deal with him according to your laws."

Caiaphas was smug, "But...must I say it? Only you are allowed to put a man to death by the order of Caesar."

Now Pilate realized that perhaps his request for this power from Caesar was backfiring on him.

"So far, I have heard of no verdict of criminal activity. First, tell me his crimes, that I might consider them. Was I present at your clandestine meeting? Do you expect me to pass your judgments when I have no proof, no knowledge of what he has done? Surely, you don't expect me to put a man to death because you simply say so?"

Caiaphas thought quickly, "He subverts this nation. He brainwashes the people, turning them against their leaders. He opposes the payment of taxes to Caesar. He claims to be the Anointed One of Israel, an unsanctioned king. Should I go on?"

"I will make no judgments until I have talked with this man myself. Need I tell you that you have given me very little reason to trust your words?" Pilate's brows joined in a scowl, making him look as threatening as the eagle that was on his standard. His arm flexed strong, his finger pointed long and sharp like a talon for his centurion to take the prisoner from the Jews. He retreated into his hall to take up his judgment seat.

Caiaphas realized the judgment of the Nazarene was far from over; he had to force Pilate's hand. He turned and said to the Sanhedrin, "No one may leave this place until that man is crucified. No one! We cannot allow Pilate to let him slip through our fingers."

**

Pilate called for the prisoner to be brought in to be interrogated. With one look, Pilate thought, 'By the gods! They must really despise this man.'

Pilate was a fighting man, swift to cut down his enemies. But he understood this abuse was something altogether different. This abuse was personal.

He thought, 'Forget what Caiaphas has said. This treatment has nothing to do with religious laws or justice. This man has been subjected to the wrath and revenge of many men."

Yeshua was still covered by their unsightly scorn from the night before. His hair and beard were matted with blood and dried spittle. His eyes were swollen to little more than purple slits making them a painful horror to look upon. His cheeks were bruised black and bright purple. Blood still oozed from his lip and the raw places where his beard had been ripped from his face. He was hunched and swaying on his feet, shaking as one in shock and great pain. Pilate recognized the work of a bully, or in this case—bullies.

Instinctively, he concluded that Caiaphas and the religious council were both jealous and afraid of this man. He shrewdly took measure of the prisoner.

Yeshua waited; his eyes were on Pilate, and something about the man seemed to tickle the edges of Pilate's memory. He made no movement, spoke no word, and made no desperate pleas. Silence stretched between them.

Finally, hoping to move things along, Pilate asked a pointed question. It was the only question that really mattered to the Roman Empire, "Are you the King of the Jews?"

"Is this your determination? Or is this what someone else has told you?" Pilate recognized his challenge.

"How should I know, am I a Jew? You heard their accusations against you. What do you say to those things?"

Staring at the tiled floor, Yeshua refused to respond. Instead, he waited for Pilate's response.

Pilate was perplexed when the man offered no defense at all for his life. He felt oddly unsettled. He rose from his seat of authority to leave Yeshua standing there. He went outside to Caiaphas and the leaders, "I am not sure what game you are playing with me, but I don't find anything to accuse this man of."

"What are you talking about? Can't you see he has stirred up all the people from Galilee?"

Pilate cut Caiaphas a sidelong glance, "Yes, well, I seem to remember another supposed uprising that went very poorly not so long ago! The Galileans had no weapons, no intention of fighting, and didn't even fight back when my men were upon them. How can I trust what you are saying about this man?"

"Yes, well, I only told you what I had heard about the Galileans! You can't blame me!

"This is different; this man has been in Galilee and Perea stirring the people towards sedition. He preached the same things here in Judea during the festivals. You tell me, what is he up to when they laud him as their 'messiah'? He is trouble. You would do well to squash this now before it is too late. He is just one man; isn't it better we handle this now before there are hundreds or thousands more to die because of *his* insurrection?" Caiaphas asked him.

Pilate flinched at a gnawing pain in his stomach. This morning's expected 'easy release' was not going as he had hoped. Caiaphas brought out the worst in him.

Then, an idea came to him, "So if he is a Galilean, why did you bring him to me? Galilee is under Herod's jurisdiction, and he is here in Jerusalem right now. I can't make this decision for one of his citizens. That decision belongs to Antipas. He is Galilee's Tetrarch."

Caiaphas tightened his jaw; he needed to get this sentence passed quickly. But, he could see he was getting nowhere with Pilate, so he agreed to take him to Herod. He had blessed Herod's marriage to Herodias. And, Herod had handled the Baptizer. Antipas was his ally who had conspired against Pilate in the past. The delay was inconvenient, but he felt sure he could get Herod to act on this.

**

Herod Antipas was thrilled for the chance to hear this 'Mysterious Miracle Man'. Now, he was being touted as the latest 'Messiah'. He had drawn people from near and far. He had no armies, no wealth, no formal education. What was the draw? He remembered how captivating the Baptizer had been. So much so that secretly, he had even feared Yohannan had been miraculously resurrected from the dead. His guilt caused him to harbor such irrational thoughts.

The Nazarene had eluded him at every turn, ghosting him on Galilee shores for months. Now, providentially, he would finally get his interview and put his irrational thoughts to rest.

Herod lounged negligently on his couch, as he so often did these days. His vigor was retreating, if not his ambitions. He languished, a bored man, anxious for new entertainment. When the guards brought the Nazarene to him, he was greatly relieved he was not Yohannan. However, there was some odd similarity between them that was not particularly physical.

"So, you are the long-awaited Messiah? Come to rule this land and free the people from their enemies?" Antipas taunted him. "I have heard all about you and the miracles you have performed. I would love to see one of your miracles for myself. Why don't you perform one now so I may know that you are the blessed Messiah?"

Yeshua did not lift his eyes, or offer even the slightest response.

Caiaphas and the other chief priests and scribes were announced and came into the hall to stand behind their prisoner. Caiaphas was anxious to share his point of view. But Herod held up a hand before they could pour out all of their accusations. He remembered how Caiaphas had used him to rid him of the Baptizer. And hadn't his reputation suffered ever since?

"I know the stakes." Herod leveled his gaze on Caiaphas. "I want to hear what our 'Messiah' has to say."

He turned to Yeshua, "So, it is up to you to rid our land of the scourge of foreigners?"

Herod scrutinized the pathetically beaten man with perverse amusement, "You do look rather kingly. Tell me, if you were king, what would you do differently?"

He gave no answer.

"How exactly do you think you would become the king of Israel? Rome chooses who rules any region. Do you have connections in Rome I know nothing about?" Herod asked with interest, waiting.

When no answer was forthcoming, Herod laughed derisively, "I see. I did not think so. You have no plan. Perhaps you should allow me to make you a king. How about that?"

He motioned to his attendant, "Go and find a suitable robe for him! Preferably something that matches his current complexion of scarlet or purple."

The man returned with one of Antipas' older robes that had been recently stained and ruined during a night of feasting. Even so, it was a luxurious garment, died a dark purplish red, the color of freshly spilled blood. It was a very regal robe with a gold lining.

"Yes, that will do nicely," Antipas said, and his men stripped off Yeshua's plain and filthy tallit, leaving only his loincloth and revealing his battered torso. They fastened Herod's old robe upon him.

"Ah, see, now you look very kingly indeed! Now the people will truly believe you are their king sent from God." Herod guffawed at Yeshua, mocking him as one would a sad court jester. But Yeshua did not play along; he refused to even look at Herod.

"Come now, what is the matter with you? Don't you want to be the King of the Jews? Guards, please show him the respect that is his due." The guards abused him in front of Herod, beating him, spat on him, and mocking him.

Gaining no reaction, Herod grew tired of his games. The man remained voiceless and self-contained. Seeing that he could get no response from him, Antipas was disappointed, "I thought you would be more animated, more like Yohannan. I thought you would teach me something I didn't know or prophesy things to me that won't come true. Now I see you are not to be compared to the Baptizer at all. I'm glad I didn't waste my time searching for you after all. How could a meek man like you ever hope to become a king?"

Herod turned to Caiaphas and those accompanying him, "Take this man back to Pilate. He is no threat to me."

Caiaphas opened his mouth to begin to advocate for a different result. But Herod told him, "I won't have you dupe me again. I will not make the same mistake of condemning this man to his death. However, do leave the robe on him. Pilate will appreciate the irony. I have had fun, but in the end, I find your king very disappointing.

As it is, I have enough troubles of my own. Tell Pilate I defer to him. However, I do appreciate his regard for my sovereignty."

~ 42 ~

FACING THE TRUTH

"I am the Lord, and there is no other.
I have not spoken in secret,
from somewhere in a land of darkness;
I have not said to Jacob's descendants,
'Seek me in vain.'
I, the Lord, speak the truth;
I declare what is right."
Isaiah 45:19

Just as there were many who were appalled at him—
His appearance was so disfigured beyond that of any human being.
and his form marred beyond human likeness—
So he will sprinkle many nations,
And kings will shut their mouths because of him.
For what they were not told, they will see,
And what they have not heard, they will understand.
Isaiah 52:14-15

Claudia awoke with a start, her heart hammering in her chest. She knew her dream was a message from the gods about the man the Jews had taken captive. She had been stricken by a fear unlike any fear she had ever known, as evil was let loose on a beloved, innocent, and holy man, the only Son of God. In her dream, she had witnessed such malice spewed out upon that innocent man. It was clear to her that he was *not* just any man. What terrified her the most from her dream was that her husband would wound up playing such a terrible part in his suffering.

"Pontius!" She called out. He did not answer. She leaped from her bed, thinking only that she had to stop him from making this huge mistake. She didn't wait to prepare her appearance. She dressed quickly and left with her guards for the fortress. Her husband would not trust anyone else, but he would receive her words of warning concerning this matter. Only she could warn him and convince him to stand down.

She entered his court, all but running to him, to fall uncharacteristically at his feet. He could see her distress and was immediately full of concern, asking everyone in the room to leave their presence.

"What is it? What has happened?" He demanded.

She began to weep, and he lifted her into his arms, searching her face. He had never seen his wife this upset. "The man, the man...."

"What, man, has someone hurt you?"

"No, no," she shook her head.

"Then... what..."

"Yeshua from Nazareth....I have had a dream from the gods. You must not hurt him. You must not kill him. He is innocent. He is not who you think. He is more... Please. He is so much more... he is...." She sought the right words but could find none. "What the Jews are doing is not right! Promise me that you will not kill him or harm him. Or ...his suffering will become our suffering." Her eyes were wild in their appeal, and her face drenched in tears.

Pilate pulled her close and said, "You know, I do not put my trust in dreams, but I can see this has shaken you. This is becoming a tense situation. I have sent him to Herod. But I will do what I can. For now, it is out of my hands."

"No. You. You will be the one that holds his life in your hands. You." She warned him in tears.

A premonition of fear made Pilate shutter. 'What if Claudia is right? Has Caiaphas trapped me in this mess? That cursed Caiaphas! Has he duped me again to do his evil?'

"I will do what I can," he promised Claudia in a hoarse whisper. He smoothed her hair to comfort her. But she wept and was not comforted.

**

Leaving Herod's palace, Caiaphas called for all remaining reinforcements to come to the Palladium. A crowd swelled, clogging the street, and the word began to circulate within the city that the religious leaders had taken Yeshua captive during the night. He had to apply every pressure to force Pilate's hand sooner rather than later before the Nazarene's followers had time to organize and add themselves to the numbers of his manufactured crowd. It was Passover, and a special sabbath would follow. The execution had to be completed before sundown. Already, worshippers at the temple were demanding answers. Caiaphas' allies hurried to the Antonia Fortress, prepared to help Caiaphas gain the death sentence they had all approved.

Pilate came out trying to reason with the gathering mob, "No one has provided me of any proof against this man that he is guilty of any crime. Would you have me condemn an innocent man?"

Caiaphas shouted, "Then you are no friend to Caesar!"

Desperate for something, anything to abate this hostility, Pilate had Yeshua brought back in before him. "Look, you must give me something to help your cause. Are you really a king? Why are they determined to kill you?"

"My kingdom is not of this world. Do you see any of my servants fighting to prevent my death by the Jewish leaders? For now, my kingdom is from another place."

"You are a king, then!" Pilate's brow furrowed.

"*You* say that I *am* a king. In fact, the reason I was born and came into the world is to testify to this truth. Everyone who searches for truth listens to me."

"What *is* truth?" retorted Pilate, as if to say, "When has the truth ever mattered?"

Again, Pilate got up and went back out to the mob, hopeful that maybe he could sway the larger crowd to overcome Caiaphas' demand. He raised his hands to speak.

The crowd grew quiet, waiting for Pilate's sentence.

"I find no basis for a charge against him," he shouted.

Objections arose forcefully.

Pilate held up his hand. "But, look now, it is your custom for me to release to the people one prisoner at the time of the Passover. People, do you want me to release to you 'the king of the Jews'?"

But Caiaphas' men were spread throughout the crowd, and they shouted, "No, not him! Give us Barabbas!"

Pilate could not believe his ears. Barabbas was a dangerous rebel who truly threatened to bring repercussions down on the heads of the people. He was a hardened criminal, an insurrectionist, and a known murderer. There were many hard proofs of *his* crimes. Unbelievably, the restless mob became even more belligerent and demanding.

Pilate thought desperately, not wanting this prisoner to die, "All right!" He held up his hands in appeasement, "I will have him flogged. That should be enough punishment for any petty crimes you hold against him. Then, I will let him go."

Another loud demand arose from the crowd. In disgust, Pilate held up his hand to the angry crowd, showing he had made up his mind, and he reentered his fortress.

Pilate told his centurion, "Take that Nazarene and have him flogged."

Only later would he wonder what had he been thinking.

Foolishly, he hoped, 'If the Jews see him punished, perhaps his supporters will show up and plead for mercy. Then I could release him. Perhaps he would relent his teachings, and peace will be restored.'

Unfortunately, it was the man who had first shoved Yeshua into dust that came forward to take charge of him. With an evil gleam in his eyes, he fastened Yeshua to the whipping post, having stripped Herod's robe from him. His fingers itched as he flexed them around his cat-of-nine handhold. With a flourish, he cracked the whip, allowing the sound to tense the man with expectation. Then, he began to methodically fray both skin and bits of sinew from Yeshua's back. There were different types of whips and different techniques, but the Syrian was very practiced with the cat-of-nine tails; with the forty lashes he was allowed, he could remove every inch of skin from a man's back.

Hungry for some gruesome entertainment, the whole regiment gathered around the periphery, whistling, shouting, and egging on the brute with the whip. Every strike drew a response from the soldiers. The Syrian was having fun, and he would have beaten Yeshua to death. But when the Centurion saw what he was doing, he snatched the whip from his hand, "Pilate did not give the order to kill him!"

"We are just having a little fun," one of the onlookers called out, defending his friend.

Someone brought forth the royal robe that had been provided by Herod and ceremoniously draped it across Yeshua's bloodied shoulders. His body wove back and forth, trembling with another gross onset of shock. The cloak clung to the bloody wetness of his back. Another man brought a crown woven with a ropey vine with long, sharp thorns. Another rushed to press a paltry reed into his hand. They became possessed with raucous laughter.

"Look, look at the glory of the King of the Jews!" Their mouths were wide with howls of laughter, making them look like a pack of hyenas ready to devour their catch. He remembered his encounter with the dogs in the wilderness during his temptation. Here they were in human form, ready to bite and tear the flesh from his body.

The were built strong like young bulls, they towered over him, angry and unrestrained in their lust for violence.

One snatched the reed from his hand and began to beat the thorns down upon his head, ripping his brow with searing pain. Blood gushed into his eyes, over his face, and onto his shoulders so that his face all but disappeared. They also took turns slapping him, punching him, and knocking him this way and that. The hot stickiness of his blood covered their hands and splattered them. He was sprinkling the nations. Another prophecy was fulfilled. He collapsed, unable to get up. Their fun and games were over. Forcefully, they took hold of him and dragged him back to Pilate.

**

When Pilate saw what his men had done, fear filled him. It was all coming true, just as Claudia had told him. This man was in his hands, and this was the result.

"By the gods! What have you done to him?" he shouted at the Centurion. "All I wanted was a simple scourging. You have all but killed him!"

The Centurion looked sheepish; he was responsible for the prisoner, and the man was in such a state of shock that he looked like he could actually die any minute.

Pilate looked at Yeshua, "I will say this: your enemies are persistent. They want you dead. I can only hope this will appease them."

When Pilate marched out onto the stone pavement, the crowd went into a frenzy, like sharks tasting blood in the water. They yelled and threw stones, threatening to riot.

'No, no, no!" He thought, desperate to keep the peace. "One more strike, and Caesar will evict me for good."

Pilate held up his hands, "Look, I am bringing the teacher out to you to let you know that I still find no basis for a charge against him."

The Centurion led his battered prisoner out onto the pavement, still wearing the crown of thorns and the purple robe.

Pilate said to them, "Look, here is the man!"

The people gasped, speechless. 'Has anyone ever been so mangled?'

Somewhere in the crowd, a high-pitched wail began.

Miriam could not hold it back. Her wounded cry accused every person, though she spoke no words. An angry outrage arose from the few believers. But the loud voices of the Sanhedrin overshadowed their cries with their demand.

Pilate waited, hoping the man's followers would arise to demand their Messiah's release. His punishment had exceeded all bounds. But, all of this was a set-up.

'Of course,' he saw it clearly.

He sputtered in utter disbelief when the priests and officials began to chant, "Crucify! Crucify!"

As heartless as he knew himself to be, Pilate saw a personal hatred like none he had ever seen at work in these men. Furious at them all, he shouted, "You take him and crucify him. As for me, I find no basis for a charge against him!"

Caiaphas ground out his words through clenched teeth, "We have a law, and according to that law, this man must die because he claimed to be the Son of God.

Pilate's jaw dropped in dismay, 'This is why Caiaphas is so keen on this man's death? He believes he is God.'

Pilate had never feared any Roman god, nor had he ever been a religious man. But now, an overwhelming fear filled him as he remembered Claudia's words, *"He is not who you think he is. He is more..."*

Once again, he led the Nazarene back into the fortress.

Standing eye to eye with him, Pilate appealed to him, "Tell me, where do you come from?"

Yeshua said nothing. He left a vacuum for Pilate, forcing him to come to his conclusion on his own.

"Come on, man, speak to me!" Pilate said with quiet desperation. "Don't you realize I have the power to free you or to crucify you?"

Yeshua rasped through obscenely swollen and throbbing lips, "You would have no power over me if it were not given to you from above. Therefore, the one who handed me over to you is guilty of a greater sin."

'Sin?' Pilate searched the depths of Yeshua's bloodshot eyes, trying to understand what he was saying. He saw this prisoner's calmness and resolution, even as he shook with pain. Claudia had been right, though he could not understand it. This man was different; he saw no hatred, no desperation, only a sorrow that seemed to Pilate to be for *his* sake. He raked his hands through his hair in frustration, searching for a way to save the man. But what could he do?

He returned to the unruly crowd to cite every reason that they should set the Nazarene free.

But Caiaphas and the Jewish leaders kept shouting, "If you let this man go, you are no friend of Caesar. Anyone who claims to be a king opposes Caesar."

Pilate brought Yeshua out once again before the people and sat down on the judgment seat before them. It was almost noon, and the mob was growing more agitated as the day progressed.

"Here is your king," Pilate said to the Jews.

Again, they shouted, "Take him away! Take him away! Crucify him!"

Pilate made yet one more plea. "Shall I crucify your king? Even Herod found no reason for his death."

"We have no king but Caesar," Caiaphas answered, and his followers nodded their agreement.

Pilate gave Yeshua a distressed and apologetic expression; then, he called for a water jar. He had his servant pour the water over his hands in the sight of the people, "This is your decision, not mine; I wash my hands of this matter. I have tried to reason with you to no avail. Now, the blood of this innocent man will be upon your hands."

"Fine," Caiaphas shouted, "let his blood be upon us and on our children!"

Filled with defeat and self-loathing, Pilate did as they demanded. He released Barabbas, a despicable, violent man, and handed Yeshua over to the Centurion to take Barabbas' place for crucifixion. He knew full well that this 'Messiah' was sinless because they had never named any crimes according to Roman law.

Pilate told the Centurion, "I want a sign placed above his head that says, 'This is the King of the Jews.' Print this in all three languages."

The Centurion gave his salute.

But he recognized something unexpected in his commander's eyes: Pilate believed his posted inscription was the truth.

~ 43 ~

THE CYRENE'S HOMAGE

"Is it nothing to you, all you who pass by?
Look around and see.
Is any suffering like my suffering inflicted on me,
That the Lord brought on me in the day of his fierce anger?
"From on high, he sent fire down into my bones.
He spread a net for my feet and turned me back.
He made me desolate and faint all day long.
"My sins have been bound into a yoke;
By his hands, they were woven together.
They have been hung on my neck,
And the Lord has sapped my strength.
And He has given me into the hands of those
I cannot withstand.
Lamentations 1:11b-14

A fresh wave of pain overtook Yeshua when they ripped the blood-drenched robe from his back and dressed him in his filthy and bloodied clothes. They brought the heavy cross beam to lay it like a yoke across his shoulders, tying his hands to it with ropes. They set out on their cruel parade of shame through a main thoroughfare to a place just outside the city walls, to the hill called Golgotha. Though crosses lined the outside city highways, this was the most prominent place of execution because it was elevated on the rock face—the Skull, and just off of a busy thoroughfare. It was a most conspicuous reminder to passersby, 'Do not cross the Romans.' And on this day, it had been preserved for Rome's enemy number one, the insurrectionist Yehu bar Rabbas. Now, Yeshua bar Yosef would take his place on this providential cross to be flanked by other criminals.

No sooner had they set out than Yeshua collapsed under its weight.

The Centurion growled at his men, "Look, you've made him too weak to carry the beam!"

Scanning the people passing by, he spotted a burley fellow who had just arrived from the great distance of Cyrene. He was very tired, and he was traveling with his two adolescent sons on his way to Passover. Before he and his sons could skirt by, the Centurion called out to him.

"You there. You look able." He pointed with his spear towards Simon, "Come and carry this man's load."

Simon knew he had no choice. Who would say "No." to a Roman Centurion? He turned quickly to his boys, telling them, "Stay with me, follow behind, and don't say a word no matter what happens."

Rufus and Alexander nodded fearfully, understanding the danger.

Simon was greatly distressed, for he greatly wanted to reach the temple in time to make his sacrifice with his boys. He needed to be washed and purified in the mitzvah to be properly prepared for Passover. Circumstances had made him run late, and now he only longed to pay his homage to God. He anticipated gathering with his relatives for the Passover Feast afterward. Now, it looked like, after his long journey and all of his best intentions—he might not make it in time. Frustration gripped him.

For the first mile, he held aloft both the weight of the beam and the prisoner, who was tied to the load and stumbling pitifully along the way. To carry the weight of the crossbeam and the condemned, he was forced to press close to the man as if in an embrace.

However, he found it strange that despite his filthy and bloodied appearance, there was a strong medicinal aroma laced with spices that permeated the man's hair and shoulders.

He tried to avoid looking at the man he was forced to support. Instinctively, he knew it would not have helped his situation. He was forced to cling to the man in order to spare his own life. He heard the labored breathing and felt the waves of shock flowing over the beaten man. Simon only hoped the man did not die on the way and make him ritualistically unclean. He would not be able to participate in Passover that day at all. As it was, he was covered in the man's blood.

The man and the beam were a heavy load. Soon, Simon was also breathing hard with his strained effort. Simon wondered what crime this man had committed that he should have been so utterly destroyed, even before he was crucified. The other two prisoners, also being paraded to the hill, had long since moved beyond them.

The man stumbled, his knees went limp, and they both tumbled to the ground. Simon heard the man whispering something in Hebrew over and over again. Simon strained to listen, "Father, help me, help me." His whimper sounded desperate, then amazingly, he pressed back to find his footing and pressed himself upward, stumbling a bit. Simon struggled to help hold him up.

There was a group of women who walked along beside them on the periphery, clearly hysterical. They wailed and cried like mourning doves. "Lord, We are here. We are here."

They came upon another group of women who were weeping and wailing at the man's bloody state. A sudden burst of energy seemed to come momentarily upon the man, and he called out to them in a loud voice that rang with authority, "Daughters of Jerusalem, do not weep for me. Instead, weep and beat your breast for yourselves and your children. Weep for what is sure to come. On that day, women will say to one another, 'Blessed are the barren, and the wombs that never bore and the breast that never nursed children. On that day, women will pray for mountains to fall on them and the hills to cover them to avoid the wrath that comes. For, if this city does *this* now while the wood is green, what will happen when the tree is dead?" Once the words were spoken, his energy was once again stripped away.

Simon caught him before he could collapse and pushed him up and forward, dragging him onward.

Simon couldn't help but wonder at the strength of his words, 'What an unexpected word of warning coming from a man stumbling to his execution. As weak as he is, why waste his breath? He was not angry or mean-spirited. Despite his words of a future retribution, his sorrow was as raw as he was. It was as if he could not bear to think they might be destroyed—much like he is being destroyed right now. He spoke with a surprising surge of power that was obviously full of urgency and authority. It seemed...supernatural, like an infusion of... what? Or the voice of... Who?'

For the second time, Simon wondered, *'Who is this man, and what has he done to warrant this death? Has his words brought this upon him?'*

Simon turned to look, really look, at the man's face for the first time. His wounds and beaten face took Simon's breath away. He was such a mess that he couldn't tell if he was young or old. Considering the tyranny of Rome, the man could be a hero rather than a criminal.

Yeshua turned his face to Simon and whispered unexpected words, "Please help me ... make it to the cross. I have to...make it...to the cross."

Something in his plea reached deep into Simon's soul, connecting to his compassion and sense of calling.

Simon himself was growing tired with the doubled weight. Now, he also stumbled. Quickly, a lash from the Syrian behind him sent a searing pain upon his back. Yeshua swung his head Simon's way to make sorrowfully empathetic eye contact.

The Centurion called out to the man with the whip, "Stop! What are you doing? He has gone his mile. Find another man to take his place."

But Simon called out to the soldier, "It is okay! I only stumbled. I can continue."

He moved to the other side of Yeshua and readjusted the load to start forward again to finish the final mile. As they walked, Simon kept his eyes on Yeshua. They connected with one another's distress and pain. They labored onward together as if they had become one. Finally, with great effort, they struggled up the last of the incline, reaching the top of The Skull.

Having arrived at the final destination, Simon was relieved of his load and set free to go on to the temple for Passover. But Simon remained with his two boys as if rooted, unable to leave the man now. Intuitively, the Cyrene waited to witness what was to follow. He thought, 'How can I desert this man now that I have had a share with him in his suffering?'

~ 44 ~

WHEN DARKNESS REIGNS

"...but this is your hour—when darkness reigns."
Luke 22:53

Having reached the destination, a strange darkness fell upon the city, a gloom unlike anything anyone had ever seen. To the righteous, it appeared as a portent of doom and gloom, a omen of God's judgement, as if an evil was present or underfoot. But the unrighteous hardly seemed to notice, thinking a storm was building.

The religious leaders followed the Roman guards up Golgotha, watching impatiently for the job to be finished, like a flock of buzzards waiting for a wounded animal to die. Caiaphas would see the crucifixion through. Once the Nazarene was on the cross, he would be satisfied. He would die because the Romans loved a tortured death.

The Syrian stripped all of Yeshua's garments from him, leaving his beaten body completely exposed. Lascivious jeers and obscene whistles came from the nearby soldiers. The Syrian shoved Yeshua backward onto the ground. Straddling him, he quickly went about the task of finding the place between the bones of his outstretched wrists to wedge the large nails through both flesh and wood. The nails found the place of the greatest agony between the median and radial nerves, which controlled the movement of the hands. With one brutal blow, an unfathomable spasm of pain shot up his arm.

The Syrian took a moment to enjoy the shock and agony that contorted Yeshua's face. He chortled, "Hurts, doesn't it?"

Yeshua's hand swiveled like a dying flower, his fingers twisted into a deformed claw. The man's overjoyed face flashed before him because he had healed his swiveled hand.

The Syrian leaned quickly to the other side and repeated his process. The pain was even worse, causing not only his hand but his whole arm to spasm terribly.

"Oh, this one was even better," He stood up and laughed out loud. He called to one of the other men, "Take hold of the other side of the cross beam to lift him up! He looked into Yeshua's face with a smirk, "Here you go, Your Majesty! It is time for you to ascend to your throne."

Together, they pulled Yeshua back to his feet and looped the ropes properly under the crossbeam. The other man climbed up the ladder along the back of the tall, ugly, leafless tree. It was rooted in place, but it was stripped of its vestige, just like the Lord. Dropping the ropes to his men below, they began lifting Yeshua from the ground onto the tree. Each jerk felt like it was ripping his body in two while scraping against the rough bark. Once again, his back stung like hornets were attacking him. When the cross beam fell into its notch, he dangled by his arms while the soldiers worked to secure the beam with ropes. They were well-practiced at their awful work. He passed dizzily in and out of consciousness while his weight pulled and tore his wounded wrists and separated his shoulder joints painfully from their sockets.

Finally, the man climbed down. They began to fight over who would pierce his feet. But the Syrian would not be denied this final pleasure. He roughly shoved Yeshua's feet up onto a small, sharp-edged platform. He twisted his feet to the left, then took up an extra-long metal peg. His helper positioned both of Yeshua's feet together in a practiced alignment. Awkwardly twisted and paralyzed in place, Yeshua thought of the poor man by the pool of Siloam, left lying helplessly. Just when he thought the pain could not get any worse, he felt the first blows just above his ankles, ripping through the ligaments between his bones. The pain was so bad that he passed in and out of consciousness.

The work of breathing in this position was excruciating. To draw each breath, he had to push up on his skewered feet again and again. Each effort to breathe caused his lower back to scream and spasm at the same time. With every movement, the rough bark of the tree raked his raw back.

He squinted into the darkened sky to gauge the time. Three o'clock was yet hours away. He had to conserve his strength to make it until the trumpet blast that would signal the Passover Lamb was slaughtered. Not until then could he allow himself the sweet relief of death.

Meanwhile, he would continue to drink the dregs of this bitter cup of his Father's wrath, the vengeance of God. So he pushed up, and he breathed. Looking downward, he dimly saw his enemies, the priests and Sanhedrin, gathered below his cross to jeer at him victoriously.

Caiaphas shouted in outrage, "This sign says, 'The King of the Jews!' Elias, go to Pilate to have this sign changed immediately to read, 'He *said* he was the King of the Jews'."

The Centurion wetted a sponge in a bucket of vinegar and gall. It was a bitter mixture meant to alleviate some of the pain and to put the victim into a stupor to help speed along the process of death. He lifted it to Yeshua's lips. But when he smelled the vinegar mixture, he refused to taste it, knowing he could not afford to lessen the pain or shorten the time. Not yet.

"Suit yourself," The Centurion studied him in consternation. "You will be sorry you didn't take it." He and his men sat down to pass the time until the three executions were complete.

Yeshua heard Caiaphas call out to him, "Look at you! Where is your boldness now? You saved others, but here you are, nailed to a cross and unable to save yourself! Some 'Messiah' you are! If you are who you say you are, let me see you come down now from the cross. Then, we will all believe in you and put our trust in you."

Yeshua recognized the taunt of the Evil One. He was clearly enjoying his momentary triumph. Caiaphas continued to mock him, "You trusted in God. But where is God now? Why won't God come to your rescue if he cares so much for you? Didn't you say to me, 'I am the Son of God?'" Caiaphas snorted with disgust, and others joined in to mock him also.

Mean-spirited strangers came to stand before him to shout obscenities. They were ruthless onlookers who were filled with resentment and bitterness. They unleashed their vitriol on him. They knew little about him and had no reason to hate him. He was simply a sanctioned and convenient target for their spleen. A few of them had even cheered him on earlier in the week. Now, they had lost their small confidence in him. They stood shaking their head, embarrassed they had ever believed.

Caiaphas shouted to him, "Didn't you tell me you would destroy the temple and then rebuild it in three days? See where your mad boasts have led you?"

"Save yourself! Come down from the cross if you are the Son of God!" they chanted loudly in unison, then broke into laughter.

The man on the cross to his left joined in, "Yes, save yourself and save us also. Aren't you the Messiah? Or are you simply the fraud they say you are?"

The man on his right rebuked his partner in crime, "Have you no fear of God? You and I are going to die today. The difference is that we are being condemned for the sins we committed. But this man has committed no sins. You should tremble in his presence."

He turned to Yeshua and cried out, "Be merciful, Lord; remember me when you have come into your kingdom."

Yeshua blinked away his tears while gratefully receiving the man's sustaining and encouraging words, glad for this one acknowledgment, "You can count on me, today you will be with me in Paradise." He gave the man a faint tremor of a smile.

Minutes ticked by, one breath after another. The pain was exhausting him. He longed for the pain to come to an end, but it grew worse, becoming even more crushing and consuming in its intensity. When he pressed up to take another ragged breath, it took all the strength he had. His breaths were shrinking as if there was no room for a breath left in his body. He felt dizzy, and dark spots danced before his eyes. Tightness was building in his chest, making it feel strained and overfilled. His stomach was extended, and also felt like it would explode. The forty days of his former temptation in the desert looked like light work in comparison to this: Satan's final opportune time.

He thought of all the prophecies, the words of Isaiah and David and the Psalmists, and of so many others which were being fulfilled on this day, word for word, just as they had been recorded hundreds and even thousands of years before.

He heard the muffled sound of the Syrian's hideous laughter, accompanied by the other men while they passed their time with a gambling game. Apparently, there was one final piece of his clothing left, the undergarment that his mother had made for him. They tossed the dice and burst into an uproar when the Syrian won it.

'Naked, I came into the world, and naked, I leave it.'

Forgiveness was all he had left to offer anyone for the taking. His forgiveness would be the catalyst for the renewal of human souls.

Yeshua lifted his voice and spoke those all-important words.

"Father, forgive them. They don't know what they are doing."

Everyone stopped that heard it. At those words, the Syrian's smile faded. The Centurion moved closer in wonder, straining to hear his next words.

'Forgiveness?' They marveled.

Yeshua's eyes swept the blurry ground below. Just then, a group of women moved forward to stand at his feet. The Syrian stood to drive them away, but the Centurion barked, "Leave them alone! It is his mother and family. Have you no heart, no couth at all?"

The women pressed close around the tree, looking up at him with glistening eyes. It was hard to see a loved one so wickedly displayed, a holy and righteous man so exposed and shamed. It was wrong. Such exposure would normally have warranted lowered eyes, but this was not the time for modesty or concern for such things. Their souls pressed past his outer visage, seeing only his self-giving soul. This was love. Real. Everlasting. Love.

Miriam called out, "Yeshua, do you see us?"

He tilted his head to see the faces that he loved.

She continued, low and comfortingly. "We are here. I am here with your Aunt Mary, Magdalene, Joanna, Salome, Susanna, Yohan, and others are here too. My son, you are not alone," her voice broke.

"We love you. We will always love you," the other women echoed her sentiment, sounding like mourning doves.

Weeping, Magdalene leaned on Joanna. She croaked, a cry of raw words, "I knew...you would...die, but...I never thought it could be...this bad. How could you do this for me? For us all, to make us yours?"

He pushed up again on his twisted and bloodied feet while Magdalene stared at them, longing to be able to reach them, for some balm that could soothe them, that she could cover them in kisses. She wanted to hold on to them and never let them go. But of course, even if she could, that would only cause him more suffering.

'Mari.' He whispered, as if sensing her thoughts. He squinted to look down to see her broken face. Mari had always adored him at his feet, but now all of the women and Yohan stood at the foot of his cross as if by his deathbed.

Each one were replaying their very personal moments with him in their mind.

Miriam thought of the day when he had slipped with such great effort from her womb, and Yosef had held him aloft. The very first thing she had glimpsed of him was his tiny baby's feet, covered in fluid and blood. She had taken him to her breast and cleaned him as best as she could before swaddling him tightly. She would be swaddling him again today.

Magdalene thought of the day he had taken a stand as her savior against Caiaphas. She had bowed face to the ground before him then. And, later, she had covered those feet with her kisses. She thought of the night she had confessed her love for him and fell asleep holding to his foot, knowing this day would come and he would be taken from her.

Yohan thought of all the miles he had walked behind Yeshua. How his Lord had at times hobbled with blisters like the rest of them. And yet, he had taught them and made them bold enough to travel out in mission. He thought of the night Yeshua's feet had walked effortlessly across the waves of the sea in the midst of the storm. He thought of his feet standing upon the mountaintop, glowing and otherworldly. Now he was standing with the women beside his deathbed just as any good son might. His youthful appearance protected him from serious consideration. With his head bowed, he wept along with Miriam and Magdalene. He looked up, searching his Master's face.

Yeshua coughed and swallowed with difficulty. His breathing was ragged and shallow when he rasped, "Dear woman, now Yohan will be your son."

To Yohan, he said, "Here is your mother."

Yohan nodded and held Miriam close.

Yeshua grew quiet again, relieved that Miriam could depend on Yohan. However, he hoped all of his disciples would keep her under their care.

They remained near to him, lifting their prayers, whispering encouragements, gazing upon him, engraving these last horrible moments into their hearts and minds.

Yeshua was becoming feverish; He was sweating yet chilled at the same time. Earlier, he had focused on prayers to make it to his goal, but now, even surrounded by loved ones, he felt utterly alone and depleted of the holy spirit. It was as if his Father had simply abandoned him in this awful unending pain and death. The heart-wrenching emptiness made him feel desperate for his Father's encouragement. He couldn't cipher the how or the why of it. It was beyond all reasoning, for they had always been one. Now, he felt the absence, the emptiness, the darkness, the void.

All of his Father's servants had at times felt abandoned by God. They had written prophetically of this feeling. Still, he had been ill-prepared for the psychic pain of it when that feeling of desolation overtook him, it's hopelessness was the worst crushing of all. His mind struggled to recall David's words, a prophesy. He spoke it in the original language, which no one spoke anymore, "Eli! Eli! Lem sabachathani?"

Miriam stumbled forward at his wail; it sounded like that of a lost child.

"Listen," Someone shouted. "He is calling for Elijah."

"Is he delirious?" Salome asked.

But Yohan and Mari knew he was quoting Psalm 22, "*My God, my God, why have you forsaken me?*"

The prophecy was being fulfilled. Yeshua's only encouragement was to remember that the song ended in praise.

He had been at his suffering for hours now. All during that time, the sun had refused to shine, as if it had shrouded it's eyes from this sight. The land was cast in dismal shadows, but he could tell three o'clock was drawing near.

He had not spoken for some time to conserve his energy. He had been breathing through his opened mouth. Now, it was dry as if filled with sawdust.

He rasped, "I thirst."

Miriam called out to the Centurion, "He is thirsty! Give him something, please!"

The Centurion had been watching Miriam's grief and thinking of his mother. As a kindness to her, he got up and brought a sponge on his spear as she requested."

Just then, the trumpet on the wall of the temple sounded its call in the distance; the Passover lamb had been slain, and the sacrifices were completed. Yeshua bent his head to receive the bitter herbs and vinegar that would speed along his death. He choked a little on the harshness of the vinegar. But it did its job, cutting through the dried flehm in his mouth and throat. He pushed up on his perch to catch one last breath, and looking heavenward, he said, "Father, into your hands, I commend my spirit."

At those words, a sudden spasm of pain exploded in his chest as if a dam had burst. He pushed up one last time, but he could not take in another breath. He craned his head to look down at those standing with him at the foot of the cross. Even as he did, he felt the darkness moving in to take hold of him. His heart, which had been loudly pounding out its struggling beat for hours, now became erratic and rapid, as if it was grasping at straws but finding nothing, no pressure or pace. Urgently, he pushed up into the pain, finding one last gasp and the strength to shout, "It...Is...Finished!"

To those who heard it, his words sounded like a mighty roar of joy. Immediately, he slumped over, deflated of all life; his body sagged against his restraints. He no longer felt the pain of his flesh at all.

~ 45 ~

SHAKEN AND SIFTED

The foundations of the earth shake.
The earth is broken up, the earth is split asunder,
The earth is violently shaken.
The earth reels like a drunkard,
it sways like a hut in the wind;
So heavy upon it is the guilt of its rebellion.
Isaiah 24:19-20

The hour was late, and Caiaphas had previously returned to his duties at the temple. Although everything had gone just as he had planned, he still felt oddly off, jangly, dissatisfied, ... anxious. He simply wanted this Nazarene's crucifixion and the Passover to be behind him.

One of the scribes approached him, "What is this blackness that has overtaken the city?"

Everyone had been asking him about the gloom as if he should know. To each, he had answered authoritatively, "It appears to be a strange change in the weather."

"Some are saying it bodes evil," the man probed him superstitiously.

Caiaphas searched the man's face to see if he was making this accusation against him, "Don't be ridiculous!"

Another priest approached him, "Good news! Iscariot returned the money early this morning while you were busy. Apparently, he had a sudden fit of remorse. He made his sad confession, claiming, 'I have sinned by betraying innocent blood.' Good thing he failed to show to witness for you; he might have spilled the beans. He revoked his deal, but it was too late. When we refused his reversal, he threw the bag of coins at us, making quite a mess. Can you believe the cheek of that man? As you know, it was a good amount. But blood money cannot remain in the temple. What do you want us to do with it?" the priest asked him, without batting an eye at the incongruity of his words.

Caiaphas hardly listened, "Figure something out."

Demonstrating his administrative prowess, the man replied, "We have discussed some possible uses. There is a piece of property just outside the city wall called 'The Potter's Field.' It is empty and unused due to its unfortunate location. We could purchase it and designate it as a place to bury foreigners who die while they are in Jerusalem. It would be the perfect place."

"Fine! Take care of it." Caiaphas said loudly to alleviate more conversation about foreigners or tainted coinage. He climbed up the tower of the precipice to look out towards Golgotha. The Nazarene was still on the cross. Descending the stairs, he called to one of his guards, "Go to Golgotha and tell the Centurion to finish the crucifixion. It is approaching 3:00, and the sunset is approaching. He must be off the cross and his body disposed of by then."

He prepared to complete his duties near the large altar. All the sheep had been sacrificed except one last straggler. He drew back the lamb's neck and readied to make the sacrifice of that Passover lamb when the trumpet sounded three blasts, signaling the end of the sacrifices for that day. He looked at the lamb, thinking, what difference does a minute make? But a sudden, earth-shattering rumble interrupted him, shaking the temple with a building intensity and moving the very stones under his feet.

"Earthquake!" came the shout. Panicked priests ran to the doorways, grabbing hold of them with bloody hands that had not yet been washed in the sea.

The last lamb panicked too; it scrambled free and bolted wild with fear through the door.

Caiaphas wondered, 'Will I die right here before the altar?'

He heard a loud ripping and looked up to see the heavy woven curtain of the Holy of Holies suddenly rip apart, starting at the top and running to the bottom. The columns swayed precariously as if a strong wind was about to blow the whole temple down. He gathered up his long robes to flee the temple for fear it would fall on him and bury him where he stood. Once outside, he found no reprieve for fear the earth would swallow him. Was there no escape?

He thought fearfully, 'Have I miscalculated Yeshua? Is this my sign? The Temples destruction?'

He remembered his prophet's words, "I will destroy this temple and rebuild it in three days." Just then the capstone of the Pinnacle arching over the sacrifices came crashing down upon the large stone altar breaking it in two, leaving the whole structure unusable. Terror struck at the hearts of everyone who saw it, 'This with the foreboding darkness? Was the world coming to an end?'

Yet, even as the altar was broken in two, Caiaphas' heart remained unmoved.

When the shaking had stopped, he was concerned with only one thing, 'Is everything finished on Golgotha?'

With frustration, he started toward the steps up to the wall to look towards Golgotha, but he found the staircase had become too unstable to use safely.

**

Pilate watched the retreat of Yosef of Arimathea, one of the most highly regarded members of the Sanhedrin. He could not have been more shocked when he had come before him to plead for the body of the Nazarene for burial.

Yosef had been concerned that the Nazarene receive a proper resting place. He was adamant, "He cannot be burned in the Valley of Hinnom where crucified bodies are burned. It is unthinkable to toss a Holy Man into the garbage heap."

Pilate, too late, realized the truth that not every Jew had been so strongly opposed to this Rabbi.

Yosef made the case that he had acquired a tomb from a friend whom Yeshua had healed. He promised he would personally be responsible for the burial.

Pilate thought, 'After I failed to preserve this innocent man's life, isn't this the least I can do, to allow him a proper burial according to his faith?'

"Yes." He'd answered, relieved, providing Yosef a sealed edict.

After Yosef left, Claudia whispered. "See, he has far more fans than Caiaphas gave us to understand."

Pilate was just wondering if the repercussions of this cursed day were finally over when a heavy rumble hit the Fortress and threw them about wildly.

A lamp was heaved from the wall, taking a chuck of stone with it. It crashed loudly to the floor. Its flame flickered and almost went out; then, it reignited in the spilled oil that was spreading across the pavement. Claudia grabbed for Pilate, holding on for dear life. They stared at the shaking ground in horror. Claudia wailed, "This is a sign of the man that you have crucified! Now, the judgment of his God will come upon us all."

A large urn tumbled from its place and shattered on the stairs below. They ran out onto the stone pavement where Pilate's seat remained from the mid-day judgment as if to remind him of what he had done. Immediately, the pavement under it buckled, and the seat fell face down upon the ground. The stone pavement cracked apart and buckled in an almost straight line from the seat and up the stairs. There was no safe place to hide.

Claudia sobbed hysterically.

They stared at the rift for some minutes after the shaking had stopped. Pilate comforted his wife, "It is over."

But as he stared at the judgment seat, he wondered if this might just be the beginning. When his men came rushing towards him, he ordered them to take the seat inside. There would be no more judgments from him today.

He stared out towards the place of the crucifixion for some minutes, turning the events over in his mind. Then he turned and carefully made his way up the cracked staircase, leading Claudia along with him, determined not to give the Nazarene another thought.

He had never believed in gods nor wallowed in regrets. The man was crucified. And that was that. But, this time, Pilate found his pragmatism failed him. He could think of nothing else.

**

Simon had sought a private vantage point from which to watch the events of the crucifixion. He saw the women, and Yohan bravely gathered around *his* master. He should have been there. He rebuked himself, 'I should have been the man who helped Yeshua carry the cross beam. I should have been there; I should have been that man. Instead, I allowed myself to be overcome by fear, by the accusations of women. What a coward!' He felt bitterly unworthy and ashamed after all his boastful promises.

"I will gladly die for you," he had said. Now, he felt he was just as much a traitor as Judas. Sobs choked him, making it hard to catch a breath. His chest ached with desolation and sorrow.

"What if I had stayed? What could I have done?" He asked himself. He watched the scene taking place on the peak of Golgotha, and he thought, 'I would be on the cross next to him. Could I defeat the Roman army or the Sanhedrin? Hadn't Yeshua known all of this would happen? Yet, he had remained in the Garden, waiting for this, all the while praying alone, while I could not even hold my eyes open. I didn't even pray with him! Alone, he has gone to the cross to be crucified, and now he is limp, lifeless, gone.'

In the midst of his confusion, he tried to remember what Yeshua had told them. He should have paid closer attention rather than pretending none of it would happen. Had Yeshua ever said an untrue word?

Suddenly, the earth shuddered heavily underneath his feet as if it would open to swallow him at any moment. Would he fall into the pit of Sheol? He clung to the tree near him in alarm. He remembered Isaiah's words, '*I will make the heavens tremble; and the earth will shake from its place at the wrath of the Lord Almighty, in the day of his burning anger.*' He was sure that if the Father were ever going to be angry, it would be today. Only then did Simon notice how dark the sky was. He had been so focused on Yeshua and his grief that he had not even wondered at it. The pain in his chest expanded to include fear. Now, he wanted to pray, but he felt unworthy to call upon God. He was unfettered and felt as lost as if he *were* falling into a miserable abyss.

When the shaking stopped, he ran towards the forsaken way. He took the path leading towards the Hinnom Ravine, weeping and wild-eyed. He veered onto the path that led to an overlook of the garbage dump. The odor of the incineration of refuse him floated up to greet him. He noticed a tree rooted right at the edge of the ravine just ahead. A frayed red rope dangled, swinging enticingly from one of the higher tree branches. He moved toward it to take a closer look. It looked like it had been cut or frayed by a heavy-weight. Now he saw it was too short for what he had in mind. Indeed, it was even too high for him to reach. He stood looking out over the stinking wasteland, full of self-contempt; he thought, 'This is me, a stinking heap of refuse.'

He leaned forward to peer down into the ravine, and... that was when he saw him. Judas lay sprawled on a crop of rocks, staring up at him, twisted at an awkward angle. His eyes and mouth were open; his limp hand was stretched out as if he were reaching toward him with a silent cry for help. Rock blanched at the sight. He could see that Judas had landed on a sharply pointed stone, and at impact, it had ripped right through his stomach. A buzzard danced around him with delight, mantling his prize and enjoying his first bites. Judas was dead. Simon looked, seeing other vultures coming quickly to the feast. It was a morbid sight. He looked for something to throw at them. He threw rocks, but they only hopped awkwardly sideways and lifted their wings, intent on their meal. The broken rope was still looped around his neck.

Simon stepped back feeling dizzy and sick, though he had not eaten since the evening before. There was nothing in his stomach but bile, but he dry-heaved anyway. Then an 'otherworldly' voice spoke to him, *"I have set before you life and death, blessings and curses. Now choose life so that you and your children may live."*

Simon raised his head. He knew that voice! The spell was broken.

Suddenly, he remembered his wife, child, brother, and mother-in-law, who depended on him. For a moment, his grief had made him actually forget about them. He couldn't consider death. He felt a tiny spark of hope. Maybe things weren't over yet. Hadn't Yeshua challenged him time and again, *"Where is your faith?"*

He straightened and went to find the others to tell them what had happened to Yeshua. And ...to tell the disciples of the horrific demise of Judas. He shivered. If the rope had been longer, ...if he had not found Judas, ...*he* might have been lying beside him at the bottom of the ravine. He straightened, determined to pull himself together. Against all odds, Simon chose life.

~ 46 ~

'THE SEED' IS PLANTED

Very truly, I tell you,
unless a kernel of wheat falls to the ground and dies,
it remains only a single seed.
But if it dies, it produces many seeds.
John 12:24

Together, Magdalene and Miriam cradled the one they loved, overwhelmed by the dead weight of him. All they could do was quietly keen and moan. Exhausted by the horror they had witnessed, the weeping had grown mute. His suffering was over, and they were in shock.

Two Pharisees pulled up with a cart to collect the body.

Miriam held protectively to Yeshua's body, "Haven't you done enough? He is dead. Leave him alone."

"It is okay," Magdalene placed a calming hand on Miriam's arm. "Yeshua prearranged that Yosef and Nicodemus would handle his burial. They are righteous men, and they follow him. They have a perfect cover, being respected members of the council. They volunteered for the task of handling his burial. They have made arrangements for the body to be appropriately secured."

Miriam bent her head and kissed Yeshua's punctured forehead, like a mother preparing to put her child to bed; then she let them take him.

The two men's faces grimaced in horror as they leaned down to roll Yeshua's bruised body onto the large cloth they had spread. They were speechless at the severity and the number of his wounds. Clearly, he had endured torture far beyond the bounds of punishment. Tears traced the lines of their distressed faces, ashamed for this evil Caiaphas' and the Sanhedrin had caused the Son of God. This wrath might have been justifiable to anyone else, but never to their Lord.

Wordlessly, Yosef, Nicodemus, and Yohan struggled to lift Yeshua's limp body onto the cart. They placed a covering over him and secured his body before they began their descent.

"I brought the linen wraps, and Nicodemus brought the myrrh and aloes; seventy-five pounds, just as it is required for a proper burial. It should do the job."

Magdalene and Miriam, as well as the other women, followed behind the cart. They had been too distraught to think to prepare such necessities. Yohan spoke a few words of thanks quietly to Nicodemus and Yosef as they led the mule down the hill of the skull. At the bottom of the hill, they turned into a lovely garden with a wine press. This vineyard garden belonged to Yosef. He reflected on how it had been here in this garden two years earlier that he had this large tomb cut into the rock face in preparation for his own burial. Yosef had been very ill with no prognosis of surviving, but now here he was with his strength renewed because of Yeshua.

The women were surprised to arrive at the tomb so quickly. But they were even more surprised by how large the tomb was. Obviously, the tomb was intended for a very rich man, making even Lazarus' tomb seem small. "This tomb is so close and much better than we could have ever hoped for," Miriam offered her approval.

"Well, as you can see, providentially, I am not using it. One might think it was planned all along," Yosef mused.

Nicodemus spoke up, "We must hurry to prepare him and place him in the tomb before sunset."

The men laid Yeshua's body in the stone trough used to catch the juice of pressed grapes. Yosef's servants had brought jars of fresh water and readied so they could wash and rinse him to remove the dried saliva, sweat, dirt, and blood from his body. They poured clean water over him, taking the time to wash his face, brush out his hair, and arrange it properly. When they released the dam, a waterfall of blood and water flowed from the press onto the ground like new wine.

They lay his body on a clean cloth. Then, they began to apply a thick coating of aloe mixed with myrrh. Methodically, they wrapped cloth strips around his limbs and then his body.

The women remained near, watching everything. Mari Magdalene was distressed that she had not brought her nard and the spices to complete the anointing, but Nicodemus assured her the job was done satisfactorily and thoroughly. There was no time now. So she stood nearby like the sentinel Yeshua had often called her.

They would have to wait for the ritual of mourning; the special sabbath did not allow for that. An appropriate time of mourning would have to wait until after the two back-to-back Sabbaths had passed.

Finally, the two men anointed his face with the aloe and pressed a separate face cloth tightly into place, then wrapped the head cloth carefully around his head to create a seal over his mouth and eyes with a separate gauze. The three men carried him into the tomb. They positioned him with his feet toward the door.

"Well, it is done. We have done our best." Said Nicodemus, laying his hand on Yeshua's chest as if touching his heart, "Rest well, Lord."

He did not understand why Yeshua had entrusted this duty to him and Yosef. He, for one, was grateful to be able to do this grim service for the Lord. He was about to snuff out the oil lamps, but

Yosef said, "Let's leave the lamp lit. There is enough oil in them for four days."

Nicodemus nodded. "Yes, you are right."

They stepped out of the low doorway into the growing shadows and took deep breaths. The three men rocked the stone upward over its brake, heaving the heavy stone into its deep trough with a thud.

An aftershock sent the earth into a second convulsion. Once again, there was a shaking with a long, low rumble. The earth was testifying that the seed of its creator had been swallowed safely into its depths.

Nicodemus turned to Yosef, "The sun is setting. We must go and wash. We must not tarry."

Yosef turned and asked Miriam thoughtfully, "Do you have a place to stay the night?"

"Yes, thank you. We have family that has prepared a place for us," Mari answered for Miriam. They took their leave, shuffling in that direction. Their feet were weighted with the trauma of leaving their beloved in the depths of the earth.

**

That night, Caiaphas' found himself feeling disturbed, afraid, and anxious. How could he not? The destruction at the temple had terrified him; the metal doors had been ripped from their hinges, and the lintel lay on the ground. The altar had been broken. Had there ever been such an earthquake in Jerusalem?

He found it hard to go to sleep. When he finally drifted off, he dreamed of the Nazarene on the cross. He had delighted in his agony. In his dream, he found he had lost his voice, and he could not plead for mercy. His fear had been so real that he awoke with his bedclothes sticking to his thighs. He had wet himself.

He left his bed to discard his damp garments and immerse himself in his private mikvah. In the chilled water, his mind wandered again over the events of that day. He should have felt satisfied. He had gotten what he wanted. The Nazarene had suffered greatly, and he was gone for good.

Yet he thought, 'He never begged. He didn't plead for mercy. He never opened his mouth to make any defense, not once. Instead, he just stared at me through those swollen eyes as if he was staring into the depths of me.' It was as if he had completely surrendered to the punishment. It left Caiaphas feeling strangely defeated.

He dressed and then looked out at the dismal darkness. His chest constricted, thinking of how the day had become unnaturally dark. He felt yet another rumble begin as the earth quivered under his feet. Another shockwave. He sensed a threatening doom he could not escape. Everyone had looked to him for answers when the temple heaved and pitched. The tall columns had rocked on their bases, threatening to toss the whole temple to the ground on top of them. But when the heavy curtains had torn from top to bottom as if someone had torn them apart and walked straight into the holy of holies, some part of him had known... God was angry with him. Fearing for his life, he had fled, and he had still not reentered.

The other priests had whispered that this was the sign the prophet had foretold, God's retribution for killing an innocent man. What if they were right? He stared at his shaking hands, pondering the Nazarene's words. *Destroy this temple, and three days later, I will raise it.'*

Only then did he realize Yeshua had never said *he* would destroy the temple. Was that someone *him*? Had his actions brought about the destruction? Then what would happen if, indeed, Yeshua's other words came true? What if he was raised back up to life again? He wondered, 'What if he is the Messiah?' Caiaphas had never allowed himself to consider the possibility. He had been in full self-protection mode.

Now he wondered, 'Can Yeshua do what he promised? Surely not.'

He closed his eyes, trying to remember once more what he had actually said. He pictured him; his hand had rested on his chest when he spoke. 'Destroy this temple....'

Had it been a challenge, or was it a command? He tried to think, 'Yeshua was looking at me when he said it.'

He sucked in a short breath, his eyes wide with realization, 'He knew I would destroy *him* all along.'

Alarm filled his face as understanding dawned, 'He was not talking about the building. He was speaking of himself. How did I miss that?'

His head turned toward Golgotha, 'Then..., he promised to raise it on the third day. As...a sign.' His mouth went dry. 'It isn't over. The man raised Lazarus back to life. I have underestimated him.'

He imagined the resurrected Messiah standing in the temple to accuse him. He saw his future unravel before his eyes. He could be put to death as a murderer, cut off from the people as the High Priest because he did not welcome the Anointed One of God. He swallowed back the sick feeling resting in the pit of his gut.

**

At sunrise, Caiaphas gathered a delegation of leaders to go with him.

Pilate growled in irritation at yet another visit, "What now?"

"We have a lingering problem," Caiaphas wet his lips, grasping his hands together in a conciliatory plead, "I have been reminded of what the impostor had said while he was yet alive."

"I have no time for guessing games," Pilate was exasperated.

"It was something he once said to me. He seemed to indicate that if he were destroyed, he would rise to life again on the third day."

"What are you talking about?" Pilate interrupted him with narrowing eyes. "Are you telling me, then, that this man not only predicted his murder...but his resurrection as well?"

Caiaphas stared at Pilate like a fish on a hook, realizing the implications of these words. Only One could do such a thing. But he pressed on with his request anyway, "No, no. We don't believe he will actually come back from the dead, but we do ask that you send a detachment to guard his tomb. I am most concerned that his followers will come and try to steal his body so they can *claim* he has risen from the dead. This deception would make matters worse than they were before and add fuel to their movement."

"Hmmm." Pilate didn't want any more trouble. He sent his servant to fetch the Centurion who had handled the crucifixion. When the Centurion entered, he looked at the High Priest with apprehension.

"Go with this man to the tomb of the Nazarene. Set a strong sealant around it and place a watch guard over it for the next three days."

The Centurion was defensive, "I can assure you, sir, without a shadow of a doubt that the Nazarene is dead. I pierced both his lungs and his heart *after* he had already died just to make sure."

Pilate held up his hand, "I do not doubt you. But now, Caiaphas fears someone will rob the grave."

"I will take care of it." He gave his salute and turned sharply on his heel.

Pilate commanded Caiaphas, "Go with him and make sure the tomb is protected to your satisfaction. I don't want to hear anything more about this sordid business."

After the priest left, Pilate sat pondering his words, 'Caiaphas does not fear the man's disciples will steal the body. He fears the man. He is terrified that this man could, by his power, come back to life!'

**

Simon found Andrew, his brother, first. He had long enjoyed Andrew's admiration. Now, he had to confess to his brother how he had failed the Lord. He sobbed in confusion and shame.

Andrew considered what he should say to comfort his brother. Andrew also felt ashamed; he had run away with the others. He embraced and wept with his devastated brother. Just glad to see him alive.

Finally, Andrew admitted, "Rock, I am proud of you. At least you tried to do something. What did I do? But what could any of us possibly do against the temple guards and the Romans?"

Simon said, "Yohan was able to get in because of his family's connection to Annas. They ignored him as if he were one of the priest's kids. But he was unable to do anything. We were all helpless."

"Best not to dwell on it," Andrew assured him.

"But...you heard all my big talk..." Simon shook his big, unruly head, embarrassed by all his boasts.

"Well, you didn't betray him like Judas. Can you believe he betrayed him like that?"

"We all betrayed him, but about Judas...," he told Andrew of his demise, confessing how he came to discover him.

"Do you think he hung himself? Or did someone murder him?" Andrew asked.

Simon was surprised at the thought, but it was completely possible, "How can we know? But it makes sense that they would want to leave no trail."

Collecting themselves, they went to search for the others in various hiding places. Even when they found them, the men were reluctant to regroup, fearing someone would report their location.

"Perhaps the group is safer if we remain split apart?"

Simon told them that he and Andrew were staying at Mari's apartment in Jerusalem, then left them to find their way. But soon, each man had found their way to Mari's door. The Passover pilgrims were angry about Yeshua's death, and some wondered, "Was he really the Messiah after all?" Others saw the earthquake as a sign from God. No one knew what to do.

The disciples looked to Simon. After all of the dreams of leading in Yeshua's place, now no one was willing to step to the plate. Their ambitions had died with him.

"What do we do now? Should we head back to Galilee or to the wilderness?"

But Simon's guilty red-rimmed eyes made him look as lost as they were. He shook his head, "I don't know...I don't know..." It was as if his brain was paralyzed by grief, though he knew they expected some words of action from him. He ran his hands over his face in an effort to awaken from his stupor. But to no avail.

Finally, he said, "Maybe we should just wait here a few days; the festival is still going on. After that, we can head back to Galilee...?"

His words offered little confidence. They shrugged, gazing feebly at one another.

**

Yohan arrived with all the women. It was dark outside, and though they had no food, no one was willing to go in search of it. Simon wondered how Yohan, the youngest of the lot, could be so strong for the women. Bereft of the comfort of the normal rituals of death, the women simply huddled together, hoping to fall into an exhausted sleep.

"This is how Jeremiah must have felt when he was told not to grieve over Jerusalem. Only worse. Yeshua was so much more than a city." Nathaniel said. "A shiva would be preferable to this silent grief."

A fearful pall settled over the lot of them. They sat together, staring listlessly into space. Nervously listening to the sounds outside, they picked at the threads of their clothes, exhausted but unable to sleep, empty but unable to eat.

"We can't even go to the tomb," Mari whispered.

They were waiting, but they were not sure if it was for death or life. Grief was like an amnesia that chased all of Yeshua's words away without any thought of resurrection. They were too traumatized and afraid to hope.

They realized he had been their righteousness and courage; without him, they were weak. If only he would walk through the door and tell them this was all just a bad dream.

As one, their souls cried, "Come back, Lord Yeshua, come back!"

~ 47 ~

NIGHT WATCH

There was a violent earthquake,
For an angel of the Lord came down from heaven
and, going to the tomb, rolled back the stone and sat on it.
His appearance was like lightning,
and his clothes were white as snow.
Luke 28:2-3

The Centurion arrived at the tomb for the changing of the guards. Petronius understood the stakes were high, so he made it a point to continuously and personally check on the guards to make sure no one was slacking off on their duties. He found his four guards, two standing on each side of the tomb just as he had left them. Better safe than sorry. Their salute was swift, and they did not speak until Petronius addressed them. There were two temple guards posted as well. 'What a strange sight, Romans and Jews together,' Petronius thought. This small army was overkill, but he knew how to take his orders. This was their third night.

"What is your report?" he asked his men.

"It has been quiet, sir. We haven't seen anyone but at a distance."

"It would seem the man from Arimathea has kept his word to keep this resting place secret."

Replacements arrived to take the night watch. Noting their commander's presence, they realized the seriousness of their detail. These were the same four men who had been given charge over Yeshua throughout his crucifixion. Now, they took up their positions while the other four left. Petronius remained, taking the opportunity to debrief his four men concerning the events of *that* day, "What do you make of all of this?"

"I have never had to guard a man's grave before," one of them commented.

These men, who had been so quick to mock and beat the Nazarene, were now very closed mouth about their experience. The Syrian, who had taken particular pleasure in his cruelties, said, "We don't know what to make of it, sir. Surely, the Hebrew God did make his fury known...the darkened sky and the earthquake."

"I have been unable to think of anything else," Petronius confessed. "That day and his words haunt me. Who has ever interceded with their God on behalf of their torturers?"

The other guard added, "And he was so determined to suffer, refusing to drink the wine that could numb his pain and stumbling back to his feet to walk to his death."

"Obviously, that Jew Caiaphas knew more about the man than he told Pilate," Petronius said. He looked toward the heavens, "Maybe in a few days, this will all simply blow over. Meanwhile, tonight—especially tonight, be on your guard. The third day will soon begin."

They gave a crisp salute then Petronius turned his horse to return to the fortress. Once he was gone, one of the men said to the Syrian, "What's up with Petronius?"

He grimaced, "Perhaps he believes the Nazarene will rise again."

"And, what about you...are you afraid?"

"Why fear a dead man? Still, if I was, would I tell you?"

**

The shift had run long, and it was in the depth of the night when the guards suddenly saw two fiery objects coming in hot, like two falling stars. At the exact same time, the earth began is rumbling complaint, that built quickly in intensity.

The attending guards dove for cover. In terror, they fell as if they were dead men.

Upon the cherubim's landing, the earth's shutter reverberated all the way to the Dead Sea. The two large cherubim stood before them, giant beings of brilliant light. They were terrifying to behold. The guards shielded their eyes in fear of going blind. They were too weak to move under the weight of their fear.

Then, another being of an even brighter, purer, light stepped through the huge gravestone that covered the tomb. Immediately, the angels bowed down on bended knees, they covered their forms with their wings and their hands rested upon their chest as in a state of worship. A supernatural sound of music filled the air, accompanied by their song of praise.

"Arise," their Lord told them.

The creatures stood with a thrill of excitement, awaiting his command.

"You know what to do," the Risen One said.

"Yes, Holy One, we do," Gabriel answered him.

Michael moved toward the huge stone that sealed the grave. At his touch, the seal was shattered, and he hoisted the stone to heave it away, leaving it tilted on its side.

Then, the cherubim tucked their wings, transforming into a less menacing version of themselves, their faces still glowing with a holy light. Their wings covered them and took on the appearance of a robe.

Gabriel spoke, "We will give them your message when they arrive, my Lord."

Yeshua disappeared while the two angels went about the work of guarding the proofs of his resurrection.

And the angels raised their shields of invisibility. When the sentries were able to stand and move. They saw that now the tomb yawned wide opened, they wailed, "What has happened?"

The Syrian went to the door of the tomb and held up his lantern, "The Nazarene is gone! What were those creatures? You all saw them, right? They must have taken him."

"I don't know! It must have been angels?" the Jewish guards surmised.

"They looked like the gods!" The Romans proclaimed, "What are we to do now? Pilate will be furious, and he will never believe us."

"I don't want to be the next to die."

"Yes, no one could have fought those creatures."

"We should go to Petronius and tell him; I think he will believe us. He will know what to do."

"First, go with us to the religious leaders, they must hear the truth from all of us, then you can go to Petronas."

They left their post since there was nothing left to guard. But the angels, Michael and Gabriel remained to guard the empty tomb, readied to share the good news with the Lord's beloveds. The two cheribum had been waiting a long, long time for this prodigious moment in time.

~ 48 ~

THE SEARCHING HEART

If you seek the Lord your God, you will find him
if you seek him with all your heart and with all your soul.
Deuteronomy 4:29

There will be heard once more the sounds of joy and gladness,
the voices of the bride and bridegroom,
and the voices of those who bring thankful offerings
to the house of the Lord, saying,
"Give thanks to the Lord Almighty,
For the Lord is good; his love endures forever."
Jeremiah 33:10-11

The jar of a thundering jolt awakened Mari, followed by yet another shaking. The clatter of falling pottery shattering on the floor made it even more real. She bolted upright with confusion and fear, oddly remembering when she had shattered the pitcher of wine. Nearby, Suzanna cried out in panic, and others came awake, and in the distance, dogs began to howl. When the shaking stopped, Mari lay in the darkness, considering what the quaking meant. She listened until everything had settled into an uneasy silence.

She thought, 'Ever since Yeshua took his last breath, I have been shaking; my world feels like it has been shaken off its foundation, and my heart has been as shattered as that clay pot.'

How could she have known how painful and traumatic her Lord's death would be? Nothing could have prepared her for the feelings of despair and utter emptiness she now felt. Not even Lazarus' death compared to this. Throughout the whole of the crucifixion, she had remained standing by, watching and experiencing the horror of it. It haunted her. She felt weak and lifeless now, unable to eat. She longed to lay down in long, deep, mindless sleep. But even *that* small comfort and escape had been eluding her. She could find no comfort for the women looking to her nor for herself.

She turned restlessly on her mat, waiting for the day to begin. Today, she could finally go to the tomb to anoint her master's body with the nard and other perfumes she and the women had prepared. She worried that the process of decomposition had already begun. Yet, she was determined to go. When the other women, Miriam, Salome, Joanna, and Suzanna, moved under their covers, and she realized no one was asleep, she stopped her pretense. She rose to light the lamp and prepare herself for the coming dawn.

Salome and Joanna picked up the shards of the broken pot. Mari rechecked her basket, which was readied, waiting by the door. The men were in the other room, and they tried not to disturb them. Impatiently, Mari went outside to look towards the east. Ducking her head in the door, she called to the others, "The darkness is receding, the break of the day draws near. I am going ahead. I want to see what we are dealing with."

"You should not go alone. Wait, we are almost ready." Miriam called out to her.

"I feel I have waited too long already. I will see you there." She needed the solitary walk to the tomb. And, though she couldn't explain it, she felt she had to go without delay."

"Okay, we will be right behind you."

After their preparation, the women wrapped their scarves around their heads, took up their baskets, and set out following Mari's path to the tomb.

They were almost there when Miriam blurted, "Oh my, why haven't we thought? Who will roll the stone away?"

But when she looked up, she saw Mari running towards them, clearly in distress.

She shouted, "Someone has taken his body! The tomb stands open!"

Mari took hold of Miriam's panicked hands, "Who did this? Why take his body? Haven't his enemies done enough already? Oh, what have they done with his body?"

"What can we do?" Salome asked, trying to comfort Miriam.

Turning away, Mari shouted over her retreating shoulder, "I am going to get Simon and Yohan."

The women watched her go, then turned back towards the tomb to see it for themselves. They would figure out what to do when Simon, Yohan, and Mari returned.

The tomb did indeed stand open, but there was no sign of life. Emboldened, Miriam moved towards the tomb. The others followed close behind her.

Two gleaming angels appeared. A weighty fear fell upon the women at their presence. The women melted to the ground in fear, trembling and hiding their faces.

In unison, as if they were one, the angels spoke, "Don't be alarmed, the Lord has posted us here for you, to tell you, 'Why do you look for the living among the dead?' Your Lord is not here. He has risen from the dead! Go in and see," they motioned toward the tomb.

The women considered the situation.

Gabriel said, "Remember what your Master told you while he was with you in Galilee?"

Miriam recognized the angel and nodded.

Michael spoke, "Didn't your Lord tell you, 'The Son of Man must be delivered into the hands of sinful men to be crucified, and on the third day he would be raised to life?'"

In unison, the two said, "Remember." At their command, the women's confusion began to clear, and they remembered. The brightness of the angels dimmed, then disappeared altogether. Once again, it was just the women.

"Mari! We must tell Mari!" Suzanna exclaimed.

They left to find her and to tell the others what they had seen. The darkness was lifting, and citizens were outside assessing damage to their homes from the latest earthquake. Smoke curled from their hearths, sending a pungent scent into the air. People began their early morning routines. The women passed them, compressing their joy, afraid to let the world in on their secret.

Yohan and Rock came running toward them but passed them by without pause or greeting, focused on their destination.

Where is Mari?" The women shouted after them. But they did not reply.

Not far behind, Mari also appeared at a run. She halted to press the stitch in her side. Then, she, too, pushed on past the women towards the tomb.

The women turned to follow, but Miriam said, "I can't keep up with her."

They slowed to walk with her.

"We will tell them when we get there," Miriam said.

**

Yohan arrived at the tomb first, pausing by the door to peer into the darkened cavern. But when Simon arrived, he bolted right into the pit without delay. Once inside, the space seemed to be illuminated by the small lamp Nicodemus had left behind. Simon took the lamp and looked around to find the wrappings lying emptied and flat where his body had lain. They were still in their wrapped form but deflated with nobody within, and the head wrap was still separate.

"How can this be?" His voice sounded amplified in the small cave. He searched wildly around the restrictive space. He tried to understand what this meant, 'Why would anyone go to such an extent to arrange the clothes like this? Is someone playing a sick prank? Or could it be... But where is he now? Wouldn't he come and find me—us? But why would he, after I denied him? After we all deserted him?'

Yohan entered the small space with Simon. Examining the clothes, he asked, "Rock, what does this mean?" He stared at Simon with a flicker of jubilation. It had to be true! Yeshua was alive, though he could not say how or where. He just felt it inside.

Simon shrugged, still unsure; he stared at them in confusion.

Magdalene arrived just outside the doorway, sobbing hysterically, "Where is he? What have they done with him?"

Simon wanted to tell her to get a grip. He could not deal with her hysteria. But he bit back his words and pushed past her. 'I shouldn't be so hard on her.' He thought. 'She stood by his cross when you ran away. And, of course, she is beside herself with grief, just as you are.'

Yohan paused to touch her shoulder compassionately. He wanted to tell her it was all okay, but he had no proof. At his touch, she collapsed, falling by the doorway of the tomb. He left her to allow her the privacy of her grief and followed Simon.

**

Mari wept with her face in her hands. She leaned into the doorway of the tomb, searching for an answer that made sense. She found it too dim to really see anything. Then suddenly, bright light filled the space. She moved further into the opening, searching for his body. She found instead two shining angelic creatures. One was kneeling at each end of the slab, and they faced one another. In between them, she saw his burial clothes. Their wings were extended over the place where the clothes remained, shedding light on them. The image reminded her of the descriptions of the ark of the covenant that had disappeared many long years before.

"Look!" They motioned to the linen strips with their hands, drawing attention to the obvious.

Mari couldn't reason through what she was seeing. Instead, she cried all the harder, not comprehending.

"Woman, why are you crying?" They spoke in unison, waiting for her to come to her senses.

But Mari was so distraught, so confused, that she could not process what she was seeing. She wailed like one lost, "They have taken away my Lord, and I don't know where to find him."

The two cherubim lowered their eyes, sensing His presence.

Mari felt the shadow of someone behind her. Was he just speaking to her? She turned from the tomb to squint toward the voice. She saw the form of a man, but her eyes were blurry. His head was covered, and his face was shadowed.

"Woman, why are you crying? Who are you looking for?" His voice was kind.

She reasoned, 'He must be the caretaker of the garden and the tombs. Surely, he knows where his body is.'

"Sir, if you have carried away the body of my Lord, then please show me where you have moved him, and I will go and retrieve him."

"Mari."

She stumbled back in surprise. The gentle timbre of his voice reached down inside her, making her confusion disperse completely. She swiped at her eyes to see him.

"Master!" She joyfully launched herself towards him.

He held up his hands to stop her, "No, do not hold onto me. The time has not come for our embrace. I have not returned to my Father."

She stopped short just in time.

He assured her, "Do not fear. We will be together just as I promised, but everything will be at its proper time and in its intended way. I must first ascend to the Father before our union is complete."

She wasn't sure what he meant. She only knew she didn't want to be separated from him again. But she heeded his warning nonetheless.

"You will understand soon enough," Yeshua told her.

"You are ALIVE! You did what you said you would do. You did it!" She was awestruck.

"You are surprised?"

She laughed, "Yes, I saw...everything that happened to you."

"Yes, you were my watchtower, my witness. But for now, I am returning to my Father... and your Father; to my God... and your God."

Mari nodded and rejoiced, "You are not dead! You are not gone! You are surely alive!"

Just then, she heard the other women reentering the garden; they were coming towards her. She greeted them with the happy news, "Guess what," she turned back, but he was not there.

She turned back to them and said, "He is alive! I have just seen the Lord!"

"What? You have seen him! Where, where is he?" They wanted to know.

Mari motioned, "He was here just now!"

Seeing no one, they exchanged looks of deepest sympathy and concern with one another.

"No!" She assured them, "I am not crazy!"

Their doubtful looks questioned her.

She chided them, "Don't treat me like I am."

Suddenly, as if to put their questions to rest, Yeshua stood before the women.

When they saw his radiance, they fell at his feet to worship him.

"Don't be afraid!" He told them, "I am sending you all to go and tell my brothers the good news. Tell them to go on to Galilee, and there I will come to them."

While they were still worshipping him, he disappeared.

"See! I am not crazy!" Mari told them, and they all danced a gig of holy joy, jumping up and down, hugging one another, and laughing.

They looked around, noticing the sun was climbing into the sky and shining brightly.

"Today is the most beautiful day," Mari Magdalene beamed.

~ 49 ~

HE IS RISEN, AMEN

For you who revere my name,
the sun of righteousness will rise with healing in its rays.
And you will go out and frolic like well-fed calves.
Malachi 4:2

In the middle of the night, Caiaphas' sleep was interrupted by a pounding on his doors. Instinctively, he knew it had to do with the Nazarene. A fresh ripple of fear flowed over him as he donned his tunic.

"What is this?" he growled. The accusations that he had murdered God's Son had put his teeth on edge. His servant entered to tell him that the temple guards had come with urgent news. He sent for Annas immediately. He was out of his depth. When Annas appeared, he had the presence of mind to interview one man at a time, allowing each man to give their eye witness separately.

Each man recounted the same fearful account but in their own words and impressions. Annas saw the truth in it; he also saw that the two fierce and burly men trembled with an inordinate fear. Each described their version of the details of the two cherubim. The clincher had been when they had told him that even before the stone had even been removed, Yeshua had emerged as a man clothed in light through the rock itself. He had risen out from the sealed tomb. And, the cherubim had bowed before that man of light and called him Lord.

Both Annas and Caiaphas questioned them. They asked if they had been sleeping or drinking. They accused them of making this up because they had been overcome and the body was stolen. They threatened them, but their story remained unchanging. And the Roman soldiers backed them up.

The men assured them, "The stone had not been removed until the cherubim hefted the stone to one side. We are not making this up!"

Annas held up his hand, knowing that, ultimately, he had no authority over the lives of these men or the Roman guards. Bribery was the best way to silence people when you had no other recourse, along with the threat that if they shared this story, an accident would likely befall either them or their family. They were paid a handsome sum in exchange for them to lie and say, 'His disciples came in the night while we were asleep and stole the body.'

"What about the Procurator?" the Roman guards wanted to know.

"I will send him the message that your services are no longer required. Hopefully, he will forget all about the man. But, if he gets wind of this rumor, we will satisfy him and keep you from taking the blame." Annas promised.

The guards understood this was the only way out of their troubles. What choice did they have? So, each was given a large sum of money. And Annas' story was spread among the Sanhedrin.

**

Armed with the great and glorious news, Magdalene, Miriam, and several other women went to the disciples to deliver the message exactly as the Lord had told them.

"I have seen the Lord," Magdalene told them.

Seeing their exchange of glances, Miriam spoke up, "We all have."

The men looked skeptical. "Where is he now?"

"We saw him near the tomb."

"Yohan and I were at the tomb. We did not see him," Simon said.

"How did it happen?" Yohan asked.

"I was looking in the tomb, and I saw two angels...."

"Wait! You...saw angels?" Yohan asked.

Miriam spoke up then, "Well, don't be so surprised. Angels do come to people, you know."

"Sorry, Ima, not to be disrespectful, but the Lord's death has undone Mari," Yohan explained.

"Yes, but look at her now. Only Yeshua could change her sorrow to joy....besides, we all saw the angels! And, then, we saw him too."

"Well, if that is true, then why wouldn't we have seen him while we were there? We didn't see him, and we saw no angels." Simon sounded angry.

"I don't know why," Mari said. "But he told me, 'Tell my brothers to go to Galilee.' He will see you there. He said that for now, he is returning to his Father, and our Father, to His God and our God."

"I don't understand. Why wouldn't he come to us first?" the other men grumbled.

Simon's mind was spinning, 'He should have come to me first, but after what I did... So, if the women are telling us the truth, he didn't show himself because of me?'

Magdalene noticed Simon's downcast demeanor, "What is it Rock? Aren't you glad to hear this good news? You will see him in Galilee."

"I am not convinced," He mumbled.

"Well, what about the rest of you?" Mari looked around the circle of men, but the disciples avoided her gaze.

"How can we believe all of this?" Thomas voiced their thoughts.

The women grew frustrated. "Are you saying you do not believe us because we are women?" Suzanna asked, incredulous.

They did not answer but looked at one another as if to admit she had hit the mark.

"What? You don't believe that he *would* appear to us? Why not?"

Magdalene put up her hand to interrupt, "Look, we came and gave you the Lord's message, just as he told us to do. If you refuse to receive it, that is up to you. Perhaps you don't want to believe he is alive for some reason. And, you struggle because he appeared to us women, then we will not beg you to hear us. We have delivered the Lord's message to you."

She turned and marched away. The other women trailed behind her. Yohan followed the women to talk more with Mari and Miriam.

The men were left staring at one another with their disparaging thoughts, glad the women had gone.

**

Early that morning, as the worship began in the Temple, the High Priest held up the Omer of grain as a first fruits wave offering unto the Lord to bless the coming harvest. The first fruits were the Lord's portion, a pleasing sacrifice. It was the day to seek blessing upon the future harvest.

The worshippers were filled with gratitude for Yahweh's gracious faithfulness to provide for their needs. They called upon the name of their Lord, praying he would provide a bountiful harvest of grain for both barley and wheat. Their words recalled God's covenant of provision.

But today, for the first time, no lamb could be offered because of the broken altar.

At the same time, in an alternate realm, Yeshua entered his Father's throne room. At the center of the throne was the magnificent flashing energy he had only seen in his dreams. He felt his Father's love and approval sweep over him. The fire on the throne had the appearance of Jasper and Carnelian. The rainbow glimmered and totally encircled the throne, top and bottom. Surrounding the throne were the twenty-four elders seated on their thrones. They remained continually in God's presence, dressed in white, with crowns of gold upon their heads. Flashes of light arched here and there to the sound of the deep rumblings and peals of thunder.

Yeshua had returned just as his Father had said he would.

Before the throne, seven lamps blazed brightly. Each lamp encompassed one of the seven spirits of God. The crystalline floor stretched between him and his Father. Creatures covered with eyes were singing, "Holy, holy, holy is the Lord God Almighty, who was, and is, and is to come."

His heart soared. It was done. He had brought honor to his Father and completed his mission.

As the singing continued, the twenty-four elders came to their feet and then fell before his Father sitting on the throne. They took off their crowns and laid them all before him in worship and allegiance. They began to speak in one accord: "You are worthy, our Lord and God, to receive glory and honor and power, for you created all things, and by your will they were created and have their being."

His Father held up his hand; in it was a large scroll. That same scroll had been written before creation began. His heart leaped with joy; it was 'The Gift.' It listed every name of every person his Father had created for the Son. It was sealed with seven seals, perfectly preserved in time.

The mighty angel of his Father stood, still holding the scroll aloft. He asked the cloud of witnesses, "Who? Who is worthy to break the seal and open the scroll?"

The flames of his eyes danced with joy.

Yeshua strode forward across the crystal floor. Every eye recognized him as the slain Lamb of God. When he reached his Father, he extended his hand, offering Yeshua the scroll.

The Son reached out to claim the scroll. He had been waiting to receive it since the foundation of the world.

As soon as he took hold of the scroll, every living creature in the room fell prostrate before him. All authority was transferred to the Son, Who Was Faithful and True. The sweet smell of incense and offerings filled the air. The whole room took up a new song, singing with heartfelt gusto, so the doorpost of heaven reverberated with the song:

'You are worthy to take up the scroll and to open its seals because you were slain, and with your blood, you

purchased children for God from every tribe and language and people and nation. You have made them to be a

kingdom of priests to serve our God, and they will reign on the earth.'

Suddenly, the celestial space began to expand to include thousands upon thousands and ten thousand upon tens of thousands of angels singing the song. The room echoed with the sound of many waters. They sang:

> *'Worthy is the Lamb who was slain to receive power and wealth and wisdom and strength and honor and glory and praise! To the One who sits on the throne and to the Lamb, we sing praises of honor and glory and power, forever and ever!'*

Heaven was filled with shouts of affirmation:

"Amen."

"Amen."

"Amen."

The Son of God had a new name. He had succeeded in his mission.

His new name was 'The Amen'.

For he had fulfilled all of his Father's words and completed his will.

~ 50 ~

SLOW TO BELIEVE

...he rebuked them for their lack of faith
and their stubborn refusal to believe...
Mark16:14

Whoever believes and is baptized will be saved,
but whoever does not believe will be condemned.
Mark 16:16

The men looked to Simon, waiting for him to take the lead as he was wont to do.

James asked, "Rock, what are we waiting for? There is nothing here for us but persecution. We should return home to Galilee, not because the women have told us to but so we can regroup and start over. The sooner, the better. If Mari is right, then when we go back to Galilee, Yeshua will meet us there," James pressed him.

"Oh, so you believe her now, do you? Do you want to follow Magdalene? Fine, follow *her*. Go back to Galilee," he sounded like a spiteful and belligerent child.

Truthfully, Rock was reeling; he didn't know what to believe. If Yeshua was alive, why didn't he come to him here in Jerusalem? Or to Yohan? He had hardly ever gone anywhere without them.

The thought that Yeshua would send him a message through the women rankled him.

Unreasonably, he thought, 'Maybe he is looking for me now.'

He told the men, "Maybe we should just wait a day or two?"

James questioned him, "To what purpose? He is not in the tomb, Simon. And, why would he stick around Jerusalem?"

Simon knew he was being contrary. He just needed time to think of a way to lift some of the burden of his guilt from his shoulders. And Mari had been a mess. If it were only her hallucination and hysteria, then shouldn't he search for his Master's body to give him a proper burial? How could he believe *her*?

James spoke sensibly to Simon, "Deborah and Ana are waiting for you. It is still dangerous here, and if something should happen to you, she would never forgive us."

"What if they took Yeshua's body and threw it in the Hinnom Valley?" He asked him, still remembering Judas' broken body lying on the stones below.

Cleopas spoke up in utter frustration, looking suddenly haggard, "My wife, Mary, is going to travel with Miriam to tell the rest of the family about the empty tomb. Magdalene is making plans for the women to travel back with her. Yohan is going with them. I am traveling to our home in Emmaus for the night before continuing to our family in Capernaum."

Zel said, "It is probably smart if we all split up to go; I will go with you. Isn't that the way we handled it when Herod was looking for Yeshua?"

Simon said to Cleopas, "I will check Hinnom today, and then I will leave tomorrow."

**

Cleopas and Zel gathered their things, along with some bread and smoked fish. For the first few miles, they said very little.

Once they were away from Jerusalem, Cleopas began to reflect, "I still can't believe this has happened."

Simon (who was called 'the Zealot') let him reminisce, but he only half listened. Lost in reflection, he roused himself to reply, "I know what you mean. I keep wondering what I could have done differently. I let him down."

All of Zel's confused thoughts clamored against one another, he said, "Toward the end, his words became so confronting, like he could no longer avoid the fight. There was only one way it could end."

"It is so sad. Look where all his words and efforts led. Now he is dead," Cleopas sighed, "I let my brother Yosef down by not trying to stop him."

Zel said, "No one could have stopped him. I cannot pretend to understand what this turn of events actually means. He was extraordinary. I mean, I saw him do some really amazing miracles. I just knew he was the One. Nothing turned out like I thought it would."

"None of us knew what to expect. We simply wanted to believe in him." Cleopas grimaced, "Even as a child, Yeshua saw all of our wrong thoughts. Even then, he had been quick to point them out, not publicly, not rudely, not with any kind of malice but out of real concern. He was always straightforward and truthful without apology.

"Who can account for his following? We were not the only ones; look at all the others who were convinced that he was actually the One who would be the great deliverer of Israel."

Unexpectedly, a voice cut into their conversation from close behind them, "I'm sorry, I couldn't help but overhear your conversation, and I am intrigued. May I ask who you are talking about?"

Cleopas and Simon both jumped in fear and spun around. They had not known anyone was near; they had not heard his approach. They were surprised to find a stranger walking only a few paces behind them. They were chagrinned. Had the stranger heard their private conversation?

With sidelong glances, they found the man's face was hidden and cast in shadow by his head covering. All they could see was the scruff of his beard.

"Well..." Cleopas sputtered at the intrusion.

"You are rather nosey," Zel responded.

"I am just a co-traveler looking for a little conversation along the way."

"We were talking about Yeshua of Nazareth," Cleopas said.

"Surely, you've heard of him?"

"Or, you would be the only person in Jerusalem who hasn't heard what has happened to him," Zel added.

The stranger asked, "What sort of things happened?"

Convinced he was clueless, Zel said, "Well, he was our friend." His throat constricted. He paused before he could go on. "He was a prophet, who was mighty in awesome deeds, a real miracle man. He preached the words of God and brought healing to all kinds of people. It didn't matter who they were."

"Is that so?" The stranger seemed to ponder this, "So, what happened to him?"

"The chief priests hated him. In the dark of night, they captured him and voted to put him to death. He was crucified on the day of Passover. He was not a violent man. The whole thing was reprehensible!" Cleopas said, clearly incensed at the injustice of his nephew's crucifixion.

"Guess you never saw that coming!"

His words niggled their memory's.

Zel said, "We put our hope in him that he would be the one to redeem Israel. Surely, you have heard of this. It has been three days since he was crucified."

Cleopas picked up the conversation, "Yes, then we had a big surprise this morning when some of our women went to the tomb. They came back with an outrageous tale to astound us. After the earthquake this morning, the tomb was found wide open. The women told us that they saw a vision of angels who told them he was not dead! He had risen."

Zel added, "Some of our friends went to look for his body but did not find him... or any angels. But, the tomb was standing wide open. His body was gone, but they did not find him."

"How foolish you are! Aren't you devout Jews?" The stranger's voice dripped with rebuke. "Surely, you know what the prophets have written! Why are you so slow of heart to believe the testimony of the prophets?"

The two men felt the sting of the stranger's words. No one had ever spoken to them like that, but their teacher. They turned toward the man, hoping to read his expression, but his head was lowered. They could not see his features.

"What do you mean?" Zel challenged him.

"Was it not necessary for the Messiah to suffer these things before he could enter into his glory?" The stranger asked authoritatively, "Surely, you must know this?"

"Well...," Cleopas was unsure how to reply, "Why don't you tell us."

His eyes cut toward Zel as if to say, 'Let's just humor him.'

Zel shrugged back, 'Why not?"

After all, the man didn't know that Cleopas was Yeshua's family or that Zel was one of his disciples. They were pretty sure they knew Yeshua far better than this man.

The traveler began to interpret the Holy Scriptures, starting with Genesis, and he worked his way methodically through the Scriptures and the ages of mankind to the current day concerning 'the Messiah. They were filled with wonder.

He recounted 'the woman's seed,' the covering of skins provided to protect Adam and Eve in their banishment in the land of knowing of good and evil, and the righteous offering of Abel from his flock. The covenant of salvation with Noah and his sons is to make a way for the righteous remnant to live. He discussed his presence at Abraham's calling and the promises made to give a special inheritance of land to Abraham's offspring, then the blood covenant in the circumcision, and the promise to bless the whole earth through Abraham's seed. The Messiah was the promise when the LORD swore by himself while he passed through the blood of the sacrificed animals. He was the ram that would take Isaac's place. He was the Passover Lamb and the one who delivered the Hebrews from death—blood, suffering, suffering, suffering. The Messiah would suffer and shed his blood.

He was present on Mt. Sinai. And he was the One they saw from the back side. His finger etched the law. He was the Bridegroom of the Covenant when God betrothed himself to his people. He was the one who met with Moses in the tent-of-meeting and talked with him as a friend. He was the covering of the Israelites in the desert. He was with them in the water from the rock and the manna from heaven. He was the one who met with Joshua as he prepared to lead the people into the Promised Land. He instructed him as the Commander of the Lord's army.

He was with Gideon on the threshing floor when he called him to action. He was present when Sarai heard she would bear a son. His work of salvation was represented in all of its elements and rituals of the Tabernacle. He was prophesied through the articles in the Ark of the Covenant. His healing work was seen in the bronze serpent that was lifted upon a pole, just as he had been in crucifixion. He was the one to turn bitterness into pleasantness. His sacrifice was represented in the Passover Lamb and the Atonement Lamb.

He is the legitimate heir to the offices of King, Priest, and Prophet of the ancient order of Melchizedek. Those offices have always been and will forever be. He was born to save, to stand on the earth as the Anointed One, to serve as the Good Shepherd sent to find the lost; he is God with us. He is the seed that was sown, the treasure that we find and give everything to have. All the Festivals are revelations of him and his work of salvation.

Cleopas and Simon were spellbound as they listened. Their broken hearts were flung open like an empty tomb, and they were filled with awe. Their minds were grasping such new understandings from the fountain of information they had never understood before. Yeshua indeed fulfilled all the promises, scriptures, prophecies, and more. Their hearts were burning within them. They had not known the Messiah nearly as well as they thought they did. How had they been so blind?

Arriving at their destination, the stranger made as if to journey onward. They were not ready for their conversation to end, even after so many hours together.

"Friend," Cleopas said, "are you going to continue in the dark? Come in, eat with us, and stay with us this evening."

"How gracious. I would be delighted to enter in and sup with you."

Their meeting had been so sudden, and the two had been so caught up in all the stranger was saying that they had failed to ask for his name or his destination.

Cleopas brought out water for washing, then brought out a filling meal of freshly baked bread made with a tasty spread of beans, olives, and herbed oil from his mother-in-law's kitchen. At the center of the table, he sat a large vegetable plate fresh from the spring sprouts. When everyone was refreshed, they eagerly came together to enjoy the simple meal.

Cleopas told his guest, "Thank you for our day of instruction; you have opened our eyes to Yeshua of Nazareth and made our hearts burn within us. My heart overflows with gladness. Would you like to bless our food tonight?"

The stranger's head was slightly lowered, and his face was hidden in shadow, so his features had not yet been seen. They were completely undone when the stranger lowered his head covering to pray. He reached to take hold of the bread, lifting both the bread and his face.

"Blessed are You, Adonai, our God, ruler of the universe, who brings forth bread from the earth; You provide seed for the sower and a bountiful harvest."

He broke the bread into two pieces, offering a part to both Cleopas and Zel. They stared slack-jawed. Their eyes were round with amazement, reminding Yeshua of the blind men he had healed when they could finally see for the first time. The two men leaped to their feet, not knowing what to do. Yeshua smiled at their surprise, but when they reached out to take hold of him, he simply vanished from their sight—leaving them astonished.

Once they had recovered, they laughed for a long time.

Zel said, "The women were right. He *is* risen. He *is* alive."

Cleopas scratched his head, "How did that just happen? Why did we not know it was him?"

"He didn't want us to know it was him. After all, hasn't he tried to tell us about these things before, and we didn't get it? If we had seen him first, we might never have listened and finally connected the dots. It was as if we just couldn't hear or see his reality before today."

"Yes, and this time, our hearts were consumed with the sound of his voice and insights."

"This news can't wait. Let's go back to Jerusalem to tell the others."

Both men felt energized even after their long walk to Emmaus.

"Yes, let us return. Everyone needs to know our Lord is alive."

~ 51 ~

PEACE, BELIEVE, RECEIVE

Peace I leave with you; my peace I give you.
I do not give to you as the world gives.
Do not let your hearts be troubled, and do not be afraid.
John 14:27

God will credit righteousness—for us who believe in him
who raised Jesus our Lord from the dead.
He was delivered over to death for our sins
and was raised to life for our justification.
Romans 4:24-25

"Receive the Holy Spirit."
John 20:22

It was still dark, not yet morning. When a pounding at the door awoke the men from their slumber. James leaped quickly to his feet, with his heart hammering in terror.

He thought, 'This is it then, the religious leaders are rounding us up too? Why didn't we just leave yesterday as I wanted? If the others are captured, it will be all my fault!'

Somehow, he was able to lower his voice and speak calmly with convincing irritation, "Who is it? What do you want."

"It is Cleopas and Zel."

James jerked the door open, "What are you doing here? You are supposed to be headed to Galilee! Everyone is trying to sleep." He glared at them.

"Sorry! We did leave; we were on the way, but something extraordinary happened," Cleopas' voice sounded like a bullhorn in his excitement.

"Sh-h-h! Not so loud." James motioned to all the men, now coming awake and some coming to their feet. He closed the door, relocking it again, and waited, glowering at the two men.

Someone lit a lamp, then another, and the other's stirred.

Zel began, "On the way...we were joined by a stranger."

"A stranger?"

"Well....we thought it was a stranger! But..."

"And he was telling us all about the Scriptures about the Messiah..."

Zel and Cleopas began to talk over one another as if they were bursting to share the news.

Cleopas held up his hands to Zel and the others in an appeal for silence. Then he blurted out, "The Lord has risen indeed, and he has appeared to us, to me and Simon."

"It's true...while we were traveling to Emmaus. He was walking with us. We saw him!"

The other disciples gathered dubiously, with their hair tussled at weird angles from sleep. They began to ask questions all at once.

James asked them, "So, where is he now? Why didn't he come with you?"

They opened their mouth to answer but didn't know what to say.

The disciples exchanged skeptical looks, clearly doubting their story.

Suddenly, Yeshua appeared--standing among them.

James glanced at the bolted door, and dread gripped him.

"Good morning," Yeshua said. "It seems that you must all see for yourselves to believe."

They stared at him as if they were seeing a ghost. Each man reacted in their own unique and comical way, with panic and anxious guilt.

Sensing their anxiety in his presence, he said, "Peace be with you. Why are you so afraid? You can see it is me. I am not a ghost. The women told you, but you had no faith. Stubbornly, you are holding on to your doubts. Why?"

They dropped their eyes guiltily to the floor.

"Neither did you believe Cleopas and Zel."

They stared at him wide-eyed.

"Look at you! Are you even doubting *me* even now as *I* stand before you? Be at peace, brothers."

But they remained huddled in fear, remembering how they had fled.

Yeshua held up his hands and waved them in the air, "Look, these are my hands and my feet."

They saw the scars where the spikes had been.

"Go ahead, touch them. It is I! Truly." He slapped his bicep and abdomen. "A ghost does not have flesh and bones; as you see, I have."

"But how can this be?" Nathaniel murmured from behind Matthew.

Yeshua allowed them to examine him.

Slowly, one by one, their faces began to transform until they all were wearing foolish grins, gawking at him with a joyful intensity.

"Pinch me," he told Rock, "I feel as if I am dreaming!" Thaddeus said, "This is too good to be true."

Yeshua went to the food baskets, searched around, and turned toward them, "Do you have anything here to eat?"

"There is not much to offer. We have been locked in here for days."

Zel took some smoked fish and day-old bread from his travel bag. Yeshua took it and ate it to prove he was not a ghost.

He took a seat at the table, and they all drew near.

He asked them, "Doesn't anyone remember?"

They looked at each other, wondering what he was talking about.

He realized then that they did not. They would require his constant help to remember anything he had ever told them. He stood up and leaned into their circle. "Receive the Holy Spirit."

He blew his breath into their faces. When they breathed in his breath, they felt refreshed, as if their mind had been cleaned and reenergized.

"My forgiveness has been given to you. From this point on, you will become the messengers of my forgiveness. Whoever you pardon will be forgiven, but whoever refuses to believe in me or the message of my forgiveness will remain imprisoned in their sins. You are my witnesses. Now listen and hear my words: What has happened to me is exactly what I told you would happen while we were all together traveling along the way.

"Remember how I told you I would rise from the dead on the third day."

The light of knowledge sparked in their eyes.

He assured them, "Everything has happened just as it was planned. It was written in my book long before I was born. What has happened fulfills all that is written about me in the Law of Moses, the Prophets, and the Psalms."

He began to open their minds so they could understand the Scriptures, just as he had done with Cleopas and Zel. He explained the prophecies, foreshadowing, and arch types that revealed how his life had been planned and prepared throughout the ages. The disciples were filled with amazement. His references explained the reality of all he had done. For the first time, it all began to make sense.

"It was written that the Messiah would suffer, be crucified, and rise from the dead on the third day. Now, I have come to you and told you! Just as the women told you on my behalf, it is time for you to go to Galilee." With those words, he vanished. Astounded disciples looked excitedly at one another.

Only Thomas had been away when the Lord appeared to the others.

When he returned, they told him, "We have seen the Lord. He was just here. You just missed him."

Thomas grew unexplainably angry at them all.

"Why are you upset with us?"

"You are ganging up on me to pull a joke, and this is no joking matter. I am not going to fall for it. I don't believe you! Only if I see him for myself, touch him with my own two hands, and put my fingers in his wounds will I believe the Lord is alive."

"We are packing up to go to Galilee. Come with us; the Lord said he would see us there."

"Well, that sounds great. I would love to go home and figure out what I am to do next."

They tried to convince him, but no matter what they said, their words lacked the power to make Thomas believe his Master was alive. Having seen the Lord, they simply couldn't understand why Thomas clung stubbornly to his disbelief.

~ 52 ~

FISH OR CUT BAIT

"But be very careful ... to love the Lord your God,
to walk in obedience to him, to keep his commands,
to hold fast to him and to serve him
with all your heart and with all your soul.
He is your life.
Deuteronomy 30:19b-20a

The Lord is compassionate and gracious,
slow to anger, abounding in love.
He will not always accuse,
nor will he harbor his anger forever;
he does not treat us as our sins deserve
or repay us according to our iniquities.
For as high as the heavens are above the earth,
so great is his love for those who fear him;
as far as the east is from the west,
so far has he removed our transgressions from us.
As a father has compassion on his children,
so the Lord has compassion on those who fear him.
Psalm 103: 8-13

Thomas' disbelief made for an awkward journey to Galilee because now that the others had seen Yeshua, he was all they wanted to talk about. Thomas kept wondering why the Lord had not appeared to him. Had he done something wrong that the others had not? He wanted to believe, but for some strange reason, he simply could not. Too many doubts floated through his mind. And, it made him angry at the others, as if they were simply making this all up. Their happiness was irritating.

The women had already left for Galilee. Everyone was speculating on what the future might hold. Did Yeshua's strange and intermittent appearances indicate he was now existing between too parallel realities? They were looking forward to seeing him again.

Arriving at Capernaum, Rock went down and stood by the water's edge, staring out at the sea. He reflected on his old life as a fisherman. Not knowing what the future held, he longed to find some comfort in this familiarity. He realized it was a beautiful day, so much like the day Yeshua had hopped in his boat and changed his life. He remembered the feeling he had when he had called him. The excitement and wonder. Now he thought, 'But I have botched all of that now.'

Yes, he had seen Yeshua, and he had offered his peace, but... Simon could not seem to accept that peace. He waded out to let the water lap over his feet. 'I have never thought myself a coward, but I was. And the words I said I can never take back. I denied Yeshua over and over again because I was afraid of the servant girls and the Romans. I will never forget that look on the Lord's face when I denied him that final time.'

Yeshua had blown his breath on him, just as he had the others. And he had opened his eyes to the scriptures, which only made Simon feel worse about his failures. He was a coward. He realized then that it was only Yeshua who had inspired him to be brave.

'The Rock,' Yeshua had called him. The others still looked to him to lead them, but his boastful confidence was gone. He was afraid he would fail them, too.

Thomas came and stood next to him. "So, what is troubling you? Are you doubting what you saw?"

Rock turned his way and shook his head, "Nah. I might doubt myself, but I would never doubt him."

**

Word was spreading that Yeshua the Nazarene had risen from the dead. People everywhere were having animated conversations about it. They kept hearing reports that he had appeared to this one or that one. No one could track his movement. Long dead prophets and martyrs had emerged to people also with real bodies. It was indeed strange. People who had heard and believed he was alive began to come to Galilee, saying they felt strangely drawn to the place. They were filled with the expectation of a glimpse of him.

One evening, when all eleven disciples were together in one place, without any forewarning, Yeshua appeared to stand amongst them. He said, "Peace be with you."

At the sound of his voice, everyone stopped what they were doing and came to their feet, Thomas most especially. He turned. His eyes grew wide and began to shimmer with the beginning of tears.

"Lord!"

"Thomas," he said. And Thomas was undone.

"Come," he motioned, "put your hand in my side and your fingers in my hands and feet."

Thomas felt too weak to move. He sank to the floor, kneeling before him, exclaiming, "My Lord and my God!"

Yeshua went to him and lifted him, so they were face to face, "Now that you have seen me, you believe. Blessed are those who have not seen and yet have believed."

Thomas felt both embarrassed and grateful all at the same time. It was really true; Yeshua had risen from the grave.

Then a moment later, Yeshua was gone again, and they all started laughing, "Is this how it is going to be? He's here one moment and gone the next."

"Perhaps he is never gone, but we just don't see him..." Yohan offered. "Perhaps he is here even now."

Their eyes widened at this thought, suspecting this was true. After all, he had known Thomas' words when it seemed he was gone.

**

A couple of weeks had passed since the last 'visitation,' as they were calling them. All they could do was wait.

Rock paced like a caged animal around the room. Finally, he said, "I cannot just sit here and wait for him to show up. Who knows when or where that will be? I have got to get out of here for a while. I am going fishing. Deborah hopes I will be able to get a catch that will pay some of our expenses that are beginning to mount up."

"I'll go with you," Andrew said, aware that his brother still struggled with the guilt of his failures.

Thomas raised his hand, "I will go, too."

Yohan said, "Yes, let's go. I will get James to come with us. I am sure the Lord will find us wherever we are."

With a little encouragement, they were joined by the others. They hopped into Simon's boat and headed out onto the sea. They tossed out their nets and then waited for the tug of a catch. But, it turned into a long wait. They moved and tried again, but nothing.

Together, in the darkness of the night, they hardly spoke. Each man was reflecting upon all their adventures upon this sea with Yeshua. Memories of the comradery, the escapes, the anticipation of the next place of mission, the conflicts, the large crowds, the miracles, the sadness, the times of righteous indignation, the Gerasene who was healed of his demons, and the pigs floating in the surf, the night Yeshua came to them walking on water in the middle of the storm and Rock walked on water to him, the night he had calmed the winds, and the sea had obeyed his command. Their thoughts kept them well-occupied.

The night wore on, and there was still no fish. In fact, there was nothing at all but disappointment. Everyone was growing drowsy as they rested with their arms tucked up in their robes.

Simon worked the nets again and again. So he would not dirty his outer clothing he had stripped down to his undergarment. His wife would appreciate that he had not dirtied his mantle. When morning was approached, Simon hauled up the empty nets, conceding that the night was a bust.

Unsettled, he turned the boat toward the shore. Standing at the helm, he looked toward the shoreline. For some reason, he had been expecting that Yeshua might show up in their boat or he might come walking across the water to join them. But he never seemed to do the same thing twice. Tears stung the corners of Simon's eyes. He hadn't shown. He roughly swiped his eyes with the back of his hand.

What would he do? He missed Yeshua's friendship, guidance, and stability. He felt lost, untethered like a boat that had lost its mooring. He released a sigh, then a loud nasally sniff.

Yohan heard Simon's sigh and came to stand beside him. The others roused themselves to see what was happening.

"What is that proverb...?" Simon asked Yohan.

It came to him, "Hope deferred makes the heart sick. That is it. My heart feels sick."

Simon placed his hand on Simon's shoulder.

Just then, a shout echoed to them from the shore across the quiet waters, "Children, have you no fish?"

Yohan leaned forward immediately at the sound of that voice, searching the shore.

"No," he called back. He spotted a man standing on the shore, barely perceptible in the earliest light of the morning. He pointed Simon toward the man.

The man called out, "Throw your net on the right side of the boat, and you will find some fish."

With those words, Rock came to attention. He waited, listening. His eyes fixed on the man on the shore. Yohan urged the others to cast their net off of the right side of the boat. Simon tore his eyes away long enough to set the net, but his heart hammered in his chest.

Almost immediately, the boat lurched as if being pulled back into the sea. Everyone scrambled to their feet to grab the nets. They pulled with all their strength, but they could not haul the catch in because the catch was so big.

But Simon left the fish to them, instead he was looking toward the shore.

Yohan came alongside him and confirmed his thoughts, "It is the Lord!"

Simon grabbed his robe and threw it over his head in one smooth motion. He launched himself into the cold waters, intent on swimming to the man on the shore. He desperately needed to speak with the Lord and make things right. He didn't know how to do that or what to say, and for a moment, he floundered. But, he forced himself to believe there was a way to be reconciled.

Simon was exhausted when he pulled through the last few strokes, and his feet touched the ground. He stood to stumble through the water that tugged at his heavy robe. He emerged dripping wet. His unruly hair was plastered to his head. He coughed and gasped for a breath. Then, with large and hopeful eyes, he came to stand awkwardly some distance in front of his master, like a loyal dog who knew he had displeased his owner and was afraid to approach. Again, he faltered.

"Come. Stand near to the fire," Yeshua told him.

Seeing the fire the Lord had built, he couldn't help remembering another charcoal fire. He simply stood there shivering.

"Bring some of your fish," Yeshua called to the others arriving on the shore. "Come, have breakfast."

Someone threw an extra blanket around Rock as they came to huddle by the fire and bask in the warmth of their Master's presence. When the fish was ready, Yeshua held up the bread and blessed it. Then, he broke the bread and passed a fish sandwich to each of his men for their breakfast.

This was now the third time Yeshua had appeared to his chosen servants since his death. The men gobbled the food down, hungry from their hours on the sea. They licked their fingers to clean them, then waited expectantly for Yeshua to speak.

"Simon, how many big fish did you bring in?"

"I counted 153," He said sheepishly.

He had counted the catch while the fish was cooking. "I can't believe the net held the weight."

"Ah, that is a good catch. That will supply plenty of money for your families."

The men nodded, "But tell me something, Simon, son of Jonah."

"What is it, Lord?"

"Do you truly love me more than these?" He motioned to the left-over fish and the fire.

Rock swallowed hard and pulled his blanket closer. He stared at the fish and then at Yeshua for an awkward moment. His brows were knit together in consternation. He squirmed under Yeshua's direct gaze and the other's squirmed with him. Simon looked around at the other men, embarrassed. But he understood the reason Yeshua would ask. His guilt was plastered on his face.

He looked up to nod a half-hearted response. Rebuked to the bone, he looked down to break the eye contact and burning with shame, he murmured, "Yes, Lord, you know that I love you."

He remembered how easily his final denial had come, "---, I don't even know the man." He remembered the pain in Yeshua's eyes when he had heard him say it. Once again, his devastation glistened in his eyes.

"Then, feed my lambs," Yeshua commanded him, "the ones young in their faith."

Rock glanced up at him, unsure he had heard him correctly.

Yeshua's eyes were still upon him, but now they were filled with forgiveness and abiding love. He waited for Rock to say something in response.

But Simon didn't know what to say. Instead, he thought, 'Who am I to feed his lambs?'

After a few more moments of awkward silence, Yeshua asked him again, "Simon, son of Jonah, do you love me?"

This question was different. It was the same words, but it had nothing to do with 'the fish, his business, comfort, security, or independence.' This question cut right to the heart of the real matter, the real question that was wedged between them.

Yeshua knew Rock's heart for him. Hadn't he recklessly tried to defend him against a regiment of Romans and the Sanhedrin? He was the only one who made a stand. He'd had to call Simon down for his own good, as well as the good of the others. And, he was the only one besides Yohan with the courage to breach the courtyard that night to remain near him, clearly putting himself in the path of imminent danger. Yohan's relationship with powerful people protected him, but there was no such protection for Simon. It had been reckless on Rock's part, but he knew he had put himself in harm's way out of love. But now, he had to remind Simon of the depth of his love and devotion to him if he was to recover and carry out his calling.

Simon began to weep openly now, feeling both foolish and unworthy. "Yes...", He sobbed, "You know that I do," but he still couldn't meet Yeshua's eyes.

Yeshua reached out and tipped Simon's chin, forcing him to look at him when he said, "Then take care of my sheep."

He held Simon's chin for a moment, searching his eyes, forcing Simon to meet his gaze.

Simon's face crumbled, and his imploring expression told Yeshua everything Simon just did not know how to say. Yeshua gave him a sympathetic smile and caressed his wet cheek like a child whose heart was broken by something he had done.

Yohan reached out and put his arm around his friend's shoulder, knowing this was an important moment for Simon's healing. Simon had been lost since that night in the courtyard.

He had not yet made an affirmative response to the charge commanded of him.

A third time, Yeshua asked his probing question, "Simon, do you love me?" His voice was challenging now, demanding even. He leaned back and speared Simon with the intensity of his direct question and eye contact.

Simon blinked, clearly hurt by this third challenging question. He felt his hackles rise, and he wondered, 'Doesn't he believe me?'

But when he saw the intensity of Yeshua's look, he realized Yeshua was asking this question for *his* sake, not for his own. He was asking so Simon would remember his love and devotion.

Suddenly, he did remember! He remembered that he had never been worthy, not even in the beginning. Yeshua had even agreed he was 'unworthy' at the time but he had loved him, called him, and chosen him despite his weaknesses and faults. His heart expanded with the unfathomable love Yeshua had for him. He well and truly felt his forgiveness. How could he have forgotten? His anger and guilt were defeated.

Now, for the first time since his betrayal, Rock willingly met Yeshua's eyes. Taking a deep and steadying breath, he said, "Lord, you *know* all things; you *know* that I love you."

Rock began to sob with grateful humility, feeling like a boulder had been lifted off of him.

Yeshua beamed at him, "Yes. You do."

"And I have forgiven you, all of you." He looked around at the wide-eyed men. "I have entrusted to you the message of my forgiveness. That is to be your life's work. How can you do that work if you will not receive my forgiveness for yourself? Haven't I given you my peace? We are good Rock, if you would only believe it."

Yeshua leaned forward and pressed his forehead against Rock's forehead as if to impart that understanding. When he leaned back, they stared at one another eye to eye. He spoke his command to Simon a third time, "Feed my sheep."

Rock stared into the unfathomable depths of his Lord's eyes and nodded. Yeshua stood and pulled him to his feet. Together, they begin to walk along the shore. Yohan got up to trail behind them.

With his hand on Simon's shoulder, Yeshua said, "You have counted the cost. You know it won't be easy. But Rock, that Passover night when I told you that Satan wanted to sift you, I told you that when your faith was restored, you were to turn back and strengthen your brothers."

Simon was surprised by the memory, surprised he had forgotten Yeshua's words to him that night. "You really do know all things," he said with awe.

"Rock, it is hard to follow me, I know. But follow me anyway. When you were younger, you dressed yourself, and you went wherever you wanted. Now you will go where I will send you. And, someday, when you are old, you will be told to stretch out your hands. Someone will dress you and lead you where you do not want to go. You will indeed drink the cup of my suffering, just as I said you would. It was just not your time for that. You will glorify me just as I have glorified the Father. Meanwhile, I have called you to be a fisher of men. Keep following me, Rock!"

They had stopped walking. Simon knew Yeshua was calling him again for the second time. He fell to his knees as he had that first day in the boat in the middle of the sea. Assured of his grace and forgiveness, he bowed his head before the scarred feet of his God. Then, he saw Yohan standing a short distance away.

Rock asked, "Lord, what about Yohan?"

"Yohan has his own path to journey. And if I want him to remain alive until I return, would it make any difference to you, Rock? Don't worry about Yohan, or anyone else for that matter. We are talking about *your* call. *You* follow me." He touched Simon's chest.

Simon looked up at him, "Lord, if you are asking me to go one mile, then let me go two. Just don't take your presence from me."

Yeshua pulled Simon to his feet. His life and purpose had been renewed, restored, and restrengthened.

~ 53 ~

THOSE BEAUTIFUL FEET

The Lord has established his throne in heaven,
And his kingdom rules over all.
Praise the Lord, you his angels,
You mighty ones who do his bidding,
Who obey his word.
Praise the Lord, all his heavenly hosts,
You, his servants, who do his will.
Praise the Lord, all his works.
Everywhere in his dominion.
Praise the Lord, my soul.
Psalm 103:19-22

"Let's go get the others," Simon said to Yohan and Nathaniel. "It will soon be time to go out to the mountain where the Lord sent us."

"The others are scattered about," Nathaniel said. "It might not be that easy."

"We have enough time."

"You don't know if they will come," Yohan said

"Did the Lord not call them to himself? They will come," Simon suddenly seemed confident.

"We have work to do," he added.

Yohan and Nathaniel's faces stretched into broad smiles. They looked at one another and said, "Simon the Rock is back!"

When the eleven and a few of the women were gathered, they got into Rock's boat, and together, they sailed to the large outdoor auditorium they had used the years before. Arriving there, they were quickly reminded of the miraculous feeding of the five thousand on this plain. A large group was waiting, but where there had once been five thousand, now a remnant of five hundred waited.

Today, no one was there for a healing or a handout. They had come to feed one more time on 'The Real Bread of Life.' They were there, anxious to learn what they should do next now that their Savior had overcome death. They came, believing Yeshua was alive. These were the faithful ones who had earnestly believed him and followed him throughout the days of his preaching. They had traveled from place to place to hear his teachings and his voice because he had touched their lives.

They were happy to see that among the number was Yeshua's family. Cleopas had corralled the lot of them, and after seeing the crucifixion and hearing about all that had happened, they had come to see their brother, the Son of God.

Rock suddenly had an attack of nerves, with no Yeshua in sight. Was he to share the good news with this crowd? They had not come here to see him. They were searching for the risen Christ. But when all who were called by his name had arrived, suddenly Yeshua appeared among them just as he had before.

The hill erupted into songs of salvation and rejoicing, filled with happy expectation to see their Lord alive. Yeshua went up on the mountain and held up his nail-scarred hands to quiet their cheers of elation. Everyone was quieted, so hushed that one could hear a needle drop. They waited for the sound of his voice.

"My return to the Father is soon before me. But today, you see me. You see that it is I—myself that stands before you. Look at my hands and my feet; they are evidence of my death and resurrection. I have glorified my Father in Heaven. Now, the time is almost here that I will return to dwell with him. But soon, the Festival of Weeks will begin. You are to go to Jerusalem for the upcoming festival. Spread the word and bring your families. Come and pray earnestly for the gift my Father is preparing to send to you."

Worship broke out among the people, and they bowed down to the ground before him. It took some time for them to become quiet again.

He motioned to his Chosen Ones, "These Eleven are my chosen ones who will serve as my ambassadors. They will go out in my name. Listen to them. They will proclaim my forgiveness. Those who receive my forgiveness will be forgiven of their sins; those who will not receive my forgiveness will remain in their sins. I am The Sacrifice that has been given for your sins. My servants will need your help in spreading the Good News. The age of salvation has begun. You will all be a part of it."

Again, they cheered with great enthusiasm so that once again, he lifted his hands to quiet them. He said, "Everything has been fulfilled that is written about me in the Law of Moses, the Prophets, and the Psalms. In the days ahead, your minds will be opened to understand the mystery of the scriptures. Keep them at your right hand, day and night.

"Having fulfilled all that was written, all authority in heaven and on earth has been given to me. Today, in your presence, I am sending these Eleven men to go and make disciples of all nations."

He turned to the Eleven in the presence of the five hundred; he said to them, "In the days ahead, you are to go forth to baptize those who profess they believe, in the name of the Father and of the Son and the Holy Spirit and teach them to obey everything I have commanded you. Surely, even when you do not see me, I am with you always. I will be with you even to the very end of this age."

The Eleven bowed before him and worshipped him with all humility, receiving anew their calling just as they had when he first invited them to follow him.

**

When the time came, the Eleven returned to Jerusalem for the Feast of Shavuot, and a large group traveled with them. This time, Rock brought his wife Deborah, daughter Ana, and his mother-in-law Abigail with him. After his many years on the road with Yeshua, he missed them, and he wasn't sure when or if he would ever return to Galilee. It was better to make his family gypsies, forced to travel with him, than to leave them behind.

"You and your family can stay with me in Jerusalem until you get things worked out." Mari offered.

Rock gave her a grateful smile. "Thank you. It shouldn't be long. We will find a place of our own as soon as we can."

"But, we are like family, are we not?" She smiled back. "I will enjoy having Deborah and little Ana around."

As they drew closer to Bethany, Yeshua appeared to travel the last of the distance with them. They stopped to visit with Lazarus and Martha. Afterward, he led them out to the clearing on the rise. From there, they could see the road behind them, and Jerusalem lay before them.

He went to each person to lay his hands on them to bless them according to the work that lay ahead. There were many tears, for they all understood the time for his departure had come, and he was returning to the Father. They all stood quietly until the last person had received his blessing.

He stood back from them all and said, "After today, I want you to go into Jerusalem and stay there until you are clothed with power from on high. Pray. My Father is preparing to send you the gifts he has promised. Having received his inconceivable gift, you will begin to share the message starting from Jerusalem to Galilee and Samaria, and then you will spread out and go into all the nations. You are my witnesses concerning my teachings, calling, miracles, signs of my suffering, and resurrection on the third day. You know of the human need for repentance. You know my forgiveness of sins," his eyes were full of love for them.

It is time for me to return to my Father, but remember what I said."

The faces of those he loved fell. They were unwilling to let him go.

"Come now, I am with you always, even to the end of the age. Do not fear."

He held up his hands to convey a priestly blessing over them. While he was blessing them, a thick cloud appeared and swirled around him. It became so thick that it obscured him--first his face, then his body, until all they could see of him was his feet as the cloud began to take him up into the sky. In mere moments, both their Lord and the cloud had disappeared. Their last glimpse of him was of his nail-pierced feet. It was then that they realized that those were the feet of their God. Scarred as they were, they were truly a beautiful sight. For in Yeshua, the God of heaven had come down to walk with them upon the earth. His presence had made wherever they followed, whoever they had stood with him, a holy place.

They were struck dumb with awe. Still, they could not stop their hearts from clamoring for him. They wanted to go with him. They found they could not move from the spot. No one knew how long they had stood there, looking up into the sky, and wondering when they would see him again, or what would happen next. The day was disappearing.

Finally, two messengers dressed in white appeared beside them, "Men of Galilee, why do you stand there looking into the sky?"

The Apostles suddenly moved as men awakened from a dream, and they remembered they had work to do. They looked down to search for what might be left behind. They found only their own weary feet, still rooted to the spot. The words from the Scripture of Isaiah came to their mind:

How beautiful on the mountains
Are the feet of those who bring good news,
Who proclaims peace,
Who bring good tidings,
Who proclaims salvation,
Who says to Zion,
"Your God reigns!"

They understood that now it would be their feet that would go and stand on the mountain to bring the good news of what God had done. Yeshua had appointed them to go and search for every lost and searching soul. If their poor, tired, and humble feet were going to ever be beautiful, they had to pray for the Lord to be with them. Didn't he say he would always be with them and he would never leave or desert them?

THE END

EPILOGUE

The story of Yeshua never ends, but now his story is poised and waiting to include you. Now that you have met God in the flesh and learned of his amazing love for you, how will you respond?

Will you cling to your unbelief? Will you go on living your life your way? Will you simply put the book away and move on?

Jesus is waiting for you to decide. His hand is extended to you. But where do you begin? I am happy to say your relationship has already begun long ago, and it can continue if you move toward him and then kneel before your Lord and God in humble submission. Confess your unworthiness and your sins. Admit your need for a Savior. Agree that you cannot heal or deliver yourself.

Ask Him to help you, save you, heal you, and make you able to follow Him and his teachings. Profess Him as the King of Kings of your existence. Invite Him to share your life with you. Make your home His home. Give Him the seat of the highest authority, the throne of your heart.

Seek His face daily, and pour out your praise to Him in worship. Join a band of brothers and sisters in Christ. Introduce Him to your friends and your family and find ways to serve Him and His purposes, whether in prayer or the labor of your hands.

Read, believe, and defend the Word of God. It is by it that you will make your stand against the dark forces of this world. Cling to the work of the cross, even though you will be hated for your faith, you will be mocked, persecuted, and pursued because of his Name and because you are set apart as holy unto the Lord. This will make you different from the world around you. Following Jesus is no small decision; by it, you choose life or death. When you choose Christ, you choose life.

Consider the price he paid to rescue you.
Are you willing to be yoked to Christ?
Then pick the cross waiting for you and follow him.
Now look down. Do you see your feet?
They were meant to be beautiful feet.
And, now you know, love requires a sacrifice.
May your feet become beautiful for Jesus
as you journey with him to your beautiful forever.

This is my prayer for you:

Father, Bless the one who puts their faith in the work of your Son Jesus, whom you sent for us. Bless their journey with companionship, with revelation, wisdom, insights, devotion, spiritual gifts, the work of their hands and their real purpose. May they know the joy of your constant presence, and live the blessed life you have prepared for them now and forevermore. In the name of the Father, Son, and Holy Spirit. Amen

AFTERWORD

In the writing of this book, many of my character's exemplify the devotion of the Bride of Christ, which is the church, and the struggles they had to overcome: Yosef, Miriam, Yohannan, Rock, Yohan, and the disciples, all of the women, but most of all Mari. Like Mari's confession, each one placed their love for Yeshua like a seal upon their hearts. Meaning, Yeshua was always their priority, their one true love. It was their intent to be faithful. They show us what it means to be the bride of Christ. Though their love was not yet perfected; it was always fierce. And, it was there to stay.

And from the moment Yeshua's feet slipped from their physical sight, they took up the prayer:

> The Spirit and the bride say, "Come!"
> And let the one who hears say, "Come!"
> Let the one who is thirsty come;
> and let the one who wishes,
> take from the free gift of the water of life.
> Revelation 22:17

ACKNOWLEDGEMENT

Praise and gratitude to the Holy Spirit who enlivens my imagination, and allows me to share life with Jesus, and helps me to see him in everything.

Thanks to Len McFarland, who has always supported my work in ministry and shared my love for Christ. From the bottom of my heart thank you for sharing this journey with me.

Love and thanks to my family.

As for me and my house, let us serve the Lord.

ABOUT THE AUTHOR

K. S. McFarland is a retired pastor with credentials of Master of Divinity and certifications in Spiritual Direction, New Church Plant, Worship Design, also, Bachelor of Business Administration and a Masters Certificate in Project Management and twenty-nine years of ministry experience.

This novel was written from a personal passion for the life, grace, and redemption offered through our Lord Jesus Christ.

Please feel free to connect with me through my website lamb58@WordPress.com.

BOOKS BY THIS AUTHOR

Way of the Lamb Way of the Lamb:
Lamb of God Series
Novel One
Kindle, Softcover, Hardcover
by K. S. McFarland (Author)
Book 1 of 1: Lamb of God Series

In WAY OF THE LAMB...

Step back in time to meet Yeshua the Messiah, and take an imaginative journey with him. Follow him along rocky paths through the wilds of Judea, sail with him on the Sea of Galilee, meet his family, neighbors, closest allies, and fiercest enemies, go with him on awe-inspiring missions, let your ears be opened to his teachings, experience the yearly festivals of Jerusalem through his eyes, become one of his inquisitive disciples free to ponder his words and ask your hard questions. Along the way, bow with him in prayer, learn of his challenges and struggles, his hopes and dreams, and his dependency on his Father in Heaven, his determination. Bow before him in worship as God incarnate, let his kingdom viewpoint change your perspectives, join forces with him.

Gain insight into the mysteries of the Lamb of God, the Prophet, the Messiah, and the Bridegroom. Experience Yeshua as both Son of God and the Son of Man, the Alpha and the Omega, and the Word of God, who was ordained and anointed to fulfill all of the

Law, the foreshadowing in the narratives, the words foretold by the prophets, and the pronouncements of the angels.

Understand the stakes of Yeshua's life. Experience his healings and miracles from new perspectives. Gain a deeper understanding of 'the game of thrones' that was operative during the first century Greco-Roman culture. Who pulled the puppet strings of power? Was it the Roman's, the Herod's, the Hasmonean's, the Sanhedrin, or the Evil One? Or was there someone else governing his times?

This first novel begins an eye opening and reflective journey. What does it means to love God with all your heart, soul and strength. to have faith, and to travel the way of the Lamb? You have nothing to lose, but everything to gain.

Come and see.

www.ingramcontent.com/pod-product-compliance
Lightning Source LLC
Chambersburg PA
CBHW061857310726
48972CB00004B/1060